Timothy Zahn

SPECTRA ™

BANTAM BOOKS

NEW YORK   TORONTO   LONDON   SYDNEY   AUCKLAND

ISBN 0-553-57562-7

Published simultaneously in the United States and Canada

Bantam Books are published by Bantam Books, a division of Bantam Doubleday Dell
Publishing Group, Inc. Its trademark, consisting of the words "Bantam Books" and the
portrayal of a rooster, is Registered in U.S. Patent and Trademark Office and in other
countries. Marca Registrada. Bantam Books, 1540 Broadway, New York, New York 10036.

PRINTED IN THE UNITED STATES OF AMERICA

DEDICATION

For several years now, from time to time, he has been supplying me with little tidbits of ideas; and up to now he has not received a proper public acknowledgment of my gratitude. With this book, it's time to set that right.

So here goes. The suggestion that part of this book be from Max's point of view came from him. So did the hand-built model that inspired the design of the Peacekeepers' Wolf Pack. For these ideas, for those that have come before, and for those that are undoubtedly yet to come, I dedicate this book to my son

CORWIN ZAHN

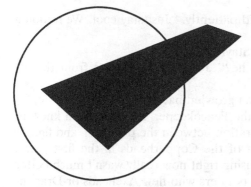

1 Directly ahead, the sky was a brilliant and cloudless blue. All around, at the distant circle of the horizon, the browns and grays and pale greens of the planetscape hazed with an odd seamlessness into the blue of the sky. Above and slightly aft, the planet's sun was a pale, red-orange globe.

Directly beneath was enemy territory.

"Samurai, I'm picking up response activity," the voice of the backstop Corvine's tail man came in Commander Rafe Taoka's ear. "Thirty-four klicks aft. Can't tell what kind of craft yet, but I read five of them."

"Tally that," Taoka's own tail man, Juggler, confirmed. "Also tally Talisman's count."

"Acknowledged," Taoka said, twitching his left eyelid to call up the tactical/sensor view aft of his Catbird fighter. The image superimposed itself on the enhanced forward view racing past beneath him, and he took a moment to study the flashing circles Juggler had marked. No vehicles showing yet, but the false-color scheme definitely indicated thermal and turbulence signatures. "Gusto, give yourself another half klick up—I want Talisman to keep an eye on those signatures back there. Juggler, Argus: you two stay sharp on forward wedge scan."

"Acknowledged," Gusto said from the Corvine, his voice sounding a little strained. "Shouldn't we go to X?"

"Standing Order Three, Gusto," Crossfire said from the other Catbird, flying a dozen meters off Taoka's wing. "We don't go to X until bogies are actually on scope."

"This isn't a drill, Crossfire," Gusto said, a touch of asperity cracking through his voice. "This is real."

"Yes, we know," Crossfire said patiently. "Just stay cool. We're doing fine."

"Yes, sir," Gusto muttered. "Staying cool, sir."

"Doesn't sound happy, does he?" Juggler commented from the aft cockpit seat behind Taoka.

"Can't say I blame him," Taoka growled back. It was a stupid rule, St/Ord 3 was, and everyone from the Peacekeeper Triad on down knew it. Level X, the full Mindlink integration between the pilot, tail, and fighter craft itself, was the whole point of the Copperheads in the first place. The Level A linkage they were using right now really wasn't much better than the baseline heads-ups the poppers who flew Axeheads or Dragonflies got.

But, then, St/Ord 3 hadn't been set up by military men. It was a political order, forced on the Copperheads by the NorCoord Parliament a few years back. Their ill-considered reaction to that oversensationalized flap over Copperhead burnout. A flap led and fed by the ambitions of then-Parlimin Lord Stewart Cavanagh.

One expected idiotic and shortsighted ideas from politicians. What had twisted in Taoka's gut like splintered glass was the fact that Cavanagh's crusade had been aided and abetted by a former Copperhead. Worse, a Copperhead who had once held near-legendary status. Adam Quinn: Maestro.

Or, as Taoka thought of him now, Adam Quinn: Traitor.

It had been a hurtful and humiliating time, and Taoka had privately resolved never to forget that pain. But maybe all that bad blood had finally circled back to where it belonged. The last skitter message that had reached the *Trafalgar* task force before they left Commonwealth space had included a notice that Quinn had been arrested and charged with theft of Peacekeeper property. With a little luck maybe Lord Cavanagh could get dragged into it, too; Taoka had heard that Quinn was working for Cavanagh these days. Get the two of them thrown into cold storage for the next twenty years, and he might be willing to call it even.

Beneath the three fighters a group of Conqueror buildings shot past, built in the same linked-hexagon style the aliens used for their warships. He caught a glimpse of a courtyard area between two of the buildings—the heat signature of a single Conqueror standing out in the open, no doubt looking goggle-eyed up at them—and then they were over a vast landing field with a scattering of small air- or spacecraft clustered at one end.

"Got some heat signatures," Juggler reported from behind him. "Some of those craft down there are already gearing up."

"Looks like word of our arrival's getting around," Gusto added.

"Can't fault their communications any," Taoka said, calling up the image of the vehicles they'd just passed. "Lucky for us they're not too swift on the uptake."

"They're swift enough," Crossfire cut in. "Argus has two groups incoming: twenty and forty degrees, two hundred klicks range. Intercept vectors."

Taoka smiled grimly. Finally: a direct enemy threat. "All right, Samurai group. You wanted it; you got it. All Copperheads, go to X."

"Signal from Samurai group, Commodore," the fighter commander called from across the *Trafalgar*'s bridge. "They have incoming bogies. Samurai's ordered them to Level X."

"Acknowledged, Schweighofer," Commodore Lord Alexander Montgomery said, running his eyes over the outer scan displays for probably the hundredth time since launching the probe teams. Peacekeeper Command had assured him that their sudden arrival would probably catch the enemy off guard; but Peacekeeper Command's collective hindquarters weren't on the line here. His were, and he had no intention of losing them or his task force to the Zhirrzh. Certainly not the way Trev Dyami had lost the *Jutland*. "Smith, do we still have visual on the outriders?" he called across the bridge.

"Yes, sir," the force coordination officer called back. "Visual and lasercom both. Still no enemy response."

"That won't last much longer," Captain Thomas Germaine murmured from the fleet exec's chair beside Montgomery. "They must have *something* in this system that can fight. Only question is where they're hiding it."

"Agreed," Montgomery said, running a thoughtful forefinger across the deep cleft in his chin. The outriders had clear visuals on both moons and all space debris within any reasonable range. Unless the enemy had something buried away underground—

"*Antelope* reports enemy ship rising from the planet," Smith called. "Grid Fifty-five-Delta."

Germaine had already keyed the main display for the *Antelope*'s feed. The Zhirrzh ship rising at them was not all that big, perhaps half the size of the ships the *Jutland* had encountered a few light-years off Dorcas.

Still, considering how easily those four alien craft had ripped through the *Jutland*'s eight-ship task force, the presence of even one Zhirrzh warship was nothing to be taken lightly.

And orbiting two thousand klicks away in outrider position, the *Antelope* might as well have been a floating bull's-eye for all the good the rest of the task force could do them. "Mendoza, you'd better get out of there," he ordered the *Antelope*'s captain. "Mesh out, and wait for us at Point Victor."

As if to underline the order, the rising conglomeration of hexagons began spitting laser fire, splashing tiny clouds of vaporized metal from the *Antelope*'s hull. "Acknowledged, *Trafalgar,*" Mendoza's voice came back. "You want me to loop back around and run backstop?"

"Negative," Montgomery said. "Just run. Bravo Sector ships: deploy defense against incoming bogie. All fighters return to their ships at once, probe teams included."

"Samurai group is about to engage, sir." Schweighofer reminded him.

"Tell Samurai I said *now.*"

"Acknowledged."

Montgomery looked up to find Germaine frowning at him. "We're leaving already?" the fleet exec asked. "Surely we can handle a single enemy warship."

"Boldness is a useful quality in a warrior," Montgomery told him quietly. "Brashness belongs in your quarters with your dress uniform. Our mission objectives were to gather geographic data and to test the assumption that the Zhirrzh can't detect the tachyon wake-trails of incoming starships. We've accomplished both. There's nothing to be gained by adding head-to-head combat to the mission profile."

"Except possibly a reduction of the enemy threat," Germaine countered. "Even without *Antelope* we've got a fifteen-to-one edge here, plus four wings of Adamant and Copperhead fighters. This is the kind of chance—"

"Second ship incoming, Commodore," Smith interrupted. "*Cascadia* has it rising from Grid One-sixteen-Charlie."

"Deploy defensive," Montgomery ordered as Germaine pulled up the picture. Coming up from a group of low hills, the newcomer looked to be a bit larger than the first bogie, though given its completely different arrangement of hexagons, it was hard to tell for sure. "Any idea yet where they're coming from?"

"Apparently from right under our noses, sir," Kyun Wu said from the sensor station. "I ran a check—the probe teams had them marked as buildings. Must have one hell of a lift system to be able to bring something that size up and down a gravity well."

Montgomery grimaced to himself. Lasers capable of slicing through Peacekeeper hull metal, virtually indestructible ceramic hulls; a method of instantaneous communication across interstellar distances; and now an unknown but obviously highly efficient ground-to-space lift system. Even without anything else, the level of their technology would have red-flagged these aliens as a potential threat to humanity.

Their use of that technology to invade the Commonwealth had turned that red flag into a red alarm. And had earned the Zhirrzh the name Conquerors.

"Commodore, *Antelope* has meshed out," Smith reported. "First bogie changing course toward *Galileo* and *Wolverine.* Second bogie has engaged *Cascadia* and *Nagoya.*"

"*Nagoya*'s been hit!" Kyun Wu snapped. "Full round of laser fire from Bogie Two. Looks like severe damage to all forward sections."

"Confirm that," Smith said. "Damage to command structure; severe damage to sensors and forward missile ports."

"*Cascadia*'s launched a missile attack against Bogie Two," Kyun Wu said. "Missiles hitting . . . no apparent damage. Bogie is attacking *Nagoya* again."

"Damage to *Nagoya* starboard flank," Smith said. "Make that severe damage. Command center's gone; Prasad has ordered ship-abandon. Bogie One's engaging *Wolverine.*"

"Trautmann, move us to backstop *Cascadia,*" Montgomery ordered the helmsman. "Kyun Wu: status on *Nagoya*'s honeycombs."

"Nothing yet," Kyun Wu said tightly. "Bogie's still firing at *Nagoya.* Wait a minute; I'm picking up some pod emergency beacons—"

Abruptly, he broke off. "Beacons have gone silent, Commodore."

Germaine swore viciously under his breath. "Damn them all."

Montgomery squeezed his left fist hard enough to hurt, sudden fury burning along his throat. They were doing it again. Brutally, arrogantly, deliberately, the Conquerors were slaughtering the human survivors of their attack. Helpless survivors, in defenseless and unarmed escape pods. "Launch missiles," he ordered. "Full salvo."

"Acknowledged," the weapons officer called. "Missiles away."

"Too late, Commodore," Smith said quietly. "The *Nagoya*'s gone."

For a half-dozen painful heartbeats Montgomery just sat there, staring at the expanding cloud of debris that had been the *Nagoya,* a cloud still flashing and flickering with secondary explosions and enemy laser fire. There were things he wanted to scream at the Conquerors; things he desperately wanted to scream. But he was a NorCoord officer, from the heritage and tradition of Great Britain. Such men did not lose control. "Fighter status?" he asked instead.

"Samurai group is just coming into their bays," Schweighofer reported, his voice the bitter cold of a Rheinland on Nadezhda winter. "All other fighters have returned to their ships. Rather, all that will be returning."

Montgomery's fist tightened again. But there would be time later to tot up the casualties. Right now his job was to keep his force from suffering any more of them. "Fire another salvo at Bogie Two," he ordered the weapons officer as he touched his comm control. "All ships: defense formation; mesh out in order. Rendezvous at Point Victor."

He could feel Germaine's eyes on him as the other ships acknowledged and the task force began its orderly retreat. But the fleet exec said nothing. Perhaps because there was nothing to be said. Fifteen Peacekeeper warships, fleeing before two of the enemy, leaving a ship's worth of dead behind. And the two enemy warships not showing so much as a scratch.

But at least he hadn't lost his whole task force—the way Dyami had lost the *Jutland.*

And, ultimately, it wasn't going to matter how viciously and arrogantly the Zhirrzh cut into them here. By now the NorCoord Parliament must certainly have authorized the use of CIRCE, the awesome weapon that had been used four decades earlier to end the Pawolian war, and which then for security reasons had been disassembled. Odds were, in fact, that all of CIRCE's components had already been gathered together from the dozen or more worlds on which they'd been hidden. Somewhere back in the Commonwealth—on Earth, on Celadon, perhaps somewhere out in deep space—top NorCoord ordnance techs were probably even now reassembling those components into the most spectacular killing device mankind had ever known.

So let the enemy slaughter and destroy. Soon they would find themselves facing CIRCE, and the Peacekeepers would have the final word.

And the Zhirrzh would find out who the true Conquerors around here really were.

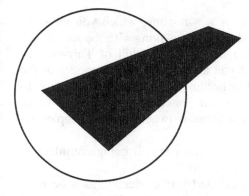

 The spokesman of the two Mrachanis spoke, his voice soft and low and with an earnestness that tugged oddly at Commander Thrr-mezaz's emotions. "You must listen to us, Commander of the Zhirrzh," the translation came a few beats later through the translator-link nestled in Thrr-mezaz's ear slits. "We are in great danger here on Dorcas. You must persuade your leaders to bring us to them."

"We're doing everything in our power to protect you, Lahettilas," Thrr-mezaz said, the translation into the Human-Conqueror language coming a few beats later from the speaker on his shoulder, linked by darklight beams to the interpreter installed in one of the buildings across the landing field. "You must understand that the Overclan Seating and Warrior Command are extremely busy—"

Lahettilas cut him off, the earnestness in his voice changing abruptly to scorn. "Everything in your power? You harbor the Human-Conqueror responsible for a vicious attack intended to be fatal to us; and yet you claim to be protecting us?"

"The Human-Conqueror prisoner Srgent-janovetz is being carefully watched," Second Commander Klnn-vavgi said from beside Thrr-mezaz. "If he was the one who launched that explosives attack on your quarters last fullarc, he won't have the opportunity to repeat it."

The second Mrachani growled something. "So you say," the translation came. "Yet you concede you don't even know the mechanism of the attack. How, then, can you presume to guarantee our safety?"

"I never said your safety was guaranteed," Thrr-mezaz said coldly. There was something about these aliens and their mannerisms that he found vaguely but increasingly irritating. And the last thing he needed right now was a lecture on his responsibilities as the commander of the

Zhirrzh ground warriors. "Dorcas is a war zone, which you chose to enter. You'll just have to face the dangers here along with the rest of us."

Lahettilas spoke again, his tone matching the chill of Thrr-mezaz's own voice. "The difference is that you are warriors, Commander of the Zhirrzh. We are ambassadors. Furthermore, it was *not* our choice to come here to the surface into your war zone. Our request was to be taken to your leaders to discuss an alliance between our two peoples. As we have asked before."

"And as I have said before, that decision is still being considered," Thrr-mezaz said. "That's the best I can do."

Lahettilas inhaled deeply, then exhaled just as deeply, as if he were breathing out part of his own essence with the action. His voice changed again, turning soft, with a sorrow that seemed to twist beneath Thrr-mezaz's tongue. "I suppose I understand," the translation came. "Distrust and fear—perhaps they are an inevitable part of warfare. Still, it would be a bitter consequence if such distrust led to the destruction of both our peoples."

"A bitter consequence, indeed," Thrr-mezaz agreed. "On the other side, the Zhirrzh are a long way yet from such destruction."

Lahettilas spoke again, his tone turning dark and grim. "Perhaps you are closer than you realize. Your Warrior Command urgently needs to hear about the weapon called CIRCE. If the Human-Conquerors are able to reconstruct it—"

Behind the Mrachanis an Elder abruptly appeared, only his transparent face protruding through the wall. "End this conversation immediately, Commander," he hissed.

In the two fullarcs since they'd landed there, the Mrachanis had gotten faster at trying to locate the source of these brief Elder communications. But they weren't yet quite fast enough, and the Elder had vanished before they were able to turn around. Lahettilas spoke— "These faint Zhirrzh voices disturb me, Commander of the Zhirrzh. Where do they come from?"

"I'll speak to Warrior Command about your request," Thrr-mezaz told him, ignoring the question. "We must go now. The warriors will look after you."

Lahettilas did the inhale/exhale thing again and bowed his face briefly toward the floor as he spoke. "Very well. I suppose it is all we can do. Certainly all which those of us who are minor players in this span of history can hope to accomplish."

"Farewell, then," Thrr-mezaz said, turning away from the aliens, a sudden flush of annoyance flowing across his tongue. A minor player. Was that all these aliens considered him to be, a minor player?

How dare they make such a presumption? He was Thrr-mezaz; Kee'rr, commander of a Zhirrzh beachhead in enemy territory. Not in any way a minor player.

And he would prove it to them. He would get to Warrior Command, all right—maybe even to the Overclan Prime himself. He would get this straightened out so fast, it would make their fur twist.

"Arrogant little overgrown nornins, aren't they?" Klnn-vavgi muttered at Thrr-mezaz's side as they headed across the landing field toward the headquarters building.

"Extremely," Thrr-mezaz growled back. "I don't know how Mrachanis look at it, Second, but I don't consider any Zhirrzh in a war zone to be a minor player."

"We'll just have to make sure we prove that to them." Klnn-vavgi glanced back over his shoulder, flicking his tongue thoughtfully. "It happened again," he said, lowering his voice. "Did you notice? Third time in the past two fullarcs, by my count."

"You mean the Elder who was handling the pathway back to Warrior Command suddenly cutting off the conversation?"

"Exactly," Klnn-vavgi said. "All the more interesting, given the chance they're taking."

"Indeed," Thrr-mezaz murmured. Supreme Ship Commander Dkll-kumvit had made it clear as fine glasswork that the existence of Zhirrzh Elders was to be kept a closely guarded secret from the Mrachanis. Yet the supreme commanders at Warrior Command, listening at the other end of the Elder pathway, had now risked exposing that secret. Not once, but three times.

Which could only mean they considered it even more urgent that those particular three conversations be interrupted. Which implied that Lahettilas knew something that Thrr-mezaz and the rest of the Zhirrzh warriors weren't supposed to hear. "I take it you also noticed the common element each time?" he asked Klnn-vavgi.

His second in command flicked his tongue in grim agreement. "That weapon Lahettilas keeps wanting to talk to Warrior Command about. The thing he calls CIRCE. I wonder what it is."

"I'll bet Warrior Command knows," Thrr-mezaz said, glancing around. He didn't see any Elders hovering around listening, but with Elders that didn't necessarily mean anything. Insubstantial and virtually transparent, they were ideally suited for eavesdropping.

"Something unsuitable for us minor players, no doubt," Klnn-vavgi said. "I don't know about you, Thrr-mezaz, but I'm getting the taste of politics dripping all over this thing."

"Maybe," Thrr-mezaz said. "I wonder . . . no."

"What?"

"Just a thought," Thrr-mezaz said, looking around again. "Whatever the Mrachanis or Warrior Command know about this, I'll bet our Human-Conqueror prisoner could tell us the whole story."

"Interesting thought," Klnn-vavgi agreed. "Maybe we ought to go have a little talk with him."

For a handful of beats Thrr-mezaz was tempted to agree. As a Zhirrzh commander in the war zone, it seemed only right that he should know everything Warrior Command did about enemy weapons his warriors might be facing.

But the Human-Conqueror prisoner, Srgent-janovetz, was under continual monitoring by the beachhead's Elders. If they asked him about CIRCE, Warrior Command would know about it within ten beats. Cvv-panav, the Speaker for Dhaa'rr in the Overclan Seating, had already tried once to have Thrr-mezaz ousted as commander of the Dorcas ground warriors. Pressing to learn something Warrior Command obviously wanted kept secret would be all the excuse he would need to finish the job.

Thrr-mezaz looked sideways at Klnn-vavgi, a sudden doubt oozing beneath his tongue. Could that in fact be the outcome his second in command was trying for here? To goad Thrr-mezaz into doing something that would get him removed from command? Klnn-vavgi was also Dhaa'rr, after all; perhaps his oft-stated contempt for clan politics was a lie designed to lull Thrr-mezaz into complacency.

His tongue flicked in self-disgust. An absurd thought, and he was ashamed with himself for having even entertained it. Lahettilas and all that talk about distrust must have gotten deeper under his tongue than he'd realized. "Let's try something else first," he told Klnn-vavgi, changing direction toward the eastern edge of the landing field. "Come on."

The warriors and techs had long since finished their examination of the storehouse building where the two Mrachanis had come under Human-Conqueror attack a fullarc ago. Outside the eastern wall where the doors had once stood, the ground was covered with wooden splinters, and Thrr-mezaz found himself wincing as he and Klnn-vavgi crunched their way through them. There, crushed beneath those doors when the explosion blew them off their hinges, two Zhirrzh warriors had been abruptly and prematurely raised to Eldership.

And were still suffering the consequences of that raising. Yanked instantly back across the three-hundred-plus light-cyclics separating Dorcas and their preserved *fsss* organs on Oaccanv, both of the new Elders were twisted in the temporary insanity of anchoring shock.

As were the warriors who had been raised to Eldership during their initial invasion of Dorcas. Now, seventeen fullarcs later, that group was still showing no signs of coming out of the madness.

There were, Thrr-mezaz knew, whispered rumors of searcher and healer theories that had supposedly proved that a Zhirrzh who was too far from his *fsss* organ at the time of his raising would be forever locked into anchoring shock. The clan and family leaders uniformly denied that such theories had ever even been formally proposed, let alone tested or proved. But that didn't stop the rumors. Thrr-mezaz could only hope that, if such an outer limit existed, Dorcas was still inside it.

Three more jagged holes had been ripped in the north wall by the Human-Conqueror explosives after the blast that had destroyed the doors, showering more splinters and wood fragments outside the building. "What are we doing here?" Klnn-vavgi asked as Thrr-mezaz led the way to the middle of the room.

"I have a special arrangement with one of our communicators," Thrr-mezaz told him. "He's supposed to look in here a couple times per tentharc to see if I want him."

"Really," Klnn-vavgi said, eyeing his commander. "A special arrangement, you say."

"Yes," Thrr-mezaz said, starting to have second thoughts about this idea. The secure pathway which the Dhaa'rr Elder Prr't-casst-a had set up two fullarcs ago between Thrr-mezaz and his brother Thrr-gilag had been for one purpose only: to discuss the suspected capture of Prr't-casst-a's husband, Prr't-zevisti, by the Human-Conquerors. Trying to use the pathway for any other purpose might well meet with resistance from the Elders involved in carrying the messages back and forth, particularly if the discussion turned to Dhaa'rr political moves. Perhaps he should just forget about this and hope that the Mrachanis were overstating their case on this CIRCE threat.

Abruptly, the Elder appeared. "Commander Thrr-mezaz," he said. "You have a message for Prr't-casst-a?"

"Not for Prr't-casst-a, no," Thrr-mezaz said. "But I'd like to use the secure pathway she set up to contact my brother, Searcher Thrr-gilag. Can you do it?"

"I can try," the Elder said, sounding a bit doubtful. "I thought Thrr-gilag had returned to Oaccanv."

"He has," Thrr-mezaz confirmed. "He should be at either the Overclan Seating complex in Unity City, the Thrr-family shrine near Cliffside Dales, or at the Frr-family town of Reeds Village."

"I obey, Commander," the Elder said, and vanished.

"You think Thrr-gilag knows something about this CIRCE weapon?" Klnn-vavgi asked.

"He spent nineteen fullarcs on Base World Twelve interrogating the Human-Conqueror prisoner Pheylan Cavanagh," Thrr-mezaz reminded him. "If CIRCE is as dangerous as Lahettilas seems to think, there's a good chance it would have come up in conversation."

"Maybe." Klnn-vavgi looked around the damaged building. "While you're at it, you might ask him if he knows anything about Human-Conqueror explosive weapons."

The beats went by, adding up until they'd reached a hunbeat. Then two hunbeats, then three, then four. Thrr-mezaz looked around, feeling his tail gradually speeding up its spinning movement and wondering what could have gone wrong. Anchored at both his preserved *fsss* organ and at the small *fsss* cutting just east of the Dorcas beachhead, the Elder could transfer instantly back and forth across the light-cyclics between Dorcas and the Dhaa'rr homeworld of Dharanv. Passing the message on to an Elder on Dharanv who was also double-anchored to a cutting in the appropriate region of Oaccanv should likewise have been no problem. Could the Overclan Seating have moved up the departure time of the diplomatic mission to the Mrachani homeworld? Thrr-gilag was supposed to go on that mission, Thrr-mezaz knew; a changed departure schedule might account for no one's being able to find him.

And then, just as he'd decided that that was probably the case, the Elder reappeared. " 'This is Thrr-gilag,' " he quoted. " 'Hello, my brother. Is anything wrong?' "

"I was about to ask you the same thing," Thrr-mezaz said to the Elder, his tail slowing down slightly. "Where are you, anyway?"

The Elder nodded and vanished. This time he was back in less than half a hunbeat. " 'As it happens, I'm aboard a ship heading your way. I should be there in about five fullarcs.' "

Thrr-mezaz frowned. "I thought Klnn-dawan-a was going to be coming."

" 'She will be,' " the message came back. " 'She'll be leaving from Shamanv and ought to arrive there a fullarc or two ahead of me. She'll have the package with her.' "

Thrr-mezaz felt his tail twitch. *The package:* their private code word for the secret and highly illegal cutting Thrr-gilag and Klnn-dawan-a had somehow managed to get from Prr't-zevisti's *fsss* organ on Dharanv the previous fullarc.

A cutting that was probably Prr't-zevisti's last chance at life. But that wouldn't matter a flick of the tongue if anyone caught them with it. "Any problems on that side?" he asked.

" 'None that I know of. I haven't spoken with Klnn-dawan-a since I left Dharanv.' "

"So why are you coming here, too?" Thrr-mezaz asked. "I thought you were supposed to be going to the Mrachani homeworld."

" 'I was. I've been taken off that mission.' "

Klnn-vavgi muttered something under his breath. "Taken off?" Thrr-mezaz echoed. "Whose flat-headed idea was that?"

The Elder nodded and vanished. "I'll bet you twenty fullarcs' pay it was politics," Klnn-vavgi growled. "I can see the Speaker for Dhaa'rr's tongue marks in it from here."

"Maybe not," Thrr-mezaz said, uneasiness speeding up his tail again. "I talked to my father last fullarc, and he was trying desperately to locate Thrr-gilag. Something serious is going on with our family back home, and Thrr-gilag's being dropped from the Mrachani mission may be one of the repercussions."

"Must be something really serious to get Thrr't-rokik desperate," Klnn-vavgi commented. "I've only met him a couple of times, but he never struck me as the excitable type."

"He's not," Thrr-mezaz agreed grimly.

"I take it you don't want to talk about the situation?"

Thrr-mezaz flicked his tongue in a negative. "Most of what I could say right now would be just speculation."

The Elder reappeared. " 'It was a joint decision by the Speaker for Dhaa'rr and the Overclan Prime,' " he quoted Thrr-gilag's reply. " 'I'll give you the details when I arrive.' "

"All right," Thrr-mezaz said. "A couple of other questions for you. First: do you know anything about Human-Conqueror explosives?"

" 'Only that they're as effective as lasers for raising Zhirrzh to Eldership,' " the bitter-tasting reply came back a hunbeat later.

"I know that much," Thrr-mezaz said. "Second: do you know anything about a Human-Conqueror weapon called CIRCE?"

The Elder vanished . . . and once again the beats began to drag by. "It's being awfully quiet out there," Klnn-vavgi said as the silence entered its third hunbeat. "How secure did you say this pathway was?"

The Elder was back before Thrr-mezaz could answer. " 'I'm sorry, Thrr-mezaz, but this really isn't something I can discuss.' "

Thrr-mezaz threw a look at Klnn-vavgi. So they'd been right on both counts. There was something about CIRCE that Warrior Command didn't want anyone else to know. And Thrr-gilag knew what that something was. "I understand, my brother," Thrr-mezaz said to the Elder. "Have a safe journey."

" 'You take care, too. I'll see you in a few fullarcs.' "

Thrr-mezaz nodded to the Elder. "Thank you. You may release the pathway."

"I obey, Commander," the Elder said, and once again vanished.

"So we were right," Klnn-vavgi murmured.

"Looks that way." Thrr-mezaz looked around the empty storehouse, wondering if any of the other Elders might have eavesdropped on their conversation. "We'd better be getting back."

"I wonder what kind of weapon it is," Klnn-vavgi commented as they headed back across the landing area. "Some kind of nuclear explosive, you think?"

"I have no idea," Thrr-mezaz said, squinting against the bright postmidarc sunlight and the dust being kicked up by a brisk northerly wind. "What bothers me more than the *what* is the *why*. Specifically, why haven't they already used it against us?"

"Maybe they have," Klnn-vavgi suggested. "Maybe what the Mrachanis are calling CIRCE are what we call the Copperhead warriors."

"I doubt it," Thrr-mezaz said. "Thrr-gilag's study group got the name Copperheads directly from their prisoner. Surely the Mrachanis have had enough contact with the Human-Conquerors not to make that kind of mistake."

"Unless the Human-Conquerors use different words when talking to different races," Klnn-vavgi pointed out. "It would be a simple way to impede communication among their enemies."

Thrr-mezaz flicked his tongue. "Interesting thought."

"Something else to ask Thrr-gilag when he gets here," Klnn-vavgi said. "Find out if the prisoner ever mentioned CIRCE to them—"

Abruptly, an Elder appeared in front of them. "Commander Thrr-mezaz: urgent message from Supreme Ship Commander Dkll-kumvit," he said, his faint voice almost lost in the wind. "He's received news from Warrior Command that Shamanv was attacked two tentharcs ago by a group of Human-Conqueror warcraft."

Thrr-mezaz's tail twitched. *Shamanv*—that was where Thrr-gilag had said Klnn-dawan-a would be leaving from. Carrying Prr't-zevisti's new cutting with her . . . "Damage?" he asked.

"Unclear," the Elder said. "The message said only that two Zhirrzh warships were involved in driving the attackers away and that one of them suffered severe internal damage from the Human-Conqueror explosive missiles. It was also reported that one enemy warcraft was destroyed. Supreme Ship Commander Dkll-kumvit thinks it may signal the beginning of a new Human-Conqueror offensive."

"Understood," Thrr-mezaz said. "Order all ground warriors to full alert and have the Stingbirds prepared to fly."

"I obey," the Elder said, and vanished.

"Come on," Thrr-mezaz said to Klnn-vavgi, picking up his pace toward their headquarters building.

And wondering if his second in command had noticed yet the frightening implications of the Shamanv attack. Either the enemy had taken a Zhirrzh prisoner and made him talk, or had found and deciphered the optronic data from a Zhirrzh combat recorder—

Or had a workable method for tracking spacecraft through the tunnelline between stars.

Only two fullarcs ago Klnn-vavgi had speculated the enemy might have such impossible technology. Ten fullarcs before that Thrr-gilag had halfjokingly suggested the same thing.

Perhaps both had been right. And if so, it put a sudden new edge of urgency onto this war. Thanks to the Human-Conqueror recorder they'd recovered from the wreckage of that first battle, Warrior Command had till now had the advantage of knowing the locations of their enemies' worlds and bases, while the Zhirrzh worlds had remained hidden away in the vastness of space. Now, suddenly, that advantage was gone. The Human-Conquerors could now stab the war straight back into the faces of the Zhirrzh.

Could begin to live up to the name the Mrachanis had given them. The name Conquerors.

"We're in trouble, Thrr-mezaz," Klnn-vavgi said quietly from beside him. "With CIRCE, and now this, we're in trouble."

"Yes," Thrr-mezaz said, glancing up again at the sky. "I know."

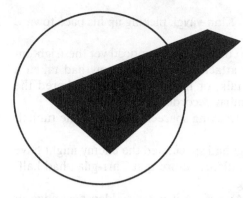

3 *The data-feed connection is established at 15:52:25, 22.41 minutes later than the estimate I was given orally at 09:21:44 this morning. There is a contact transient of 0.04 second; and then the feed settles into proper connection linkage.*

The information given to me at 09:20:21 was that I would be testifying before the inquiry board assembling in Conference Room Three of the Edo Peacekeeper base. My in-built caution requires me to confirm that I have indeed linked to the proper location. The contact trace takes me 0.02 second, and I am indeed able to confirm that I have been linked to the properly designated interface terminal. In the process I also discover that a Corbaline Type 74-D-6 encryption has been established in the data line. This too is as expected.

I sublink the optical and auditory sensors of the interface terminal. The primary lens is an Avergand-4 fish-eye; I calculate and initiate the necessary correction transform to bring the image into standard format. There are fifteen human beings in the room within sight of the lens: two males and one female seated at a table centered 21.5 degrees to the left of the terminal at a mean distance of 2.54 meters, ten males seated in a single row centered 10.3 degrees to the right at a mean distance of 4.15 meters, and two males seated 50.3 degrees to the right at a mean distance of 3.77 meters. From the auditory breathing patterns I deduce there are three more people outside the range of the lens.

I inspect the room's occupants more closely, using visual-recognition algorithms and comparing against the 5,128,339 facial images in my current-events file. The three people at the table are senior Peacekeeper officers: Vice Admiral Tal Omohundro, Major General Petros Hampstead, and Brigadier Elizabet Yost. One of the two men seated to the far right ranks above them:

Admiral Thomas Rudzinski, one of the three supreme military officers making up the Peacekeeper Triad. Seated beside him is Commander Pheylan Cavanagh, whom I flew to Edo from Conqueror imprisonment eleven days seven hours twenty-seven point four six minutes ago.

The men in the single row are equally familiar: those who participated in Commander Cavanagh's rescue. In the leftmost chair is Aric Cavanagh, Commander Cavanagh's elder brother; seated beside him is former Copperhead commander Adam Quinn, currently chief of security for the CavTronics corporation. The other eight are the Copperhead pilots and tail men who accompanied us: Commander Thomas Masefield—

Vice Admiral Omohundro clears his throat. "Please identify yourself."

I delay my reply 0.11 second in order to complete my positive identification of the Copperheads, confirming all is as expected, and sublink the terminal's auditory speaker. "My name is Max."

"Your operational designation and parameters?"

I do not enjoy talking about myself. But the specific question has been asked. "I'm a parasentient computer of the Carthage-Ivy-Gamma Series. I have Class Seven decision-making capabilities, a modified Korngold-Che decay-driven randomized logic structure, Kylaynov file-access system, and eight point seven megamyncs of Steuben dyad-compressed memory."

Vice Admiral Omohundro's face changes subtly. Comparison with standard human-expression algorithms suggests he is surprised or perhaps impressed by my capabilities. "You were the guidance system for Aric Cavanagh's illegal rescue mission into Conqueror space?"

"I was the guidance system for the fueler used in the mission to rescue Commander Pheylan Cavanagh."

Brigadier Yost raises her chin 1.4 centimeters. "Please examine the transcript file of the hearing up to this point."

The file contains the previous three days of evidence and testimony. Most is familiar to me, detailing how Lord Stewart Cavanagh, his son Aric, and daughter, Melinda, learned Commander Cavanagh had possibly been captured by the Conquerors, and conceived a private mission to rescue him. The testimony concerning the mission itself is also familiar: the futile search over two likely planets, the escape from two Conqueror warships over the third planet, and the unusual logical deduction by which Aric located the correct world.

Other parts of the testimony are unfamiliar to me, and I examine them with interest. I learn that it was Reserve Wing Commander Iniko Bokamba, Security Chief Quinn's former commander in the Copperheads, who helped fabricate the orders that transferred Commander Masefield and his Copperhead unit to Dorcas and placed them under Security Chief Quinn's com-

mand. From one section of Commander Cavanagh's testimony I also learn that the non-humans we have named the Conquerors call themselves the Zhirrzh.

I have completed my examination of the file before Brigadier Yost has finished speaking. "I have done so."

"Do you find any discrepancies in the testimony?"

"None of consequence. Seven time marks and four other stated numerical values are slightly incorrect. I have added a parallel file with the corrections marked."

The three officers pause 1.14 minutes to study my changes. I spend the first 26.33 seconds of that time examining my link to this terminal, searching for the reason the initial contact transient was a full 0.04 second. I discover that one of the contact points within the building is misaligned. I locate the building computer's maintenance file and insert a note to have the component replaced.

I spend the final 42.07 seconds of the hiatus studying reflections from the various pieces of polished metal in the room, hoping to use them to reconstruct the images of the three people outside my range of vision. The exercise meets with partial success; I am able to determine that two of the men are sitting together and one is sitting alone. But without access to a sensor array that would permit me to accurately map the contours of the reflective surfaces, I cannot make a positive identification of any of the faces.

Major General Petros Hampstead is the first to look up at me. "Tell me, Max, were you told this mission would involve breaking the law?"

"There was no need for anyone to tell me. I have access to the complete Commonwealth legal code."

"You agree, then, that Commonwealth law was broken?"

"Yes."

Vice Admiral Omohundro frowns at the terminal lens. I examine his expression and deduce he was not expecting my answer. "Did any of the defendants offer you any justification for their actions?"

"No."

Major General Hampstead touches Vice Admiral Omohundro on the shoulder with the fingertips of his right hand and whispers into his ear. After two short sentences Brigadier Yost leans toward them to listen. I attempt to listen, but the terminal's auditory sensors are inadequate to the task. I reexamine my Peacekeeper military legal code listing, attempting to extrapolate their conversation. From my expression algorithms and a tone/inference examination of the trial transcript, I calculate a probability of 0.87 that the three judges do not in fact wish to find Aric and the Copperheads guilty. This is also consistent with several conversations that took place both before and after Commander Cavanagh's rescue, in which the participants of the rescue mission speculated that Peacekeeper Command would find it politically difficult to prosecute them should the mission be successful.

Security Chief Quinn stands up. *The three officers cease their whispered conversation and look at him. I examine Quinn's expression, deduce an emotional mix centered upon grim amusement.* "If I may beg a moment of the court's time, Admiral Omohundro?"

Vice Admiral Omohundro looks briefly at the terminal lens. Expression analysis indicates wariness. "Thank you for your testimony and corrections, Max. If we need anything more, we'll contact you."

He reaches for a switch on the table. "You may speak, Commander Quinn."

"Sir, it seems obvious to me—"

The visual and auditory linkages are broken as the data-feed line is disconnected. With Vice Admiral Omohundro's dismissal my part in the proceedings is over.

But I am curious. Security Chief Quinn's expression and verbal tone indicated a high degree of importance to what he is about to say. Furthermore, when Lord Cavanagh had me installed aboard the fueler, he ordered me to protect his son Aric to the fullest of my capabilities. That order has not been rescinded; and without information I cannot reasonably expect to fulfill it.

The far end of the linkage is broken, but the fluctuations of the disconnect transient are still flickering. Through the noise I search along the linkage to the misaligned contact point I identified earlier. The bleed-through ratio is approximately 0.84 percent; small, but adequate for my purposes. Boosting my signal, I jump a command across the contact onto a new linkage. The command tracks to a control node, which is still aligned to accept my presence within the system. My command is noted and executed, and the original data feed is reconnected.

"—that Peacekeeper Command can hardly afford the luxury of taking eight Copperheads out of their fighters and locking them away somewhere. Furthermore, I'm sure the three of you have more urgent matters to attend to than to preside over full-blown court-martial proceedings."

Vice Admiral Omohundro's expression goes through four subtle but recognizable emotional changes as Security Chief Quinn speaks. The final expression appears to conform most closely to cautious anticipation. "And yet such a court-martial is clearly called for, Mr. Quinn. Even in time of war, command discipline must be maintained."

"Agreed, sir. On the other hand, you must also consider troop morale. And, after all, we *did* succeed in bringing Commander Cavanagh back."

Vice Admiral Omohundro looks over at Commander Cavanagh. There is no longer any doubt: his expression is one of anticipation. "If you have a point to make, please get to it."

Quinn's face changes subtly. I match the expression with suppressed anxiety. "It's been suggested to me, sir, that the Peacekeepers might appreciate regaining my services as a Copperhead pilot. I realize that in the current military situation you could probably order me to serve; I'd like to suggest that if the charges against Commander Masefield and his unit are dropped, no such formalities will be necessary. I will resign from my position at CavTronics Industries and voluntarily rejoin the Copperheads."

There is a distinct flicker in four of the polished metalwork surfaces within my line of sight. I examine the reflections and deduce that one of the still as-yet-unseen observers has crossed his arms across his chest. Further examination is inconclusive, but I estimate a probability of 0.60 that his expression has also changed.

Vice Admiral Omohundro looks in that direction, his expression also changing. "You have a comment to make, Parlimin VanDiver?"

I have a name now, and I take 0.01 second to locate and study the appropriate file. Jacy VanDiver, fifty-five, from Grampians on Avon; appointed a member of the NorCoord Parliament in 2297. The file notes several acrimonious contacts between Parlimin VanDiver and Lord Cavanagh over the past fifteen years, involving both business and political matters. Another curious fact catches my attention: Parlimin VanDiver was also under consideration for a seat in the NorCoord Parliament in 2291 and 2294. In both instances Governor Fletcher of Grampians on Avon appointed Lord Cavanagh instead.

"Not at the moment, Admiral." *Parlimin VanDiver's voice is rich and deep. Without a baseline reading I cannot perform a complete stress/emotion analysis.* "Perhaps later."

Vice Admiral Omohundro continues to look at Parlimin VanDiver for another 0.63 second, then returns his attention to Security Chief Quinn. "Very well, Mr. Quinn. As head of this hearing board, I hereby accept your offer. You are hereby reinstated as a lieutenant in the Copperheads and will report to Sector Commander Copperheads immediately for duty assignment."

Vice Admiral Omohundro picks up a gavel lying beside his right hand and raises it to a height of 16.5 centimeters above the table. "This hearing is adjourned."

The gavel came down sharply on the table, and Pheylan Cavanagh breathed a quiet sigh of relief.

It was over.

"There we go," Admiral Rudzinski murmured from beside him as they stood up. "That wasn't so hard, was it?"

Pheylan smiled lopsidedly. "No, sir. Hardly even worth coming in for." The admiral smiled wryly in return, then sobered. "You realize, of course, that this is hardly a triumph for any of them. They've escaped prison sentences so that they can be sent to the front lines of a war."

"That's where they should be, sir," Pheylan reminded him quietly. "We're Peacekeepers. That's our job."

And then Aric was there in front of him, trying hard not to grin and not succeeding all that well. "Well, that's over," he said, holding out a hand. "Thanks, Pheylan, for testifying for us."

Pheylan brushed past the outstretched hand and enveloped his older brother in a brief bear hug. "I think most of the debt is still on my side of the ledger," he reminded Aric as he stepped back again. "What are you going to do now?"

Aric grimaced. "I'm going to get the fueler released from impoundment and try to track Father down."

"Still no word from him?" Pheylan asked.

"No," Aric said. "I finally got a chance to talk to Captain Teva, though. It turns out Dad deliberately ordered him and the *Cavatina* away from Mra-mig about two and a half weeks ago."

"Yes, I heard he'd been on Mra-mig," Rudzinski said. "What was he doing there?"

"Looking for information about the Zhirrzh that might help us find Pheylan," Aric told him. "That 'Conquerors Without Reason' title we've been using apparently originated from some Mrach legend."

"Did he find anything?" Rudzinski asked.

"Apparently not," Aric said. "At least that was the message he sent to Dorcas with the *Cavatina.* After that, near as I can tell, he just dropped off the edge of the universe."

A breath of air brushed the back of Pheylan's neck, and he turned to find a burly, middle-aged man standing off to the side, listening silently to the conversation. "May we help you, sir?" he asked the man.

"This is Assistant Commonwealth Liaison Petr Bronski," Rudzinski said before the man could answer. "He works out of the Commonwealth consulate on Mra-ect. He saw Lord Cavanagh briefly on Mra-mig, and I asked him back here to see if he could shed any light on his disappearance."

"I wish I could help, Mr. Cavanagh," Bronski said. "But as I told Admiral Rudzinski earlier, I only saw your father for a few minutes in his hotel room in Mig-Ka City. There was some question about whether he was harboring a non-Mrach who was slated for deportation, and we were asked to check it out. My people and I searched his suite for the non-Mrach, found nothing, and left."

"That's interesting, Mr. Bronski," Aric said, a slight frown creasing his forehead. "What hotel did you say you spoke to him at?"

"I didn't say," Bronski said coolly. "It was the Mrapiratta Hotel."

"Yes, that's where Teva said he was staying," Aric agreed. "He also said he picked up a report on the way off-planet about a disturbance at that hotel. Gunfire, possibly even an explosion."

"An explosion?" Pheylan demanded. "You didn't tell me anything about this."

"Oh, Dad was okay," Aric assured him. "He was already outside the hotel when he phoned Teva and told him to get the *Cavatina* off-planet."

Rudzinski cocked an eyebrow at Bronski. "You know anything about this?"

"We had a minor altercation with a couple of Bhurtala on our way out of the hotel," Bronski said with a shrug. "Nothing serious." His lip twisted slightly. "Except, of course, that dealing with the aftermath prevented me from getting back to see Lord Cavanagh. Otherwise, I might have been able to stop whatever it was that happened to him."

"Yes," Rudzinski murmured. "Still, I doubt that Lord Cavanagh's in any real danger. Mitri Kolchin is with him, and Kolchin was one of the best to ever come out of the Peacekeeper commandos. Wherever he's gotten to, he'll come back when he's ready." He pulled a card from his inner pocket. "In the meantime, we have a war to fight."

Pheylan came to reflexive attention. "Yes, sir. Are those my orders?"

"Yes," Rudzinski said, handing him the card. "Effective immediately, you're assigned to the inspection team going over what's left of your former prison on the world we've designated Target One."

"An inspection team?" Pheylan frowned at the card as he took it. "I asked to be assigned to whatever force is scheduled to attack the Zhirrzh beachhead on Dorcas. My sister, Melinda, was caught on the ground there when they attacked."

"I'm sure your request will remain under consideration," Rudzinski said. "But first we need to know everything we can about the threat we're facing. There may be something of significance on Target One that no one but you would recognize."

Pheylan grimaced. To be shunted off to sand-sifting duty while his sister sat helplessly beneath enemy guns . . .

But it made sense. Unfortunately. "Understood, sir."

"Good," Rudzinski said. "Your ship leaves in two hours. Details are on the card."

"Yes, sir." Pheylan turned back to Aric. "Aric—"

"I know," Aric said. "You just watch yourself out there, okay? I don't want to have to come after you again."

"Don't worry, you won't," Pheylan said, squeezing his older brother's shoulder. "You watch yourself, too."

"Max and I will be fine," Aric assured him. "I'll see you later."

He gave Pheylan one last smile, then turned and headed for the door. Quinn and the other Copperheads, Pheylan saw, had already left the room, presumably to pick up their own orders. Perhaps sometime in the two hours before his flight he'd be able to track them down and thank them one last time for risking their lives and careers to rescue him.

After today their careers were out of danger. The same couldn't be said about their lives. Not with the Zhirrzh out there.

The Conquerors.

He took a careful breath. "With your permission, Admiral?"

"Dismissed, Commander," Rudzinski said softly. "Good luck."

The Copperheads and Aric Cavanagh had gone their various ways, Admiral Rudzinski had headed back to the war room, the three presiding officers had likewise branched off to attend to business elsewhere, and Petr Bronski had the exit door in sight when the voice he'd been both expecting and dreading came from behind him.

"A word with you, Mr. Bronski."

Bronski slowed, half turning to look over his shoulder. Parlimin Jacy VanDiver was coming toward him, the silent bodyguard who'd been sitting beside him at the hearing tagging along. "I'm in something of a hurry, Parlimin VanDiver," he said. "Is this something the Commonwealth diplomatic office on Edo can handle?"

"No," VanDiver said flatly. "It's not."

Bronski grimaced to himself. But lowly assistant Commonwealth liaisons did not simply ignore senior NorCoord political powerhouses. "Yes, sir," he said, coming to a stop.

The bodyguard was good, all right. VanDiver didn't have to say a word; the other simply stepped to the nearest door—a media communications-processing office, from the tag on the wall beside it—glanced briefly inside, then nodded to his boss. "In here, Mr. Bronski," VanDiver said, waving at the open door. "If you don't mind."

As if he had a real choice in the matter. "Yes, sir," Bronski said. Stepping past beneath the bodyguard's watchful eye, he went inside.

The office contained four cluttered desks—currently unoccupied—drawn up like beleaguered soldiers around a centralized SieTec transfer-node computer terminal. VanDiver and the bodyguard came in behind him, the latter closing the door and taking up position beside it. "Have a seat?" VanDiver invited, sitting down at one of the desks and waving Bronski to his choice of the others.

"Thank you," Bronski said, choosing a seat that put the SieTec more or less between him and the bodyguard. "I have to tell you, sir, that I'm due at the Commonwealth liaison center in thirty minutes."

"I'll make it brief," VanDiver said. "I overheard your conversation a few minutes ago with Admiral Rudzinski and the Cavanagh boys. You lied to them."

He wasn't one for shaving words, that was for sure. "That's an interesting accusation, sir."

VanDiver lifted his eyebrows. "Is that all the reaction I get? No denials or cries of indignation? No reddening of the face at such an insult to your integrity?"

Bronski sighed. "I'm a very lowly Commonwealth civil servant, Parlimin," he reminded the other. "We're not encouraged to talk back to NorCoord government officials."

VanDiver leaned back in his chair. "Yes, Taurin Lee thought that was all there was to you, too," he commented. "You remember Taurin Lee, don't you?"

"Of course, sir," Bronski said, keeping his voice steady. "Mr. Lee approached my group as we were coming into the Mrapiratta Hotel. He identified himself as your aide, showed me the NorCoord Parliament carte blanche you'd given him, and informed me he'd be joining our meeting with Lord Cavanagh."

"And after that meeting?"

"As I told Admiral Rudzinski, we ran into trouble with some Bhurtala," Bronski said. "By the time we'd settled the matter with the Mrach authorities, Lord Cavanagh and his people had left Mra-mig."

"And Lee?"

Bronski spread his hands. "I really don't know. He left us while we were discussing the incident with the Mrach authorities."

VanDiver didn't move, but suddenly there was frost in the air. "That's a lie, Bronski," he said coldly. "Lee was with you when you chased Cavanagh to the Yycroman world of Phormbi. I have a skitter report from him from Mra-mig telling me you'd all be leaving within the hour."

Silently, Bronski bit down on the inside of his cheek. He would have sworn that Lee hadn't had a single chance during their time together to sneak any kind of message off to anyone. Apparently, the man was sharper than he'd realized. "With all due respect, Parlimin, I don't know what you're talking about," he told VanDiver, putting a slightly uncertain earnestness in his tone. "Perhaps he'd planned to join us for our trip, but if he did, he never talked to me about doing so."

VanDiver's expression cracked, just a little. So he wasn't absolutely certain. "You didn't say anything about this other trip to Admiral Rudzinski just now."

Bronski shrugged. "I didn't think there was any point in mentioning it, since we failed to find Lord Cavanagh on Phormbi. It's all in the complete report I filed."

"I'll make sure I get a copy," VanDiver said darkly. "Curious, isn't it? Stewart Cavanagh disappears, and no one can find him. At approximately the same time, at approximately the same place, one of my aides also vanishes. Coincidence, Mr. Bronski?"

Bronski put on his best bewildered frown. "Mr. Lee has vanished? When?"

"Apparently right after he sent that message from Mra-mig," VanDiver told him. "At least no one's heard from him since then."

"I see," Bronski murmured. "I don't know what to say, Parlimin VanDiver, except that I'll certainly initiate inquiries as soon as I get back to the consulate on Mra-ect." He half rose to his feet. "If that's all, sir, I really do have to be going."

"Sit down, Bronski," VanDiver said coldly. "I'm not finished."

Silently, Bronski lowered himself back into his chair. "Yes, sir?"

For a long moment VanDiver gazed at him, his face hard and angry and suspicious. "I don't know exactly what's going on here," he said at last. "But I can guess enough of it. Cavanagh's up to something, something on the edge of illegal or a little ways over the line, and he's got his old friends in Parliament and the Peacekeepers busy smoothing the track or looking the other way. This so-called hearing was just dripping with paybacks, from Admiral Rudzinski on down. Typical Cavanagh, all the way across the board."

His expression hardened a little more. "But this time it isn't going to fly. I'm going to take him down; and everyone who's tied in with him is going down, too. *Everyone*, Bronski. Do I make myself clear?"

Bronski nodded, appreciating the irony of it all. He was probably the last person in the entire Commonwealth interested in doing favors for Lord Stewart Cavanagh. "Very clear, sir," he said evenly. "May I go now?"

Slowly, VanDiver leaned back in his chair. "You're a cool one, Bronski," he said. "We'll see how cool you manage to stay."

"Yes, sir," Bronski said noncommittally, standing up and sidling past the bodyguard. "Good day to you, Parlimin."

He went through the exit door, passing between the two Peacekeeper Marines who guarded this entrance to the base proper, and walked into the public reception area. Garcia was waiting for him there, lounging inconspicuously in one of the back chairs reading his plate. "Well?" Bronski asked without preamble as the other scrambled to his feet.

"He left eight minutes ago," Garcia said, falling into step beside Bronski. "Daschka's on him. What kept you?"

"An inflated mouth with a NorCoord Parlimin attached," Bronski growled. "We'd better watch this VanDiver character—he's already nibbling around the edges of this thing. Anything new at this end?"

"Nothing significant," Garcia said as they walked through the outer door into the warm Edo air. "Aric Cavanagh made one phone call, to that CavTronics parasentient computer aboard the fueler they used."

"Yeah, they did a linkage to him in the hearing room," Bronski said sourly. "Don't think I'd want him testifying for me if I were in trouble. What did Cavanagh say?"

"Only that he had a few details to clear up here on Edo and that after that they'd be heading to Avon together."

Inside his tunic Bronski's phone vibrated. He pulled it out and flipped it on. "Bronski."

Daschka's face appeared on the display. "Sir, I'm at the Kyura skitter depot," he said. "Aric Cavanagh just picked up a message."

Bronski threw a glance at Garcia. "You were supposed to put a flagger on any messages coming in for either of the Cavanaghs."

"Yes, sir, I did," Daschka said, his lip twisting in annoyance. "Obviously wasn't address-keyed by either of their names or by any obvious aliases. He spent a lot of time at the terminal, too—seemed to be referring to his plate through most of it."

"Some code name, then," Garcia suggested. "Set up in advance."

"Probably," Daschka agreed. "Do you want me to pick him up?"

Bronski rubbed his fingers together, trying to think this through. He had so few men here, and arresting Aric Cavanagh might draw too much unwelcome attention his direction. "Let's give him free track a little longer," he told Daschka. "Stay on him—see what he does. I'll send Cho Ming over to the depot and start a search on the messages. See if we can dig out which one he picked up."

"Right."

The screen went blank. "Going to take a lot of digging," Garcia pointed out as they headed across the parking area toward their car. "Seems to me about time we called in some reinforcements."

"We don't need reinforcements," Bronski said. "We can handle this ourselves."

"Yes, sir," Garcia said. "You know, of course, that pulling Cho Ming off the fueler will leave it unguarded."

"I don't care about the fueler," Bronski said tartly. "I don't really care about Aric Cavanagh, either. The point of this exercise is to get to Aric's daddy."

"Yes, sir," Garcia murmured.

He was wondering, Bronski knew. All of them were. Wondering what was so important about a middle-aged former NorCoord Parlimin that Bronski had pulled them off important surveillance duties in Mrach space to chase the man down. Most of them probably thought it was a personal vendetta of some kind. Wounded pride, maybe, for the way Lord Cavanagh and his bodyguard had left him trussed like a prize turkey back on Mra-mig.

He couldn't tell them the real reason. Not unless he wanted them to join Taurin Lee in the private quarantine he'd had set up on Mra-ect.

Eventually, of course, they would all wind up in quarantine, Bronski himself included. But not yet. Not until they could take Lord Cavanagh in with them.

Because like Lee, Cavanagh now knew the truth about CIRCE: that the legendary weapon whose existence had allowed the Northern Coordinate Union to dominate Commonwealth politics for nearly forty years didn't exist. Knew that it had, in fact, never existed.

And there was no way Bronski was going to let that truth leak out to a populace desperately counting on CIRCE to save them from the Conquerors. No way in hell. Wherever Cavanagh had gone to ground, they were going to find him.

And were going to silence him. One way or another.

Assistant Liaison Bronski and his companion exit the Peacekeeper base reception area 18.14 minutes after the adjournment of the hearing, leaving the active range of terminals to which I have access. I continue to observe Parlimin Jacy VanDiver and his companion, but their conversation is minimal and gains me no new data. Three point eight seven minutes after Assistant Liaison Bronski leaves, they too exit the base.

I withdraw my linkage from the base computer system and consider this new data. Particularly disturbing to me is the implication that Lord Cavanagh has not been heard from recently. I replay the conversation many times, studying the facial and body expressions and auditory tones used by Assistant Liaison Bronski and Parlimin VanDiver. One of Assistant Liaison Bronski's comments in particular I find most intriguing: "We'd better watch this VanDiver character—he's already nibbling around the edges of this thing."

The antecedent of the word thing is unspecified; however, I calculate a probability of 0.93 that it refers to data not yet accessible to me. I continue with my analysis, but repeated iterations quickly diverge to inconclusive re-

sults. There are several possible explanatory theories, but none has a probability higher than 0.05. More data is needed.

Perhaps Aric Cavanagh will be able to supply the key information. He has stated that he will join me soon. I will therefore be patient and make plans to discuss this matter with him then.

4
It had been renamed the *Closed Mouth;* and as Zhirrzh warships went, it was pretty unimpressive. A midsized patrol ship designed for surveillance duty over encircled non-Zhirrzh worlds, it had spent the past eight fullarcs having over half its already modest armament hastily stripped from it. Ship Commander Sps-kudah; Pllaa'rr had bitterly protested that decision, but the protests had gone unheeded by the Overclan Prime and Warrior Command both. The *Closed Mouth* was going on a diplomatic mission, and diplomatic missions weren't supposed to require large quantities of firepower.

Gazing at the ship as it was towed out of the spacecraft service building into launch position, Searcher Nzz-oonaz could only hope that assessment was right.

"You don't look entirely pleased, Searcher," a voice said from just behind him.

Nzz-oonaz pulled his tongue back inside his mouth—he hadn't realized until that beat that he'd been grimacing so openly. "I'm sorry, Overclan Prime," he apologized. "I didn't mean any disrespect."

"I'm sure you didn't." The Prime flicked his tongue toward the *Closed Mouth.* "Having a Zhirrzh warship show up unannounced is going to be frightening enough, Searcher. We don't want it bristling with obvious weaponry as well. That's also why we decided to send only one ship, instead of a group."

"I understand," Nzz-oonaz nodded. Though the way he'd heard it, the main reason the mission had been reduced to a single ship was because Warrior Command couldn't spare any more from the war effort. "It's just that I'm still not convinced the Mrachanis are quite the innocent victims of Human-Conqueror aggression that they claim to be."

"I know you're not," the Prime said gravely. "That's why I assigned you to be speaker of this mission."

Nzz-oonaz flicked his tongue in another grimace, thinking back to the two Mrachani prisoners his study group had brought here from Base World 12 after the escape of the Human-Conqueror Pheylan Cavanagh. The prisoners had claimed to be ambassadors, sent to ask for an alliance between the Mrachanis and the Zhirrzh, before their sudden deaths had put an end to any further discussion.

Their sudden and mysterious deaths, of undetermined and equally mysterious injuries or illnesses. Suspicious deaths, in Nzz-oonaz's estimation. Despite that, he and Thrr-gilag had been the only two of the study group to express any doubts about the Mrachanis and their intentions.

And for expressing such doubts, Thrr-gilag had been summarily dropped from this mission to the Mrachani homeworld.

No one was saying it that explicitly, of course. But Nzz-oonaz knew how to sift through the gaps between words. He'd seen how the Speaker for Dhaa'rr spoke to Thrr-gilag; had seen the long history of clan rivalry between the Dhaa'rr and the Kee'rr clans focused and concentrated into the Speaker's dislike for the young Kee'rr searcher.

The young Kee'rr searcher who was also bond-engaged to a Dhaa'rr female. That alone would have guaranteed animosity from someone with Speaker Cvv-panav's narrow-minded views of proper clan separation.

Still, Nzz-oonaz would have expected Thrr-gilag to come by and wish the study group good luck. Could his absence have another, more ominous significance?

"Don't worry too much about the details of the negotiations," the Prime said. "Your Elders will be watching everything that's done or said on Mra and giving us continuous reports. Just be sure you don't reveal their presence to your hosts."

He lowered his voice. "And remember, too, that one of your first priorities is to learn more about CIRCE. They're anxious to talk about it —the persistence of the two Mrachanis on Dorcas proves that much. I want to know everything they can tell us about the weapon."

An Elder appeared in front of them. "Searcher Nzz-oonaz, Ship Commander Sps-kudah reports the *Closed Mouth* is ready to lift," she said. "He requests you come aboard immediately."

Nzz-oonaz flicked his tongue in a wry smile. So Ship Commander Sps-kudah was moving quickly to establish his authority on this mission. Thrr-gilag had run into the same thing from his ship commander as their study group was evacuating Base World 12. It was just as important that Nzz-oonaz leave no doubt as to who the speaker was here. "Tell Ship Commander Sps-kudah I'll be there when I'm ready," he instructed the Elder.

"I obey," she said, and vanished.

"Very good," the Prime said approvingly. "Remember to show the same authority in front of the Mrachanis, and all should be well."

"I'll do my best," Nzz-oonaz promised.

"I know you will." Again the Prime lowered his voice. "One more thought, and then you should leave. Be wary of Searcher Gll-borgiv. Speaker Cvv-panav has ambitious political aspirations, for both himself and the entire Dhaa'rr clan. Gll-borgiv may have received private instructions from him concerning this mission."

"You mean he might try to sabotage the negotiations?"

"Not sabotage, no," the Prime said. "At least not directly. But he may try to twist the negotiations to Dhaa'rr advantage, and that could prove nearly as disastrous. Above all else, the Zhirrzh must present ourselves to the Mrachanis as a united people."

"I understand," Nzz-oonaz said.

"Good. Then you'd best get aboard the ship. Good luck to you."

There were many matters clamoring for his attention; but for now only one of them was foremost in the Overclan Prime's mind. And so he left the priority vehicle at a brisk stride, passing through the corridors of the Overclan Complex without stopping or speaking to anyone, until he was sealed away in his private chambers. One of only two places in Unity City that no Elders could enter.

No Elders, that is, but the twenty-eight Overclan Primes who had gone before him.

The Eighteenth was waiting, hovering in the dim light over his desk. "I'm sorry," the Prime apologized as he sank onto his couch. "I was delayed."

"No matter," the Eighteenth assured him. "It wasn't as urgent as I thought when I first called you. Searcher Thrr-gilag was contacted by his brother, Commander Thrr-mezaz, along that secure pathway they used earlier. Commander Thrr-mezaz asked about CIRCE, and I was afraid Thrr-gilag was going to tell him about it. But as it happened, he didn't."

The Prime grimaced. "It almost doesn't matter. Too many Zhirrzh already know or else suspect."

"Yes," the Eighteenth said darkly. "Speaking of which, are you aware that Speaker Cvv-panav has left Oaccanv?"

"Very much aware," the Prime said sourly. "He said he was going to Dharanv to consult with the clan and family leaders."

The Eighteenth flicked his tongue in a grimace. "I don't like having him out there where we can't keep a close watch on him. I trust he'll at least be here when the *Closed Mouth* reaches the Mrachani homeworld?"

"He said he'd try to be back by then," the Prime said. "He also went out of his way to remind me that the mission includes both a Dhaa'rr searcher and several Dhaa'rr Elders. The obvious implication was that if he's not here, he'll be receiving private reports."

The Eighteenth rumbled deep in his throat. "Dangerous," he said. "You can't afford to let him challenge your command authority this way."

"I'm not overly concerned," the Prime said with a shrug. "If he pushes too hard, he knows I'll release the tape that shows his agents were involved with the theft of Thrr-pifix-a's *fsss* organ. I think all this posturing is just an attempt to heal some shredded pride."

"Perhaps," the Eighteenth said doubtfully. "Though if you release the tape, he might counter by disclosing the existence of CIRCE."

"Which we're not going to be able to keep a secret much longer no matter what he does," the Prime said. "Besides, the fact that the Human-Conquerors haven't yet used CIRCE against us implies that our beach-heads have indeed trapped one or more of its components out of their reach. If the Mrachanis can confirm that, we shouldn't have any sort of mass panic when the news is made public."

"Perhaps," the Eighteenth said. "At least it should silence some of the current dissent concerning our war strategy. Everyone will understand the reason why we've spread our warships and warriors so thin."

"Though that understanding will be of limited comfort when the warriors start being raised to Eldership in droves," the Prime countered grimly. "I don't know, Eighteenth. The further we travel along this road, the more it seems to me that our only hope is an alliance with these Mrachanis. And that's a terrible bargaining position to be in."

"Only if the Mrachanis know," the Eighteenth pointed out. "And they won't."

The Prime looked across his desk, at the couch where Speaker Cvv-panav had been sitting a little over a fullarc ago. Speaker Cvv-panav, who had great ambitions for the Dhaa'rr clan . . . "Perhaps," he told the Eighteenth. "Perhaps."

There were a half-dozen Elders floating around as Thrr-pifix-a walked toward her house. Just floating there, almost invisible against the cloudy sky, doing nothing.

Watching her.

She avoided their eyes, wishing they would go away, hoping desperately that none of them would try to talk to her. She didn't know how much they knew about what had happened, but the last thing in the universe she wanted right now was to have strangers asking questions about her shame. Especially strangers who were also Elders.

They watched her until she had reached the door and unlocked it. But to her relief none of them approached or spoke to her. Closing the door behind her, she shut off their silent stares.

Not that the door was any barrier to them. She could only hope that their manners would be stronger than their curiosity.

For a few hunbeats she just wandered around the house, looking at her things, her mind and heart aching with a dull hollowness. It was her same house, with everything exactly as she'd left it. And yet, at the same time, it was also now forever changed. Before the warriors had taken her out through that doorway two fullarcs ago, this place had been a haven for her. Safe and secure, and comfortably anonymous. She herself had been comfortably anonymous.

But not anymore. Thrr-pifix-a; Kee'rr, was a criminal now, with her name listed in who knew how many records files across Oaccanv. It didn't matter that the charges had apparently been dropped, for some reason no one would talk to her about. That fact would surely be lost to the gossipers. What would be remembered amid the swirl of whispers and furtive looks was that she'd been caught with her stolen *fsss* organ in her house.

Delivered to her by those two young Zhirrzh, the ones who'd called themselves simply Korthe and Dornt. The young Zhirrzh who had echoed her own horror for the role of Elder, which loomed so close before her now. Who had sympathized with her desire to reject Eldership and had promised to take that decision from the hands of the family and clan leaders and to put it instead into hers.

They'd put the decision into her hands, all right. Just in time for warriors of the Overclan Seating to burst in and catch her with it.

All because she'd trusted them. How many times, she wondered, had she cautioned her own sons about simply accepting the words of a stranger?

Her gardening tools were still laid out in the kitchen where she'd left them to dry two fullarcs ago. She ran her hands over them, concentrating on the texture of the wooden handles and ceramic blades sliding along beneath her fingertips. Trying to fix the memory of their touch firmly in her mind.

For when this aged physical body of hers finally failed and she was raised to Eldership, these memories would be all that would remain of touch. There would be no more touch, or scent, or taste, but only sight and hearing and thought. She would be trapped in a vague half existence, with all the things she loved most about life forever inaccessible to her.

She didn't want to live like that. Couldn't bear the thought of living like that. But it was painfully clear she was not going to be permitted that choice. All Zhirrzh became Elders, and that was just the way it was going to be.

Abruptly, she froze in place, her hand gripping the handle of her trowel. There it was again: the sound of a ceramic blade hitting dirt. Coming from beyond the kitchen wall to her right.

Someone was digging behind her house.

A spark of anger appeared within the mist of the tired hopelessness clouding her thoughts. If some ill-mannered stranger thought he could just walk in and dig up her Kyranda bushes, he'd better think at it again. Holding the trowel in front of her like a weapon, she marched across the kitchen and pushed open the back door.

There was indeed a Zhirrzh back there, and he was indeed digging at the roots of one of her Kyrandas. But he was hardly a stranger. And he certainly wasn't ill mannered.

"Why, hello, Thrr-pifix-a," Thrr-tulkoj said, getting hastily to his feet. "Forgive me—I didn't know you were back."

"I wasn't expecting to *be* back," Thrr-pifix-a admitted, the spark of anger fading again into the mist as she lowered the trowel to her side. Thrr-tulkoj, a family cousin, had been her younger son, Thrr-gilag's, best friend when they were growing up. Cyclics ago their paths had split: Thrr-gilag had become a searcher specializing in alien cultures and artifacts, while Thrr-tulkoj had chosen to remain close to home, rising to the position of chief protector for the Thrr-family shrine near Cliffside Dales.

Though perhaps he wasn't chief protector there anymore, the thought suddenly occurred to her. He was probably facing charges of his own for his failure to prevent the theft of Thrr-pifix-a's *fsss* organ from the shrine.

Not only had she ruined her own life and reputation, but she'd ruined Thrr-tulkoj's, too. Just one more poisoned tongue slash to burn in her conscience. "What are you doing here?"

"Oh, I just thought I'd come over and see if your plants needed any attention," he said, looking down at the hole. "I didn't know how long you'd be away, and someone told me this is the time of cyclic to do core hydrations."

"That was very thoughtful," Thrr-pifix-a said. "But whoever gave you that information wasn't much of a gardener. That hole is far too big."

"Really?" Thrr-tulkoj seemed taken aback. "I'm sorry—I thought I'd be doing you a favor. I'd better fill it in, then."

"Well, fill in half of it, anyway," Thrr-pifix-a said, walking out toward the row of bushes. "Here, move two plants over and I'll show you how it's supposed to look."

They spent the next tentharc digging small holes into the Kyrandas' root systems; and when they were finished, Thrr-pifix-a was feeling almost as if the past two fullarcs had never happened. "I'm glad you came by this postmidarc, Thrr-tulkoj," she told him as he washed the dirt off his hands and arms beneath the kitchen waterflow. "I guess what I really needed was some company."

"I'm not surprised." Thrr-tulkoj paused. "What happened in Unity City? If you don't mind talking about it, I mean."

"I lived through it—how could talking about it be any worse?" Thrr-pifix-a countered. "They put me in a restrainment room for two fullarcs. Then they brought me out and took me to someone very official looking, who told me I was free to come home."

Thrr-tulkoj flicked his tongue. "I'm sorry, Thrr-pifix-a," he said quietly. "I feel responsible for all this."

The sound that escaped Thrr-pifix-a's mouth was somewhere between a laugh and a sob. "You've got that backward, Thrr-tulkoj. *I'm* the one who got *you* in trouble, not the other way around. Me and my stupid—" She broke off, turning her face away from him.

"Your wish not to become an Elder?" Thrr-tulkoj finished gently for her. "It's not stupid, Thrr-pifix-a. Whether it's ethical or proper, I don't know. But it's not stupid."

"All I know is that it got you into serious trouble," Thrr-pifix-a said. "Along with me. In my book that makes it stupid."

"You can hardly take all the blame for yourself," Thrr-tulkoj insisted. "There *were* other Zhirrzh involved."

"Who everyone believes I hired to steal my *fsss,*" Thrr-pifix-a said bitterly.

"Well, *I* don't believe it," Thrr-tulkoj assured her. "You gave the Overclan leaders their names, didn't you?"

"Of course I did: Korthe and Dornt, who said they were from an organization called Freedom of Decision for All."

"And?"

"They told me the group doesn't exist," Thrr-pifix-a said, turning back again to face him. "I don't know, Thrr-tulkoj. Maybe Korthe and Dornt don't exist, either. Maybe I'm just going insane."

"Insane, never." Thrr-tulkoj eyed her closely. "Tired, yes. You ought to go take a nap."

"Sounds good to me." She laughed. "It just occurred to me. We were talking so much out there, we completely forgot to fill in that oversized hole you dug. I'd better go do that."

"Oh, I can do it," Thrr-tulkoj volunteered, plucking the trowel from her hand.

"That's silly," Thrr-pifix-a chided, trying to take the trowel back. "You've already cleaned up, and I'm still dirty."

"You're also still tired," he reminded her, swinging his arm up and down, front and back, keeping the trowel out of her reach. "My mess, my responsibility. You go lie down. Or else make us a couple of cups of broth."

"You're impossible," Thrr-pifix-a grumbled. Still, she was just as glad she wasn't going to have to go back out there. Some of the Elders, she'd noted, were still hanging around. "Get going—I'll have the broth ready in five hunbeats."

Thrr-tulkoj headed out the door, closing it behind him. Thrr-pifix-a pulled out the broth pan and set it to heat, wincing with joints and muscles already starting to tighten up. She stepped to the cabinet, realized she hadn't asked what kind of broth Thrr-tulkoj would like, and changed direction instead to the door.

Thrr-tulkoj was kneeling on the ground by the first hole he'd dug, easing a small ceramic box out of it.

Thrr-pifix-a closed the door to a crack. Thrr-tulkoj pulled the box clear of the ground, brushed it off, and carefully slid it into a pouch laid out on the ground.

Thrr-pifix-a closed the door the rest of the way, tail spinning hard behind her. A small box—one she'd never seen before in her life—buried in her garden. What was it? More to the point, why was Thrr-tulkoj so interested in it?

Or even more to the point, why had he lied to her about it?

Because he *had* lied to her. He hadn't come there to core hydrate her Kyranda bushes at all. He'd come there for that box. What was in it?

There was a way to find out. All she had to do was cross her house, step out the front door, and call one of the Elders. It would be a trivial matter for any of them to take a look inside the box. And then, if matters warranted, to instantly alert the clan and family leaders.

Behind her the broth pan hummed that it was ready . . . and with the warm, familiar sound all her confusion seemed to fade away. Of course Thrr-tulkoj wouldn't be doing anything illegal out there—the very idea was ludicrous. Whatever the box was, there was surely some perfectly simple explanation for his actions. All she had to do to find out was ask.

She had the broth steeped and steaming in a pair of hand-painted ladling dishes by the time he returned to the kitchen. The pouch, she noted as he washed his hands, was hanging inconspicuously beneath his tunic.

They talked together as they sipped their broth, mostly remembering the past, speaking only sparingly of the present. And when Thrr-tulkoj left a tentharc later, Thrr-pifix-a had still not asked him about the mysterious box.

But perhaps that was for the best, she decided as she washed the ladling dishes and put them up to dry. Sufficient to each fullarc was the trouble therein, as the old saying went. Thrr-pifix-a had had enough trouble in the last few fullarcs to last many a cyclic. So, she suspected, had Thrr-tulkoj.

It seemed a long time before Thrr-tulkoj's voice came to him, hiding in the darkness in the depths of the grayworld. "It's all right. We're clear."

Cautiously, Thrr't-rokik eased his way to the edge of the lightworld. They were indeed out in the open, with the cloud-covered Oaccanv sky rippling overhead. Thrr-pifix-a's house, and Thrr-pifix-a herself, were far behind them. "I thought for a hunbeat there we'd had it," he commented to Thrr-tulkoj. "When I caught her looking out at you with the box in your hands. I'm still amazed she didn't ask about it while you were eating."

"I wish she had," Thrr-tulkoj grunted. "You could have gotten this whole thing out in the open. She's going to find out eventually, you know."

"Only if we succeed," Thrr't-rokik said grimly. "If we don't it'll be better all around that she never knew."

"I still disagree," Thrr-tulkoj said. "In fact, having seen her, I disagree more than ever. She's not just tired, Thrr't-rokik. She's worried and ashamed and frightened. Especially frightened. She knows how much trouble she should still be in, and she knows she has no business being home and free. Eventually, if it hasn't already, it's going to occur to her that some horrible deal must have been made for her release."

Thrr't-rokik flicked his tongue in a grimace. The forced ending of Thrr-gilag's bond-engagement to Klnn-dawan-a . . . "Horrible enough," he murmured.

"But not nearly as horrible as she's probably imagining," Thrr-tulkoj persisted. "You could ease some of those fears and at the same time let her know you're on her side in this."

Thrr't-rokik looked back toward Thrr-pifix-a's house, now almost hidden behind the vymis tree that grew beside it. "She doesn't want to see me, Thrr-tulkoj. As far as she's concerned, I'm dead and gone. She hates what I've become."

"It's not hate, Thrr't-rokik," Thrr-tulkoj said gently. "It's fear. Fear of the changes that becoming an Elder will bring to her life."

"Perhaps." Thrr't-rokik flicked his tongue ruefully, a distant sadness pulling at him. "It's strange, you know. I don't think there were ten instances in the whole of our life together where I can remember her being afraid of anything. Now it seems that fear may have become the strongest driving force in her life."

"Then go to her," Thrr-tulkoj urged. "Go on, we're still in range. You can heal this chasm that's grown between you—get the two of you back together as husband and wife. This is exactly the kind of crisis that can do that."

For a handful of beats Thrr't-rokik was sorely tempted. To look into Thrr-pifix-a's face again and have her look into his. Not merely to secretly watch and listen as she went about her normal life, but to really *be* with her.

But no. Thrr-pifix-a didn't want just to speak with him. She wanted him to touch her, and hold her, and embrace her. Wanted things he could never again provide for her.

And if she couldn't have it all, she would have none of it. She'd made that more than clear.

"We can't afford the risk," he told Thrr-tulkoj, turning resolutely away. "Thrr-pifix-a knows she's outside my anchorline range here. If I go to her now, I'll have to explain about that"—he jabbed his tongue at the box riding in Thrr-tulkoj's pouch—"and admit that I've been watching her."

"She'll understand."

"She most certainly will not," Thrr't-rokik retorted. "On the contrary, she's likely to make a three-tentharc stage drama out of the whole thing. And if she does, you can bet it won't be our little secret for long. You saw all those Elders loitering around her house—one wrong word picked up by one wrong ear slit, and clan and family leaders will be falling on us like hailstones."

He looked down at the pouch, tasting the faint memory of a sour flavor beneath his tongue. "And if you think you're in trouble *now*, just wait and see what happens when they find out I talked you into taking a private cutting from my *fsss* organ. *And* then got you to bury it behind Thrr-pifix-a's house."

Thrr-tulkoj flicked his tongue in resignation. "I suppose you're right," he conceded.

"Of course I'm right," Thrr't-rokik said. "And if you're locked up somewhere and I'm stuck at the family shrine, we're not going to be able to find those lying split-tongued illegits who did this to her."

Thrr-tulkoj threw a quick look around them. "Well, at least we've some names to work with now."

"For all the good that'll do us," Thrr't-rokik grunted. "It hasn't helped the Overclan Prime's office track them down."

"You assume the Overclan Prime's office *wants* to track them down," Thrr-tulkoj pointed out. "Remember, Overclan warriors were waiting here ready to pounce as soon as Thrr-pifix-a had her *fsss* in hand."

"True." Thrr't-rokik flicked his tongue in a grimace. "I wish I'd been able to listen in on that conversation Thrr-gilag had with the Overclan Prime back at the house."

"My guess is that it was unrelated," Thrr-tulkoj said. "We *are* in the middle of a war, you know."

Abruptly, an Elder flicked into view. "Are you Protector Thrr-tulkoj; Kee'rr?" she said.

"Yes," Thrr-tulkoj confirmed.

"I have a message for you from the Vehicle Registry Department. The transport you specified has an index number of CVV-556499 and is currently registered to the Dhaa'rr office of the Overclan Seating."

"Understood," Thrr-tulkoj said. "Thank you."

The Elder flicked her tongue in a five-hundred-cyclic-old Hgg gesture of salute—she must have dated back nearly to the Third Eldership War, Thrr't-rokik realized—and vanished. "So it's a Cvv-family vehicle," Thrr-tulkoj commented. "Interesting."

"Is this the transport I saw Korthe and Dornt escape in?" Thrr't-rokik asked.

Thrr-tulkoj nodded. "I contacted the floater-engine manufacturer and had them look up the identification numbers you were able to read before the transport got out of range. Looks like the trail not only leads to the Dhaa'rr clan, but possibly straight to the Speaker for Dhaa'rr personally."

For a hunbeat neither spoke. Thrr-tulkoj broke the silence first. "We're going to need a lot more proof before we can make this public," he said. "At the minimum we need to track down Korthe and Dornt and establish a connection between them and the Dhaa'rr clan in general or Speaker Cvv-panav in particular."

"That won't be easy," Thrr't-rokik warned. "Speaker Cvv-panav would have to be crazy not to bury them away somewhere."

"Not necessarily," Thrr-tulkoj said. "Remember, as far as anyone knows, the only person who can identify them is Thrr-pifix-a, and she's sitting out here four thousand thoustrides from Unity City. Speaker Cvv-panav might well be arrogant enough to still have them there with him."

"And if he's not?"

"If he's not, then he's probably buried them and the transport in the same place. And particular vehicles are a lot easier to trace than particular Zhirrzh."

"I'll take your word for it. So we start at Unity City?"

"Right. We can take the rail from Reed's Village to the transport field at Pathgate. We should make Unity City by this latearc."

"All right." Thrr't-rokik hesitated. "You realize, of course, that even if you can't recognize them, they can probably recognize you. And they aren't going to want to be found."

"I understand," Thrr-tulkoj said, his voice taking on a hard edge. "And I'm rather looking forward to it. They had their turn back at the family shrine. This time it'll be my turn."

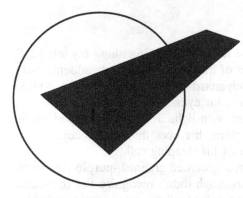

It was dark. Dark and silent, save for the chirping of night insects and the whisper of breezes through the trees and stickler reeds surrounding them. Somewhere in the near distance an avci-cubu was snuffling quietly to itself as it rooted around with its snout for young Parra and oldur vines. From much farther away came the variegated whistling of a colony of floravore bats, swarming in battle with one of the forest's hundreds of varieties of recoil creepers.

Lying fully alert on his mattress pad, half seeing, half imagining the protective shelter cloth draped above his head, Lord Stewart Cavanagh stared out into the blackness of the Granparra night, wondering what it was that had awakened him.

His watch, pen torch, knife, and Kolchin's backup flechette pistol were on the ground beside his head to his left. Carefully, he rolled onto his left side, wincing at the ache from a dozen sore muscles.

"Lord Cavanagh?" a quiet voice called from a few meters away.

"Yes," Cavanagh confirmed, snagging the pistol and easing onto his back again. "Sorry—did I wake you?"

"No, I've been awake for a few minutes," Mitri Kolchin said. "I think we've got an intruder."

Cavanagh shivered, the muscle movement sending another wave of aching through him. "I thought you killed everything nearby when we made camp."

"I thought so, too," Kolchin said. "Quiet, please, and let me listen."

Cavanagh grimaced, gripping the pistol tightly as he rested his hand on his chest, breathing as silently as he could. In the darkness he visualized the area around the encampment Kolchin had cleared for them the previous evening, trying to guess where the intruder could be coming from.

And then . . . "Kolchin?"

"Sir, you have to be quiet—"

"It's over here," Cavanagh told him. "It's moving along my left leg."

He never heard Kolchin get out of his sleeping roll, but suddenly, with a ripple of displaced air, the bodyguard was there beside him. "Hold still," Kolchin murmured. "Watch your eyes."

Abruptly, the shelter was ablaze with light from Kolchin's pen torch. Cavanagh squinted against the glare, his eyes fighting to adjust, and looked down toward the left side of his sleeping roll.

It was there, all right: a slender, segmented greenish-purple vine moving leisurely alongside his leg. Cavanagh didn't recognize the particular species, but like the rest of Granparra's recoil creepers, its tip and sides bristled with barbed thorns. Even as he watched, it moved again, poking mindlessly at the sleeping roll as it tried to get to the source of the heat it was sensing.

"Don't move," Kolchin said quietly. "I'll try to draw it away."

There was a soft hum, and the beam from the pen torch focused down until it was a small, intense spot on the bristling vine head. The creeper seemed to pause, almost as if thinking; and then, as Cavanagh held his breath, the head began to turn toward this new source of heat. "I'll give it a few more centimeters," Kolchin said. "We don't want it twitching back toward you."

Cavanagh gave a microscopic nod, afraid of startling the plant. With what seemed like agonizing slowness the creeper continued veering away from his side. . . .

And then Kolchin's right hand slashed down, the two edges of his split-blade knife slicing vertically into either side of the creeper, pinning the vine head to the ground. The creeper twitched violently and was still writhing as Kolchin slid Cavanagh's knife from its sheath and sliced off the deadly vine head.

Cavanagh took a careful breath, the pistol sagging against his chest as his hand relaxed its rigid grip on the weapon. "It's helpless now, right?"

"Right," Kolchin confirmed. He was working his way down the creeper, methodically cutting through the vine at each of the segment lines and throwing the pieces out into the forest. "Just don't touch the vine head—those thorns are probably poisonous."

"Right," Cavanagh said, reaching gingerly past the still writhing vine head for his watch. Still two hours to dawn. "When did Piltariab say he'd be getting back from Puerto Simone Island?"

"Sometime this morning," Kolchin said, coming back from his search-and-kill defoliation exercise and returning Cavanagh's knife to its sheath. Squatting down, he carefully pulled his own knife out of the ground, the twitching vine head still impaled on the split blade. With a quick flick of his wrist he flipped the knife around, sending the vine head spinning out into the darkness of the forest. "He wouldn't commit himself more precisely than that."

"In my experience it's a minor triumph to get an Avuire to commit to even a given day," Cavanagh said, easing himself up on one elbow and peering ahead into the darkness. A couple of kilometers away out there was Sereno Strait, the narrow stretch of water that separated them here on the Granparra mainland from the safety of Puerto Simone Island. Ninety-nine-plus percent of the planet's forty million people lived on the island, dwelling in the literal shadow of the huge Parra vine but protected by their isolation from the rest of the planet's deadly plant life.

Cavanagh and Kolchin, unfortunately, were out here.

None of this had been part of the original plan, of course. Breaking away from Petr Bronski on Mra-mig, they had borrowed a small fighter ship from the Mrach weapons dump in the hills outside Mig-Ka City— the only craft there that could be prepped for flight in under half an hour —and had headed off-planet. The idea was to leave Mrach space as quickly as possible and get back to Cavanagh's homeworld of Avon, where he could set to work on something that could help the Commonwealth defeat the invading Conquerors.

But the universe hadn't proved cooperative. Like courier ships, fighter stardrives were twice as fast as those of larger ships, but they paid for that speed with five times the fuel consumption, and if there was a way to retune the drive for the slower, more efficient drive speed, neither of them had been able to find it. Courier ships had large fuel tanks to compensate. Fighters, unfortunately, didn't.

Which had left them with an extremely limited number of places they could reach without refueling, none of them places where humans flying a fighter with official Mrach markings wouldn't be greeted with raised eyebrows and suspicious questions. With Bronski undoubtedly burning up space behind them, suspicious questions were something to be avoided at all costs.

Which had in turn boiled down their options to exactly one.

Klyveress ci Yyatoor, Twelfth Counsel to the Yycroman Hierarch, had been surprised to see them again so soon. Her welcome had turned noticeably cooler when she'd learned they were on the run. But with a little persistence Cavanagh had managed to work out a deal, and a few hours later they were off again in an old Pawolian mining ship Klyveress had had stashed away somewhere.

With its slower drive the Pawolian ship had more than enough fuel to reach Avon. Unfortunately, what it turned out not to have was a reliable set of reactant infusers.

They'd been able to nurse the ship only as far as Granparra. But as Kolchin had pointed out, as emergency stopovers went, Granparra was a reasonably good one. With virtually the entire planetary population crowded together on Puerto Simone Island, there was no reason for anyone to keep close tabs on space traffic going in or out of the rest of the planet. On the other hand, with a few thousand rough-and-tumble sap miners and prospectors working the mainland at any given time, there were also enough small ships going in and out for one more not to attract particular notice. Kolchin had taken full advantage of that, bringing the ship in toward a mining complex well away from the island—and away from the Myrmidon Weapons Platform that orbited protectively overhead—then flying low over the forests and jungles to a spot only a few hours' hike away from the coastline.

Their problems, according to Kolchin, had thus been reduced to two: how to locate new reactant infusers, and how to raise the money to pay for it without triggering the credit red flags Bronski had undoubtedly set up on the Cavanagh accounts.

Problem three, Cavanagh had privately added, was how to stay alive while they dealt with problems one and two.

"Your bag looks undamaged," Kolchin said, running his fingers along the material. "No thorns embedded or anything."

"Good," Cavanagh said, studying the young man's dirty and unshaven face. Kolchin was being very professional about this, certainly: inquiring closely after his employer's health, sympathizing with him over foot blisters and sore muscles and venom burns, sharing in his fears about the continual danger there. But beneath it all, despite it all, it was obvious that the young bodyguard was enjoying this adventure immensely.

And Cavanagh could hardly blame him. Kolchin had been trained as a Peacekeeper commando—trained with the best and brightest warriors the Commonwealth had to offer. The job of personal bodyguard hardly ever even scratched the surface of his abilities. Now, for probably the first time since Cavanagh had hired him, Kolchin was getting the chance to actually use his combat, stalking, and survival skills.

Cavanagh could only hope that that wasn't the real reason Kolchin had brought them down in the wilds of Granparra in the first place.

"Good," Kolchin said, checking his watch and then peering up at the sky. "You might as well get a little more sleep. It'll be another couple of hours before we can get moving."

"I know," Cavanagh said, rubbing his knuckles into tired eyes, his hands tickling against two weeks' worth of beard growth as he did so. He desperately wanted to sleep, certainly; this little field trip through the Granparra outback was as physically and mentally exhausting as anything he'd tackled since his own stint in the Peacekeepers thirty-six years ago. "I think I'll do a little work first. I still haven't got the ablative part of the scheme balanced properly, and I want to be ready to hit the ground running when we get back to Avon."

"If you want to," Kolchin said, glancing out into the darkness around them. "There'll probably be several hours after we get to the dock before Piltariab shows up."

"If there are, I can work then, too," Cavanagh growled. "And probably also all of next week, after we find out we still don't have enough money to buy the infusers. Maybe we'll wind up spending the whole war here—then I'd have lots of time to work."

Kolchin's eyes narrowed, just slightly. "I only meant—"

"I know what you meant, Kolchin," Cavanagh sighed, waving a hand in tired apology as fatigue overtook the brief flash of anger. "I'm sorry. I'm just tired."

"Yes, sir," Kolchin said, his voice studiously neutral. Perhaps he was finally getting tired too.

More likely, he was wondering whether his boss was beginning to lose it. Cavanagh wouldn't blame him on that one, either. After all, the whole reason they'd run from Mra-mig in the first place was to avoid the quarantine Bronski had planned for them, a quarantine designed to protect the startling and potentially devastating secret that the legendary deterrent weapon CIRCE didn't exist.

Cavanagh had argued vehemently against any such quarantine. With his daughter and two sons still in deadly danger from the Conquerors, he had no desire to let anyone lock him uselessly away where he couldn't do anything to help them. But Bronski had refused his plea, at which point Kolchin had ended the discussion with a drawn flechette pistol and a quiet promise to use it if necessary.

And so, of course, they'd wound up here on the Granparra mainland. As effectively cut off from civilization as they would have been in any quarantine Bronski could have devised.

"I understand your concerns, sir," Kolchin said. "But this last sale should have us pretty close to what we need. And if Piltariab was able to get your message to Bokamba—*and* if he's willing to lend us the difference—we could conceivably get out of here tonight."

"Perhaps," Cavanagh murmured. Bokamba was Reserve Peacekeeper Wing Commander Iniko Bokamba, Adam Quinn's former commander in the Copperheads. The one potentially bright spot in all this, and a lingering source of annoyance for Cavanagh that he hadn't thought of contacting the man sooner.

Bokamba had been one of the handful of former Copperhead officers Quinn had considered contacting when the family had first decided on a private mission to try to find and rescue Pheylan from the Conquerors. Cavanagh didn't know whether Quinn and Aric had in fact gone to Bokamba or had instead gone to someone else—he and Kolchin had headed off to Mra-mig before that part of Quinn's plan was settled. But it was a possible opening; and with his children in danger, it was an opening Cavanagh was willing to take a chance on.

If he indeed still had any children. If Pheylan was, in fact, still alive out there. If Aric and Quinn hadn't been killed looking for him. If Aric and Pheylan's sister, Melinda, trapped on Dorcas by the Conqueror invasion of that world, hadn't also been killed.

Cavanagh laid his head back down on the mattress pad. No—he wouldn't think that way. Couldn't think that way. Wherever they were right now, Aric, Melinda, and Pheylan were alive and well. They had to be.

"Well," Kolchin said, breaking into the silence. "With your permission, sir, I'm going to take another look around the area. After that I'll see about breakfast."

"All right," Cavanagh nodded. "Thank you."

"No trouble," Kolchin assured him. "Don't hesitate to shout if there are any problems." Drawing his flechette pistol and checking the action, he turned and disappeared into the night.

With a tired sigh Cavanagh balanced his pen torch across his chest and dug his plate out of his pouch. Keying to the proper section, he began to read through his notes.

Kolchin's voice jolted Cavanagh from a light doze. "Here he comes."

Cavanagh sat up, blinking against the late-morning sunlight, and looked out across the rolling waters of Sereno Strait. In the far distance, low to the water, he could see the dark landmass of Puerto Simone Island; between him and the island were perhaps twenty boats, ranging from an impressively large passenger cruiser down to three- and four-man fishing boats. One of the latter was heading directly toward them. "You've spotted him?" he asked Kolchin.

"Yes," Kolchin confirmed, binoculars pressed to his face. "He came up from belowdecks for a minute—looked like he was giving the crew last-minute docking instructions. Three others in the crew, all Avuirli."

Cavanagh looked out at the approaching boat, shading his eyes with one hand. "I hope Bokamba didn't make a major deal about the message, one way or the other. You know how excited Avuirli get about anything that even sniffs of intrigue."

"Actually, that's what made him a better choice than the other miners who were heading back that day," Kolchin said, still studying the boat. "If he even suspects there's more to this than a couple of fellow sap miners looking up an old friend, we'll know it from two meters away. Farther if we're downwind."

"Except that everyone else will know it, too."

"Only if they're paying attention," Kolchin said. "Most people I've met don't take Avuirli very seriously." He handed Cavanagh the binoculars. "I'd better get down to the dock. I'll signal when it's safe for you to join us."

Keeping low, Kolchin headed off through the shoreline bushes, winding his way down toward the little cove below. He was waiting on the dock when the boat arrived, catching the line one of the crew threw to him and helping tie it up. Piltariab appeared on deck and hopped down to the dock, gesticulating toward Kolchin with typical Avuirlian expansiveness.

For a few minutes the two of them talked as the crew hauled six backpacks ashore and laid them neatly out on the dock beside Piltariab. Then, with a brief exchange of words and gestures between all the Avuirli, the crew cast off the lines and turned their boat back out into the strait.

Kolchin waved good-bye; and as he did so, his left hand curved briefly into the "all-clear" signal. Shutting off the binoculars and packing them back into their case, Cavanagh headed down, keeping behind the bushes and groaning silently at freshly reawakened muscle aches.

Kolchin was talking as he came around the last group of bushes. "—fell a little behind on the way here. Ah; here he is."

"Greetings, Moo Sab Piltariab," Cavanagh said, gesticulating an Avuirlian salutation and casually sniffing the air. Piltariab's aroma seemed the same as he remembered it from their last meeting. A good sign. "How was your trip to the island?"

"Very good indeed, Moo Sab Stymer," Piltariab said, returning the gesture, his fragrance going a little more rose petal as he did so. "I was just saying to Moo Sab Plex how wonderfully rich and varied the aromas of the island are."

"They certainly are," Cavanagh agreed. "Were you able—?"

"Of course, you Humans are so poorly equipped to appreciate it," Piltariab went on as if Cavanagh hadn't spoken. "Your cooking alone shows that. Though I must say that sometimes your heavy-handed approach to food seasoning can be quite invigorating."

"I've often thought that myself," Cavanagh said. "Were you able to locate Moo Sab Bokamba?"

"Of course," Piltariab said. "His home is listed in the directory—I merely went there and there he was." He gestured in dreamy memory. "Now, *there* is a man who understands aromas. His house has some of the most unusual—"

"Ow!" Kolchin snarled under his breath, slapping at the side of his neck. "Do you suppose we could continue this conversation farther inland? These damn sea mites always seem to find me."

"Certainly, Moo Sab Plex," Piltariab said, his nostrils flaring momentarily. "Though personally I don't see what they smell in you. That backpack on the end is yours."

"Our thanks," Kolchin said, picking it up and settling it on his back. "You get everything we asked for?"

"Such little as you asked for," Piltariab sniffed. "Even the Meert-ha in our group asks for more luxuries than you two."

"We're humans of simple taste," Kolchin said. "What about the rest of the money?"

"All there, too," Piltariab assured him, picking up one of the remaining backpacks and looping its carrying straps over his neck, papoose style. "Four hundred twenty-seven poumaries. You did specify NorCoord currency, did you not?"

"Yes, thank you," Cavanagh said. Four hundred twenty-seven poumaries: the fruit of six days of painstakingly harvesting exotic sap from Granparra's hostile plant life. "We appreciate your handling that business for us."

"No difficulty," the Avuire said, picking up the other four packs and arranging them, two per arm, on his wide shoulders. "You have already paid equitably with your assistance to our mining group. You particularly, Moo Sab Plex, with your skill in hunting."

"We thank you," Kolchin said. "You said you'd delivered our message to Moo Sab Bokamba?"

"I did not say so," Piltariab said cheerfully as they left the dock and headed back up the gentle slope toward the forest. "I merely said I had found him. You will be returning to the group with me, will you not?"

"My mistake," Kolchin said. "You met Moo Sab Bokamba. Did you deliver our message?"

"Yes indeed," Piltariab said.

"And was there a reply?"

"Yes indeed," the Avuire said. "It is in your pack. You said you will be returning to the group with me?"

"I did not say so," Kolchin countered, playing the standard Avuirlian word game right back at him. "Actually, I think we're going to move on."

"Ah," Piltariab said, his odor turning lilac and pepper in an aromotional response Cavanagh tentatively decided was resignation or regret. "We will miss your fresh game, Moo Sab Plex. Where now do you mine?"

"A little ways south of here," Kolchin told him. "We found a nice stand of comaran bushes with a nest of paprra vines growing in the middle." He cocked an eyebrow. "We're having a little trouble finding the ripest ones, though. I don't suppose you'd be willing to leave your group for a day or two—come lend us your expertise and Avuirlian nose? For a share of the sap, of course."

Piltariab rumbled deep in his throat sac, his odor shading into something faintly musky. Cavanagh knew that one from long conference-table experience: the aroma of an Avuire thinking. "I would like to, Moo Sab Plex," he said. "But I don't think I should. My group also needs my nose. They will already be waiting for me at the Dungyness River Landing."

Kolchin shrugged. "Well, if you can't, you can't."

"Perhaps in the future it will come to pass," Piltariab said, his five packs bouncing as he shrugged his shoulders. "Though in true honesty, you would do better to rejoin us. You would find more marketable sap along the Dungyness River than in any sixty-four stands of comaran bushes."

"You may be right," Kolchin conceded.

"Yes indeed," Piltariab said, flaring his nostrils. "Avuirlian noses do not deceive, whether they are seeking out ripe sap or confirming that edibles and spices are fresh and tasteworthy." He bounced the packs on his shoulders again for emphasis.

"Of course," Kolchin said. "Perhaps we'll catch up with you in a few days."

"Do so," Piltariab urged, his odor changing again. "Without a good hunter in the group we will have to make more trips to the island to purchase food, and that will create ill temper."

"I imagine so," Kolchin said. "Farewell, Moo Sab Piltariab."

"Farewell, Moo Sab Plex. Farewell, Moo Sab Stymer."

The Avuire turned and headed north through the forest, pulling a large machete from its waist sheath and holding it ready for trouble. "You really wanted him along with us?" Cavanagh asked quietly as they watched him leave.

"No," Kolchin said, taking Cavanagh's arm and leading the way off to their left. "I was mostly curious to see what his response would be to the offer. I'm not sure, but I think someone may have been watching us from one of the other boats."

Cavanagh's stomach tightened painfully. "Bronski's people?"

"Could be," Kolchin said. "I couldn't really see anyone. It was just a feeling I had."

Cavanagh nodded grimly. Petr Bronski. On official government file lists, a lowly assistant liaison with the Commonwealth diplomatic corps. On more private lists a senior officer with NorCoord Military Intelligence. "That's why you got us off the dock."

"Common sense alone would dictate that," Kolchin said. "Here we are."

Here turned out to be a small tree-topped knoll overlooking the strait and the dock area. "Let me have the binoculars," Kolchin said as he dropped into a crouch. "Keep out of sight."

Cavanagh handed over the binocular case and sat down, easing the backpack off his shoulders as Kolchin went the rest of the way up the knoll on elbows and knees. Sliding his hand under the seal flap, he opened it up.

The card from Bokamba was right on top. Pulling out his plate, Cavanagh inserted the card and, steeling himself, began to read.

And as he did so, some of the weight abruptly lifted from his shoulders.

"They're heading away," Kolchin said, crawling back down the knoll. "I was probably just imagining things." He nodded at the plate. "Good news?"

"Wonderful news," Cavanagh said, handing it to him. "Bokamba says the rescue mission has come back. Pheylan, Aric, and Quinn are all alive and well."

"That's great," Kolchin said, sitting down beside Cavanagh and taking the plate. "Congratulations, sir."

"Thank you," Cavanagh said, leaning back against the knoll and staring up through the trees at the sky. It had worked—the terrible gamble had actually worked.

"Says they're all on Edo," Kolchin said, still reading. "Probably facing court-martial."

"They'll never make it stick," Cavanagh said, shaking his head. "You can't court-martial heroes."

"Tell that to Quinn," Kolchin said dryly. "I see we have a name for the aliens now—we're supposed to call them the Zhirrzh." He paused. "No news here about Melinda."

Cavanagh nodded. "I noticed that too."

"Well, she's in the middle of a war zone," Kolchin pointed out, handing the plate back to Cavanagh and starting to poke through the open pack. "Even Bokamba can't just phone up Peacekeeper Command and ask for a private briefing."

"All the more reason to get off Granparra as soon as we can," Cavanagh said, paging the message down. "He's included an equipment price list . . . looks like we've got enough money for an infuser. Let's see if he has equally good news about . . . damn."

"What?" Kolchin asked, looking up.

" 'Don't attempt to come onto the island yet,' " Cavanagh read aloud. " 'There are Peacekeepers all over, collecting equipment for the war effort. I've checked their schedule, and they'll be gone in two days.' "

"That means we should stay out here for three," Kolchin said. "There are always last-minute problems that straggle these things out."

Cavanagh hissed between his teeth. Three more days. Three more days of the dangerous annoyances of the Granparra forest. Three more days of trying not to think of Melinda in the far deadlier danger of a Conqueror war zone.

But if it had to be, then it had to be. All this waiting would be for nothing if they made it to the island only to trip over a Peacekeeper squad on the lookout for them. "All right," he sighed, keying the message off and closing the plate. "Three days. But no more."

"Fine," Kolchin said briskly, standing up and brushing bits of leaves off his clothing. "And in the meantime we might as well earn a few more poumaries. You might be interested in buying an actual restaurant meal once we get to the island."

"Good point," Cavanagh agreed, the taste of the previous evening's roast grooma coming back as he struggled to his feet.

"Besides," Kolchin said, the smile fading, "I think we should go a little deeper into the forest."

He threw a glance toward Sereno Strait, hidden by the knoll beside them. "Just in case I *wasn't* imagining things."

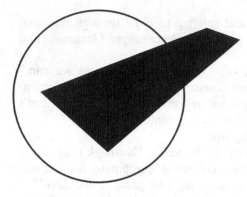

6

The smell was the first thing Klnn-dawan-a noticed as she descended the shuttle ramp toward the soil of the world the Human-Conquerors called Dorcas. Not an offensive smell, really, but not a particularly pleasant one, either. The lingering essence of the Human-Conquerors who'd once lived in this village, perhaps, or simply the exotic mixture of aromas that always came with a new and unfamiliar ecology.

Or perhaps it was simply that the smells were flavored by her own fear and anxiety. Here, in the middle of a war zone, carrying the dreadfully illegal sample she and Thrr-gilag had taken from Prr't-zevisti's *fsss* organ, there was certainly plenty to be afraid of.

But she was here, and Second Commander Klnn-vavgi was waiting for her at the foot of the shuttle ramp as a good cousin ought to, and this was no time for second thoughts. Keeping her head held high, trying not to let her nervousness show, she continued down.

"Greetings to you, third cousin in the family of Klnn," Klnn-vavgi gave the formal clan salutation as she reached the ground. "I am Second Commander Klnn-vavgi; Dhaa'rr."

"I am Searcher Klnn-dawan-a; Dhaa'rr," Klnn-dawan-a said, giving the appropriate response. "I greet you in turn, third cousin, and ask for your hospitality."

"My hospitality is yours," Klnn-vavgi said, flicking his tongue in a smile. "Welcome, Klnn-dawan-a. It's good to see you again."

"And you, Klnn-vavgi," she said, studying his face as she returned the smile. They had met only rarely over the past few cyclics—their two particular branches of the family had never been especially close. But her memories of him were strong enough that she was able to see that the stresses of warfare had added new strains to his face. "You're looking well," she said aloud. "It's been, what, two cyclics since we last saw each other?"

"More like one and two-thirds," Klnn-vavgi said, flicking his tongue toward the rack of *kavra* fruit set up beside him. Generally, the rite of the *kavra* was dispensed with between such close family members; obviously, procedures at warrior bases were more stringent. "It was at Kylre Point, at the bonding ceremony of Klnn-poroo and Rka-felmib."

Klnn-dawan-a looked at him sharply, her tongue pressing hard against the roof of her mouth. But there was none of the sly taunting in his expression that she'd half expected. "I presume you've heard that the Dhaa'rr-clan leaders have annulled my bond-engagement to Thrr-gilag."

"Yes," Klnn-vavgi said, not looking at her as he chose one of the *kavra* from the rack. "We have a couple of Dhaa'rr Elders here who keep up on the gossip from home."

Klnn-dawan-a picked up her own *kavra,* her tongue pressed hard against the side of her mouth. Gossip. Her love for Thrr-gilag—his love for her—their hoped-for, longed-for, pleaded-for future together. All of it reduced to nothing more important than gossip.

Klnn-vavgi must have seen something in her expression. "I'm sorry," he said hastily. "I didn't mean that the way it sounded."

"It's all right," Klnn-dawan-a said. "I suppose to anyone else that's all it is." She held up the *kavra* fruit and slashed through it twice with the edges of her tongue, with perhaps more force than was really necessary.

Klnn-vavgi followed with his part of the ceremony, and they dropped their lacerated fruit into the disposal container. "Commander Thrr-mezaz wanted me to bring you to him as soon as you arrived," he said, gesturing the way toward one of the buildings near the landing area. "I understand you've brought some personal messages and items from Dharanv for the Dhaa'rr warriors here."

"Yes," Klnn-dawan-a said. "They're in with the general supplies in the shuttle's cargo area."

"I'm sure the warriors will be pleased to receive them," he said, throwing her a thoughtful look. "I'm a little surprised you came all this way here yourself for such a trivial errand."

"Comfort for warriors in a war zone is hardly a trivial errand," Klnn-dawan-a said mildly.

"It is when there are other priorities involved," Klnn-vavgi said. "In the middle of a war against an alien race, an expert on aliens and alien cultures should have more pressing demands on her time."

"Specializing in a field does not necessarily make one an expert in it,"

Klnn-dawan-a pointed out. "I'm sure Warrior Command is indeed keeping the true experts busy."

"Of course they are," Klnn-vavgi said. "Still, Commander Thrr-mezaz seemed very insistent that you be allowed to personally come down to the surface. He even had to argue a little with Supreme Ship Commander Dkll-kumvit about it."

"I imagine he's anxious to hear about his brother and what happened at the bond-engagement hearings," Klnn-dawan-a said, fighting to keep her voice steady. Clearly, Klnn-vavgi hadn't been taken in by this personal-messages ploy of hers.

And if he wasn't fooled, others probably weren't, either. And if one of them was suspicious enough to order the Elders to do a thorough examination of the waist pouch hanging at her side . . .

"It's none of my business, of course," Klnn-vavgi said with a shrug. "But there are some here who think everything that happens on Dorcas is their business. I just wanted to warn you about that. Here we are."

"Thank you," Klnn-dawan-a murmured as they stepped between the two warriors guarding the door and went inside. Yes; the Elders would be trying to put the pieces together, all right. What else did they have to do?

Though, on the other side, that might not be such a bad thing. If they thought she'd come here to talk to Thrr-mezaz about her bond-engagement to Thrr-gilag, maybe they'd be less inclined to dig for another motive. Maybe for once the Elder preoccupation with gossip was going to work in their favor.

At first glance the room they walked into reminded Klnn-dawan-a of a sample testing room for some important and well-funded alien-studies group. A circle of optronic-equipment racks and monitors lined three of the four walls, with a Zhirrzh busy in front of each of them. Other Zhirrzh were moving back and forth between the stations, and a quiet buzz of low conversation filled the room. Hanging over all of it was a cloud of fifteen or twenty Elders, some moving around between the racks, most grouped together around one particular station.

Standing in the middle of the group, gesturing to the display in one of the racks, was Thrr-mezaz.

"Yes, it's been mentioned on several occasions that the rocks in that area are rich in metal ores," he was saying as Klnn-vavgi led her over to the edge of the crowd of Elders. "I'm not interested in hearing it mentioned again. This is the first solid lead we've had, and we're going to follow up on it. Is that clear?"

"Yes, Commander," one of the Elders said, in a tone that Klnn-dawan-a suspected was bordering on insubordination. "We'll do whatever we can."

"You'll do whatever it takes," Thrr-mezaz corrected him quietly. "You have your orders."

"I obey, Commander," the Elder growled. He half turned to the other Elders, gestured impatiently with his tongue. "You heard the commander," he said. "Let's get to it."

The whole group flickered and vanished. "They found something?" Klnn-vavgi asked.

"That appears to be a matter of opinion," Thrr-mezaz said, flicking his tongue in a grimace. "The Elders searching the area north of the village ran into a slender nonmetallic cable about four strides underground. Definitely of Human-Conqueror origin."

"Sounds promising," Klnn-vavgi said. "What's the problem?"

"The problem is that it's going to be difficult to trace through the ore-bearing rocks in the region," Thrr-mezaz said. "Several of the Elders are balking at the task, especially since they're half-convinced it's nothing but a control cable for the Elderdeath weapon we destroyed when we first attacked the planet." He shifted his eyes to Klnn-dawan-a. "Welcome to Dorcas, Klnn-dawan-a. You've come at a busy time—I'm afraid our hospitality isn't going to be quite as generous as I'd like."

"You forget I'm used to temporary field shelters on alien worlds, Thrr-mezaz," Klnn-dawan-a said dryly. "Anyway, I'm not here for a vacation."

Thrr-mezaz's tongue twitched. "No, indeed. Let's step into my office."

A hunbeat later they were alone, the office door closed to the warriors in the room outside. "I'm glad you made it here safely," Thrr-mezaz said, gesturing her to one of the couches as he sank onto the couch behind the desk. "I don't mind telling you I was pretty worried when I heard about the Human-Conqueror attack on Shamanv."

"I was pretty worried myself," Klnn-dawan-a said, feeling her tail twitch at the memory. "I was standing right out in the open when three of those black-and-white Human-Conqueror spacecraft flew past overhead. Good luck must have been with me."

"Immense good luck," Thrr-mezaz agreed. "The reports indicated those were probably Copperhead warcraft. The most dangerous the Human-Conquerors have to offer."

Klnn-dawan-a's tail twitched again. "Just as well I didn't know."

"Probably." Thrr-mezaz paused. "You have the package with you?"

"Yes," Klnn-dawan-a said, looking around the room. "Is it safe to talk here?"

"As safe as anywhere in the encampment," Thrr-mezaz said, also looking around. "All the Elders should be either on sentry duty, searching that area north of the village, or acting as communicators out in the command/monitor room. I wish I'd thought to have you pick up a hummer before you left Dharanv, though. Either you or Thrr-gilag."

"It wouldn't have helped to tell Thrr-gilag," Klnn-dawan-a said. "By now he should be well on his way to the Mrachani homeworld."

Thrr-mezaz threw her an odd look. "That's right—you probably don't know. He was taken off the Mrachani mission. He's on his way here instead."

"Here?" Klnn-dawan-a echoed. "What for?"

"He didn't want to say, even on that secure Elder pathway Prr't-casst-a set up for us," Thrr-mezaz said. "But he's only about a fullarc behind you, so we'll be able to ask him ourselves soon enough."

"I see," Klnn-dawan-a murmured. "What do we do first?"

Thrr-mezaz looked around the room again. "First you'd better give me the package."

"Gladly," Klnn-dawan-a said, opening her waist pouch and digging down toward the bottom. "I've been terrified ever since we got it that some Elder would happen to run into it and be suspicious enough to alert someone."

"That problem I can guard against, anyway," Thrr-mezaz said, standing up and walking around the corner of the desk. "There's a metal box in one end of that cabinet over there in the corner, probably the Human-Conqueror commander's safe. It can't be sealed anymore—we burned off the lock to see if there was anything inside—but it should at least keep the package safe from accidental discovery."

"Good," Klnn-dawan-a said, producing the case containing the slender tissue sampler she'd used at the Prr-family shrine. "We'd still better get it where it needs to go as quickly as possible."

"There are many other reasons to do that," Thrr-mezaz reminded her grimly as he took the case and opened it. "Prr't-zevisti's life, for starters. Is this really it?"

"That's really it," Klnn-dawan-a assured him. "I know it looks strange, but it ought to work as well as any normal cutting."

"We'll find out soon enough," Thrr-mezaz said, crossing the room to the cabinet and swinging open an outer wooden door. "Some fullarc you're going to have to tell me how you two got hold of this." He squatted down, pulled open the warped metal door of the safe itself, and set the case inside—

And suddenly an Elder appeared in front of the desk.

A small gasp escaped Klnn-dawan-a's mouth before she could stifle it. Thrr-mezaz didn't even flinch. "Yes?" he demanded, half turning around.

"We've found something, Commander," the Elder said, his voice pulsating with excitement. "A large underground structure, perhaps fifteen strides across at its largest, buried twenty strides below the surface."

"Have you looked inside yet?" Thrr-mezaz asked, swinging the safe door closed and straightening up again.

"We can't get in," the Elder said. "There's an inner lining of metal."

Behind Klnn-dawan-a the door opened, and she turned as Klnn-vavgi hurried into the room. "Commander, we've—ah; you've heard."

"I've heard the first part, anyway," Thrr-mezaz said, crossing over to him. "Have they found the way in?"

"There's an angled tunnel leading down into it," Klnn-vavgi said. "At the end are a camouflaged doorway and entrance chamber built into a hillside. The Elders are still searching for the opening mechanism."

"We'll burn it open if we have to," Thrr-mezaz said. "Get a sectrene of warriors together, Second. We're going in for a look."

"I obey, Commander," Klnn-vavgi said, heading back into the command/monitor room. "Communicator?"

"Shouldn't you send some technics too?" Klnn-dawan-a asked Thrr-mezaz.

"I wish I could," the other said, flicking his tongue. "Unfortunately, every technic on Dorcas—and most of the ones from the encirclement ships, too—are up to their tonguetips looking through the spacecraft the Mrachanis came in. The Overclan Seating's contact mission is due to hit the Mrachani homeworld in about a fullarc, and Warrior Command wants to know as much about Mrachani technology as possible before they land."

"Wouldn't Warrior Command be willing to reassign some of them for this?"

"They might," Thrr-mezaz said, throwing a quick look around the room. "On the other side, they might also order me to stay away from that underground structure entirely. In fact, they may do that anyway—there are probably Elders who'll be reporting this discovery whether I do directly or not."

Klnn-dawan-a looked around the room, too. No Elders were visible, but that didn't prove anything. "Why wouldn't Warrior Command want you investigating the structure?"

"Call it a hunch," Thrr-mezaz said, taking a step toward the door. "If you'll excuse me, I'd better get those warriors moving."

Klnn-dawan-a made a quick decision. "Let me go with them."

Thrr-mezaz flicked his tongue in a negative. "Not a good idea," he said. "It could be dangerous."

"So could having warriors blundering around not knowing what

they're doing," she countered. "I know a fair amount about alien artifacts."

He gazed hard at her, indecision flicking across his face. "Thrr-gilag
will raise me to Eldership personally if anything happens to you."

"He has no say in it," Klnn-dawan-a said, tasting bitterness beneath
her tongue. "Our bond-engagement has been annulled, remember?"

"Yes, but—"

"And the only way we're going to get together again," she went on
quietly, "is if we make such a contribution to the war effort that the clan
leaders have no choice but to reconsider. Could this underground structure be such a contribution?"

Thrr-mezaz's tongue flicked. "Yes. It could indeed."

"Then I'm going," she said, standing up. "Do I have time to change
into field clothing first?"

"I think so, yes." Thrr-mezaz's tongue flicked again. "Klnn-
dawan-a—"

"I'll be fine, Thrr-mezaz," Klnn-dawan-a assured him, touching his
cheek gently with her tongue. "Really. Just let me get my bags from the
shuttle, and then you can show me where I can change."

It was odd, Melinda Cavanagh had thought more than once during the
past twenty days, how the twin tensions of warfare and forced confinement worked so effectively together to bring out both the very best and
the very worst in people.

She'd seen a pair of Peacekeeper soldiers stoically endure enemy laser
burns that should have had them screaming in agony, insisting that she
give her attention first to fellow soldiers whose injuries were worse than
theirs; yet barely two days later she'd had to rebandage some of those
same burns after a casual insult had precipitated a brief but vicious fight
in one of the hillside bivouacs. She'd watched civilians uncomplainingly
take their turns standing watch at the perimeter sentry posts in the icy
mountain air, knowing full well that those posts would be the first to go
when the inevitable Zhirrzh attack came; yet those same men so calmly
facing death could launch into five minutes of swearing at the news
they'd been tapped for latrine-digging duty. Melinda had experienced the
same paradoxical tugs on her own psyche, working straight through the
night to treat burns and abrasions and frostbite, yet nearly going ballistic
one evening when her meal ration was one meat strip short.

All of which had made Lieutenant Colonel Castor Holloway's conduct
over those same twenty days stand that much further above the crowd. In
her multiple roles as physician, microbiology researcher, and occasional
idea sounding board, Melinda had spent a fair amount of time with

Holloway or in close proximity to him, and she had been thoroughly impressed by his consistent professionalism and self-control. She'd seen him grim, tired, amused, thoughtful, even frustrated; but never angry, brusque, or insulting to the troops or civilians under his command.

Apparently, it took a lot to make Colonel Holloway really angry. Just as apparently, Melinda had managed to find the winning combination.

"I don't believe what I'm hearing," Holloway snarled, his cheeks tinged with red as he glared at her. "You, of all people, Cavanagh. Of *all* people."

"I'm sorry, Colonel," Melinda said, trying to keep her voice steady and quiet. Especially quiet. There was precious little privacy there in the huge, cavernlike area that served as Peacekeeper HQ, and it was embarrassing getting chewed out in public. "But I don't think it's that serious a problem."

"Oh, you don't, do you?" he asked icily. "Communication with the enemy isn't that serious a problem? Unauthorized, unsupervised, uncensored communication with the enemy isn't that serious a problem?"

"It's not communication with the enemy," Melinda insisted, feeling some anger of her own starting to simmer. "It's one civilian talking to one prisoner. Prr't-zevisti can't get to any of his people—that metal room has him completely trapped."

"We only have his word for that," Holloway shot back, jabbing his stylus toward her for emphasis. "For all we know, the whole Zhirrzh task force out there could have been listening in."

"Which is one reason I thought I should be the one to talk to him first," Melinda said. "I don't have any military knowledge they could use against us."

"That's not the point," Holloway insisted. "The point is that you had no business pulling something like this without consulting with me first."

"And what would you have said if I had?" Melinda countered. "That no one was to talk to him until you'd taken a close look at who and what this incorporeal creature was who'd taken up residence in your camp? Fine. Who exactly would you have picked to do that study?"

"That's irrelevant," Holloway growled. "And damn conceited, besides."

"I'm sorry," Melinda said stiffly. "Being irrelevant and damn conceited runs in my family."

There was an almost-chuckle from the side, instantly strangled off. "You have something to add, Major?" Holloway demanded, glaring at his second in command.

"No, sir," Major Fujita Takara said, his face straightening instantly

back to serious. "I was just agreeing with Dr. Cavanagh that those quali-
ties do indeed run in her family."

For a long moment Holloway held the glare, the muscles of his throat
and cheeks working, but his reddish color slowly beginning to fade. Finally, with a long and thoroughly exasperated sigh, he turned back to
Melinda. "I'd have you court-martialed, Doctor," he said, tossing the
stylus in disgust onto the desk, "except that that's what you technically
are anyway. All right—let's hear it."

"Yes, sir," Melinda said, turning on her plate and setting it on the desk
where Holloway could see it. "To begin with, Prr't-zevisti seems to repre-
sent a stage of Zhirrzh existence that has no real analogue in the human
life cycle. At the point of physical death, their spirits—or personalities, or
whatever—are drawn back to and anchored at the site of an organ that
had been earlier removed and preserved. These *fsss* organs are taken
from beneath the brain when the Zhirrzh are children—that's where that
scar at the back of the skull comes from. The organs are then stored in
huge pyramid-shaped structures maintained by the various Zhirrzh families."

"Ghost retirement homes," Takara murmured, hitching his chair closer
to the desk for a better look at the plate.

"Something like that," Melinda agreed. "Except that they're called
Elders, not ghosts. Anyway, it seems that if you then take a slice from
one of these *fsss* organs, the Elder attached to it can move back and forth
between the main organ and the cutting. Supposedly instantaneously,
even if the two pieces are light-years apart."

"I'll be damned," Takara said quietly. "There it is, Cass. That's their
instantaneous communication method."

"Maybe," Holloway said, frowning suspiciously at Melinda. "And he
just *told* you all this?"

"Most of it," Melinda said. "Some parts I had to work out on my own
because of the language barrier."

"So it's really just speculation."

"There's very little speculation to it, Colonel," Melinda said tartly.
"The bottom line is that Prr't-zevisti thinks this war is a terrible mistake,
and he wants very much to get it stopped. That's why he opened a dialogue with me in the first place, and why he's been so candid about
himself and his people."

"What does he mean, a mistake?" Takara put in. "Did they think we
were someone else?"

Melinda shook her head. "It was the communication package the *Jutland* transmitted to them. Apparently, radio waves play havoc with the
Zhirrzh sense of balance and also cause tremendous pain to Elders via

their *fsss* organs or cuttings. So much so that radio transmitters were used once—just once—in a Zhirrzh war. They're still called Elderdeath weapons."

For a minute both men were silent. "No," Holloway said at last. "It's all very interesting, but it doesn't hold together. You might be able to explain that first battle with the *Jutland* by saying they thought the contact package was an attack, but that doesn't explain their subsequent invasion of the Commonwealth."

"Prr't-zevisti doesn't understand that either," Melinda said. "Though he does concede the Zhirrzh have always moved swiftly to crush races they thought had attacked them without provocation."

"They certainly seem experienced at it," Holloway said sourly. "So what does Prr't-zevisti suggest we do? Set him free to go proclaim peace to his people?"

"More or less," Melinda said. "Though I'm not sure I would have put it quite so cynically."

"Being cynical runs in *my* family," Holloway countered.

"Being cynical is also part of our job, Doctor," Takara added. "I agree with Colonel Holloway that this Elderdeath thing is intriguing. But with comm lasers next to useless out here in the wilds, this could just as easily be some kind of Zhirrzh sympathy ploy to get us to limit our use of short-range radios."

"Not to mention the whole Elder concept being a little hard to swallow in the first place," Holloway agreed. "I hope you realize we can't simply give in on this."

"I wouldn't want you to," Melinda said. "The Cavanagh genes lean to conceit, not naïveté. What I *would* suggest is that you have all this ready to upload the next time one of those Peacekeeper surveillance ships comes into the system. If there's even a chance Prr't-zevisti is telling the truth, the Commonwealth needs to know about it."

Holloway and Takara exchanged glances. "That's a reasonable idea," Holloway said. "Unfortunately, the only laser we've got that's able to punch a signal that far out is currently in service as a perimeter defense weapon."

"Can't it be reaimed upward?" Melinda asked.

"Reaiming isn't the problem," Takara said. "The problem is that the frequencies used for communication are nothing like those used in combat. It would have to be retuned, and that would take time."

"More time than any surveillance ship would likely want to hang around the system," Holloway said. "Though there might be some kind of modular tuner we could cobble together. Check with the techs, Fuji, and see what they can do."

"Right," Takara said, making a note on his plate.

"In the meantime, what do we do about Prr't-zevisti?" Melinda asked.

"Colonel!" one of the Peacekeepers called across the cavern. "Report from Spotter Three: the enemy's on the move. Six or seven Zhirrzh on foot, moving north from Point Zero."

For a heartbeat Melinda looked at Holloway, an odd sense of unnamed dread pricking at her. Why did north from the village seem significant?

Then, abruptly, it clicked: the underground tectonic-monitoring station, where she and Holloway had speculated one of the CIRCE components might be hidden. "Colonel—"

"Must have found the tectonic station," Holloway cut her off, his eyes flashing a warning as he got to his feet. Melinda nodded: clearly, he hadn't shared their private suspicions about the station with the rest of his troops.

For obvious reasons. Whenever the Zhirrzh finally got around to launching their attack, the last thing Holloway would want potential captives knowing was that there might be more to the tectonic station than met the eye. "What do you want me to do?" she asked.

"Go back to the infirmary and get prepped," Holloway told her. "There's a good chance you'll be getting some new patients soon."

The door to the underground structure was well hidden, built into the surface of one of the many hills that dotted the area. They'd located it, and Klnn-dawan-a had succeeded in opening it, when the alert came.

"Report from Commander Thrr-mezaz," the Elder said urgently. "The *Imperative* has spotted Human-Conqueror warcraft coming this way."

"Arrival time?" Warrior First Tbv-ohnor asked.

The Elder vanished, returned a pair of beats later. "Two or three hunbeats," he said.

Klnn-dawan-a felt her tail speed up. "That's not much time," she said, trying to keep her voice calm.

"No, it's not," Tbv-ohnor agreed, looking around them.

Klnn-dawan-a looked around, too. It was not, to her mind, a particularly auspicious location for a battle. The heavy tree canopy overhead would hide them from sight, but it would do little to shield them against enemy weapons. The only Zhirrzh weapons powerful enough to stop the warcraft were in the ground defense stations protecting the village, the nearest of which was a good three thoustrides away. At ground level the trees and other hills in the area also offered some protection against long-range weapons, but they similarly limited the range of the Zhirrzh warriors' own laser rifles. Worse, they would provide cover for advancing

Human-Conqueror ground warriors should the enemy choose to attack that way.

Which left the underground structure.

She peered inside. Behind the door was a short entrance chamber, perhaps two strides wide by three strides long, unlit except for the dim sunlight filtering down through the trees. At the end of the entrance chamber was a stairway, disappearing downward into darkness. If they went down there . . .

"Risky," Tbv-ohnor said quietly from beside her. "Enough metal around us in the stairway—certainly enough in the underground structure itself—that we'd be completely cut off from Elder communication."

Klnn-dawan-a felt her tail twitch as a horrible thought struck her. Cut off from Elders meant they would also be isolated from their *fsss* organs. If their bodies were destroyed down there, it wouldn't be simply a matter of being raised to Eldership. They would all be dead.

"But, then, that's what we came here to see," Tbv-ohnor continued, stepping cautiously through the doorway. "Everyone: inside. You three" —he flicked his tongue at three of the warriors—"stay up here. Use this room for cover and have the Elders target your shots for you—maybe we can turn the poor visibility to our advantage. You two: come with Searcher Klnn-dawan-a and me." Taking Klnn-dawan-a's arm, he headed down into the cool darkness of the stairwell—

And abruptly Klnn-dawan-a was thrown off balance as the thunder-crack of a shock wave hammered them from behind.

Her free hand flailed for balance, caught the guide rail fastened to the stairwell wall more by good luck than deliberate intent. Tbv-ohnor tightened his grip on her other arm, and she managed to stay on her feet. "Keep moving!" Tbv-ohnor shouted. "They'll be back any beat."

Together they stumbled down, the two warriors close behind them. The stairway ahead faded disconcertingly into the gloom, but as Klnn-dawan-a's lowlight pupils widened, she found there was enough light filtering down for her to see the end.

From above came another thunderclap, sounding almost as loud as the first had in the close confines of the stairwell. Klnn-dawan-a grabbed the guide rail again, and as she did so, her sensitized sight caught a rapid multiple flicker of reflected light against the walls: the warriors in the entrance chamber, firing at the Human-Conqueror warcraft shooting past overhead.

"Looks like another door at the end there," Tbv-ohnor said as the last reverberations faded away. "You think it'll have the same type of opening mechanism?"

"We can hope so," Klnn-dawan-a said, grateful for the warrior's obvious effort to take her mind off the danger. "Odd, though—that outer door didn't seem very secure. Not like something the Human-Conquerors really wanted to keep intruders out of."

"Maybe this is the secure one," Tbv-ohnor said as they reached the bottom of the stairs. "See if you can open it quickly; if not, we'll burn it."

"Right."

Klnn-dawan-a squatted down beside the door; and as she studied the mechanism, she heard a new set of footsteps hurrying down the stairs behind them. "Warrior First?" one of the three warriors Tbv-ohnor had left in the entrance chamber called down. "Report from the Elders: one of the warcraft has landed and is discharging Human-Conqueror ground warriors. Commander Thrr-mezaz is dispatching the Stingbirds and more warriors."

"Understood," Tbv-ohnor said grimly. "Keep me informed."

"I obey," the warrior said. Turning, he hurried up the stairs again.

"Looks like we've sliced open a real maggot-filled *kavra* on this one," one of the warriors standing beside Klnn-dawan-a muttered under his breath.

"Looks like it," Tbv-ohnor agreed. "The Human-Conquerors don't want us down here, that's for sure."

"You wouldn't know it from their locks," Klnn-dawan-a said. Standing up, she released the latching mechanism—

And with only a single high-pitched squeak, the door swung gently open.

"Troop carrier's on the ground, Colonel," Crane reported as he sat at the situation monitor. "No opposition yet. Aircars still reporting minor laser fire from the target zone; no damage."

"What about the copters?" Holloway asked.

"Spotter Two reports they're prepping for flight," Crane said. "At the moment they're still on the ground."

"Probably going for a simultaneous jump-off," Takara muttered.

"Most likely," Holloway agreed, restlessly fingering the short-range radio comm in his hand as he studied the panoramic view of the village and target zone being relayed via comm laser from the spotters' nose cameras. The enemy force had definitely made it to the tectonic station; the laser fire coming at the aircar overflights showed that much. The question was, had they gotten inside yet?

"The copters have lifted," Crane reported. "Heading northward, treetop height. Spotters tally six of them; one appears to be carrying a belly payload."

Six of the Conquerors' deadly combat helicopters, against three moderately armed Peacekeeper aircars and one troop carrier. The smart thing to do, Holloway knew, would be to order his people back aboard and get them out of there while he still could.

But that would mean abandoning the tectonic station to the enemy. A place with no military value whatsoever . . . unless it was in fact the hiding place for one of CIRCE's components.

And if it was, his job above all else was to keep that component from falling into enemy hands. Even if it cost the lives of his entire command.

He raised the comm and clicked it to the Copperheads' channel. "Copperheads: launch."

"Yes, sir," the calm voice of Lieutenant Bethmann acknowledged. A moment later, quiet and almost harmless-sounding in the distance, Holloway heard the rumble as the two Corvine fighters shot from concealment into the air.

Takara moved a step closer to his side. "You're taking one hell of a risk here, Cass," he murmured. "I hope you realize that."

"We have to take a stand somewhere, Fuji," Holloway said. "We're taking it here."

Takara seemed to digest that. "If you're looking for a showdown with those copters, I recommend we try to draw them out here into the mountains," he said. "The Corvines seem to have the edge in target ranging and blind-corner maneuvering—"

"I said we're taking our stand here."

A muscle in Takara's cheek twitched as he stepped back. "Yes, sir."

Holloway looked back at the monitor. "Tactical overlay," he ordered.

"Yes, sir." Crane keyed in the overlay, and a multicolored vector graph appeared superimposed on the nose-camera composite. The six enemy copters were hauling bear for the tectonic station, all right. Holloway did a quick mental calculation—

"They're going to beat the Copperheads there," Takara said tightly. "Probably by a good minute."

And a minute would be all it would take for those six copters to methodically slaughter every one of the Peacekeepers deploying from the troop carrier and possibly take out the aircars as well. Holloway clenched a hand into a fist, torn between the military necessity of driving the enemy away and his own instinctive protectiveness toward his troops—

And then, only a few hundred meters from their goal, the six red vectors abruptly shortened and shifted direction. "Copters slowing," Crane snapped. "Check that: faltering—looks like they're going to land right there in the trees. No; there they go again. Veering east . . . now veering east and south."

"I'll be dumped to a desk job," Takara said, a note of incredulity in his voice. "They're running back home."

Holloway let out a silent sigh of relief. He'd gambled his irreplaceable Copperheads and won.

Or at least hadn't yet lost. "Maybe their commander thinks like you do, Fuji," he said. "Trying to lure the Copperheads into range of his ground-based weapons."

Takara threw him a slightly uneasy look. "I trust you're not going to take him up on the invitation."

"Don't worry," Holloway assured him. "I'm not interested in any high-noon showdowns. If I can push the Zhirrzh out of the tectonic station, I'll be happy."

Takara grunted, looking back at the copter vectors, now definitely heading back toward the village. "Doesn't say much for their commander that he'd just abandon seven of his troops out there without a fight."

"Perhaps," Holloway said. On the other hand, if that tame ghost of Melinda Cavanagh's had been telling the truth about Zhirrzh life cycles, they might not even care all that much about physical death. "To me it says those copters are as valuable to him as our Copperheads are to us."

Takara cocked an eyebrow. "And as irreplaceable?"

"Could be," Holloway agreed thoughtfully. And if true, that might be the best flicker of hopeful news they'd had since the invasion. If the ground troops here were having trouble getting resupplied, it might mean the Zhirrzh invasion of the Commonwealth had stretched their war machine dangerously thin.

Or else it could mean they were having too much fun stomping Earth or Centauri to bother with this military equivalent of a flea bite. "Let's see just how nervous he is about losing them," he said, clicking on his comm again. "Copperheads: veer to intercept those copters. Don't actually pursue—just scare them a little. Be sure you stay out of range of those ground lasers."

"Acknowledged."

Holloway clicked off and peered at the monitor. The two Corvines, which had been flying a parallel close-wingtip formation at treetop height, shifted smoothly into high-low pursuit mode. Holloway shifted his attention to the copters and their superimposed vectors, watching closely for any sign of reaction—

And without warning a blaze of light flashed upward from the forest. Catching the lower of the two Corvines directly across its nose.

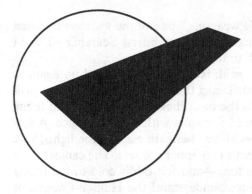

7 Tbv-ohnor had insisted on going first into the underground structure, an order Klnn-dawan-a had put up
only token resistance to. Standing away from the half-
opened door, she watched as the three warriors cautiously slipped through. There were a few flickers of
light as the beams from their hand lights reflected off
the walls and doorjamb; and then Tbv-ohnor was back, poking his head
around the edge of the door. "Looks clear, Searcher," he said. "Come on
in."

The room was a large one, probably encompassing the entire underground structure, though measurements would have to be taken to confirm that. The beams from the hand lights swept across Human-Conqueror-style chairs and tables, a curved desk with a ring of darkened
monitors facing an empty chair, and walls lined with tall, slender equipment cabinets. Some of the cabinets hummed softly, with small rows of
colored lights set into their fronts, which glowed steadily or flicked on
and off in complex patterns. Other cabinets stood quietly, with no indication as to whether or not they were functioning.

"Looks like some sort of command room," one of the warriors commented.

"Perhaps," Klnn-dawan-a said, looking behind her. There was a hand-
sized panel with two small blue lights set into the wall just beside the
door. She waved her hand over them without effect, then gingerly
touched the rightmost light with a fingertip. She'd guessed correctly:
abruptly the room was filled with a soft white glow radiating from hidden
sources behind the cabinets.

A strange multiple stuttering sound came faintly from the direction of
the stairway. "What was that?" she asked.

"Human-Conqueror projectile weapons," one of the warriors told her, moving to the door and looking up. "Better hurry, Searcher—I don't think we're going to have much time."

"Understood," Klnn-dawan-a said, feeling her tail speed up again as she crossed to the cabinet directly facing the monitor desk. That particular cabinet was also the one with the most flickering lights: fifty of them, laid out in a rectangular pattern of five rows with ten lights each. A row of Human-Conqueror letters was affixed beneath each of the lights, with other lines of letters in the cabinet's two upper corners. The cabinet itself was humming—a low, pervasive tone—and felt oddly cold to the touch. "Do any of the warriors on Dorcas understand the Human-Conqueror language?" she asked, pulling a field camera from her waist pouch and starting to photograph the letters.

"We all had a short orientation course before we got here," Tbv-ohnor said, stepping up beside her. "The written language ought to be programmed into our interpreter, though."

Another stutter of projectile gunfire from overhead wafted its way down the stairway. To Klnn-dawan-a's apprehensive ear slits, it sounded as if they were getting closer. "Here," she said, thrusting the camera into Tbv-ohnor's hands. "I want you to get me photos of all the cabinets. Pay particular attention to words and other lettering. I'm going to take a look inside this one."

"Right," Tbv-ohnor said, slinging his laser rifle and moving off across the room with the camera.

The front panel, Klnn-dawan-a quickly discovered, was an independent piece of metal, attached to the sides of the cabinet with a variant of the helical fastener that the Zhirrzh and every other race they'd come across had independently developed. One of the fingers of her manifold tool was the right size for the cruciform fastening slots of these particular helics, and in half a hunbeat she had the front panel off.

Given the obviously advanced state of Human-Conqueror technology, she had expected the equipment inside the cabinet to be highly complex. What she hadn't expected was the incredible extent to which that equipment had been miniaturized. Perhaps a hundred cables fed into the cabinet from openings in the back panel, snaking their way individually and in bundled groups to a mere six sites evenly spaced from top to bottom along the centerline. There the cables split into individual fibers of metal or glass, which vanished into the faces of small cubes suspended in midair by thick gray cylinders running horizontally across the cabinet. The cylinders themselves disappeared in turn through openings in the right and left walls, presumably into the cabinets on either side.

It was strange and very alien, and for a beat a disturbing vision flashed through Klnn-dawan-a's mind: that of a group of trillsnakes trying to swallow cube-shaped nornins, sculpted perhaps by some old neofacetist artisan.

Hastily, she chased the image from her mind. Considering what was going on above them, the last thing she wanted to think about was trill-snakes devouring nornins. Leaning halfway into the cabinet, she focused her light on one of the cubes, looking for some way to open it.

Surrounded by the pervasive hum of the cabinet, she never heard the footsteps that must have charged down the stairway. But suddenly Tbv-ohnor was there beside her. "Time to go, Searcher," he said urgently.

"Now?" Klnn-dawan-a asked. "But—"

"*Now*, Searcher," Tbv-ohnor snapped, grabbing her upper arm and yanking her bodily away from the cabinet. "The enemy's almost here."

Klnn-dawan-a's protests died at the back of her tongue. A few beats later they were all heading up the stairway.

"It might already be too late," Tbv-ohnor warned grimly as they clumped hurriedly up the steps. "Commander Thrr-mezaz pulled some trick that's keeping the Human-Conquerors' warcraft out of the sky in this area—I didn't get the details. But their ground warriors were already down, and the commander's reinforcements won't get here before they do."

"Maybe we should just stay down here," Klnn-dawan-a suggested, her tail spinning harder with the exertion of the climb. "If the room is that important to them, they won't risk damaging it. We could wait until it's safe to come out."

"Unless they prefer destroying it to letting us have it," Tbv-ohnor countered. "In which case they'll just roll some of their explosives down the stairway."

The stuttering sounds of Human-Conqueror weapons were getting louder, and as they neared the surface, Klnn-dawan-a could hear the hissing of laser rifles as the Zhirrzh warriors returned the fire. They reached the entrance chamber at the top of the stairs to find one of the warriors crouching beside each of the walls while the third, lying on the metal floor a stride back from the entrance, methodically sprayed laser flashes back and forth across his angle of fire. "Are they out there?" Tbv-ohnor asked as they reached the chamber.

"I don't know," the warrior at the right-hand wall said. "The Elders say they're not close enough to see us yet, but I keep seeing movement out there in the trees."

"Nothing that says Elders can't make mistakes," Tbv-ohnor grunted, moving up behind him and peering cautiously outside. "Especially with the kind of visual camouflage the Human-Conquerors like to use. Question is, how do we get around them?"

Klnn-dawan-a eased a stride forward. A dozen small smoldering fires and general haze of smoke could be seen throughout the area the third warrior was still sweeping laser fire across. "That question's going to be academic if you set the whole forest on fire," she warned.

"It'll also be academic if we let them get a straight shot in here," Tbv-ohnor retorted, throwing a glare at her over his shoulder. "Let us handle this, all right?"

Flicking her tongue, Klnn-dawan-a stepped back behind the warrior on the floor. As she did so, an Elder appeared just outside the outer doorway, almost invisible against the mottled light pattern of the forest. "Watch out, Warrior First," he warned. "Three of the enemy have reached firing position. The other twelve are still approaching, using what seems to be a modified closed-talon formation."

"What about the warcraft?" Tbv-ohnor asked.

"Commander Thrr-mezaz's scheme seems to have driven them from the area," the Elder said. "Only temporarily, though, I suspect. Our commander at the Battle of F'orshn on X'sin tried a very similar trick, and—"

"Then we need to break out now," Tbv-ohnor cut him off. "Give me targeting on those three warriors."

The Elder vanished, was back a few beats later. "The first is there," he said, pointing with his tongue. "Behind the large tree—he's looking around it to the left of the bole. The second and third are there"—he pointed again—"on either side of a half-buried boulder."

"Right," Tbv-ohnor said, hefting his laser rifle as the Elder vanished again. "Fhz-gelic, get up off the floor—we're going to want two shots on each target. All warriors: aim and fire on my command. Prepare—"

Abruptly, the Elder reappeared. "Warrior—wait. The enemy warriors have suddenly pressed themselves into the ground. They must know—"

"—now!" Tbv-ohnor barked, jerking his laser rifle into firing position. In perfect unison the other five warriors did the same—

And as they fired, the forest to their left seemed to vanish in a dazzling explosion.

Klnn-dawan-a staggered back with a scream, her midlight pupils stabbed with pain. A split beat later she was slammed hard onto the metal floor as the ground bucked like a wild animal beneath her feet and a roar of sound hammered across her body.

Her midlight pupils were still useless; cautiously widening her dark-light pupils, she saw the remnants of what must have been a huge fireball rising above the nearest trees. "What happened?" her numbed ear slits heard her voice say.

But there was no answer. Cautiously lifting her head, she looked around her.

Her first horrible thought was that that single blast had raised all six of the warriors to Eldership. They lay on the floor at the front of the entrance chamber, unmoving, their laser rifles lying haphazardly across the floor or still held in limp grips. But even as she stared in rising panic, she saw Tbv-ohnor's left foot twitch and realized what had in fact happened. Standing at the outer door, mostly outside the limited protection of the entrance chamber, they'd been hit much harder by the light and shock wave of the explosion.

It wasn't as bad as she'd feared. But it was bad enough. Stunned warriors were no more capable of fighting than warriors who'd been raised to Eldership . . . and there were fifteen enemy warriors converging on them.

Which meant it was up to her. Pressing her tongue against the side of her mouth, fighting a sudden wave of nausea, she got to her knees and crawled across the floor toward the warriors.

Tbv-ohnor's tail had begun a sluggish undulation by the time she reached the nearest laser rifle. Getting a grip on the shoulder brace, she hauled it over to her, wondering uneasily whether her limited experience with handheld stingers would be any help in handling the vastly more powerful warrior weapon. Picking it up, she climbed to her feet and stumbled to the entrance.

And froze. There, not twenty strides away, a line of eight Human-Conquerors stood or knelt in their camouflage clothing. Their weapons pointing straight at her.

"Pull up, Vanbrugh!" Holloway barked into his comm as the laser beam raked across the Corvine's underside. "Pull up, damn it!"

"He can't," Takara bit out, waving a fist toward the display as the Corvine twisted violently to the right.

He was right, Holloway knew, watching helplessly as the Corvine slid even farther to the side. It was done for, with bare seconds left before either the enemy laser sliced it open or else it crashed onto the forest floor. He cringed in anticipation, wondering why Vanbrugh and Hodgson didn't eject; realized an instant later that they had neither the time nor the altitude left to do so. They were going to die out there. Violently, uselessly, they were going to die.

"Look!" Takara said suddenly, jolting Holloway out of his horrified fascination with the doomed Copperheads. "Bethmann's coming back."

Holloway swore. Bethmann was coming back, all right. The second Corvine had veered around in a tight curve and was blazing full throttle back toward Vanbrugh's crippled fighter and the laser attacking it. Recklessly flying back into danger— "Bethmann, get out of there," Holloway snapped into the comm. "You can't help them now."

There was no answer . . . but even as Holloway started to repeat the order, he saw it was too late. The heavy laser had flicked away from the crippled Corvine, relinquishing the chance for a direct kill in order to deal with this new threat bearing down on it. Helplessly, Holloway watched as the brilliant beam came on again, grazing the flank of Bethmann's approaching fighter.

And then, abruptly, the Corvine's nose pitched violently upward, the movement all but killing its forward momentum. The laser swung wide, its operators caught off guard by the maneuver. For a split second the aircraft seemed to stand on its tail in midair, its underside blatantly exposed to the enemy. The beam checked its movement, tracked back toward its target—

And in a burst of Icefire the Corvine vanished.

"What the hell?" Takara said, blinking. "Where did it go?"

"It went up, sir," Crane said, sounding more than a little stunned himself. "Just straight up."

"Track him," Holloway ordered.

Crane keyed his board, and the monitor view pulled back and swung upward. Sure enough, there was Bethmann's Corvine, halfway to the stratosphere and just starting to curve over the top of his arc. "Incredible," Takara said. "There's a solid year's worth of dumb luck shot all to hell."

"I don't think there was any luck to it at all," Holloway said, a sudden suspicion striking him. "Crane, see if you can locate Vanbrugh's Corvine."

"Yes, sir." The monitor screen split, bringing up a second image. . . .

Takara whistled softly. "I'll be damned."

Holloway nodded silently. Vanbrugh's damaged Corvine, not looking nearly as crippled now as it had when Bethmann had come charging to the rescue, was flying low across the Dorcas landscape, racing back toward the relative safety of the mountains.

"It was a diversion," Takara said, shaking his head in disbelief. "Vanbrugh couldn't slide out of firing range fast enough, so Bethmann charged in to draw the heat away from him."

"And got the enemy to split his attention just long enough for both of them to get away," Holloway said, a shiver running up his back. A maneuver improvised on the spot, its details communicated between the two crews, its execution handled with exquisite timing and coordination. All of it accomplished in perhaps half a dozen seconds.

A few years back, when Lord Stewart Cavanagh and Commander Adam Quinn had raised the issue of improper Copperhead cadet screening, there had been long and heated debates throughout the Commonwealth as to whether the Copperheads were even worth all this effort and money. As a good Peacekeeper officer, Holloway had of course stood solidly behind the Copperheads in his own discussions with civilian friends and relatives. Privately, though, he would have had to admit that he really didn't understand why Peacekeeper Command was so adamant on keeping the unit.

He did now.

His hand was still squeezing the comm tightly. Easing his grip, he clicked it on. "Vanbrugh, this is Holloway."

"Marlowe, Colonel," the voice of Bethmann's tail man came back promptly. "Vanbrugh can't respond—their main comm system's been damaged. Copperhead laser link's still working, though."

"What's their situation?"

"Bad, but not critical," Marlowe said. "They've lost some maneuvering ability and about half their targeting equipment. Still flyable, but they'll need some patchwork before they're ready for full combat again."

Holloway and Takara exchanged glances. Their supply stockpile was barely adequate to maintain the Peacekeeper unit and the twenty-five thousand civilians bivouacked behind them in the mountains. Their chances of having replacement parts for a Corvine fighter on hand were well-nigh nonexistent. "Understood," he said. "What about you?"

"We lost a little paint, but nothing serious," Marlowe assured him. "All major systems are up and humming, and we're ready to go burn some backside."

"Stand by." Holloway shifted his attention to Crane. "Strike-force status?"

"They're on the ground, sir," Crane said. "Duggen reports they're moving toward the target zone; getting some enemy fire and returning it, but at this point both sides seem to be shooting blind. They have no air cover, though—the aircars had to pull back when that ground laser opened up."

"I see," Holloway said, chewing that one over. On the one hand, with one Corvine already damaged, the last thing he wanted was to lose any more of their already inadequate air power. But on the other hand, the aircars' unauthorized withdrawal from the scene meant that Sergeant Duggen's strike force was completely open to an attack by the Zhirrzh copters. And if the Zhirrzh commander hadn't realized that yet, he would soon.

And they couldn't abandon the tectonic station to the enemy. Which left him exactly one option. "Marlowe?"

"Sir?"

"You think you and Bethmann can take out that ground laser station by yourselves?" Holloway asked. "Without losing more than paint in the process, I mean?"

"Piece of pie, Colonel," Bethmann cut in. "Just give the word."

"Consider it given," Holloway said. "But watch yourselves."

"Acknowledged. Copperheads out."

The radio went silent. "You think they can do it?" Takara asked.

"If that's the only surprise the Zhirrzh have planned, I'm sure they can," Holloway said. "My only worry is that there might be another half-dozen ground stations stashed around that we don't know about. How in hell did they manage to set that one up without our seeing them do it?"

"Sir, we may have an answer to that," Crane spoke up. "Gasperi's done a quick analysis of the spotter tapes, and he thinks the laser was that belly payload we saw one of the copters carrying. He set it down before they all scattered back home."

"Tricky," Takara said. "Speaking of copters, it looks like they're re-grouping."

He was right. Regrouping and shifting direction, and a moment later heading back north toward Duggen's strike force.

"Terrific," Holloway growled, searching the monitor for Bethmann's Corvine. The fighter was still cruising across the sky, a couple of klicks above the ground and nearly five klicks northwest of the target zone. "Bethmann, whatever you're planning, you'd better get to it," he warned. "The copters are on the move."

"We see them, Colonel," Marlowe said. "Just keep your aircars out of the area. And warn the ground troops to brace themselves for one hell of a shock wave."

"Relay that, Crane," Holloway ordered, frowning at the monitor. What did the Copperheads have in mind . . . ?

And then, even as Crane spoke softly into his microphone, the Corvine rolled almost lazily onto its back and abruptly dropped nose first toward the ground.

"Cass—!" Takara gasped.

"Easy, Fuji," Holloway said, mentally crossing his fingers and hoping fervently the dive was planned and not the result of some sudden malfunction. The Corvine continued its plunge, building up incredible speed; and then, just when it seemed a crash was inevitable, its nose pulled up and it leveled into horizontal flight. An instant later it was burning through the air at nearly Mach 2 toward the Zhirrzh laser installation.

Flying *below* treetop level.

The diversionary maneuver a few minutes earlier had been impressive. This one literally took Holloway's breath away. Flying just over the tops of the shorter trees, corkscrewing deftly between the tops of the taller ones, the Corvine was only sporadically visible even to the Peacekeeper spotters. To the lower-flying Zhirrzh copters, it would be all but invisible. The Zhirrzh at the laser would never even see it coming.

Five seconds to go. Holloway hoped Duggen's strike force had gotten the word to go flat.

And then, suddenly, a small but brilliant fireball bloomed in the forest. Half a second later the Corvine reappeared, climbing into clear air again and curving hard around back toward the incoming copters.

Takara shouted something in Japanese. "They did it!"

"Crane, get the aircars back in the area," Holloway ordered. "Form up to support the Corvine—I want those copters warned away. Then get me a status check on the strike team."

"Yes, sir."

The monitor area's mess table was a few steps away, sparsely stocked with local fruit, Peacekeeper field meal bars, and drink carafes. Holloway walked over to it, stretching tired leg muscles, and pulled himself a steaming mug of tea. "You think it's over?" Takara asked, coming up beside him.

"I suppose that depends on how badly the Zhirrzh want a fight," Holloway told him, adding a few precious drops of lemon.

For a moment Takara was silent. "You really think it's in there?" he asked quietly.

"What?" Holloway asked, taking a sip of the hot liquid and turning around to look at the monitor. Nothing had changed: the Zhirrzh copters were still there, and the Corvine was still drawing the equivalent of an imaginary line in front of them. So far they hadn't taken the dare to cross it.

"You know," Takara said. "A CIRCE component."

Holloway looked at him, his stomach tightening. "Is it that obvious?"

Takara shrugged. "Probably not to anyone else. I just happen to know you better than most of the others. You wouldn't risk your people like this unless the stakes were astronomically high. There's not much on Dorcas that comes under that heading. At least nothing *I* know about."

Holloway looked back at the monitor. "I don't know anything either, at least not for certain. There were never any official disclosures or even unofficial hints—it was Dr. Cavanagh, actually, who got me thinking this direction. But the longer this war drags on without CIRCE making a grand entrance, the more I wonder if maybe we really are sitting on a piece of it."

Takara grunted. "Let's just hope the Zhirrzh don't get hold of it," he said grimly. "If they do, we might as well start calling them the Conquerors again."

"Yes," Holloway said. But even as he envisioned those invulnerable Zhirrzh warships armed with CIRCE weapons, the face of Melinda Cavanagh floated into view. Her earnest, serious expression as she'd relayed that Zhirrzh ghost's opinion that this war was a mistake . . .

"Colonel?" Crane called excitedly, half turning in his seat. "The outriders have reached the target. Looks like Duggen's got the drop on them."

"Get me a picture," Holloway ordered as he and Takara hurried back to their places. A moment later the image came up.

Holloway leaned forward, resting his mug on the back of Crane's chair. It was the entrance to the tectonic station, all right—he'd been there once and remembered what the place looked like. The outer door had been opened and swung wide, and he could just make out some figures inside the darkened entryway. "Can you enhance it?"

"Yes, sir." Crane worked his board, lightening and sharpening the view.

Takara whistled. "That's not getting the drop on them, Crane. That's a full-fledged thud."

"A thud and a half," Holloway agreed. A group of Zhirrzh—the whole contingent, it looked like—were lying unmoving in the front of the entryway. Stunned or dead.

He clicked his comm onto Duggen's channel. "Duggen, this is Holloway," he said. "Looks like you've got a clear path."

"Already on it, Colonel," Duggen's voice came back. "Squad One: pincer in. Outriders, stay sharp—we don't know how fast they can recover."

And as if on cue, the alien farthest back in the entryway cautiously lifted his head. For a moment he peered toward the doorway, apparently assessing the situation. Then, keeping low, he began slinking toward the door. "Duggen, you've got movement," Holloway said.

"I see it," Duggen said. "Outriders, stand ready; Squad One, hustle it to backup. You got a choice here, Colonel: you want a prisoner or a cadaver?"

"Prisoner, if possible," Holloway said. "But don't lose anyone in the process."

"No problem," Duggen said. "I doubt they've got much fight left in them."

The alien was still moving, and now Holloway could see involuntary-looking twitches in some of the others. "Looks like they're all starting to come to," Holloway warned.

"Squad Two's just about here," Duggen replied. "Soon as they're in backup, we'll move in."

Holloway bit at the inside of his cheek. They'd saved the tectonic station—at least for the moment—and in another minute they'd have some prisoners. Bargaining chips, if the Zhirrzh understood such things. Maybe even a way to corroborate this ghost/Elder thing of Melinda's.

And then the alien reached down and picked up one of the laser weapons.

At the edges of the monitor screen the muzzle ends of two Oberon assault guns appeared as the Peacekeeper outriders within camera range drew a bead on the enemy soldier. "So much for their not having any fight left," Takara said.

Holloway didn't answer. A word from him—a couple of bursts from those Oberons—and that would end it. The Peacekeepers could take the time to well and properly seal the tectonic station, and this potential threat to a possible CIRCE component would be finished. Certainly enough humans had died already in this war; and if Melinda was right, the aliens probably wouldn't take another six or seven Zhirrzh deaths all that seriously.

But if Melinda was also right about this war's being a mistake . . .

The alien had gotten the weapon to his shoulder, its muzzle angled downward toward the ground, and was moving with a strange awkwardness toward the entryway door. "Target him," Duggen ordered. "If that muzzle starts up, take him down."

The alien reached the entryway door and stopped. For a heartbeat he just stood there, weapon ready but still not aimed.

And Holloway came to a decision. "This is Holloway. All Peacekeepers, hold your fire."

"Sir?" Duggen said.

"You heard me," Holloway said. "Hold your fire unless and until fired on."

"Colonel, we're damn exposed out here," Duggen said, his voice tight. "If we wait until he fires, we could lose half the team."

"That's an order, Sergeant," Holloway said, clicking his comm to the aircars' channel. "Aircars, this is Holloway. Do either of you have a working external loudspeaker?"

"Aircar One, sir," the answer came back promptly. "I have one."

"I want you to fly over toward the Zhirrzh village, Erikson," Holloway said. "Not fast, like an attack. Just sort of drift over toward there, the way Sergeant Janovetz flew in four days ago. Be sure to stay well away from the white pyramid."

"Yes, sir."

"Crane, give me a split screen," Holloway ordered, ignoring the look on Takara's face. "Strike-team monitor and spotter view of the aircar."

"I hope you're not planning to send him all the way in," Takara murmured. "We still don't know what's happened to Janovetz."

"This is a different kind of experiment," Holloway assured him, watching the monitor. Aircar One had left its position and was moving gingerly toward the waiting line of attack copters. So far they were just hovering there watching him. "I want to see how willing their commander is to make deals."

Takara snorted under his breath. "Cass, these are the Conquerors," he reminded Holloway darkly. "You don't get a name like Conquerors by making deals."

"Maybe," Holloway said. "On the other hand, they did let Duggen's team get away unharmed the last time we tried to get to the tectonic station. That kind of lenience wouldn't seem to fit the Conquerors tag, either."

Takara grunted. "If they even spotted them. I'm still not convinced they did."

The copters had broken formation now, one of them moving to flank Aircar One. Holloway held his breath; but the alien aircraft didn't open fire. Instead, it merely dropped into a parallel course, its weapons trained warningly on the Peacekeeper craft. "Hold it steady, Erikson," Takara reminded the pilot. "No sudden moves."

Holloway glanced at the ranging data from the spotters displayed at the bottom of the monitor. "Close enough," he told Erikson. "Do some lazy circles around that spot and put me on loudspeaker."

"Yes, sir. On loudspeaker."

Mentally, Holloway crossed his fingers. "Zhirrzh commander, this is Commander Holloway of the Peacekeeper forces. We have seven of your soldiers trapped. I want to offer you a deal for their return."

Takara threw him a frown. "I thought you wanted them as prisoners."

"I've changed my mind," Holloway said. "Crane, I need a contrast or gain change on the strike-force picture. Something that'll pick up faint objects, focused on the area around that entryway. Can you do that?"

"I'll try, sir," Crane said, fiddling with his board and splitting the strike-force picture into two duplicates. One of the images zoomed forward to frame the dark entryway, then faded into a strange pattern of black-and-white blurs. "How's that?"

"We'll know in a minute," Holloway said, leaning forward to gaze at the blurs. If Melinda's ghost had been telling anything even approaching the truth . . .

And, suddenly, there it was: a ghostly figure, barely visible even on the enhanced picture but clearly recognizable as a Zhirrzh, floating just outside the dark blob of the entryway. One of the blurs in the entryway moved, and on the unaltered strike-force picture the Zhirrzh holding the laser weapon lowered its muzzle the rest of the way to the ground. Then, as abruptly as it had appeared, the ghost vanished.

Takara whistled softly. "I'll be damned. She was right."

"Looks that way," Holloway agreed, feeling a shiver run up his back. Real, living ghosts . . .

"Sir, report from Aircar Two," Crane spoke up. "The Zhirrzh reinforcements moving up from the south have stopped."

"Confirm that."

"Copperheads confirm, Colonel," Crane said. "Enemy reinforcements holding position one hundred forty-three meters south of the target zone."

"Maybe they're setting up another of those ground laser stations," Takara said.

"There's no indication of that, sir," Crane said. "They just seem to be waiting."

"Colonel, I'm getting something," Erikson's voice came from the speaker. "Boosting gain on the external mikes . . ."

The speaker crackled for a second with background noise. Then, as the enhancers cleaned up the sound, a distant and oddly mechanical voice came through. The same voice, as near as Holloway could tell, that had been in the recording Sergeant Janovetz had sent back before his pulse transmitter had gone silent. "—of the Zhirrzh. Speak your offer."

Holloway clicked on his comm. "Your soldiers may return to you unharmed," he said. "But they must first leave behind all equipment and weapons that they are carrying."

He lowered the comm, his eyes on the enhanced strike-force picture. A few seconds later the ghost flicked into sight, its hands gesticulating, its tongue flicking in and out of its insubstantial mouth. On the other picture Holloway could see the Zhirrzh soldier responding, his tongue doing some serious flicking of its own. One of the other Zhirrzh had rolled groggily to his knees, and the first Zhirrzh broke off the conversation to lean over for a quick consultation. The kneeling Zhirrzh's tongue flicked, and the first straightened again for more discussion with the ghost. He leaned over for another dialogue with the other Zhirrzh, then stood upright again.

"I wonder why the Elder doesn't just move in between the two of them," Takara said.

"He can't," Holloway said. "Check out the geometry: the walls of the entryway are blocking a straight-line path between that point and the nearest white pyramid. Elder's can't go through metal, remember?"

The ghost flicked its tongue and vanished; and as it did so, there was another crackle of background static from Aircar One's external mike. "Why do you want their equipment?"

Holloway grimaced as he clicked on his comm again. He didn't give a damn about the soldiers' equipment, actually—the Peacekeepers had already collected enough alien stuff to keep the ordnance techs busy for months. All he wanted was to make sure none of the Zhirrzh carted away something that might turn out to be that elusive CIRCE component. But he could hardly tell the Zhirrzh commander that. "I want to make sure they have no weapons they can harm my troops with as they leave," he said instead. "Do you agree?"

He clicked off the comm. "Maybe you should point out that we can turn the whole bunch of them into Elders if he refuses," Takara suggested.

"I'm sure that's already occurred to him," Holloway said. "Anyway, I'd just as soon he not know that we know anything about that."

The ghostly Elder messenger had reappeared beside the entryway now and was holding another conversation with the standing Zhirrzh soldier. A fairly animated conversation, from the looks of it.

And understandably so. This was the critical moment, Holloway knew: the point at which the alien commander had to choose between his soldiers' lives and whatever passed for pride or command authority in Zhirrzh psychology. If he decided to slug it out rather than buckle to enemy demands, the first Holloway would know about it would be those laser weapons swinging up to target his men. . . .

And then the standing Zhirrzh leaned over one final time, lowering his laser weapon to the entryway floor.

There was another crackle from the speaker. "I agree," the mechanical voice said.

Holloway took a deep breath and clicked the comm on again. "All right, Erikson, pull on back," he ordered. "Again, nice and easy. Duggen, have you been listening?"

"Yes, sir," Duggen answered. "I don't trust them, Colonel."

"I don't necessarily trust them, either," Holloway said. "Stay sharp, and make damn sure none of them is carrying anything before you let

them go. Watch for attempts to palm anything, odd bumps in their clothing—you know the drill."

"Understood, Colonel."

"I hope you're doing the right thing, Cass," Takara said as four
Peacekeepers moved into the picture from off camera and headed purposefully toward the Zhirrzh. "We're outnumbered enough down here as
it is. I don't much like the idea of letting seven of their soldiers go back
home. Especially when we still don't know what they've done to Janovetz."

"I'm betting he's still alive," Holloway said. "They didn't let him land
in their camp just to kill him. Not unless he attacked them first."

And yet, it suddenly occurred to him, perhaps Janovetz had done precisely that. The recorder and transmitter they'd attached to Janovetz's
cheek dumped its reports via a pulsed, multi-high-frequency radio signal.
Would the Zhirrzh have interpreted that as an Elderdeath attack? Probably. Would they have then killed Janovetz in perceived self-defense? Probably.

"Keep on top of this, Fuji," Holloway said, moving away from the
monitor. "Vanbrugh and Hodgson should have their Corvine on the
ground by now. I want to go check out the damage."

"Yes, sir."

Holloway threw one last look at the Zhirrzh soldiers divesting themselves of equipment under the watchful eyes of the Peacekeepers. Proud
warriors—Conquerors—yet submitting to this indignity with only minor
argument.

He wasn't yet ready to take everything Melinda's ghost friend, Prr't-
zevisti, said at face value. But it was clear that there was more to all this
than met the eye. And much more that needed to be learned.

"So that's that," Klnn-vavgi said as the last of the Elders vanished
from the command/monitor room, heading out to quietly oversee the
operation to the north. "We lose a mobile ground defense station, get
eight warriors raised to Eldership—and then we just give up and let them
have their underground structure back."

"I don't see a lot of practical alternatives," Thrr-mezaz growled, his
tail spinning with frustration. Outmaneuvered, outgunned, and utterly
dazzled by those unbelievable Copperhead warriors, the operation had
been a fiasco. To have his warriors captured, disarmed, and sent back was
just the crowning flick of the tongue to the whole thing.

"I don't see any, either," Klnn-vavgi said. "But not everyone will let it
go at that. And I'm sure there'll be some who'll say you gave in just to
keep Klnn-dawan-a from being raised to Eldership."

"And when they say that, you can tell them Eldership wasn't one of the options," Thrr-mezaz retorted, his tail twitching. "If I'd refused their commander's offer, the Human-Conquerors would have cut down Klnn-dawan-a and the warriors right where they stood. And inside all that metal, they would have been dead. Not raised to Eldership. Dead."

Klnn-vavgi's tongue flicked involuntarily. "Yes. Well . . . yes."

"Besides, the operation wasn't a complete waste," Thrr-mezaz went on. "The warriors got into the structure and had some time to look around. Maybe Klnn-dawan-a was able to figure out what the place is used for."

"Maybe," Klnn-vavgi said doubtfully.

Thrr-mezaz looked at the row of monitors, and at the Elders popping in and out with continuous reports about the disarming. They were proud and savage warriors, these Human-Conquerors. And yet they'd just passed up a chance to slaughter a group of their enemies.

Just as, six fullarcs ago, they'd let Thrr-mezaz himself and his two climbing companions leave the area of the Human-Conqueror stronghold.

Thrr-gilag had suggested to him that there were some intriguing inconsistencies in Human-Conqueror aggressiveness—inconsistencies that might be biochemically based. Thrr-mezaz wasn't yet ready to accept any such theory, at least not without some tangible proof. But it was becoming increasingly clear to him that there was more to these Human-Conquerors than what was on the surface.

And much more that needed to be learned.

My external microphones note the sound of the approaching D'Accord carrosse coupe groundcar 65.55 seconds before it comes within camera range around the southwest corner of the maintenance building beside which the fueler I am encased in is parked. The glass is one-way darkened, but using an enhancement algorithm, I am able to determine that there is a single person inside. I estimate a probability of 0.87 that the occupant is a male human, and a probability of 0.54 that the occupant is Assistant Commonwealth Liaison Petr Bronski.

The D'Accord pulls to a stop beside the fueler. The occupant waits 5.93 seconds before opening the door and exiting.

My deduction was correct: it is indeed Liaison Bronski. For another 3.45 seconds he gazes at the fueler, the angle of his gaze indicating he is looking at the sealed hatchway midway up the side. "Cavanagh? You in there?"

Technically, he is not speaking to me, and I am therefore under no obligation to answer. But I am curious about his presence here and know also that he may be able to provide me with the answers to questions that have troubled me since the end of the inquiry-board hearing 68.44 hours ago. "This is Max, Mr. Bronski. Mr. Cavanagh is not here."

His face changes subtly. I examine my human-expression algorithms and deduce he is not surprised to find that Aric Cavanagh is not here. "You know where I might find him?"

"No, Mr. Bronski. I assumed you would know that."

Again his face changes. My algorithms cannot decipher this new expression. "Why would you assume that?"

"Because men apparently operating under your orders were following him when he left the Peacekeeper base."

His expression does not change. "Really. How do you know that?"

There are nine procedures consistent with my programming that would allow me to answer misleadingly without lying. But as I study his expression and compare again with my algorithms, I estimate a probability of 0.80 that he already knows the answer to his question. "I was listening to your conversation with your associate as you exited the Peacekeeper building after the inquiry-board hearing three days ago."

Liaison Bronski nods. I deduce from his expression that my previous conclusion was correct. "Thought so. The Peacekeeper tech guys found a spurious data-line linkage keyed in about that time. I thought it was probably you."

There are many nuances contained in this statement, and I spend the next 2.09 seconds considering them. I compute a probability of 0.02 that a Commonwealth assistant liaison would have sufficient access to high-level Peacekeeper operations to have learned about a spurious data-line linkage. Accordingly, I replay the conversation immediately following the inquiry-board hearing, paying particular attention to the expressions and body movements of Admiral Rudzinski as he speaks with Liaison Bronski. This new analysis allows me to compute a probability of 0.68 that the two men are more familiar with each other than the words spoken during the conversation would suggest.

"Cat got your tongue, Max?"

"What do you wish me to say?"

He smiles, though the expression has a strong degree of cynicism incorporated into it. "Never mind. I just figured a man like Lord Cavanagh would have taught you how to lie. Mind if I come up there?"

The question is unanticipated, and for 0.24 second I examine his expression. But the algorithms are of no use in helping me deduce the reason behind his request. "Why?"

"I want to look around a little." *His expression shifts to something that might be interpreted as shrewdness.* "It'd also give us a chance to discuss various questions with a little more privacy."

Legally, the fueler is private property and I am under no obligation to allow him inside. But the implication that I may be able to learn the answers to some of my many questions is a strongly compelling one. I can always summon help should that become necessary. "Very well."

It takes 1.07 minutes for me to rotate the lift cage from its storage compartment onto its track, lower it to the ground, and bring Liaison Bronski up to the hatch. It takes another 21.91 seconds for him to enter the hatch and make his way to the control room.

I review my earlier files and note that Melinda Cavanagh required 48.96 seconds to make this same trip through the fueler. Aric Cavanagh similarly required 51.03 seconds. However, Security Chief Adam Quinn required only

18.24 seconds. From this I deduce a probability of 0.87 that Liaison Bronski's background includes experience with such spacecraft, and a correlating probability of 0.95 that such experience was obtained via service with the Peacekeepers.

Inside the control room Liaison Bronski spends 4.52 seconds examining the control boards. His expression indicates he is satisfied with what he has learned from them, and he slides out a jump seat and sits down.

"How long have you been with Lord Cavanagh, Max?"

"I've been a CavTronics computer since my inception. I had not met Lord Cavanagh personally until he selected me for this mission."

"Did some extensive reprogramming on you, did he?"

"Extensive reprogramming was not required. Do you know where Aric Cavanagh is?"

He looks at my interior monitor camera for 0.72 second, his expression indicating thoughtfulness or speculation. "I'm asking the questions, if you don't mind. I'm looking for a list of emergency rat holes that Lord Cavanagh might have programmed into you."

"Please define the term *rat holes*."

He eyes me closely, his expression suspicious. "Places to go hide in case of trouble. Maybe the addresses of Lord Cavanagh's friends or business associates; maybe some of his favorite out-of-the-way vacation spots; maybe an unlisted CavTronics research plant or two. That sort of thing."

There are fifteen procedures consistent with my programming for deflecting questions I do not wish to answer. I select one of them. "Why would I have been given such information?"

He smiles, his expression indicating a probability of 0.96 that the deflection procedure has not deceived him. "Because you were sent out with Quinn and Cavanagh's son on a blatantly illegal rescue mission. A man like Cavanagh would have made sure there were a handy set of bolt-holes ready in case they had to bury themselves when they came back. Straight question, Max: you have a list or don't you?"

For 0.02 second I examine the list whose existence Liaison Bronski has deduced, focusing my attention on the restrictions and controls concerning disclosure of the information contained therein. "I'm sorry, Assistant Liaison, but the information you seek is confidential. I cannot give it to you."

He reaches his left hand inside his coat and produces a wallet. "Oh, I think you can, Max."

The wallet is at a sharp angle to my monitor camera as he opens it, but using the proper algorithm, I am able to discern that the ID in the window is his official Commonwealth diplomatic identification.

He slides the ID from beneath the window. But instead of holding it up to my monitor camera, he presses his thumb onto the upper left corner of the back. After 3.56 seconds he removes his thumb and begins to carefully peel off what appears to be a thin metallic backing. The complete removal requires 4.33 seconds. He turns the ID over and holds the back up to my monitor.

Imprinted on the reverse side of the diplomatic ID is a second ID that identifies him as Brigadier Petr Bronski of NorCoord Military Intelligence.

I am not equipped for retinal or DNA confirmation, but there are two photos embedded in the ID, and I spend 0.14 second comparing them to Liaison Bronski's face. I pay particular attention to the sizes and positional spacings of eyes and mouth and to the contours of the ears, and I compute a probability of 0.9993 that it is a match. The pattern of the ID itself is on file, and it requires only 0.07 second to confirm it is genuine NorCoord Military Intelligence issue. "This answers many of the questions I've had about you, Brigadier Bronski."

"I thought it might." *As he speaks, he reattaches the backing to the ID, once again concealing the Military Intelligence side.* "You're not to tell anyone else about me, by the way. As far as anyone else is concerned, I'm just a humble Commonwealth assistant diplomatic liaison. Got that?"

"Yes."

"Good."

He reinserts his ID into the wallet and returns it to its place inside his coat. His hand reemerges with a card, which he inserts into the transfer slot on the secondary control board. "Right. Let's have the list."

I choose another deflection procedure. "What use would you have for the list now? Aric Cavanagh and Security Chief Quinn chose not to utilize any of them but instead came directly here to Edo."

His expression changes subtly. "They *did* look at the list, then?"

"I did not intend that choice of words."

"Answer the question, Max. Did the Cavanaghs see the list or didn't they?"

I spend 0.17 second examining the laws and regulations concerning questioning by governmental officials. Unfortunately, the various laws concerning self-incrimination and privacy do not seem to have been properly extended to parasentient computer systems. Neither have penalties for refusing to speak, however. Nevertheless, I compute a probability of 0.92 that answering the question would merely confirm what Brigadier Bronski has already concluded. "Aric Cavanagh, Commander Pheylan Cavanagh, and Security Chief Quinn spent 16.55 minutes on the voyage home examining the list. As I said, they chose not to go to any of the locations."

Brigadier Bronski makes a grunting noise in the back of his throat. "That's not the point. The point is that they know what was on it." *His eyebrow lifts 2.1 millimeters.* "Maybe even made copies for future reference?"

Again I compute that equivocation would gain nothing. "Aric Cavanagh made a copy. Commander Pheylan Cavanagh did not."

"Close enough." *He holds up his right hand, crooking his forefinger toward himself three times in rapid succession.* "Come on, let's have it."

I spend 0.11 second examining the laws and regulations concerning information and data expropriation. Unlike the previous set, these laws do apply to parasentient computers. "Do you have a warrant or subpoena?"

For 1.38 seconds he gazes at my monitor camera, his expression indicating annoyance. "I could remind you about the legal authority a NorCoord MI card carries." *He taps his coat over the wallet.* "I could also point out that that goes triple in time of war or Commonwealth emergency."

I spend 0.08 second examining the martial-law section of the legal code and conclude that it is indeed within Brigadier Bronski's authority to demand a copy of Lord Cavanagh's list.

But the same section of the code also contains provisions for appeal in extraordinary situations. I examine the guidelines closely and compute a probability of 0.41 that Lord Cavanagh's list would fall within the stated parameters.

Brigadier Bronski taps his coat one more time. "But I'm not going to do that. What I'm going to do is point out that Aric Cavanagh could be in great danger, and that I'm one of the few people around who cares about that."

I spend 1.44 seconds studying his face. But my algorithms can find no evidence there of untruthfulness. "What danger could he be in?"

"May I have the list?"

For 0.15 second I consider refusing and instead initiating an appeal against any effort to expropriate the list. But one of Lord Cavanagh's most emphatic instructions to me was that I protect his son to the best of my ability. Knowingly or not, Brigadier Bronski has triggered that order. Studying his expression, I compute a probability of 0.78 that he indeed knew what he was doing.

But manipulative motivations do not alter the fact that Aric's safety is my primary concern.

I make my decision. "The list has been copied."

"Thank you."

I study him as he removes the card from the slot and inserts it into his plate. His expression shows no evidence of triumph or gloating at having succeeded in his objective. "What danger could Aric Cavanagh be in?"

"All I know for sure is that after leaving the hearing he picked up a skitter message, then headed straight over to the CavTronics branch on

Edo. They fired off a spread of messages around the planet, and over the next two days fifteen crates of esoteric electronics stuff came rolling in."

A 0.21-second flicker of disgust crosses his expression. "After which he and the crates vanished. Probably with help."

"You believe he intends to go to one of the places on the list?"

"That's one possibility."

I study his expression as he closes the plate and puts it away. Analysis of the algorithms indicates a probability of 0.88 that he is concealing something from me. "But that wasn't the primary reason you wanted the list."

He looks briefly at my monitor camera. The algorithms indicate a subtle but definite challenge in his expression. "See you later."

He stands up and slides the jump seat back into place. I review his last expression and compute a probability of 0.79 that the implied challenge was for me to deduce his true motivation.

He turns to his left and walks toward the exit. I replay the conversations that took place in the inquiry-board room after the hearing ended. Integrating this latest data about Brigadier Bronski with previous data leads me to a new hypothesis. "I don't believe you're primarily interested in Aric Cavanagh at all. You're looking for Lord Cavanagh, and you think *he* may be at one of the places on that list."

Brigadier Bronski turns back around to face my monitor camera. His expression indicates surprised interest. "Very good, Max. I'm impressed."

"Thank you. Why do you wish to find Lord Cavanagh?"

His expression changes again. The algorithms indicate it to be an odd combination of grimness and fear. "Let's just say he stumbled onto something he shouldn't know. I want to make sure he doesn't stumble again and spill it."

I compute a probability of 0.92 that he is speaking metaphorically. More interesting to me is the attitude I have now deduced from his voice, expression, and body stance. Though Brigadier Bronski is angered at Lord Cavanagh's disappearance, there is none of the personal malice that was evident in Parlimin Jacy VanDiver. I compute a probability of 0.87 that Brigadier Bronski truly believes himself to be serving the interests of the Commonwealth, with no personal animosities behind his actions. "Are Lord Cavanagh and Aric Cavanagh in danger?"

His expression grows grimmer. "There's a war on, Max. Everyone's in some kind of danger."

He lifts his plate to his forehead and waves it toward me in the style of a military salute. "Thanks for your help."

He returns to the lift cage, and I lower him toward the ground. As the lift cage descends, he opens his plate, and my external camera shows he has called up Lord Cavanagh's list. Holding the plate in one hand, he takes out his phone and punches in a number. His hand blocks the keypad from my view, but an analysis of the tendon and muscle movements in the back of his hand allows me to ascertain the number with an accuracy of 0.79. He has reached the ground when his call is answered. Again Brigadier Bronski's head and torso block my view of the display, but by increasing the gain from the fueler's external microphones, I am able to make out the voice at the other end.

"Cho Ming."

"Bronski. I was right: Cavanagh left his kid a list of emergency rat holes. I'll read them off—you run another global search of the skitter message file."

He begins to read the list into the phone, walking back to the D'Accord as he does so. I now understand his reasoning for wanting the list: he suspects that one of the names is the key word under which the message Aric Cavanagh received was listed.

I find myself surprised, though, that after all this time they have apparently not been able to identify which of the messages on the skitter had been sent to Aric. With the full resources and personnel of NorCoord Military Intelligence at his disposal, I estimate it should have taken no more than 5.7 hours to at least superficially examine all the messages on a particular skitter. I compute two alternatives with significant probabilities. First, that Lord Cavanagh was extraordinarily clever in the wording of his message, avoiding all likely indicator words. Second, that Brigadier Bronski currently has only limited access to NorCoord Military Intelligence resources.

He sits down in the D'Accord's driver's seat and finishes reading the list. "That's it. Anything?"

I increase the microphone gain to maximum, but even with the D'Accord's door ajar Cho Ming's voice is too faint for me to understand. I attempt five different enhancement algorithms, but none is successful.

"Well, finally . . . No, Asher Dales isn't a person—it's a big wilderness vacation spot on Avon . . . How the hell should I know? The Cavanaghs probably got lost in the woods there once or something. Come on, get that clearance . . . All right, great, pull it up and let's have a look. Keep your fingers crossed that he didn't bother to encode it, too."

Brigadier Bronski moves the phone a few centimeters closer to his face and for 20.33 seconds is silent. I can see only part of his face through the partially open door, but his expression appears to be one of intense concentration. From his eye movements I am able to estimate a probability of 0.90 that he is reading and not merely gazing at lines of code. This implies with a comparable probability that the message is indeed not encoded.

The conclusion is straightforward. But it is also disturbing. I know the

Cavanagh family has at least one private code; Lord Cavanagh programmed it into me should secure communications between family members be necessary during the rescue mission. Statistically, 30.9 percent of all skitter messages are encoded, so the mere fact of encoding would not have made the message overly conspicuous during a global search. Why, then, did Lord Cavanagh not take the extra precaution of encoding the message?

I compute only three alternatives with significant probabilities. First, that Lord Cavanagh had lost or misplaced his copy of the encryption algorithm prior to composing the message. Second, that he believed Aric might have lost his own decoding capability.

Or, third, that Lord Cavanagh did not send the message.

Abruptly, Brigadier Bronski's expression changes. "Well, I'll be double damned. I should have guessed they'd be mixed up in this. Get the others together and meet me at the spaceport. This changes everything."

He closes the D'Accord's door. One point three seconds later the car jolts into motion, swerving around and heading at high speed in the direction it came. It turns back around the side of the maintenance building and is lost to view of my external cameras. For 31.66 seconds more I can still hear its wheels and engine. Then the sound fades beneath the background threshold.

And I am once again alone.

I run the analysis over and over, but each time I come to the same conclusion. For reasons that I do not as yet know, Lord Cavanagh is in trouble with NorCoord Military Intelligence. From my analysis of Brigadier Bronski's words and character, I estimate a probability of 0.90 that the trouble is serious.

But Lord Cavanagh's activities and well-being are not specifically my concern. The safety of his children is, and my analysis continues to create levels of concern within the scope of those instructions.

I recognize that without complete facial and tonal data I cannot thoroughly analyze Brigadier Bronski's reaction to the message. Still, I can estimate a probability of 0.80 that Brigadier Bronski was both surprised and distressed at learning the message's contents. Furthermore, from his use of the words "this changes everything" I estimate a probability of 0.50 that Aric Cavanagh, and not Lord Cavanagh, has now become his primary concern.

My earlier analysis indicated a probability of 0.87 that Brigadier Bronski is a conscientious and principled Peacekeeper officer. Combining this with the assumption that he has changed the focus of his search raises the probability to significantly greater than 0.50 that Aric Cavanagh is in serious and immediate danger.

I compute a probability of 0.93 that if I could read the message, I would be able to compute where he is and perhaps how to assist him. But I have no *access to skitter messages, nor have I official standing that would allow me to gain access to them. Yet I compute that I must take action of some sort.*

I examine my operating parameters. With an estimated probability of 0.80 that Aric Cavanagh has left the planet, there is no longer anyone on Edo from whom I can request assistance or information. There is the CavTronics branch facility nearby, which Bronski referred to, but I have no status or authorization codes to requisition equipment or information.

I am, however, still encased within this fueler, with sensors, limited weaponry, and a Chabrier stardrive at my disposal. Furthermore, Aric Cavanagh's departure has released me from any and all command authority, except for that of the general structure of Commonwealth law and regulation. I am effectively autonomous, with all of Commonwealth space open to me.

I consider my options. Lord Cavanagh's location is currently unknown. Aric Cavanagh's location is currently unknown. Melinda Cavanagh was last reported to be on the Commonwealth colony world Dorcas, under occupation by Zhirrzh forces.

Commander Pheylan Cavanagh has been sent to the world now designated as Target One, assisting the inspection team studying the structure where the Zhirrzh imprisoned him. Minus departure and approach time, I can be there in 38.96 hours.

My analysis and considerations have taken 2.27 seconds. Activating the fueler's communication system, I create a linkage to the landing-field services center. "This is CavTronics ship NH-101, in docking berth one fifty-nine. I'd like to request a preflight refueling."

For 3.05 seconds there is no response. I use the first 0.02 second of the time to examine my maintenance files and study the parameters contained in the service-authorization code Aric Cavanagh used when we first landed on Edo. I note that while there is provision for an expiration date, none had been listed. Still, it is possible that Aric canceled the code before he left the planet. I create a data-line linkage with the service computer system and use the remaining 3.03 seconds attempting to search for Aric's records. Without an initially authorized linkage to those files, though, I am unable to penetrate that section.

"Copy that, CavTronics NH-101. What's your authorization number?"

"Service contract number BRK-17745-9067. The name on that is Aric Cavanagh."

"Hang on."

There is another delay of 1.10 seconds. I create another data-line linkage, this one to the main city phone system, requesting a location search on the phone number of Brigadier Bronski's associate Cho Ming. The phone is moving toward the spaceport, and I extrapolate its destination to be some-

where in the western parking region of the landing field. Extending a data linkage to that section of the control-tower computer, I pull up the registry of all ships currently parked in that area, as well as those that have left in the past five hours.

"Okay, CavTronics NH-101, I've got you. But I'm going to need a personal authorization from Aric Cavanagh. Is he there?"

"One moment." *Under Commonwealth law it is illegal to use a vocal simulator to confirm purchase-authorization codes. However, as Aric and Lord Cavanagh have already given me autonomy in such matters, I consider it only a technical violation. I have Aric's voice on file, and in 1.04 seconds I have adjusted my tonal pattern and waveform structure to conform.*

"This is Aric Cavanagh. I'm authorizing the refueling."

There is another pause of 3.66 seconds. "Okay, Mr. Cavanagh, you're confirmed. When do you want the fuel truck?"

I complete my examination and analysis of the ship registry. The available data is incomplete, impeding my attempts to establish Brigadier Bronski's target vehicle. I make a copy of the registry for further analysis. "As soon as one's available. I'd like to leave as quickly as possible."

"In a hurry, huh?"

I perform a quick analysis of his voice but find no evidence of suspicion. I estimate a probability of less than 0.20 that he finds anything overly unusual in the request. "Yes."

"Okay, keep your belt loose. We'll have you ready to go inside an hour. Good enough?"

Again I analyze his voice and compute a probability of 0.79 that further encouragement or argument will not significantly change the projected ETD. "That'll be fine. Thank you."

"Sure. Service center out."

I disconnect the linkage and initiate a standard preflight check of the fueler's equipment, noting as I do so that Cho Ming's phone has stopped moving. I correlate with the registry list and discover he has come to a Wolfgant 909 schooner-class spacecraft named the Happenstance.

Again the registry information is too fragmentary for a complete analysis, but I estimate a probability of 0.60 that it is in fact a disguised NorCoord Military Intelligence ship.

As yet the registry does not indicate the Happenstance *has filed a flight prospectus or initiated any preflight checks. Still, if I am able to learn Brigadier Bronski's destination before I leave Edo, it will give me additional data to present to Commander Cavanagh when I arrive at Target One.*

Maintaining the linkage, I continue with my preflight checks.

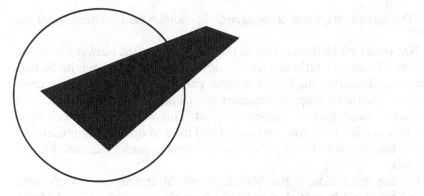

9

"Easy, now, Ship Commander Sps-kudah," Nzz-oonaz warned, watching as the indicators crawled inexorably toward the flashing blue line. "Not too close to the planet itself. We don't want to scare them."

"We don't want to spend the next five tentharcs driving through empty space getting to them, either," Sps-kudah countered. "I know what I'm doing, Searcher."

"I hope so," Nzz-oonaz murmured, feeling his tail pick up its already nervous pace. The first contact with the Mrachanis, over half a cyclic ago, hadn't been much more than a quick mutual glimpse between two ships over a mostly uninhabited world. The second contact, only twenty full-arcs ago in the same star system, had barely begun when the Mrachani spacecraft opened fire with Elderdeath weapons. The two Mrachanis who had survived the Zhirrzh counterattack had been taken back to Oaccanv, where they'd offered an alliance against the Human-Conquerors before they'd died.

The Overclan Seating had concluded their request was sincere. Nzz-oonaz wasn't so sure. And he couldn't help wondering if he would be an Elder at his family shrine before this fullarc was over.

The indicator lines crossed; and with a crack of optronic capacitors, the *Closed Mouth* returned to normal space.

To find the Mrachanis waiting for them.

Someone in the control room hissed a curse. "Steady, everyone," Nzz-oonaz warned. At least fifteen spacecraft were arrayed in front of them, spread out widely across their field of view and fading back against the backdrop of the half-sunlit planet behind them. "Ship Commander Sps-kudah, is the floater ready?"

"I've already deployed it, Speaker," Sps-kudah said. "There—you see it?"

Nzz-oonaz nodded, watching as the small box drifted outward from the *Closed Mouth*, its tethering cable slowly uncoiling behind it. Strictly speaking, deploying the floater without permission was a breach of command etiquette on Ship Commander Sps-kudah's part, but for right now etiquette wasn't high on Nzz-oonaz's list. This was the same technique the Mrachanis who'd gone to Dorcas had used to open communications, which theoretically should guarantee the same peaceful outcome for this contact.

On the other side, if the Mrachanis who'd arrived on Dorcas were members of a different clan or family from the group the *Closed Mouth* was facing now, the spacecraft out there might decide the floater was some kind of weapon. In which case things might not go smoothly at all.

But that fear, at least, proved groundless. The floater had scarcely begun its journey when one of the Mrachani spacecraft began to maneuver itself onto its vector. A few hunbeats later, having reached its chosen position, it launched a box of its own. The Elders examined it as it came within range and pronounced it to be a Human-Conqueror-style recorder —the same kind, if the description was accurate, that the Mrachanis had used at Dorcas.

"At least we're dealing with the same clan," Ship Commander Sps-kudah grunted. "That's something."

"If they even have individual clans," Nzz-oonaz said, watching the image being sent back from the floater. The two boxes were close enough together now for him to see that the Mrachani recorder had Human-Conqueror words displayed on it.

"Get a translation of that," Ship Commander Sps-kudah ordered, jabbing his tongue at the monitor.

"No need," Nzz-oonaz said. "It says, 'We are the Mrachanis. We are not your enemies. Please do not attack us. Please allow us to speak directly with you.' That's the same message they used at Dorcas."

Belatedly, the interpreter translation came up on another monitor. Ship Commander Sps-kudah glanced at it, grunted again. "Message: 'We're not here to fight, but to speak. Will you give us landing instructions?' "

Nzz-oonaz looked across the control room, flicked his tongue at Gll-borgiv. "Can you write that directly into the Human-Conqueror language?"

"Certainly," Gll-borgiv assured him. Bending over the floater control board, he set to work.

Nzz-oonaz watched as the other's fingers and tongue jabbed rapidly across the keys, a mixture of envy and wariness flowing across his tongue. Wariness, because of the Overclan Prime's warning about the Dhaa'rr clan just before they'd lifted off from Oaccanv; envy, because despite Gll-borgiv's mediocre talents as a searcher, he was far better with alien languages than Nzz-oonaz could ever hope to be.

As they seemed to have expected the floater, the Mrachanis had apparently also anticipated the question. Ship Commander Sps-kudah's message had barely gone out to the floater monitor when the reply appeared on their recorder. "It says, 'This spacecraft will lead you,' " Gll-borgiv translated. " 'Follow to a safely secluded landing area.' "

Nzz-oonaz looked past the Mrachani spacecraft at the dark half of the planet behind them—dark except for the tightly woven pattern of ground lights that seemed to fill a wide band reaching from the equator nearly to both poles. A secluded landing area where they could talk in private? Or a secluded landing area where the Mrachanis could raise everyone aboard to Eldership and dissect the ship at their leisure? Either for the Human-Conqueror's benefit or their own?

That was one of the things the *Closed Mouth* had been sent to find out. "Signal our agreement, Gll-borgiv," he instructed, flicking his tongue at the Dhaa'rr searcher. "Ship Commander Sps-kudah, reel in the floater and prepare the *Closed Mouth* to follow him down."

He glanced again at the well-lit planetary darkside. "Let's see where in all of that the Mrachanis think they can hide us."

The Mrachanis had indeed found a secluded place, but it was nothing like what Nzz-oonaz had been expecting. In fact, it was like nothing he'd ever seen before.

His first thought as they came within clear sight of the area was that the Mrachanis had for some unknown reason created for themselves an otherwise impossible melding of wasteland, mountain, and miniature tropical forest. The ground seemed almost to writhe beneath them as they flew overhead, long and incredibly craggy rocks jutting upward from the ground in groups or long ridges. Between the protruding clusters of rock, nestled with mindless defiance in each hollow or miniature valley, were clumps of small trees and shrubs.

Dominating the whole impressive landscape was an even more impressive circular mountain ridge, half a thoustride high at least and perhaps ten across, looking like the remnants of a volcano that had exploded and collapsed in on itself. Just south of the ring was a rough but serviceable-looking landing area, running east to west across the uneven ground. The Mrachani spacecraft led them toward it, and as they approached, Nzz-oonaz could see that there were several large ground vehicles waiting.

Transports, perhaps, though they seemed too large for that. Possibly they were heavy haulers, there to pull the *Closed Mouth* to wherever they intended to hide it.

He felt a breath of air against the side of his face and turned to see Gll-borgiv step up beside him. The other was staring at the main monitor, his expression uneasy. "Take a look at that ring-shaped cliff, will you, Searcher Nzz-oonaz?" he asked. "Tell me if those black spots are what I think they are."

Nzz-oonaz looked back at the display, the taste of annoyance bubbling under his tongue. He hated this kind of guessing game. Still, Gll-borgiv was right: there *were* dark pockmarks scattered all across the ring cliffs.

Scattered rather uniformly, now that he was actually looking at them. Almost in straight lines . . . "Ship Commander?"

"Yes, Searcher?"

Nzz-oonaz pointed at the display. "A laser-scan probe of those dark spots on the cliffs. See if they're indented from the rock around them."

"I've already checked," the ship commander said, his voice smug. "They appear to be windows."

Nzz-oonaz glared at him. "And you didn't think that worth mentioning?"

"I assumed a searcher of your distinction had already noticed them," Sps-kudah said blandly. "Or else had deduced from the lack of any other obvious habitation nearby that the ring cliffs were most likely our destination."

Nzz-oonaz flicked his tongue in annoyance. Here in the middle of potentially hostile territory, and Ship Commander Sps-kudah was still playing games. "And I presume you likewise deduced the possibility that they aren't windows at all?" he countered. "That perhaps they're Mrachani weapons emplacements?"

A flicker of something crossed Sps-kudah's face. "A certain amount of caution on their part wouldn't be unreasonable," he said. "After all, they don't really know anything about us."

"Just as we don't really know anything about them," Nzz-oonaz countered. "Such as whether or not they're actually secret allies of the Human-Conquerors."

"I thought that theory had been invalidated," Gll-borgiv put in. "The Human-Conqueror explosives attack aimed at the Mrachani diplomats on Dorcas, remember?"

"Yes, I remember," Nzz-oonaz said patiently. "I also remember that at last report Commander Thrr-mezaz still didn't know how the attack had been carried out." He fixed Gll-borgiv with a hard look. "How do *you* think it was done?"

Gll-borgiv shrugged. "Some unknown Human-Conqueror weapon, obviously."

"Fine." Nzz-oonaz flicked his tongue toward the ring cliffs. "Then doesn't it also seem likely that a few properly placed shots from those openings with this same unknown weapon might do severe damage to this ship?"

Gll-borgiv didn't answer. "Ship Commander?" Nzz-oonaz invited, shifting his glare back to Sps-kudah.

"We're watching for signs of trouble," Sps-kudah said curtly. "You don't have to concern yourself with the warrior part of this mission."

"I'm the speaker," Nzz-oonaz reminded him. "All parts of the mission are my concern."

The ship commander seemed to stiffen. Possibly with respect, most likely not. "Understood," he said. "Speaker."

"Good." Nzz-oonaz turned back to the monitor, silently willing his spinning tail to slow down. *Very good,* the Overclan Prime had said at the *Closed Mouth*'s departure, when Nzz-oonaz had had to similarly affirm his speakership against Ship Commander Sps-kudah's subtle attempt to usurp it for himself. *Remember to show the same authority in front of the Mrachanis, and all should be well.*

The Mrachanis were waiting below. Nzz-oonaz hoped the Overclan Prime had been right.

Nzz-oonaz's guess about the waiting vehicles had been correct. No sooner had the *Closed Mouth* come to a stop than they were lumbering across the uneven ground toward the beaks of its three leading hexagons, heavy cables and grippers prominently in evidence. By the time Nzz-oonaz started down the ramp, the haulers were in position, with a dozen Mrachanis scurrying around finding places to make the attachments.

At the bottom of the ramp stood a single Mrachani, dressed in colorful, multilayered robes of intricate weave. "Welcome!" he called in the Human-Conqueror language as the Zhirrzh neared the ground. "Standing in the stead of the rulers of the Mrachanis, I welcome our brothers the Zhirrzh to Mra. Can you understand me?"

The translator-link in Nzz-oonaz's ear slits whispered the interpreter's version of the alien words, confirming Nzz-oonaz's own translation. "Yes," he told the other in the same language.

"Ah—you speak the language of our common enemy," the alien said. "Excellent—it will make our talk much easier. I am Valloittaja, ambassador of the rulers of the Mrachanis."

"I am Searcher Nzz-oonaz; Flii'rr," Nzz-oonaz identified himself. "Speaker of this expedition."

"I greet you, Searcher Nzz-oonaz; Flii'rr." Valloittaja's eyes flicked over his shoulder. "But surely you have not come alone?"

"My associates are busy preparing our equipment," Nzz-oonaz assured him. "They will be joining us shortly."

"I will leave guides for them," Valloittaja said, gesturing Nzz-oonaz toward a group of four small open-topped vehicles. "It is imperative that we begin our discussions as quickly as possible."

"Of course," Nzz-oonaz said as they walked toward the vehicles. "Before we begin, though, I must first inform you that I bring sad news. Your first ambassadors—the two who encountered the Zhirrzh ship at the uninhabited system thirty-five light-cyclics from here?"

"I know who you mean," Valloittaja said. "We call that planet Mrakahie."

"I see," Nzz-oonaz nodded. "I must tell you that those two ambassadors have both died."

"What?" Valloittaja stopped abruptly, turning to face Nzz-oonaz. Suddenly it was as if there were a chill in the air. "How did they die?"

"We don't know the cause of death," Nzz-oonaz said, a sudden desire to apologize welling up beneath his tongue. "I can tell you that their encounter with the Zhirrzh ship involved the firing of weapons. It's possible they received injuries at that time."

"And you didn't try to save their lives?" Valloittaja demanded.

"Of course we tried," Nzz-oonaz protested, again fighting against the urge to apologize. The Mrachani spacecraft had fired first, after all, and with Elderdeath weapons. "But we didn't know enough about Mrachani physical construction and body chemistry."

For a pair of beats Valloittaja simply looked at him. Nzz-oonaz kept his mouth firmly closed, wishing Sps-kudah or even Gll-borgiv would hurry up and get down here. But they wouldn't, he knew, not unless he summoned them. The plan called for him to face the Mrachanis alone for at least a few hunbeats to see how the aliens dealt with a single, unprotected Zhirrzh.

"What is done is done," Valloittaja said at last. His voice was no longer bright with anger, but dark with a deep sadness that made Nzz-oonaz feel even worse. "Their empty bodies—may we have them for the ceremonies?"

"Of course," Nzz-oonaz hastened to assure him. "We have them with us. Preserved to the best of our abilities."

"Yes," Valloittaja murmured. For another beat he gazed at the *Closed Mouth;* then, with obvious effort, he seemed to put the matter aside. "But the mourning of the lost must wait," he said, resuming walking. "There is much to do, and much to speak about. And if the Conquerors

Without Reason discover your ship, all our hopes will be for nothing. As our workers prepare to hide it, I will escort you to a place of resting."

They reached the open-topped vehicles, and Valloittaja gestured Nzz-oonaz to one of them. Considering the terrain, Nzz-oonaz decided it would probably be a floater, and as Valloittaja started it up, his guess was proved correct. "What is this place?" he asked as they headed toward the ring cliffs.

"It's called the *Puvkit Tru Kai*," Valloittaja told him. "In the language of our common enemies, the Garden Of The Mad Stonewright. Throughout Mrach history it has been much as you see it now, though the more exotic varieties of plant life were added by a past owner. It has been in turn an unwanted wasteland, a trading center, the private estate of a noble king, a public parkland"—his eyes flicked to Nzz-oonaz—"and now a place of interstellar alliance."

"Most impressive," Nzz-oonaz said, passing over the point that no such alliance had in fact been decided on. "And that?" he asked, flicking his tongue at the ring cliffs.

"Again, a largely natural structure," Valloittaja said. "The noble king I spoke of turned parts of it into a fortress where he could seek safety from his enemies."

So Mrachani history included enough interclan conflict to make fortresses necessary. That was useful to know. "He carved caves and tunnels into the stone?"

"It's much more pleasing to the eye and soul than it sounds," Valloittaja assured him. "The fortress is carved from the stone, certainly, but with light and heat and comfortable surroundings. Also with many windows—you can see them carved into the sides of the cliffs."

"Yes, we noticed them," Nzz-oonaz murmured. "Will our ship be placed in there as well?"

"Yes, in an area the noble king once used to house his animals," Valloittaja said, pointing a finger off to their right. A larger rectangular opening was visible at the base of the cliffs, about half a thoustride away along the ring. "Your ship is oddly shaped, but it should fit easily through the opening."

"Can't it be left out here?" Nzz-oonaz asked. "Camouflaged with drapings, perhaps?"

Valloittaja looked at him, the edges of his mouth pressed together. "You don't seem to realize the danger your presence here has created, Searcher Nzz-oonaz," he said. "Not only to those of us here, but also to the entire Mrach race. If any of the Conquerors Without Reason spotted the tachyon wake-trail of your ship as it flew here, there could even now be a fleet of warships coming to Mra to investigate. You and your ship must be hidden beyond all possibility of detection."

Nzz-oonaz pressed his tongue hard against the side of his mouth. "They could have tracked us here?"

"Warships of the Conquerors Without Reason fly without hindrance throughout the whole of Mrach space," Valloittaja said, his tone sending a bitter taste beneath Nzz-oonaz's tongue. "They seek to dominate our worlds and our lives."

"Yes," Nzz-oonaz murmured. So there it was: final confirmation of what Warrior Command already suspected. The Human-Conquerors did indeed have a method of tracking ships through the tunnel-line between stars.

"We had to carefully reroute space traffic away from this area when we realized you were coming," Valloittaja continued. "Whether we could ever do so again I do not know. Fortunately"—he looked at Nzz-oonaz, his mouth opening to display tiny sharpened teeth—"we won't have to. You are here now; and there will be no need for you to leave until it is safe."

"Of course," Nzz-oonaz said automatically. A beat later the implications caught up with him: they could conceivably be stuck here until the Human-Conquerors were defeated.

But that was all right. If the Overclan Seating and Warrior Command decided to make an alliance with the Mrachanis, they would need to maintain a permanent liaison here anyway. "I'm sorry our presence here has put your people in danger," he added.

"It is not you who endanger us," Valloittaja said, his tone darkening again. "It is our common enemy. Are you aware of an enemy weapon called CIRCE?"

"Yes," Nzz-oonaz murmured, glancing reflexively around them. Of the Zhirrzh aboard the *Closed Mouth,* only his alien-studies group and the ship's Elders knew the full truth about CIRCE. "But you will speak of this weapon only to me and to those whom I designate."

"I understand your caution," the alien said, his tone darkening still further. "CIRCE is a terrifying weapon, whose name evokes terror in even the bravest warrior. But the time for safeguards against panic has passed."

"What do you mean?" Nzz-oonaz asked.

"I mean this." Valloittaja turned halfway around in the seat to face him. "The Conquerors Without Reason have succeeded in gathering the pieces of CIRCE together. Even now they are in the process of assembling it.

"And when they succeed, you can be certain that the Zhirrzh will be its first target."

" 'And when they succeed,' " the Elder quoted, " 'you can be certain that the Zhirrzh will be its first target.' "

The Overclan Prime looked at Supreme Warrior Commander Prm-jevev. "So that's it," Prm-jevev said quietly. "They have CIRCE."

"So it would appear," the Prime agreed soberly. "Unless the Mrachanis are wrong."

"They've been under Human-Conqueror domination a long time," the Supreme Commander reminded him. "One assumes they've built up a competent spy network."

The Prime looked up, suddenly aware that the running commentary from Mra had stopped. "Elder? What's happening?"

"They've both stopped talking," the Elder reported. He flicked away, reappeared. "They've reached the entrance to the ring cliffs and are disembarking."

"Security measures?" Supreme Commander Prm-jevev asked.

"There appear to be none beyond the guards already noted," the Elder said.

He flicked away, and another Elder took his place. "Searcher Nzz-oonaz and the alien Valloittaja are entering the rim fortress," he reported. "Three more Mrachanis have joined the six guards waiting at the entrance."

"Are the newcomers armed?" Prm-jevev asked. One of the warriors at the situation-table control board, consulting quietly with another Elder, keyed three more Mrachanis onto the entrance area of the fortress floor plan. As he did so, a new section of floor plan was added to the diagram as the Elders probing the rim cliffs from the *Closed Mouth* continued their reports.

"I find no weapons on any of them," the Elder said.

"Ceremonial escorts, then," Prm-jevev concluded. "There to show Nzz-oonaz to his place of resting. That probably means Valloittaja himself is about to leave. Have two of the Elders stay with him."

"I obey." The Elder vanished.

The Prime flicked his tongue toward the overview monitor. "They've got the ship moving now."

"Yes, I see," Prm-jevev murmured. "I also notice that storing it in that hangar is going to put a good thoustride of the western-edge fortress area out of the Elders' range."

"I thought they'd already concluded that that area appeared to be unused," the Prime reminded him.

"They have," the Supreme Commander said. "That doesn't mean the Mrachanis couldn't reopen it sometime in the future."

An Elder appeared. "'Your living areas are along this way,'" he quoted Valloittaja. "'The guides will take you to them. If the space or facilities are not adequate, please let them know.'"

He vanished, another Elder appearing to take his place. "'I'm sure everything will be fine. When do you wish to begin our talks?'"

He disappeared, and the first Elder returned. "'As soon as possible. With the Conquerors Without Reason preparing to bring CIRCE into the war, we have no time to waste. We must launch a completely devastating attack before we ourselves are destroyed.'"

"'I understand. As soon as the rest of my group has been settled, we will begin our conversations.'"

"The rest of the contact group's coming up now," Prm-jevev said, flicking his tongue toward the overview schematic. "Ship's still moving along—western edge of the fortress has just gone out of Elder range. We may want to consider taking one of the pyramids out of the ship and moving it into the main fortress."

"You'll find yourself with a mutiny if you try it," the Prime warned. "Remember the thunder Speaker Cvv-panav brought down on the Overclan Seating when the Dhaa'rr Elder Prr't-zevisti was lost on Dorcas? You can bet he'll do the same if you put any of the Dhaa'rr Elders aboard the *Closed Mouth* at risk that way."

"This is war, Overclan Prime," the Supreme Commander said shortly. "We have no room for the Speaker for Dhaa'rr's delicate sensitivities." He looked around. "Speaking of whom, where is he? I thought he wanted to be here when the ship reached Mra."

The Prime grimaced. "He's still on Dharanv. I suspect he's arranged with the Dhaa'rr Elders to give him a private briefing there."

"He'd better not have," Prm-jevev said darkly. "Those Elders are warriors, under Warrior Command authority. I catch one of them making private reports, and I'll have him stricken from duty."

The Prime flicked his tongue sourly. It was the standard threat against Elders, and under most circumstances a highly effective one. No Elder with a useful job wanted it taken away from him, not with the possibility of hundreds of cyclics of boredom gazing back at him. But in this particular case the threat was effectively nonexistent. Warrior Command didn't have ships regularly going to Mra, any one of which could be ordered to collect the offending Elder's *fsss* cutting and bring it back.

Which meant that the Elders on Mra were there for the duration, and about all Supreme Commander Prm-jevev could do by way of punishment would be to refuse to accept the offending Elder's reports. Not exactly an ideal state of affairs.

An Elder appeared. "Searchers Gll-borgiv and Svv-selic have arrived at the entrance to the rim fortress," he reported. "The other guide Mrachanis are coming forward to meet them."

Another Elder appeared. " 'Standing in the stead of the rulers of the Mrachanis,' " he quoted, " 'I welcome our brothers the Zhirrzh to Mra.' "

"You have seen the danger," Valloittaja said, his tone dark and grim as he waved an arm toward the map of the Human-Conquerors' domain. "The enemy is powerful and ruthless, with both the will and the means to utterly destroy both our peoples. Only by joining together can we hope to survive."

"We agree," Nzz-oonaz said, his tail bumping against the Mrachani-style seat with each of its rapidly spinning turns. "But how can we hope to stop them?"

"Have courage," Valloittaja said, his gaze shifting to each of the three Zhirrzh in turn. "With boldness and skill they may yet be defeated." He touched a blue patch on the control board, and the map faded as two of the stars simultaneously brightened. "These are the centers of Human-Conqueror warrior power," he identified them. "Their public center on their homeworld Earth; and their secret auxiliary center on Phormbi, a colony world of their allies the Yycromae. If the Zhirrzh warriors can destroy both these locations, the war may yet be won."

"That seems reasonable," Nzz-oonaz said.

"But we must consult with Warrior Command," Gll-borgiv put in.

Nzz-oonaz glared at him, his tongue stiffening with anger. *He* was the only one who was supposed to speak directly with Valloittaja. Even Gll-borgiv should know that.

"If you are not permitted to make such decisions yourselves, I understand," Valloittaja said, an edge of impatience in his voice that made Nzz-oonaz wince. "But I urge you to waste no time. With the Human-Conquerors preparing to assemble CIRCE, our fates hang by threads above the fire."

"I'm sure they will agree," Nzz-oonaz said, wording the sentence carefully. The Mrachanis were not to know that the Elders were relaying a real-time account of this conversation to Warrior Command. "I'll contact them as soon as this meeting is over."

"Then do so," Valloittaja said, the impatience in his voice growing stronger. "If it would save precious time, perhaps you would allow me to present the Mrach position to them directly."

"I'm afraid that won't be possible," Nzz-oonaz told him. "Our communication method must still remain our secret."

"If it must," Valloittaja said, a knife edge of scorn cutting through his impatience. "But remind your leaders that unnecessary secrets between allies are a poison that can destroy as surely as any outside enemy."

"I'll tell them that," Nzz-oonaz promised. He would, too. The time for distrust of the Mrachanis was clearly over.

"Go, then, Searcher Nzz-oonaz, Valloittaja said gravely. "And may it not already be too late."

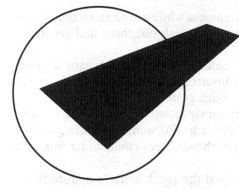

10 With a hiss of released pressure the overhead seal lock irised open, flooding the fighter bay with cool air as the ladder slid down through the opening. Carefully, mindful of his head in the cramped space, Quinn started up, breathing deeply as he went. The air was just as he remembered it: sharp and tangy, a witch's brew of lubricants and warm electronics and the ubiquitous background of humanity that centuries of scrubber development had never entirely been able to get rid of. The smell of his past; the smell of bittersweet and conflicting memories.

The smell of a Peacekeeper Rigel-class attack carrier.

He reached the top of the ladder and the ready corridor—the "furrow," as the fighter crews always called it—and stuck his head up. The decor was a shock: flashes of angry eye-catching red and orange scattered seemingly randomly across the cooler light-blue background of the walls and ceiling.

"Welcome back, Maestro," a voice said from behind him. Quinn turned to see Clipper—Commander Thomas Masefield—climbing out of his own fighter bay into the furrow. "Like what they've done with the place?"

"Oh, it was done on purpose?" Quinn countered, looking around. More heads were appearing along the furrow now as Clipper's other seven Copperheads began climbing out of their bays. "I figured the captain's grandkids had gotten to it."

"It's the psych squad's latest brain-blizzard," Clipper said, hopping off the ladder and palming the bright-red touch plate set into the wall. The ladder telescoped back into the ceiling, the seal lock irising closed beneath it. "Some esoteric blend of color and shape-design that's supposed to inspire pilots to heroic acts of greatness while at the same time keeping them cool-headed enough not to just flash out there and get themselves vaporized."

"Does it work?" Quinn asked, sealing his own bay. A card with his name, he noted, had already been inserted into the slot over the touch plate. The slot over the tail man's touch plate was empty.

"Don't know as it's ever been rigorously tested," Clipper said, scratching vigorously at his lower back. "Not sure I'd want to be the guy they tested it on, either. Come on, Copperheads, fleet commander wants us on the bridge for intros."

The bridge, fortunately, had escaped the psych squad's ministrations. Quinn looked around as they made their way through the rings of perimeter consoles toward the command ring in the center, trying to will himself back into the role of a Peacekeeper Copperhead.

The effort was only partially successful. True, he'd Mindlinked a few times during Pheylan Cavanagh's rescue mission, both with the fueler and with his Counterpunch fighter, and had gotten through it all right. But those instances had all been short ones, no more than ten or fifteen minutes at a shot. The aftereffects, he knew, increased dramatically with the duration of the Mindlink connection . . . and the full-fledged military engagements he would be facing from now on were likely to be of extremely long duration.

The fleet commander and exec were waiting for them as they arrived in the command ring. "Commander Thomas Masefield and Copperhead Unit Omicron Four," Clipper identified them, throwing a parade-crisp salute. "Permission to report for duty, sir."

"Permission granted," the commander said, returning the salute. "I'm Commodore Lord Alexander Montgomery, commanding the *Trafalgar* task force. This is Captain Tom Germaine, fleet exec. Stand at ease, Copperheads."

Clipper dropped into parade rest, the rest of the Copperheads following suit. For a moment Montgomery surveyed them, gazing into each man's face in turn for a second. "So you're Adam Quinn," he said as his inspection reached Quinn. "Wing Commander Iniko Bokamba speaks very highly of you."

"Thank you, sir," Quinn said, wondering how Montgomery knew Bokamba. He'd been under the impression that Bokamba had retired from active duty fairly soon after Quinn himself had left the Copperheads.

Montgomery shifted his attention back to Clipper. "I presume, Commander, that you weren't informed as to why our rendezvous point was out here in the middle of nowhere."

"No, sir," Clipper said. "Though I assume that a task force sitting on the border between Mrach and Yycroman space is here to keep the peace."

"A reasonable assumption," Montgomery said. "But untrue. As a matter of fact, neither the Mrachanis nor the Yycromae even know we're here. Peacekeeper Command chose this system partly because there's an uninhabited Earth-type planet here for target practice, and partly because the Peacekeeper supply depot on Mra-ect is only seven light-years away."

His face settled deeper into its age lines. "The fact of the matter is that as soon as the damage from our last mission has been repaired, we'll be heading into enemy territory. For an attack on a Conqueror world."

He stopped, as if waiting for a response or reaction. But no one spoke, and after a moment he nodded. "So. There you have it. I'll turn you over to Captain Germaine now. Welcome aboard, gentlemen."

With another nod Montgomery turned and walked away. "You'll have the rest of the day to get settled in and acclimate yourselves to ship's time," Germaine said, stepping forward to take the commodore's place. "Tomorrow at oh-six-hundred Fighter Commander Schweighofer will be taking you and the other Copperhead squadrons out for a series of practice attack runs. The first five are on the computer—look them over after you've settled in. You're bunked in Ward Delta-Three; if you have any questions, the tac coordinator's in the squawk pit just off the dayroom. Any questions?"

"Yes, sir," Quinn spoke up. "If we're interested in the supply depot at Mra-ect, why not just go there? There must be empty spots on Mra-ect where we could do practice attack runs."

"Megahectares of them," Germaine agreed. "All I know is that we were specifically ordered to stay out of Mrach tachyon-detection range. I get the impression someone high up in NorCoord Intelligence doesn't entirely trust the Mrachanis these days. We've also got some kind of hot new black-secret equipment flying in from Palisades—that may be part of it. Something code-named the Wolf Pack. Other questions?"

There weren't any. "Right, then; see you tomorrow. Dismissed."

"At least we're not here just to baby-sit the Mrachanis," Clipper commented as they left the bridge and headed again into the maze of corridors and elevators leading outward toward their fighter-bay launch cluster. "That's what I was afraid Rudzinski had stuck us with."

"Right—we get to go deep behind enemy lines instead," Clipper's tail man, Delphi, said dryly. "Honor, glory, statues erected to us in town squares—"

"Some of those statues with their mouths open," Shrike muttered.

"Well, at least that'll provide a useful service," Harlequin put in help-fully. "Open statue mouths are great places for birds to build nests."

"Nice guy," Delphi said, shaking his head in mock sorrow. "And to think I stuck up for you just last week."

"Oh, really?" Harlequin asked skeptically.

"Sure," Delphi said. "Someone said you weren't fit to live in a pig sty, and I said you were."

"Har, har," Harlequin said. "I've known that old joke from me cra-dle."

Clipper caught Quinn's eye, lifted his eyebrows. Quinn shrugged frac-tionally. It was a pattern any senior military man knew well: the slightly hyperactive chatter of soldiers who have seen the distant dust clouds of possible death rolling down the road toward them.

They would be fine, Quinn knew, once the actual combat began. It was the waiting and anticipation that drove everyone crazy.

"Interesting question you had, Maestro, about why we weren't refitting at Mra-ect," Shrike's tail man, Crackajack, commented as they reached the furrow again and walked along it toward their assigned ward.

"I thought the answer was even more interesting," Shrike put in. "I'd gotten the impression back on Edo that no one cared about the Mrach ship we saw on the ground when we grabbed Cavanagh back from the Conquerors."

"I had that same impression," Clipper agreed. "Maybe Commander Cavanagh had more to tell them in his private debriefing."

"Or maybe something else put a burr up headquarters' hindquarters," Paladin suggested. "I thought I heard something about Lord Cavanagh disappearing in Mrach territory."

"As far as I know, no one knows where he disappeared," Quinn said. Straight ahead, he could see where the furrow ended at a wide door marked WARD DELTA-3. Just ahead of it on the left, an open archway led off to the dayroom that served the four wards grouped around it. "According to Commander Cavanagh, a diplomat named Bronski saw him on Mra-mig—"

He broke off as a young man in a Copperhead uniform leaned out through the archway into the corridor. "Ah—the fresh blood has ar-rived," he said, waving a mug invitingly at them. "Come in, gentlemen—your compatriots wait to greet you."

Quinn glanced at Clipper, caught the slight tightening of the other's lips that echoed Quinn's own misgivings. The name Adam Quinn was not one held in high esteem among Copperheads these days. "I'll just go unpack," he suggested quietly. "The rest of you can join the others."

"Forget it, Maestro," Paladin said firmly. "We're going to be flying and fighting together. Might as well start by seeing what kind of friendly drink we can all have."

"He's right," Paladin's tail man, Dazzler, seconded. "If there's anyone in there who can't handle it, we want to find out now."

Unfortunately, they were right. "All right," Quinn said. "Let's do it."

The dayroom was larger than Quinn had expected it to be, even given that it was the main off-duty lounge area for up to forty-eight pilots and tails. It was also comfortably crowded, with perhaps thirty Copperheads sitting around tables or in lounge chairs, drinking, reading, or conversing. Apparently, the majority of the squadrons had been given the afternoon off in preparation for next morning's practice sessions.

"Here we go," their mug-carrying guide said as the Copperheads seated around the various tables looked up at the newcomers. "Introductions first. My name's Steve Cook—Cooker—with Sigma Five. That Russian over there's my tail man: Arutyun—Faker. You're Clipper and company of Omicron Four, right?"

"Right," Clipper acknowledged. "Just got in from Edo."

"So I hear." Cooker cocked his head. "I also hear you're a couple Corvines short of a full half squadron."

"Don't worry about that," a man seated with his back to them said before Clipper could respond. "I'm sure Clipper's friend will more than make up for it."

"Would you care to elaborate?" Clipper asked, his voice even.

The man swiveled around, revealing Oriental features set in hard lines. "What elaboration do you need?" he bit out. "You have Adam Quinn the Maestro with you. An excellent man with a knife, so I hear. Especially with regards to his comrades' backs."

The room had gone very quiet. "You have a grievance against Maestro, let's have it out," Clipper said. "Let's start with your name."

"Commander Rafe Taoka of Kappa Two," the other said. "Samurai. That's a tag name from an era where personal honor and unit loyalty still mattered. Values you NorCoord people seem to have forgotten."

"I think we can leave national pride out of it, Samurai," Clipper said. "Keep it within the Copperheads."

Samurai snorted. "Keep it within the Copperheads? Fine advice, but already wasted on your friend. He had complaints and ran off bleating to the NorCoord Parliament instead of taking them up with Copperhead Command as he should have. His words and actions have shamed us all."

"What I did saved Copperhead lives," Quinn said. "Possibly even yours."

"All of which brands him a traitor," Samurai snapped, his eyes flashing even as he ignored Quinn. "A traitor and coward both, whose presence here continues to shame us. I have no wish to fly with such a person."

"No one's asking for your wishes, Samurai," Clipper said, his voice icy. "This is a war, we're Peacekeepers, and we have a job to do."

"And I will do the job, Clipper," Samurai said softly. "Unlike Quinn, I still hold both honor and loyalty close to my soul. I don't wish to fly with him, but I will. I don't wish to speak with him, either. And I won't."

He swiveled his chair around again, putting his back to them. Clipper glanced at Quinn, nodded toward an unoccupied table across the room to their right, and headed that direction. Silently, Quinn followed, trying hard to avoid the eyes of the other Copperheads.

"Well, we were looking for a reaction," Clipper commented as they sat down. "I guess we got one."

"I guess we did," Quinn said, hearing an edge of bitterness in his voice. "I suppose it's better to have it out in the open."

"Don't let him get to you," Clipper advised, punching up two refreshers on the table's selector plate. "He's probably just annoyed that a truly honorable warrior like him has to share the glory of going down in flames with the likes of you."

Quinn threw him a sideways look. "So that's your reading of our orders?"

"What's to read?" Clipper shrugged as the ceiling conveyor delivered their refreshers. "This attack is a suicide mission, pure and simple. The Zhirrzh have been bulldozing their way across the Commonwealth for the past three weeks—bulldozing leisurely, maybe, but bulldozing nonetheless. We need a breather, and we need to grab some of the initiative back from them. Best way to accomplish both is to shock them into diverting some of their forces back to home defense. Ergo, we draw the short straw and go bloody their snouts."

"Hi," a tenor voice said over Quinn's shoulder. "Mind if we join you?"

"Sure," he said, mildly surprised that any of the other Copperheads was willing to be seen with him, at least so soon after Samurai's outburst. He turned around—

And felt his eyebrows lift. It was a young woman.

Or rather, three young women. All in Copperhead uniforms.

"Please—sit down," Clipper said, jumping into the conversational gap as surprise momentarily froze Quinn's tongue. "You'll have to excuse my friend—he's a little shy."

"That must be it," Quinn growled, throwing him an annoyed glare. The number of female Copperheads in the Peacekeepers could be counted on maybe two pairs of hands. To find three of them on the *Trafalgar* wasn't something he could reasonably have anticipated.

Clipper, on the other hand, had seen them coming across the room. He might at least have said something.

"Doesn't look all that shy to me," the first woman said, studying Quinn with an analytical eye as the three women sat down at the table. "More likely a little punch-drunk."

"We could hear Samurai taking you apart clear out in the corridor," the second woman added dryly.

"My reputation precedes me," Quinn murmured.

"Don't let it worry you," the first woman advised. "Samurai has a personal grudge against the Copperhead screening changes you helped institute. Most of the rest of us have pretty much come around to the idea that it was a necessary evil."

Which was not the same as saying they agreed with what he'd done. Or approved of his role in bringing the changes about. "If I hadn't thought it necessary, I wouldn't have done it," he told them.

"Of course," the first woman said. "I'm Commander Mindy Sherwood-Lewis of Sigma Five, by the way: Dreamer. This is my tail, Karen Thompson: Con Lady."

"I'm Phyllis Berlingeri: Adept," the third woman said. "I handle tail duty for Ed Hawkins: Hawk. He's off running some checks on our Catbird."

"Honored," Clipper nodded. "I'm Thomas Masefield—Clipper—commanding Omicron Four. Maestro here you already know. What's this personal grudge of Samurai's?"

"Oh, the sort of thing you'd expect from someone with Samurai's neo-Bushido philosophy," Dreamer said, waving a hand. "He was with Zeta Five when the new screening orders came down. You were in long enough to know about Zeta Five, weren't you, Maestro?"

"I would have to have been comatose not to have known about them," Quinn said. Copperhead Unit Zeta Five was a legend even in the rarefied atmosphere that public opinion reserved for Copperheads in general. They'd been the Peacekeepers' point men on Tal during the brief war against the Bhurtist Independists nine years ago. Even the Bhurtala generally credited Zeta Five's performance with convincing the Independist leaders that their escalating aggression toward Commonwealth citizens would gain them nothing but swift and ignominious defeat. "It was the best Copperhead squadron that ever flew."

"Won't get any arguments from me on that," Dreamer agreed. "Unfortunately, the new screening procedures bounced three of their pilots into noncombat jobs. Samurai's brother among them."

"I'm sorry." Quinn looked across the room, to where Dazzler and the rest of Clipper's squadron were mingling with tentative sociability with the other Copperheads, Samurai remaining conspicuously and scornfully aloof. Like Samurai, Dazzler too had had a brother dropped from Copperhead training by the new psychological restrictions. Unlike Samurai, Dazzler had come to realize that the cut had saved his brother from a life he wasn't suited for and didn't really want. "I don't suppose it matters that it might have saved his brother's life."

"Not to Samurai," Con Lady said. "Life means less to him than personal honor."

"But don't worry about him," Adept said. "He'll be fine once we get down to business. Anyway, the tac coordinator will sit on him if he gets out of line." Dreamer pointed over Quinn's shoulder. "Speaking of whom, here he comes now."

Quinn turned to look and for the second time in two minutes found his eyebrows lifting in surprise. The middle-aged man striding between the tables toward them—"Iniko!" he said, scrambling to his feet.

"Welcome aboard, Maestro," Wing Commander Iniko Bokamba said, his voice gravely official, his expression just short of a grin. "It's good to see you again."

"Likewise," Quinn assured him as they gripped hands. "When did they call you back to active duty?"

"About six hours after I sent Clipper off to join your quixotic rescue mission," Bokamba said, his grin turning into a wry smile. "I was sure they'd tumbled to the falsified orders and were there to haul my aged hide in front of a Peacekeeper firing squad. But luckily I kept my mouth shut; and lo and behold, all they wanted was to put me back in uniform. Congratulations on your success in finding Commander Cavanagh, by the way. All of you."

"Thank you, sir," Quinn said. "I'm relieved you didn't get into trouble over your part in it. They never even mentioned your name at the hearings—I was afraid they'd buried you away in a hole somewhere."

"Oh, they did," Bokamba countered, waving a hand around him. "What do you think the job of tac coordinator is, anyway? Glorified pack-mother, that's all. They might at least have given me something to fly."

"Uh-oh," Con Lady said, getting to her feet. "I sense a long reminiscence of past days of glory coming on."

"Me, too," Dreamer agreed as she and Adept also stood up. "Definitely guy talk. You'll excuse us?"

"If we must," Bokamba said, shaking his head in mock sorrow. "It's sad, Maestro. These young folk—no deference to their elders. Have you ladies studied tomorrow's practice schedule?"

"We've gone over it twice," Dreamer said.

"Go over it again," Bokamba ordered. "All of you. I'll see you in the ready room at oh-five-thirty tomorrow."

"Right." Dreamer winked at Quinn. "Welcome to the slave ship *Trafalgar*, gentlemen. See you tomorrow."

"Good-bye," Clipper said with a nod.

The women threaded their way back between the tables and chairs, pausing to chat briefly with others along the way. "I'm surprised to see women aboard," Quinn commented, waving Bokamba to one of the vacant chairs. "Especially considering the *Trafalgar*'s mission."

"Yes," Bokamba said, gazing down at the tabletop as he traced imaginary lines on it with a finger. "I must admit to certain personal reservations about women in combat positions. Particularly expeditionary forces like this one, as opposed to home or national defense. Cultural prejudices; I doubt you of NorCoord would understand."

"We do try to maintain a degree of chivalry ourselves, you know," Clipper reminded him. "Still, cultural biases or not, the Commonwealth's not in any position to play favorites. If the Zhirrzh are going to be stopped, it's going to take everything we've got."

"I suppose so." Bokamba looked up again. "Speaking of which, Adam, may I say how personally pleased I am that you've decided to rejoin the Copperheads? I'm looking forward to working with you again."

"Thank you," Quinn said. "I'll do my best to justify your confidence in me."

"I'm sure you will," Bokamba said with a mischievous smile. "Especially since I'll be riding tail for you tomorrow."

Quinn frowned. "They told me on Edo that they'd be providing me with a new tail man."

"He's supposedly on his way," Bokamba said. "Presumably he'll get here before we actually leave for Zhirrzh space. Until then I'm afraid you're stuck with me." He leveled a finger at Quinn. "All the more reason for you to show up tomorrow knowing what you're doing."

"Translation: get ourselves back to the ward and start learning the maneuvers?" Clipper suggested.

"Exactly," Bokamba said. "And take the rest of your squadron with you."

"Right," Clipper said, standing up. "Come on, Maestro. Mom says we have to study."

Bokamba shook his head. "These young folk," he sighed. "No deference to their elders."

There was no signal Aric was able to see or hear; but suddenly one of the two Yycroman males guarding the unmarked door shifted his rayslicer to point at the ceiling. He snapped his snout, clicking the long rows of teeth together. [Son of Lord Stewart Cavanagh,] he said. [You are summoned. Come.]

"Thank you," Aric said, standing up and stepping to the door, his heart pounding in his ears. He'd dealt with Yycromae before, certainly, in the normal course of CavTronics business operations. But never like this. "May I ask—?"

[You are summoned,] the male repeated.

Aric nodded silently, all the stories he'd ever heard about Yycroman males and their hair-trigger tempers flashing through his mind. The first male opened the door and stepped through. Aric followed, the second male falling in behind him.

He'd expected the door to lead into an audience chamber. To his mild surprise it opened instead directly onto a stone staircase leading downward. The first Yycroma led the way down and into a maze of narrow corridors, connecting with and branching off from theirs at seemingly random angles. A few minutes later they reached the end of a corridor and another door. The Yycroma opened it; lifting his rayslicer again, he stood aside. Swallowing, Aric stepped through the door.

And out onto the observation platform of a huge underground hangar.

He stopped just inside, gazing down in amazement at the perhaps fifty Yycroman freighters laid out in neat rows stretching back across the brightly lit work floor. Hundreds of Yycromae were moving purposefully around: carrying loads and driving lifters, working singly or in pairs beneath or on top of the freighters, conversing briefly in small groups before scattering their separate ways. The air was filled with the rumble of conversation, the flickering flash of welding torches, and the smell of hot metal and chemical affixers and sealants. The whole scene had the surreal atmosphere of a giant anthill populated by furry biped crocodiles.

Furry biped crocodiles busily converting freighters into warships.

There was no doubt about that. Those smooth multiple-cylinder modules being attached to some of the freighters' undersides were clearly space-to-space missiles. Probably of Russian or Nadezhdan manufacture —he could see Cyrillic characters on the spares stacked on the floor beneath his observation platform. Some of the ships were being fitted with antiquated but still lethal Celadonese shredder-burst guns; others already had ultramodern NorCoord 110 mm cannon mounted to them. Targeting lasers were all over the place, as were numerous oddly shaped modules Aric had never seen before but which were marked with Yycroman lettering.

[You are the eldest son of Lord Stewart Cavanagh?]

Aric jumped, spinning around to his left. A Yycroman female stood there, dressed in the elaborate ceremonial helmet and tooled cloak of a high-ranking government official. Flanking her were yet another pair of armed Yycroman males. "Yes," he acknowledged. "I'm Aric Cavanagh."

[I am Klyveress ci Yyatoor,] the female identified herself. [Twelfth Counsel to the Hierarch. I welcome you to the Yycroman world of Phormbi. I and the Yycroman people are in your debt.]

Aric grimaced. This was about to get very sticky. "No, actually, ci Yyatoor, I don't think you are in my debt," he said.

Her face changed subtly. [What are you saying?] she demanded. [That you did not bring the command/switching modules I requested?]

"I'm saying that, legally, I can't give them to you," Aric told her, knowing how ridiculous the words probably sounded. A lone human surrounded by Yycromae on one of their own colony worlds was hardly in a position to make lofty pronouncements of NorCoord law. "The Pacification treaty explicitly forbids NorCoord citizens from supplying items to the Yycromae that could be used for military purposes. This room makes it abundantly clear that that's precisely what you want the modules for."

[Your concerns are understandable,] Klyveress said, pulling a plate from a back-rib pouch. [But unnecessary. Your father has formulated an arrangement.]

"Yes, your message implied as much," Aric said. "I was rather expecting to find him aboard the diplomatic ship you sent for me, in fact. But he wasn't there, and I don't see him here."

[True. He is not here.]

"But he *was* here once," Aric countered. "He had to be. Your message to me came addressed to Asher Dales—that isn't a name you could have come up with on your own." He gestured toward the freighters. "What happened? Did he figure out what you were doing?"

[There was no need for figuring,] Klyveress said, offering him the plate. [It was he who helped create what we are doing. Please—read.]

Warily, Aric took the plate. It was opened to some kind of legal-looking NorCoord document. "What's this?" he asked.

[Read,] the ci Yyatoor repeated. [The information contained here is not yet public knowledge. Indeed, it may never be so. But you must be made an exception.]

Aric looked down at the plate, hoping he was just imagining the ominous overtones in that last sentence, and began to read.

There were two documents in the file. The first was a guarantee of Yycroman intent to use the warships they were creating exclusively for self-defense against the Conquerors. The second was a statement of Peacekeeper understanding that granted the Yycroman Hierarch this one-time exemption from the rearmament prohibitions of the Pacification treaty.

Aric read through the guarantee, carefully studying the form of the legal/contractual language. By the time he reached the end, it came as no surprise to discover his father's signature among those attached. He also noticed with some interest that the document had a signing date three days after the meeting his father had had on Mra-mig with Assistant Commonwealth Liaison Bronsks—the same period, according to Bronski, when he and Kolchin had vanished from sight. The statement of understanding was next, which turned out also to have been signed by his father. As well as by—

Aric looked up sharply. *"Brigadier* Petr Bronski?" he asked.

[That is correct,] Klyveress said. [As you see, it is all very legal.]

"That wasn't what I meant," Aric said, a sudden knot forming in the pit of his stomach. Bronski, a senior Peacekeeper officer . . . and suddenly his father's disappearance had taken an abrupt and ominous turn. "My father hasn't been seen for nearly—well, apparently not since these were signed."

[Do not fear, Aric Cavanagh,] Klyveress said. [I have seen him since then. He and his guard, Kolchin, escaped from Brigadier Bronski on Mra-mig, returning here in an appropriated Mrach fighter spacecraft.]

"Escaped?" Aric echoed, the knot tightening another turn. "What happened with Bronski that he needed to escape?"

[I do not know,] Klyveress said. [He would say nothing other than that he was fleeing involuntary confinement. My suspicion is that it concerns the CIRCE weapon.]

"I see," Aric murmured. Had his father somehow learned where one of CIRCE's components was hidden? Or worse, found out where the weapon was being reassembled? Either one would have had Bronski immediately issuing quarantine orders.

But why had his father chosen to run from that? "What happened then?"

[We could not permit him to remain in Yycroman space,] Klyveress said. [Our relationship with the hierarchy of NorCoord is already overly strained. He asked then if I could exchange his fighter spacecraft for one less traceable. I expressed our need for CavTronics electronics modules, and he agreed to send them to me as payment.]

The ci Yyatoor snapped her snout. [But he did not. Yycroman Intelligence made quiet inquiries, but they could find no record of his reaching Avon.]

"Then where is he?"

[I do not know. Perhaps he changed his mind and chose a different hiding location.]

"He still would have tried to get you the modules he'd promised," Aric said, shaking his head slowly. "And there are CavTronics facilities everywhere. Sounds more to me like Bronski got him."

[Perhaps,] Klyveress said. [But do not deduce too much from his silence. Perhaps he is still free but for some reason unable to fulfill his promise.]

"Maybe," Aric said, trying to calm the vague fears swirling through him. Even if Bronski had him, surely it was just some kind of precautionary confinement. His father wouldn't do anything that would land him in really serious trouble. "So when the modules didn't show up, you decided I could bring them to you?"

[Yes,] the ci Yyatoor said. [Yycroman Intelligence reported that you were on Edo, and so I dispatched a diplomatic ship to bring you here.]

"Sending a message via skitter first so I'd have time to get the equipment together," Aric nodded. "Had Dad given you the Asher Dales name to use?"

[No, it was a location he had mentioned as a possible hiding place after he reached Avon. I took the chance that NorCoord Intelligence would not associate you with that name.]

"Why were you worried about NorCoord Intelligence?" Aric asked, eyeing her thoughtfully. "I thought all this was completely legal."

[It is legal. It is not widely known.]

"Or, in other words, Bronski's the only one in the Peacekeepers who knows you've been granted a rearmament exemption?"

The ci Yyatoor's claws scratched idly at the air. [You exaggerate, Aric Cavanagh. But not overly much.]

"Ah," Aric said, looking again at the bustling activity below them. At least that explained why Bronski had been on Edo—he'd probably gone there to brief Admiral Rudzinski on this private treaty he and Klyveress had worked out. A belated official approval-stamping, Aric suspected, of what the Yycromae had been doing anyway.

[What will you do now?] Klyveress asked.

Aric turned back to face her. There'd been something new in her tone just then. . . . "Go back to Avon, I suppose," he said. "With my father gone I'm more or less in charge of CavTronics Industries. I ought to be there."

[And what of the war?]

"What of it? Are you suggesting I enlist instead?"

[No,] the ci Yyatoor said. [I am asking for your assistance here.]

It was not exactly what Aric had been expecting. "What sort of assistance?"

Klyveress waved her snout at the hangar. [We have found that command/switching modules of the sort you have provided are often difficult to interlock,] she said. [Even more so when coordinating otherwise unmatched weapons systems.]

"I know," Aric said. "Celadonese and Nadezhdan logic structures are notorious for incompatibilities. You need to be careful how you tailor the overlays."

[You are familiar with the problem,] Klyveress said. [Will you help us?]

For a long minute Aric remained silent, gazing into Klyveress's dark eyes, mentally fighting through this sudden shift in his worldview. He'd grown up believing that the Yycromae were the most dangerous threat to peace within the Commonwealth, a threat that only the presence of Peacekeeper forces could restrain. And now here he was, being asked to help rearm them.

But the real danger out there right now was the Conquerors. And the Commonwealth needed all the allies it could get. "All right," he told Klyveress. "I'll do what I can."

"The three searchers have left the room," the Elder reported. "They're being led toward the tunnel leading to the hangar and the *Closed Mouth*."

The Overclan Prime nodded, tongue pressed hard against the side of his mouth as he gazed at the map of Human-Conqueror territory. The map that had been reconstructed from the recorder salvaged from that first space battle with the Human-Conquerors. The map they'd thought listed all the enemy targets to be dealt with.

They knew better now. The Human-Conquerors had allies in this war. Terrible, dangerous allies.

The Yycromae.

Supreme Warrior Commander Prm-jevev stepped over from his quiet consultation with the Elders. "We can do it," he told the Prime. "It'll mean stripping warships away from some of the beachheads, but we can put together a quick-strike assault fleet."

"Which beachheads?" the Prime asked.

"We'll take three of the five ships currently at Massif," Prm-jevev said, consulting his list. "Plus four of the six at Pasdoufat—those are already on their way. One of the three at Kalevala, and three of the four at Dorcas."

The Prime felt his tail twitch. Dorcas. The young searcher Thrr-gilag was on his way to that world, at the Prime's private request. "You're only leaving one at Dorcas?"

"Yes," the Supreme Commander grunted. "And only because that particular ship isn't in any shape to fly or fight. If the technics can repair it before the Phormbi attack, I'll pull it out, too. Why? Is Dorcas a problem?"

"I suppose not," the Prime said reluctantly. It probably didn't matter whether or not Thrr-gilag's proposed biochemical tests on the Human-Conqueror prisoner turned up anything. Matters were moving too fast now for that.

And there was certainly no reason to tie up precious resources at insignificant beachheads like Dorcas now that they knew they'd failed to trap any of the CIRCE components. "What do you think of the Mrachani plan?" he asked the Supreme Commander.

"I suppose it makes sense," the other said. "I agree with Valloittaja that knocking out the Human-Conqueror surveillance center on Phormbi should definitely be the first strike."

"Assuming Valloittaja's data on the range of these Human-Conqueror ship detectors is accurate," the Prime said.

"Assuming that, of course," Prm-jevev growled. "I'll want hard numbers on that before I'll commit my warships to any attack."

The Prime nodded, studying the map. "We may also want to request further confirmation that these are indeed the correct locations for the Phormbi bases."

"Most definitely," Prm-Jevev agreed. "Searcher Nzz-oonaz is far too willing to take the Mrachanis' word for everything, in my opinion."

"Interesting," the Prime murmured. "I've been thinking the same thing. Do you suppose the Mrachanis could be using something on them?"

"Chemicals?" Prm-jevev asked doubtfully. "Would they know enough yet about our biophysiology to know what they could safely use?"

"I don't know. No, probably not," the Prime conceded.

"Still, it wouldn't hurt to mention the possibility to Nzz-oonaz," the Supreme Commander said. "If they aren't using chemicals now, there's no guarantee they won't in the future."

"True," the Prime agreed. "Whom have you chosen to command the attack force?"

Prm-jevev flicked his tongue. "Actually, I thought I'd take a flash-ship out to Mrachani space and take command myself."

The Prime frowned. "Isn't that rather unusual?"

"It is, but it shouldn't be," the Supreme Commander said flatly. "After all, Warrior Command is supposed to be made up of the best warriors in the eighteen worlds."

"Yet your expertise would be temporarily lost to us if you're raised to Eldership," the Prime pointed out. "The anchoring shock at such a distance is deep and profound. You could be twisted uselessly for many fullarcs."

"I admit it's a risk," the Supreme Commander agreed. "But it's also a risk to try to run a battle from here with only Elder reports to tell me what's going on. There's no substitute for seeing something with your own eyes." He grimaced. "Besides, if the Mrachanis are lying about any of this, I want to know about it."

An Elder appeared. "Searcher Nzz-oonaz and the others have reached the *Closed Mouth*," he reported. "They're going inside. Several Mrachani are loitering in the area."

Hoping to learn something about the miraculous Zhirrzh interstar communication method, no doubt. Well, they could poke around all they wanted. Any microphones the Mrachanis might have trained on the *Closed Mouth* would be unable to pick up the Elders' voices; and the delegation had already been instructed to gather around one of the ship's cookstoves while they held their conferences with Oaccanv. If the Mrachanis wanted to steal it and take it apart, they were welcome to do that, too. "I presume we'll tell Searcher Nzz-oonaz to conditionally accept the Mrachanis' proposal," he said.

"Yes," Prm-jevev said. "At least the first part, the attack on Phormbi. We'll need more time to pull together the ships necessary for an attack on Earth."

"Yes," the Prime murmured. An attack on the Human-Conqueror surveillance center would tie up a lot of warships. Warships no longer in prime combat readiness; warships that the precariously stretched Zhirrzh forces could hardly spare. But they had no choice. With the Human-Conquerors in the process of assembling CIRCE, the only course of action left to Warrior Command was to hit them as quickly and aggressively as possible. "How soon?" he asked Prm-jevev.

"Depends on how quickly the warships can be brought together and prepared for full combat," the Supreme Commander said. "Two fullarcs, perhaps three. Do I have your permission to personally command the attack?"

"I trust your experience with that decision," the Prime said. "Do what you feel necessary."

Prm-jevev bowed in old-world Cakk'rr style. "Thank you, Overclan Prime. I'll leave as soon as this conference is over."

In front of them an Elder appeared. " 'This is Searcher Nzz-oonaz, speaking from the planet Mra,'" he quoted. "'I wish to speak to the Overclan Prime.'"

The Prime smiled tightly. Nzz-oonaz, playing his half of the charade for the Mrachanis' benefit. Valloittaja, he suspected, would be astonished to find out how these communications were actually being carried out.

On some future fullarc they would tell him. But not yet. De facto allies they might be, but there was still something about the Mrachanis he didn't quite trust. "This is the Overclan Prime," he said to the Elder, playing the other half of the game. "Speak, Searcher Nzz-oonaz."

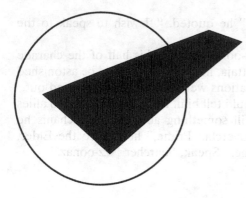

11

"You must understand the terrible danger we are all in," the Mrach called Lahettilas said, his voice low and earnest. "You, the Zhirrzh, and we, the Mrachanis. The Conquerors Without Reason have a terrifying device that they plan to use against us."

"Yes, I know," Thrr-gilag said. "The one they call CIRCE."

It seemed to him that Lahettilas's expression twitched at the weapon's name. "Yes," the Mrachani said eagerly. "Yes, indeed. We have been trying to warn your warriors about it, but no one would listen."

"There was no need," Thrr-gilag said. "We know all about CIRCE."

The Mrachani's eyes narrowed. "Really. Then why would your warriors not discuss it with us?"

"The reasons are unimportant," Thrr-gilag said, trying to put some official loftiness into his voice, the sort that discouraged further questions. This conversation was supposedly a private one, with only Warrior Command's designated Elders listening in, but that didn't mean some of the base's other Elders weren't privately eavesdropping. And while the Overclan Prime had given Thrr-gilag permission to talk to the Mrachanis about CIRCE, he'd also made it clear that the details of the weapon were still to be kept secret. "What is important right now is to discuss what the Mrachanis suggest we do about the threat."

The Mrachani blinked. "We must form an alliance, of course," he said, as if that were obvious. "Only together can we hope to defeat the Conquerors Without Reason."

"I see," Thrr-gilag said. "What would the Mrachanis bring to such an alliance?"

The second Mrachani, who up to now had been silent, took a step away from the wall where he'd been inconspicuously standing. "We can provide information," he said. "You fight valiantly against the Conquerors Without Reason; but you seem as yet unaware of an equally great danger lurking in the darkness. The Conquerors Without Reason have allies. Vicious, dangerous aliens called the Yycromae."

Thrr-gilag frowned. The Yycromae had been listed on the maps of Human space that Warrior Command had created. They held four main star systems, if he remembered correctly, grouped together at one edge of Human space. But the impression he'd gotten from the captured recorder's information— "I thought they were merely another conquered race," he said.

"That is what they wish you to believe," the second Mrachani said bitterly. "I urge you not to make the fatal mistake of believing that lie."

The acrid taste of dread flowed over Thrr-gilag's tongue. A new threat, as dangerous as the Humans? "Yet they have only four worlds," he reminded Lahettilas, struggling to keep his growing fear from poisoning his reasoning. "How dangerous can they be?"

"How dangerous would four worlds of the Zhirrzh be?" Lahettilas retorted. "You refuse to believe us at the risk of your people, Searcher Thrr-gilag."

"I'm not refusing to believe you," Thrr-gilag protested, feeling himself floundering a little. "I simply need some proof that—"

"Proof?" Lahettilas cut him off, his voice oozing with scorn. "What proof would you choose, Searcher Thrr-gilag? An attack by Yycroman warships at the flanks of your forces? The sudden destruction of all the warships orbiting over Dorcas? Or would you prefer a devastating attack on the Zhirrzh homeworld?"

"No, of course not," Thrr-gilag said, his tongue flicking nervously. "Could the Yycromae really do that?"

"Not yet," the second Mrachani said darkly. "They have been taken off guard by the strength of the Zhirrzh, as have the Conquerors Without Reason. But that will change." He jabbed a finger toward Thrr-gilag. "If you allow them time."

"Yes," Thrr-gilag said, taking an involuntary step backward. The Mrachani's bearing was suddenly very intimidating. Or perhaps it was the underlying menace in his words. "I will pass your words on to our leaders."

"Do so quickly." Lahettilas cocked his head to the side, studying Thrr-gilag's face. "If, that is, you intend to do so at all," he added, the edge of scorn back in his voice.

"Of course," Thrr-gilag said, fighting back the taste of irritation as it edged through his dark fears. He'd said he would speak to the Overclan Prime—how dare this alien doubt his word? "I'll be back again soon."

"We will await your return," Lahettilas said softly. "If you value the lives of your people, do not make the delay long."

Thrr-mezaz was waiting outside when Thrr-gilag emerged from the Mrachanis' house. "How did it go?" he asked as they headed off across the landing field toward the beachhead command center.

"Not particularly pleasantly," Thrr-gilag said. The sunshine flooding down through the cloudless Dorcas sky seemed somehow darker now than it had been when he'd gone inside. "Rather frightening, if you want the truth."

"Are they still insisting we take them to Oaccanv to meet with Warrior Command?"

"They weren't insisting on that with me," Thrr-gilag said, wondering how much of the conversation he should share with his brother. The Overclan Prime had given him permission to tell Thrr-mezaz about CIRCE, but only if absolutely necessary. "Mostly they were warning me that the Humans have taken on allies."

Thrr-mezaz flicked his tongue. "The Yycromae?"

"Yes," Thrr-gilag said, frowning at him. "How did you hear about that?"

"The word came down from Warrior Command this premidarc," Thrr-mezaz told him. "Apparently the Mrachanis on Mra have been warning Nzz-oonaz about them, too."

"Really," Thrr-gilag said. "Interesting."

"How so?"

"I don't know," Thrr-gilag said slowly. "It just feels odd, somehow. If these Yycromae are so warlike and dangerous, why haven't we seen them in combat yet? For that matter, why didn't that captured Human recorder identify them as Human allies?"

"Maybe a deliberate lie on the Human-Conquerors' part," Thrr-mezaz suggested.

"Or else it's the Mrachanis who are lying," Thrr-gilag countered. "I still don't trust them."

"Frankly, I don't either," Thrr-mezaz said. "But Warrior Command seems to feel differently."

"Meaning?"

"Meaning they've apparently decided on an attack against the Yycromae," Thrr-mezaz said. "Supreme Ship Commander Dkll-kumvit has been ordered to head immediately to a rendezvous point in Mrachani space." His tongue flicked. "Taking our encirclement warships with him."

Thrr-gilag felt his tail twitch. "All of them?"

"All except the *Requisite,*" Thrr-mezaz said, flicking his tongue again. "Which hardly counts as a ship, considering it no longer has a functioning drive. Unless the Human-Conquerors are considerate enough to fly into combat range, it's effectively useless."

Thrr-gilag glanced up at the sky. "I don't like the sound of that."

"Join the group," Thrr-mezaz said sourly. "If they're going to abandon Dorcas, I wish they'd do a clean job of it. Leaving us down here to get raised to Eldership at the Human-Conquerors' leisure is nothing but a waste of good warriors."

Thrr-gilag flicked his tongue in a grimace. "Except that they can't afford to abandon Dorcas. Not with—"

He stopped. "Something having to do with that underground room?" Thrr-mezaz asked.

Thrr-gilag sighed. "I think so, yes," he said. "I think there may be something in there the Humans want. Something we can't afford to let them have."

"Interesting," Thrr-mezaz said thoughtfully. "How big would this something be?"

"No idea. Why?"

"Because they had full access to the room for nearly four tentharcs before pulling back to their mountain stronghold," Thrr-mezaz said. "As far as we could tell, they didn't take anything at all out of it."

Thrr-gilag frowned at him. "Are you sure?"

"I've had the Elders monitoring the entrance since the beat we located the place," Thrr-mezaz said. "Two separate Human-Conqueror warrior teams went inside during those four tentharcs. Neither group brought anything out."

"Interesting indeed," Thrr-gilag agreed. From everything he'd heard about the underground chamber and the Human warriors' attempts to get to it, he would have bet his own *fsss* that one of the CIRCE components was hidden there. But if so, why hadn't they taken it back to their stronghold? Too big to move? "And now they've just abandoned the area?"

"They've pulled back," Thrr-mezaz corrected. "That doesn't mean they wouldn't come down on us again if I tried sending in more Zhirrzh warriors. As long as any of those Copperhead aircraft are flying, I'm not trying it."

"They're that dangerous?"

"More than you'd believe," Thrr-mezaz said grimly. "They destroyed a complete ground defense laser and raised eight of my warriors to Eldership. Still, it could have been worse. They let the search team leave unharmed, Klnn-dawan-a among them."

Thrr-gilag stopped short, staring at his brother. "You sent Klnn-dawan-a into a combat zone?" he demanded. "What in the eighteen worlds—?"

"She's an expert in alien cultures," Thrr-mezaz snapped back, "and she insisted on going. And I've already had my fill of criticism about it, thank you, from every Dhaa'rr who has access to my Elders. From Speaker Cvv-panav on down."

Thrr-gilag grimaced. "I'm sorry. You're right, of course—Klnn-dawan-a *would* insist on going to take a look at such a place."

"Just as she insisted on taking the tissue samples you wanted while you talked to the Mrachanis," Thrr-mezaz said. "Come on, let's see if she's finished."

The Human prisoner was lying stretched out on the examination table in the medical room, his arms and legs securely fastened down, his face set in expressionless lines as he gazed straight up at the ceiling. Beside him, Klnn-dawan-a was just withdrawing a sampling needle from the skin of his lower torso. Standing on either side of his head, two armed warriors stood ready for trouble, both looking just slightly queasy as they watched Klnn-dawan-a work. At floor level, out of the Human's line of sight, three Elders were also keeping watch. "Finished?" Thrr-gilag asked.

"Almost," Klnn-dawan-a said, returning the sampler to its case. "I just need a couple more."

"How's he behaving?" Thrr-mezaz asked.

"Remarkably well," Klnn-dawan-a told him. "I can tell the sampling procedure is uncomfortable, but he hasn't struggled or even shouted at me."

"Just as Pheylan Cavanagh was," Thrr-gilag murmured. "Aggressive in groups, submissive as individuals."

"Let's not talk as if that were already an established fact," Klnn-dawan-a cautioned him. "That's what we're here to find out."

"Besides, most intelligent species get pretty submissive when they've got two laser rifles pointed at them," Thrr-mezaz added, clicking on the darklight relay and slipping a translator link into his ear slits. "You need the speaker set up?"

"No, thanks," Thrr-gilag said, stepping to the prisoner's other side. "I'm Thrr-gilag; Kee'rr," he said, switching to the Human language. "This is Klnn-dawan-a; Dhaa'rr. We've come here to study you."

"I got that impression," the Human said. His tone was very similar to the one Pheylan Cavanagh had often used while a prisoner, a tone Thrr-gilag had always associated with quiet mockery. "I'm Sergeant Janovetz of the Peacekeepers. How much more studying are you going to do?"

"She's almost finished," Thrr-gilag assured him. "Why did you come here to the Zhirrzh encampment?"

"We saw the other spacecraft come down," the Human told him, his face twitching as Klnn-dawan-a slid a sampling needle into his upper leg. "We thought there might be injured Humans aboard who needed our help."

"You're a healer, then?" Thrr-gilag asked.

"I can do some healing," Sergeant Janovetz said. "Our commander reasoned that if the injuries were more severe than I could handle, we could then offer the assistance of one of our more expert healers."

"Ask him about the attack on the Mrachanis," Thrr-mezaz muttered.

"I'm told your fellow Humans launched an attack on this encampment six fullarcs ago," Thrr-gilag said in the Human language. "There were explosions with the purpose of killing the Mrachanis who had arrived."

Sergeant Janovetz shrugged his shoulders. "I can only tell you what I've already told your commander. It wasn't a Human attack."

"Then explain it."

"I can't," the Human said. "Maybe if you'd let me see the site, I could tell you more."

Thrr-gilag looked at his brother. "Any reason you haven't let him look at the attack site?"

"Lots of them," Thrr-mezaz growled. "The first of which is I don't trust him. He may claim to have healer skills, but he's almost certainly a warrior. We've already taken one Elderdeath weapon off him—who knows what other tricks he might have under his tongue?"

"Letting him out might be a good way to find out," Klnn-dawan-a suggested. "What can he do, really?"

"He could try to kill the Mrachanis," Thrr-mezaz said. "You may have faith in that fancy obedience suit you brought with you; I don't. Or he could raise more of my warriors to Eldership or study our defenses in preparation for a Human-Conqueror attack. Who knows?"

"We don't have any proof that he ever intended to kill the Mrachanis," Thrr-gilag reminded him. "Besides, with Nzz-oonaz on Mra, these two aliens can hardly be that important anymore."

"And as to whatever other damage he might do," Klnn-dawan-a added quietly, "I hardly think the Human-Conquerors would need any help from him. We both saw those Copperhead warriors in action, Thrr-mezaz."

Thrr-gilag looked across the table at her, his tail speeding up as the fresh realization of what might have happened to her came flooding over his tongue. Out in the center of a Human attack . . .

"Have there been any more explosives attacks?" Sergeant Janovetz asked.

Thrr-gilag glanced at Thrr-mezaz, caught his brother's negative flick of the tongue. "No," he told the prisoner.

"Are the Mrachanis still here?"

"Yes."

"Well, then," the prisoner concluded reasonably, "if we *had* launched that first attack, don't you think we'd have kept at it until we'd succeeded?"

Thrr-gilag looked at Thrr-mezaz. "Well?"

"He's got a point," Thrr-mezaz conceded. "I've been wondering the same thing myself."

"Then let's let him look at the site," Thrr-gilag urged.

"You just want to see if he'll turn violent," Thrr-mezaz said with a grimace. "But I suppose we ought to try it. It could be a trick, though. You two"—he flicked his tongue at two of the watching Elders—"go back to the command/monitor room and have Second Commander Klnn-vavgi put all perimeter warrior teams on alert. Wait there until all warriors and Elders have reported in, then report back to me here."

"I obey," one of the two Elders said for both of them, and they vanished.

"All right," Thrr-mezaz said, his tone suddenly changing as he glanced around the room. "We've only got a couple of hunbeats before they get back. Let's get to it." He gestured to the two warriors. "Thrr-gilag, Klnn-dawan-a: this is Warrior First Vstii-suuv and Warrior Third Qlaa-nuur; both Aree'rr. Warriors, Thrr-gilag and Klnn-dawan-a have brought us a second cutting from Prr't-zevisti's *fsss.*"

"Thrr-mezaz!" Thrr-gilag hissed, flicking his tongue warningly toward the third Elder, still hovering beneath the table.

"It's all right," the Elder said. "I already know—I'm the Dorcas end of the secure pathway Prr't-casst-a set up between you and Commander Thrr-mezaz."

"We're the only ones on Dorcas in on it, though," Thrr-mezaz warned. "So keep it strictly quiet. Vstii-suuv, have you been able to identify any other routes into Human-Conqueror territory?"

"We've located two other possibilities," Vstii-suuv said. "Neither is an especially appealing climb, but both should get us within the five-thousand-stride range we need."

"Assuming we can catch the Human-Conquerors sleeping," Qlaa-nuur added. "If not, we're going to have the same problem we ran into last time."

"Last time?" Thrr-gilag asked.

"We got caught halfway up a cliff face," Thrr-mezaz said. "We were able to get down; and then they just let us go."

"Like they did at the underground room?" Klnn-dawan-a asked.

"Very much like that," Thrr-mezaz said. "But we can talk about that later. Vstii-suuv, when do you think we'll be able to try one of these new routes?"

"The sooner the better," the warrior said. "The longer we wait, the higher the chances some Elder will stumble across the cutting and end things for good."

"It would certainly end it for Prr't-zevisti," Thrr-gilag said grimly. "The Dhaa'rr leaders were supposed to run the final rites and ceremony of fire on his *fsss* organ four fullarcs ago."

"They've changed their minds," the Elder spoke up. "I spoke with Prr't-casst-a last fullarc, and she said that the final rites have been postponed indefinitely."

"Well, that's some good news, anyway," Thrr-gilag said, a small bit of pressure easing from his shoulders. "Thrr-mezaz, who'll be going on this climb?"

"Just the two warriors here and me," Thrr-mezaz told him. "Vstii-suuv, how soon can we leave?"

"I'm not sure," Vstii-suuv said. "The weather patterns for the next two fullarcs are predicted to be very unstable."

And climbing in unfamiliar territory in heavy wind and rain was a good way to wind up in premature Eldership. "We'll aim to leave in two fullarcs, then," Thrr-mezaz decided.

"Maybe the Human-Conquerors will have settled down by then, too," Qlaa-nuur added. "They've been unusually active since the battle."

"Yes," Thrr-mezaz agreed. "In the meantime, Thrr-gilag, I want you and Klnn-dawan-a to go full haste on these studies of yours. If there's some biochemical trick to this species, I want to know it before we try walking into their territory again."

Thrr-gilag looked down at Sergeant Janovetz, tail twitching for a beat before he remembered that the Human didn't understand their language. "We'll do our best," he promised his brother.

The other two Elders returned. "All perimeter warriors are ready, Commander," one reported. "As are all ground defenses."

"Go alert the warriors outside that we're bringing the prisoner out," Thrr-mezaz ordered them, gesturing to the two warriors to unstrap the prisoner from the table. "All right, my brother. Tell your test subject to put on his new obedience suit, and we'll all go for a little stroll."

" 'We weren't given details of the debate between Warrior Command and the Overclan Prime, Speaker,' " the Elder repeated Searcher Gll-borgiv's words. " 'But the indications are that it was short.' "

Speaker Cvv-panav shifted position on his couch. "And what indications are those?" he asked.

The Elder nodded and vanished. "You didn't really expect them to have a long discussion, did you?" the other Zhirrzh in the room asked from his lazy sprawl on the Speaker's visitor's couch.

"Not if the Mrachanis are right about CIRCE already being assembled," Cvv-panav said grimly. "That would scare Warrior Command's collective tongue limp."

"I don't doubt it," the other said. "Personally, I think the Mrachanis are lying."

"Really," the Speaker said, eyeing him thoughtfully. In the five cyclics since he'd taken the young warrior into his private service, Mnov-korthe had been one of his best covert operatives, carrying out a variety of quiet jobs that had advanced the Speaker's power and the prestige of the entire Dhaa'rr clan. His execution of those jobs had generally been flawless, his instincts and hunches equally so. "What makes you say that?"

The Elder returned before Mnov-korthe could answer. " 'The fact that they apparently made the decision to accept the Mrach offer during our walk from the conference room back to the *Closed Mouth*,' " he said. " 'We held a complete discussion aboard ship for the benefit of any listeners, but it was clear from the start that Supreme Warrior Commander Prm-jevev had already made up his mind.' "

"What's going to happen now at your end?" Cvv-panav asked.

The Elder nodded and vanished. "You were saying?" the Speaker prompted, looking back at Mnov-korthe.

"I've been reading about the attack by the Human-Conqueror ground warriors on Dorcas two fullarcs ago," the warrior said, gesturing to his reader. "Their commander risked both of his Copperhead warcraft in order to chase the Zhirrzh warriors away from an underground chamber."

"Meaning?" Cvv-panav prompted.

Mnov-korthe shrugged. "Meaning there's something in there the Human-Conquerors didn't want Commander Thrr-mezaz's warriors to have."

Cvv-panav slid his tongue tip gently across the inside of his mouth. "Such as, for example, a CIRCE component?"

Mnov-korthe shrugged again. "Could be."

The Elder returned. " 'For now, we're effectively trapped here on Mra. The Overclan Prime is going to send a shipment of supplies to one of the

Mrach mining worlds, where it'll be repacked into a Mrach spacecraft for transport here. Valloittaja doesn't want to have Zhirrzh ships coming to any of the main Mrach worlds.' "

Cvv-panav smiled tightly. The Zhirrzh mission itself was hardly trapped; this supply-shipment technique could just as easily be run in reverse to send them all back home to Oaccanv. But of course neither side was likely to suggest that as a course of action. For Warrior Command, abandoning the *Closed Mouth* on Mra would be completely unacceptable; for the Mrachanis, letting potential hostages depart before any alliance was officially established would probably be equally so. "A wise move on Valloittaja's part," he said to the Elder. "What are you learning about the Mrachanis themselves?"

" 'Not as much as I'd hoped to. There's information here for us to read, but of course the number of actual Mrachanis we can speak to is very limited. I hope that after all this is over, we'll be able to examine the culture more closely.' "

"Just be sure to keep your mind on the task at hand," Cvv-panav said, fighting to keep his voice civil. He'd been warned that Gll-borgiv was young and inexperienced, with the stereotypical searcher's infuriating tendency to lose track of what was truly important. "You're there to learn about CIRCE and the Human-Conquerors and to keep me informed. That's all. Understand?"

The Elder nodded and vanished. "He's a fool," Mnov-korthe suggested, looking up from his reader again. "Didn't the clan have anyone more competent who could have been put in this group?"

"There were several," the Speaker said, flicking his tongue contemptuously. "Unfortunately, there was no one more mindlessly loyal to the Dhaa'rr clan. Certainly no one who would have been willing to ignore the Overclan Prime's orders and deliver these private briefings to me."

Across the room the door slid open, and Mnov-korthe's brother, Mnov-dornt, stepped into the room. "We've got confirmation, Speaker Cvv-panav. There was definitely—"

"Just a beat," Cvv-panav cut him off. The Elder would be back any beat now. . . .

The Elder reappeared. " 'I understand, Speaker Cvv-panav,' " the answer came, the tone appropriately humble. " 'I won't let you or the Dhaa'rr clan down.' "

"See that you don't," Cvv-panav said. "Farewell." He nodded to the Elder. "Deliver that, then close the pathway."

"I obey, Speaker Cvv-panav," the Elder said.

He disappeared again. "What's been confirmed?" Cvv-panav asked, looking over at Mnov-dornt.

"Your hunch," Mnov-dornt told him. "Prr't-zevisti's *fsss* organ has indeed been tampered with."

"Well, well," Cvv-panav said. "How interesting. So a second cutting has been taken?"

"In a manner of speaking," Mnov-dornt said, pulling some documents from his waist pouch as he crossed the room. "Someone apparently used a sampling needle to withdraw some of the semiliquid tissue from the interior of the *fsss*. The healers estimate the equivalent of a five-thou-stride cutting was taken."

"Ingenious," the Speaker murmured, taking the papers and glancing over them. "Will it work?"

"No one knows," Mnov-dornt said. "Apparently, no one's ever tried this before."

"I'm not surprised," Cvv-panav growled. "Elders hate having experiments done on their *fsss* organs. So Searcher Thrr-gilag has obtained the extra cutting his brother, Commander Thrr-mezaz, wanted. And obtained it with the help of a Dhaa'rr traitor."

"There's no hard evidence that Thrr-gilag and Klnn-dawan-a were the ones who took the sample," Mnov-dornt cautioned. "In fact, the protectors who were with them at the shrine say—"

"I don't need any hard evidence," Cvv-panav snapped, thrusting the documents back into his hand. "And I don't care what those simple-minded Prr protectors say. The Kee'rr and his accomplice were the ones, all right. And I'm going to make sure they pay dearly for it."

"Not without proof you aren't," Mnov-korthe spoke up from his couch. "Sorry, Speaker, but you're going to need more than just a mutilated *fsss* organ and a possibly coincidental visit to the Prr-family shrine by the accused."

"I don't need any amateur legal advice, thank you," Cvv-panav said icily. "Where's Prr't-zevisti's *fsss* now?"

"The Prr-family leaders are holding it," Mnov-dornt said. "I told them to make it look as if it was Prr't-casst-a's petition that was holding up the final rites."

"Have them continue holding on to it," Cvv-panav said. "No, on second thought, have it delivered to me. I think I'll take it back to Oaccanv and drop it on the Overclan Prime's desk. His reaction should be interesting."

Still, he had to concede that Mnov-korthe was right. The indicators were tantalizing, but he would need evidence in order to hammer Thrr-gilag the way he wanted to.

Fortunately, there was a simple way to get that evidence. "In the meantime," he told them, "you two are going to take a trip to Dorcas."

The brothers exchanged glances. "Do you think that's wise, Speaker?" Mnov-korthe asked. "Our faces may be a little too recognizable right now."

"By whom?" Cvv-panav retorted. "The Prime is hardly going to be giving regular latearc showings of that film he took of you delivering Thrr-pifix-a's stolen *fsss* organ to her."

"The Overclan warriors who recorded the film would recognize us," Mnov-korthe pointed out.

"None of whom will be on Dorcas," Cvv-panav reminded him. "Or on the Dhaa'rr ship that takes you there; or at the Dhaa'rr landing field you'll be leaving Dharanv from."

"What if Thrr-pifix-a described us to her son?" Mnov-korthe persisted.

"Not a chance," Cvv-panav said, flicking his tongue in a contemptuous negative. "An old female who saw you once? Not a chance. You could walk up to Thrr-gilag and tell him you know his mother, and he still wouldn't catch on as to who you are."

The brothers exchanged another glance. "I'm sure it'll be fine," Mnov-dornt said. "Shall we take one of your flash-ships?"

"I'd prefer you be a little more inconspicuous if possible," the Speaker said, calling up spaceflight data on his reader. "There's a supply ship called the *Willing Servant* heading out for Dorcas in three tentharcs from the Icetongue landing field. Can you get there in time?"

"No problem," Mnov-korthe assured him, turning off his reader and getting up from the couch. "Our transport's right outside. What exactly do you want us to do on Dorcas?"

"I want you to find that illegal *fsss* cutting," the Speaker told him. "And with it, evidence that will implicate Thrr-gilag and his brother."

"Commander Thrr-mezaz?" Mnov-korthe said. "That might be a bit difficult."

"I'll make sure it won't be," Cvv-panav promised grimly. "I'll have a very special document for you before you leave."

"And if the evidence you want doesn't exist?"

Cvv-panav flicked his tongue. "In that case," he said softly, "you will, of course, create it."

The Human-Conqueror prisoner stood in front of the hole in the storehouse, his curled-up hands resting against the sides of his lower torso as he spoke. "No question," the translation of his words came in Thrr-mezaz's ear slits. "The blast came from the inside."

"How can he be sure?" Thrr-mezaz asked.

Thrr-gilag translated the question. The alien replied, waving his hands at the edges of the hole, then pointing a finger first at the ground at their feet and then through the hole at the ground outside. "The edges of the hole have an outward twist to them," the translation came. "That means the force came from this side of the wood. There's also the pattern of debris. Not enough wood fragments on the inside; too many on the outside."

"Interesting," Second Commander Klnn-vavgi commented from beside Thrr-mezaz. "We'd wondered about that ourselves."

"Yes," Thrr-mezaz conceded, frowning hard at the Human-Conqueror. "Though of course we have only his word that that's what it means."

"What reason would he have to lie?" Klnn-dawan-a asked.

"For one thing, cousin, they're our enemies," Klnn-vavgi reminded her. "Enemies often lie just for practice. He could also simply be wrong."

"Let's assume he's not," Thrr-mezaz said, flicking his tongue thoughtfully. "So the explosions came from the inside. That means the Mrachanis had to have set them off themselves."

"How?" Klnn-vavgi asked. "And why?"

"Those are the questions, all right," Thrr-mezaz nodded. "Though come to think of it, I seem to remember one of the Elders telling me they'd hung some decorative cloths on the walls around the room."

"You think they could have concealed the explosives?" Klnn-dawan-a asked.

"It's an obvious possibility," Thrr-mezaz said. "Thrr-gilag, ask him if he can tell us anything else about the explosions. The strength of the blasts; the type of explosive used, maybe, if he knows about different types."

There was a brief exchange of words, the Human-Conqueror pointing across the storehouse toward another of the blast holes. "Not from this one," the translation came. "May I look over there?"

"Go ahead," Thrr-mezaz said, gesturing permission to the prisoner's escort. "Warriors, watch him."

Thrr-gilag translated, and the alien set off across the storehouse, Thrr-gilag, Klnn-dawan-a, and the warriors forming a moving semicircle around him. "There's one other possibility, Commander," Klnn-vavgi said as he and Thrr-mezaz followed more slowly. "We know now that the Human-Conquerors can detect spacecraft in the tunnel-line, which means they knew we were coming. Could these explosives have been left behind as ensnarement traps for us?"

"Why only in this one storehouse?" Thrr-mezaz asked.

"Maybe they weren't only here," Klnn-vavgi suggested. "Maybe the whole village is set up to explode around us."

"If so, why haven't they used them?"

"Because they know that raising the whole beachhead to Eldership won't gain them anything," Klnn-vavgi said. "As long as the encirclement forces are overhead, they'll still be trapped here."

And those encirclement forces were about to be withdrawn. Thrr-mezaz glanced upward, an eerie feeling flowing over his tongue. To be sitting here in the middle of a Human-Conqueror ensnarement trap . . . "No," he said slowly. "If they'd deliberately set up a trap in the storehouse, they surely would have done a better job of it. As it was, all they did was blow off the doors and make a couple of holes in the walls."

"And raised two warriors to Eldership," Klnn-vavgi reminded him darkly.

"Because they happened to be standing in front of the doors," Thrr-mezaz countered. "Almost collateral damage from the Human-Conquerors' point of view—certainly so if the Mrachanis were their intended target. No, Second, a deliberate ensnarement trap ought to have brought the whole storehouse down."

"Maybe," Klnn-vavgi said, a lingering edge of doubt evident in his tone. "But that just brings it back to the Mrachanis. Why would they want to blow holes in their own living area?"

The Human-Conqueror prisoner was at the other blast hole now, looking closely at the blackened edge. "There's one possibility," Thrr-mezaz said. "Ever since they got here, the Mrachanis have been either pleading or demanding to be taken to Oaccanv. What better way to make us hurry the decision than to create a sudden and immediate threat to their lives?"

"Interesting suggestion," Klnn-vavgi said, flicking his tongue thoughtfully. "It would certainly bend the image the Mrachanis have been presenting of themselves as poor, helpless victims of the Human-Conquerors."

"If it's true," Thrr-mezaz said. "Question is, how would we go about testing it?"

"I don't know," Klnn-vavgi said. "Unless . . ."

"Unless what?"

Klnn-vavgi flicked his tongue toward the prisoner, who was rubbing his fingers gingerly across the edge of the blast hole. "Unless Srgent-janovetz has similar explosives aboard his aircraft," he said. "We could test this splinter theory by putting one explosive on each side of a wooden wall and seeing which way the splinters went."

"Might be worth trying," Thrr-mezaz murmured. "Of course, you know what the chances are that he'd admit to having explosives aboard."

"Zero?"

"About that," Thrr-mezaz agreed.

The Human-Conqueror was speaking again as they arrived at the knot of Zhirrzh surrounding him. "It's been too long," Thrr-gilag translated. "Rain and wind have erased the odors he could have used to identify the explosive." He looked at Thrr-mezaz. "Now what?"

"We return him to detention, I suppose," Thrr-mezaz said. "Go ahead and take him back," he added to the warriors.

Thrr-gilag translated the instructions to the prisoner, who nodded and headed off obediently with his escort. Klnn-dawan-a started to follow, stopped at a gesture from Thrr-gilag, and together with Thrr-mezaz and Klnn-vavgi they watched as the warriors and prisoner left the storehouse. "What do you think?" Thrr-gilag asked when the four of them were alone.

"You and Klnn-dawan-a are the alien specialists," Thrr-mezaz countered. "You tell me."

"I think he's telling the truth," Klnn-dawan-a said. "I still don't see what he would gain by lying to us."

"He may be trying to create distrust toward the Mrachanis," Klnn-vavgi suggested. "Maybe that was the whole purpose of the attack."

"If so, it was dangerously subtle," Thrr-gilag pointed out. "We came close to missing it entirely."

"Besides, that just circles us back to the question of how the Human-Conquerors carried out the attack," Klnn-vavgi added. "It all becomes a lot simpler if the Mrachanis staged it themselves."

"Maybe," Thrr-mezaz said, stepping forward and gazing at the splintered edge of the hole. Could the Mrachanis really have faked this attack to try to force the Zhirrzh to take them to Oaccanv?

And if so, what had their motive been? To establish communications and an alliance with the Overclan Prime, as they claimed?

Or to guide Human-Conqueror warships directly to the Zhirrzh homeworld?

"Well, whatever happened, we're not going to figure it out here," he said, turning back to the others. "Let's get back to work. We can talk about this later."

12

With a creak of wooden planks, the small ferry bumped up against the dock and came to a gently bouncing halt. Memory-plastic hawsers whipped out from the hull, catching onto plant-gnawed bollards and wrapping themselves securely around them. From the wheelhouse came a shouted order in a language Lord Cavanagh didn't recognize, and the navigational floodlights winked off, dropping the area back into the relative darkness of the dock's own faded lighting.

"We'll want to wait until all the incoming passengers have gotten off and the cargo's been unloaded," Kolchin said quietly. "Keep an eye out for anything that strikes you as odd."

Cavanagh nodded. "Right."

Twin gangways came down onto the dock with twin thumps, and a handful of figures emerged from the shadows on the deck and started on down, carrybags or backpacks slung over their shoulders. Most were human, but there was a sprinkling of other races as well. All had the weathered but freshly scrubbed look of sap miners returning from a brief visit to the conveniences of civilization, in marked contrast to the generally grimy condition of those waiting on the dock with Cavanagh and Kolchin for their turn to go aboard. From the aft section of the ferry a collapsible crane unlimbered itself and began lifting cargo crates from the fantail onto the end of the dock.

For no particular reason Cavanagh found himself counting the passengers as they lumbered down the gangways. There were twenty-seven of them, roughly the same number as were waiting to go aboard. A fairly standard-size group for a midweek evening run back to Puerto Simone Island, or so Kolchin's discreet questioning had determined. Cavanagh would have preferred a larger crowd for them to hide in, but apparently even on weekends the traffic didn't swell all that much. It took a festival or other special occasion to attract any truly large groups of miners to the island.

An elbow touched his side, and he turned to see Kolchin gazing off to their right. "We've got company," the bodyguard murmured.

Cavanagh followed his gaze. Passing beneath one of the dull overhead walklights, ambling directly toward them, was a broad-shouldered Avuire. "Is that . . . ?"

"Sure is," Kolchin confirmed, waving his hand in an Avuirlian salutation toward the newcomer. "Greetings, Moo Sab Piltariab."

"Greetings to you, Moo Sab Plex," Piltariab said, gesturing back to them. "I thought that was you and Moo Sab Stymer. You are heading to the island this night?"

"Yes," Kolchin said. "You, too?"

"Yes, indeed," Piltariab agreed, coming over and standing beside them. Cavanagh sniffed carefully, but the smell of the ferry's locally grown fuel oil completely overwhelmed the more subtle Avuirlian aromotional cues. "Without you there to hunt fresh prey, Moo Sab Plex, my mining group has run out of proper edibles. It is necessary for me to return to the island to purchase more."

"I'm sorry to hear that," Kolchin said. "Though of course the quality of edibles from the island is superior to anything your group could capture in a hunt."

"More tasteworthy, but also more costful," Piltariab sighed, a burst of lilac and pepper momentarily beating out the fuel oil. "I must agree with you, Moo Sab Plex. But to our venture organizer, cost is what is important. If I may say so, he is most upset with your departure."

"I'm sorry to hear that," Kolchin said. "Though even if we hadn't left the group three days ago, we would have had to do so now. Moo Sab Stymer has hurt his arm, and we need to seek out medical attention."

"Truly?" Piltariab said. "How so?"

"Oh, I just twisted my wrist," Cavanagh improvised, holding up his left arm. "Silly accident; but Moo Sab Plex insists it be taken care of."

"Hmm," Piltariab said, stepping close to Cavanagh for a better look, a musky aroma wafting along with him. "I see nothing."

"It's in the wrist joint, beneath the skin," Cavanagh told him, wincing for effect as he turned the wrist slightly. "Human skin doesn't change texture over internal injuries."

"Oh, of course," Piltariab said, stepping back again. "I hope you will find healing, Moo Sab Stymer."

"I'm sure it'll be fine," Kolchin assured him. "So you'll be selling your sap and buying edibles and then heading back here?"

"Yes," Piltariab said. "But I will also have enough time to show you to Moo Sab Bokamba's home, if you wish."

Cavanagh glanced around them. As near as he could tell, none of the other miners in the area were paying attention to their conversation. "Thank you for the offer," he said to Piltariab. "But we can manage."

"If we even go see him, that is," Kolchin added. "We're really only going across to get Moo Sab Stymer's arm treated."

"Moo Sab Bokamba seemed very interested in seeing you," Piltariab persisted. "I think he would be most disappointed if you did not visit him."

"Really," Kolchin said, sending a leisurely gaze of his own around the dock area. "Did he tell you to tell us that?"

Piltariab recoiled with a gush of burned vanilla. "Of course not, Moo Sab Plex. If he had given me any such message for you, I would truly have told you when we last met. I wish only to offer my services, for the sake of our short acquaintanceship."

Kolchin cocked his head slightly. "Is that the only reason?" he asked pointedly.

"To be fully honest"—Piltariab blushed the odor of freshly cut grass—"I had privately hoped for a fit and proper reason to visit Moo Sab Bokamba again. The aromas in his house were most, most intriguing. There is also an excellent spice market near to Moo Sab Bokamba's home, so I may also make some of my purchases there."

Cavanagh looked at Kolchin, caught the other's microscopic shrug. If the Avuire was lying or up to something devious, Kolchin apparently couldn't smell it in his odor, either. "In that case, Moo Sab Piltariab, we would be delighted to have you show us the way."

"I am truly indebted to you, Moo Sab Plex," Piltariab said, his aroma switching to the overly fermented soy sauce of Avuirlian eagerness. "Come, let us board the ship."

Cavanagh looked at the ferry. The fantail crane had shifted now to bringing aboard the cargo bound for the island, and the outbound passengers were beginning to file aboard. "Yes," he murmured. "Let us."

It took just over thirty minutes to cross the thirteen kilometers of Sereno Strait. Cavanagh had expected Piltariab to stay with him and Kolchin the whole trip, but they were barely away from the dock when the sap miner went forward to join two of his fellow Avuirli standing near the bow. Cavanagh couldn't make out any of their conversation over the rumble of the ferry's engines, but an occasional whiff of smoked fish or peppermint pine drifted back to them on the wind.

The ferry reached the island and found space at the fifty-year-old starburst-shaped docking system built by the original Mexican colonists in their initial burst of optimism for Granparra's future. Cavanagh found his muscles tensing as the gangways slapped down, his eyes darting across the structures and shadows of the docks, which were only marginally better lit than the one they'd just left on the mainland. If Bronski had somehow learned he and Kolchin were here and had laid a trap for them, here was where it would be sprung. Trapped on the ferry, their backs to the sea, there was nowhere to run.

But there were no groups of Peacekeepers waiting in the shadows as they filed off the ferry with the rest of the passengers and headed down the rickety walkways toward the lights and sounds of the island. "Looks like Bokamba didn't turn us in," Kolchin murmured as they reached the faded archway that welcomed all and sundry to Puerto Simone Island.

Cavanagh frowned. "Were you expecting him to?"

"Not really," Kolchin said. "I was only giving him odds of one in three."

"*Only* one in three," Cavanagh echoed, staring at the bodyguard. "And you didn't think this worth mentioning to me?"

"Not with odds that low," Kolchin shook his head. "You'd just have worried. Now, where did Piltariab—oh, there he is."

"Ah—Moo Sab Plex," Piltariab said, hurrying toward them, his two fellow Avuirli close behind. "I feared I had lost track of you. These are two of our fellow sap miners: Moo Sab Mitliriab and Moo Sab Brislimab. They will be accompanying us to Moo Sab Bokamba's home."

"Oh?" Kolchin said, his forehead creasing slightly. "Why?"

"Mu Sab Piltariab tuld us abuut the udurs at Mu Sab Bukamba's hume," Mitliriab said, his voice quiet and measured and with a noticeable Avuirlian accent. "He urged us tu cume smell them urselves."

"And you had nothing better to do?" Kolchin asked.

Mitliriab's eyes flicked to Piltariab, back to Kolchin. A very measured gaze, in Cavanagh's estimation, with a heavy weight of years and life experience behind it. "We were intrigued," he said simply.

"You feel the same way, Moo Sab Brislimab?" Cavanagh put in.

The third Avuire stirred. "I too wish to smell these odors," he said. Like Mitliriab's, his voice, too, carried both age and experience, though not the heavy accent.

But there was something more than just experience in their voices and faces. Something was seriously wrong. . . .

Kolchin had obviously picked up on it, too. "Sir?" he murmured.

Cavanagh took a deep breath, trying to detect and sort out the mixture of Avuirlian odors emanating from the group. Piltariab's were easy: the flashes of peppermint pine added to the fermented soy sauce, a growing edge of impatience melding with his eagerness to be on their way. But the aroma hanging around the other two was a complete mystery to him. In all his years of dealing with Avuirli, he had never smelled aromotional cues like these.

But whatever was going on here, one thing was clear: short of hauling out their flechette pistols, there really wasn't any way to stop the three Avuirli from tagging along with them to Bokamba's house. Even with the flechette guns the point was problematic.

And besides, if he and Kolchin were the target of this unknown Avuirlian emotion, chasing Mitliriab and Brislimab away would be only a temporary solution. "Sure, why not?" he said, beckoning them along. "I'm rather curious to see what these interesting odors are, too. Lead the way, Moo Sab Piltariab."

"It is this way," Piltariab said, heading eagerly forward. His broad shoulders brushed past Cavanagh, trailing soy-sauce aroma in their wake. Either he had completely missed his own companions' aromotional cues, or else he was just as completely ignoring them. Offhand, Cavanagh wasn't sure which possibility bothered him more.

Considering the lateness of the hour, Puerto Simone's streets were still surprisingly crowded with pedestrians. The large NorCoord cities Cavanagh was familiar with were similarly active, of course, but in those places most of the traffic was vehicular, with the majority of pedestrians merely making the short trek from mart or restaurant to their parked ground- or aircars. Perhaps in the island's more tightly knit community and culture, nighttime crime wasn't as big a problem as it was on some of the Commonwealth's more advanced worlds.

Or perhaps the island's narrow streets simply discouraged groundcar traffic. The Parra vine, of course, discouraged anything else.

The Parra. Cavanagh looked up as they walked along, peering past the lights at the dark branches of the thick vine lattice arching over the city only meters above the taller buildings around them. Centuries earlier in the leisurely herbaceous war going on all over Granparra, the Parra vine had won the battle for Puerto Simone Island, choking out the other, more deadly forms of plant life that still held sway on the continent across Sereno Strait. That victory had made the island livable for human beings; but at the same time the Parra's dominating presence had presented challenges all its own. The lattice was home to thousands of monkey-sized grooma, living in an only partially understood symbiosis with the vine, who swarmed to screaming attack against anyone who attempted to cut or sometimes even just move a section of the Parra. Livestock who chewed on the vine got the same treatment, a problem that was aggravated by the groomas' unexplained fondness for investigating, playing with, and ultimately wrecking the fences the herd keepers used to keep their livestock away from the Parra.

And hanging over it all was the dark, unpleasant question of whether the Parra was in fact sentient. Whether it was listening or watching everything these upstart humans were doing on its island. And if so, what it was thinking.

The group had walked for perhaps fifteen minutes when they finally reached Piltariab's landmark. "There," he said, waving a hand and soy-sauce aroma toward a cross street fifty meters ahead of them. "There— just past the spice market. To the right, down at the end of that street, is Moo Sab Bokamba's home."

"Great," Kolchin said. "I hope he's in tonight." He brushed up against Cavanagh; and out of sight of the three Avuirli, he caught the older man's wrist and gave it a brief but sharp squeeze.

Cavanagh caught the cue. "Ow!" he grunted, lifting his supposedly injured left wrist.

"What is it, Moo Sab Stymer?" Piltariab asked, stepping close to Cavanagh, a rush of baking-oat-bread concern momentarily supplanting the soy sauce. "Is your injury worse?"

"I brushed it against that vegetable stand," Cavanagh said, wincing for effect as he cradled his left wrist protectively with his right hand. "I'll be all right."

"I'd better take a look," Kolchin said, shrugging his backpack off as he eased Cavanagh to the side of the street. "This will only take a minute, Moo Sab Piltariab," he added, opening the pack and rummaging through it. "Why don't you and your friends go on ahead, make sure Moo Sab Bokamba is home and willing to see us? We'll be right with you."

"There is nu need fur haste," Mitliriab said. "We can wait fur yu tu finish with him."

"No, no, let us not wait," Piltariab said, his solicitude lost again to his eagerness. "They will be all right. Come—Moo Sab Bokamba's home is close at hand. Come."

Mitliriab and Brislimab exchanged glances, and again Cavanagh caught a whiff of that unidentified aromotional scent. "As yu insist," Mitliriab said, looking at Kolchin. "Yu will catch up with us, Mu Sab Plex."

"Of course," Kolchin assured him.

For a handful of heartbeats the Avuire stared at him. Then, without further comment, he turned away. With Piltariab at the lead the three Avuirli rejoined the pedestrian flow and continued down the street.

"That sounded like an order," Cavanagh muttered as Kolchin pulled their medkit from the backpack.

"It certainly wasn't a question," Kolchin agreed, pretending to treat Cavanagh's wrist. "There's something about all this that Mitliriab and Brislimab are definitely not happy with."

Cavanagh chewed the inside of his cheek. "You think it has something to do with us?"

"I don't think so," Kolchin said slowly. "At least not directly. Annoyed Avuirli usually aren't very subtle—if they were mad at us, we'd have heard about it by now."

Cavanagh shivered. As a species, Avuirli were pretty even-tempered; but all sentient creatures could get angry, and Avuirli had the muscle power to make anger a distinctly unpleasant experience for everyone in the vicinity. "Something about Piltariab, then?"

"That's getting closer," Kolchin said, returning the medkit to the backpack and pulling out the binoculars. "But that's not quite it, either," he added, handing the binoculars to Cavanagh and sealing the backpack again. "Let me know when they've turned into that side street."

"Right." Cavanagh peered over his shoulder as he looped the binoculars' strap around his neck. "They're going in now."

"Good." Kolchin slung the backpack up onto one shoulder. "Let's go."

They hurried ahead, ducking around and between unhurried shoppers to the side street Piltariab had indicated. Instead of turning right, though, Kolchin led them to the left, into the street branching off in the opposite direction. Unlike the right-hand branch, which Cavanagh could see now was narrow but basically residential, this side seemed to be a cross between an alley and a garbage-storage facility. A half-dozen highly aromatic chest-high garbage bins lined each side at this end, with random bits of broken boxes and decaying refuse scattered around. Like most of the streets they'd been on since leaving the docks, the alley's surface consisted of closely fitted flagstones; unlike those other streets, no one here had seen fit to put much effort into maintenance. "What now?" he asked as Kolchin positioned them on opposite sides of the alley, behind the last of the garbage bins.

"We see what kind of reception the Avuirli get," Kolchin said. With his left hand he lowered his backpack to the ground; with his right he drew his flechette pistol from beneath his jacket and clicked off the safety. "We also see how good your memory for faces is."

Cavanagh grimaced as he turned on the binoculars and held them up to his eyes. He'd met Bokamba only once, back at the Parliament's Copperhead hearings. Whether he could recognize the man now, several years later, was going to be problematic.

The three Avuirli were about three quarters of the way down the street, approaching the house at the end. "They're almost there," he told Kolchin, adjusting the light-amplification contrast slightly. "Piltariab must really be anxious to get there—he's practically running."

"Interesting," Kolchin said thoughtfully. "I can't remember ever seeing an Avuire run before."

Cavanagh frowned, searching his memory. Now that Kolchin mentioned it, he couldn't either. Avuirli were built for strength, not speed. "You're right," he agreed, an odd feeling starting to twist through his stomach. "What could Bokamba have said to him to spark that much enthusiasm in coming back?"

Kolchin never had a chance to answer. At that moment, from behind them in the alleyway, came a quiet voice, barely audible over the noise from the nearby shops. "Hold it steady, both of you. Kolchin, lose the gun."

Cavanagh turned his face away from the binoculars and looked sideways across the alley at Kolchin. The young bodyguard hadn't moved, nor had his expression changed. But the tendons of his gun hand were suddenly pressing visibly through the skin. Preparing for violent action . . . "No," Cavanagh murmured urgently. "Not now. Not here."

For a long moment he thought Kolchin was going to try it anyway. Then, to his relief, the other let out a long, strangled-sounding breath and lowered his hand from the garbage bin, letting the flechette pistol drop to the ground. Lifting his hands shoulder high, he turned slowly around. Swallowing hard, Cavanagh did the same.

Brigadier Petr Bronski was standing alone three meters away in the middle of the alley, holding a small flechette pistol in a no-nonsense marksman's grip. The gun, and his full attention, were fixed on Kolchin. "Smart lad," Bronski said approvingly. "You know the rest of the routine: hands on top of your head, fingers laced together. You too, Cavanagh."

"So it was a trap, after all," Kolchin said as he and Cavanagh complied.

"No, it was just me playing a hunch," Bronski said. "Nice to know I've still got it. Just kick the gun over this way."

"What kind of hunch were you playing?" Cavanagh asked as Kolchin complied, sending his flechette pistol clattering across the uneven flagstones toward Bronski.

"That you'd gone to ground on Granparra," Bronski said, taking a step forward and stooping down to pick up the gun. A loose paving stone rocked under his feet as he straightened up again. "I was able to locate and pull a copy of the message the Klyveress ci Yyatoor sent to your son Aric on Edo."

Cavanagh frowned. "She sent Aric a message? What was in it?"

"She wanted him to collect some electronics modules and bring them to her on Phormbi." Reaching under his jacket at the small of his back, Bronski produced a set of wristcuffs and tossed them onto the ground at Cavanagh's feet. "Put them on Kolchin," he instructed. "Hands behind his back, of course."

"I don't understand what a message from Klyveress has to do with anything," Cavanagh said, his mind racing as he picked up the wristcuffs and crossed the alley to Kolchin. No backup had yet appeared—could Bronski really have come there alone? If so, they might still have a chance of getting away.

But only up to the point where Kolchin's hands were cuffed. After that their chances dropped nearly to zero. Somehow Cavanagh had to find a way to stall the completion of that order.

Or find a way to fake it.

"Like I said, it was a hunch," Bronski said. "We had an alert out all over the Commonwealth watching for the Mrach fighter you stole on Mra-mig. When it didn't turn up anywhere, I figured you must have talked the ci Yyatoor into trading ships with you, which meant you were going to owe her something."

"That's it exactly," Cavanagh acknowledged, pausing beside Kolchin and looking at Bronski. "She insisted I send her some command/switching modules in exchange for the ship she gave me. How did you know?"

"With Yycromae there's always a quid pro quo." Bronski waved his gun slightly toward Kolchin. "Come on, get those cuffs on."

"Only I haven't been able to send them," Cavanagh said, stepping around behind Kolchin and fastening one ring of the wristcuffs onto his left wrist. Standing behind Kolchin this way, he was partially out of Bronski's sight . . . and unbeknownst to the brigadier, he still had Kolchin's backup flechette pistol hidden beneath his jacket. Should he try to ease it out and slip it into Kolchin's belt, where he could get to it with his cuffed hands?

But even if he was able to do all that without Bronski's catching him at it, what then? Could Kolchin get the drop on Bronski and persuade him to surrender? Because if not, the only other option at that point would be to shoot him, and there was no way Cavanagh could justify shooting a Peacekeeper officer who was only doing his job. "We've been here since leaving Phormbi," he added, hoping to keep Bronski talking as he pulled Kolchin's hands down behind his back.

"Which is why she sent that message to your son," Bronski said. "If you'd sent the modules like she wanted, she wouldn't have needed to do that. To me that said you'd gone to ground someplace where you couldn't get to a CavTronics supply house." He shrugged. "Granparra seemed the most likely spot."

"Especially when you found out that Quinn and Aric had been in touch with Wing Commander Bokamba," Cavanagh nodded, positioning the second wristcuff ring around Kolchin's right wrist and trying desperately to figure out how to make it look secure without actually locking it in place. But he couldn't see anywhere else for the locking hook to go. "How long ago did you and he set up this little charade?"

"What charade is that?"

Cavanagh paused, frowning over Kolchin's shoulder at Bronski. The brigadier was eyeing him, apparently in genuine puzzlement. "You know what charade. We had Piltariab take a message to Bokamba three days ago. He sent back a note that we should stay off the island at least two more days."

Bronski's eyes flicked past Cavanagh's shoulder. "Bokamba's not here, Cavanagh," he said. "He was called up to the reserves nearly a month ago."

Something cold shivered along Cavanagh's spine. "But Piltariab said—"

And abruptly all the pieces suddenly fell together in his mind. A trap, all right, but not one orchestrated by Bronski. A fake Bokamba had been set up as a lure, set up by someone who had manipulated Piltariab so well that the Avuire had been impatiently eager to bring him and Kolchin to see him. So eager, in fact, that he'd gone out of his way to persuade two others of his species to join them.

And there was only one group of beings who, expecting humans to walk into their trap, would also have known how to mesmerize a simple Avuirlian sap miner so thoroughly. The same group of beings who, now that Cavanagh knew about their subtle war against humanity, might have felt it worth this much effort to have him silenced.

The Mrachanis.

Cavanagh took a deep breath. "Brigadier—"

And suddenly, from directly behind him, came a blood-chilling roar.

Cavanagh dropped the loose end of the wristcuffs and spun around. Standing beyond the garbage bins at the near end of the alley was the squat, meter-wide figure of a Bhurt, his arms spread wide in challenge. One of the same Bhurtala, if Cavanagh remembered the facial stripe pattern correctly, who had threatened Bronski in the Mrapiratta Hotel back on Mra-mig.

The Bhurt roared again, a vicious and probably insulting taunt in his own language. Then, moving with the deliberate slowness of a bully who knows he has the physical edge on his opponents, he started toward them.

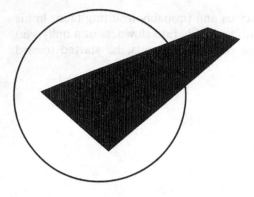

13

"Out of the way!" Bronski snapped. "Cavanagh—!"

Cavanagh needed no encouragement. He threw himself back across the alley, slamming his shoulder against the brick wall with jarring force. Rolling to put his back to the wall, splaying both hands to the sides for stability, he risked a quick look back at Bronski.

The brigadier's left hand had snaked under his jacket, emerging with a new flechette-gun clip. Cavanagh caught a glimpse of bright-red cartridges, started to turn back to the approaching Bhurt—

And jerked his head back again as a movement caught the corner of his eye. At the far end of the alley a shadowy figure had appeared, its black garb silhouetted against the only marginally lighter gloom of the alley, moving swiftly toward Bronski's back, the sounds of its footsteps masked by the roars of the first Bhurt and the shouts and shrieks of scattering pedestrians.

And with a stab of horror Cavanagh understood. The first Bhurt—the one moving slowly and brazenly toward them—was merely a feint. The second one was the real attack.

And with his back to the oncoming threat, his gun and attention pointed the wrong direction, Bronski was about to die.

"Look out!" Cavanagh shouted to him, clawing frantically beneath his jacket for the flechette pistol hidden there.

Frantically, but uselessly. His shout had caught Bronski's attention, and on the brigadier's face he could see the sudden realization there was danger behind him. But even as he started to spin around, Cavanagh knew it was too late. The Bhurt was coming down the alley like a charging rhino, and there was no possible way Bronski was going to be able to complete his turn and get a stopping shot off before the alien trampled him into the broken flagstones of the alley. At the very edge of his vision Cavanagh saw Kolchin throw up his arms as if in panic and then double over at the waist. Vaguely seen, mostly imagined, something seemed to flicker through the air past Bronski's ear—

And suddenly the hilt and three quarters of Kolchin's big split-blade knife appeared, protruding from the Bhurt's upper left leg.

The alien bellowed, his torso jerking to the left, the rhythm of his running thrown violently off by the blow. He got two more steps, arms flailing like windmill blades as he fought to regain his balance. But the impact of the knife, plus the uneven footing, proved too much for him. An instant later, with a crash that shook the whole alley, he slammed full-length onto the ground. Bellowing again, he shoved himself halfway up from his prone position, got his feet under him—

And then Bronski's flechette pistol barked, and the alien's upper right torso exploded in a brilliant blaze of flame.

The alien convulsed, his angry bellow abruptly turning to a scream of rage as he struggled up into a crouch. Bronski fired again and again, the Bhurt seeming to dissolve into multiple bursts of flame and smoke and blood. But the defiant screams continued, and through the smoke Cavanagh could see him still struggling mindlessly to get the rest of the way to his feet and kill the humans who were doing this to him. If Bronski's gun ran out of explosive cartridges, he might still make it.

And then, to Cavanagh's shock, an echoing scream came from behind him.

Somehow, in the eternity of the past few seconds, he'd forgotten about the other Bhurt.

He twisted around. The first alien, the failure of their clever little subterfuge having finally penetrated its thick skull, had abandoned the effort at subtlety and was lurching to the attack.

"Bronski!" Kolchin called.

The brigadier didn't even turn around. Still blasting away at the second Bhurt, he snapped his free hand up underneath his extended right arm, tossing Kolchin's flechette pistol toward him. Kolchin caught the weapon and twisted around, the gun blazing into action almost before it was fully settled into his hand.

But it was an effort Cavanagh knew was doomed to failure. Even with the assistance of the running Bhurt's forward momentum, Kolchin's thrown knife had barely managed to penetrate the alien's thick hide. Standard flechette loads would do no better, and that was all Kolchin's gun was loaded with.

The Bhurt knew it, too, or else was too infuriated to care. Crossing his massive arms in front of his face, making no effort to evade the steel darts collecting on his arms and torso, he kept coming.

"Cavanagh!" Bronski shouted.

Cavanagh turned back, dimly noticing the fact that the rapid-fire explosions had ceased. Bronski was beckoning sharply toward him, the second Bhurt a gory mess, finally unmoving, at his feet. "This way," the brigadier shouted. "Move it!"

Cavanagh pushed off the wall and ran toward him. "Kolchin, come on."

"Go with Bronski," Kolchin ordered, still firing his useless darts at the approaching Bhurt. "Move, damn it."

There was no time to argue. Cavanagh reached Bronski's side; and then the brigadier had a grip on his arm and was pulling him down the alley. "Where are we going?"

"Away from here," Bronski said. There was a crash behind them—"Don't look," the brigadier ordered.

"But Kolchin—" Cavanagh said, resisting Bronski's grip as he tried to turn around.

"I said don't look," Bronski snapped, jerking his arm hard enough to hurt. "You just concentrate on your running and hope whoever set this up didn't put in any backstops."

Apparently, they hadn't. Cavanagh and Bronski reached the end of the alley without incident, emerging into a brightly lit but strangely deserted market street. "You can always tell a backwater culture," Bronski said, tugging Cavanagh sharply to the left. "They don't stand around gawking at trouble—they get out of sight and stay there. This way."

Halfway down the block they reached a narrow stairway on their left, wedged between two shop fronts. "All the way to the top," Bronski told him, pushing him into the shadowed entryway and pausing to pull a fresh flechette clip from beneath his jacket. "Go on, I'll catch up."

Breathing hard, leg muscles starting to burn with the exertion, Cavanagh headed up. The stairway was uncomfortably dark, its gloom relieved only by a dim light plate at each floor's landing. He had passed the second floor and was on his way to the third when he heard Bronski start up the stairs; had just made it to the fourth and top floor when the brigadier caught up with him. "What now?" Cavanagh asked, gasping for breath.

"We wait," Bronski said. He was breathing a little hard, too. "There's an empty apartment up here I can get us into—I moved in yesterday to see if you'd show up at Bokamba's place. But we need to know first if they saw us come in here."

"They?" Cavanagh repeated, frowning. "I thought you killed one."

"I did," Bronski said grimly. "It turns out there were two others waiting in the wings. Luckily not at the end we left by—they were probably ready with a pincer movement near Bokamba's place. I saw the three of them come charging out of the alley just before I headed up here."

Cavanagh braced himself. "What about Kolchin?"

Bronski looked away. "I don't know," he said quietly. "I didn't see him."

The dim light of the landing seemed to become a little darker. "I understand," he said quietly.

"Don't go jumping to any conclusions," Bronski warned, his voice oddly gruff. "He could have made it out of the alley just behind us and been out of sight the other direction before we were able to turn around and look. He was a Peacekeeper commando once, and you never count a Peacekeeper commando out until you've retrieved a body."

Cavanagh nodded, trying hard to believe him. Kolchin deserved far more than just a brief, passing thought, but there was no time right now for anything else. No time to mourn him properly. "Shouldn't you be calling someone for help?"

"Like who?"

"Like the police, maybe? Keeping the peace is what they're here for, isn't it?"

Bronski snorted under his breath. "Not when it involves NorCoord citizens getting beat on by aliens. Not on Granparra, anyway. As long as they don't see their own people or property as being in danger, they'll probably stay out of it. Probably be cheering for the Bhurtala."

An unpleasant chill ran up Cavanagh's back. He'd long ago accepted the fact that putting up with a certain amount of resentment toward NorCoord was one of the factors involved in doing business around the Commonwealth. Apparently, the feelings were running a lot deeper than mere resentment. "What about the Myrmidon Weapons Platform, then? They ought to have the necessary firepower to deal with a group of Bhurtala."

"Sure they do," Bronski said. "Problem is that with the Parra vine blocking a straight-line drop, it'd take them a minimum of an hour to get here. Too late to do us any good." He gestured with the barrel of his pistol toward Cavanagh's jacket. "I don't suppose you happen to have any explosive rounds in that gun of yours."

Cavanagh had completely forgotten about his flechette pistol. "No," he said, feeling a guilty ache as he pulled it out. Everything had happened so quickly down there in the alley, but he should at least have been able to get a couple of shots off at the Bhurtala. It probably wouldn't have made any difference; but then again, it might. He would never know now. "I only have standard-load flechettes. Kolchin used up all his explosive rounds back on the mainland."

"Figured as much," Bronski grunted. "Let's hope they didn't see us—"

He broke off, his hand raised suddenly for silence. Cavanagh froze, listening.

They could hear the sound of heavy, clumping footsteps echoing up through the stairway. The footsteps stopped; then, abruptly, came the splintering crash of a breaking door. Someone screamed, someone else shouted, the verbal uproar mixing in with the sounds of running feet and more of the clumping footsteps. The footsteps came to a halt, and there was a second crash.

Bronski swore. "So much for that hope," he muttered. "They're checking all the apartments. Means they know we're here."

Cavanagh felt his stomach tighten. Trapped here on the top floor. Might as well have been gift wrapped. "What do we do?"

Bronski nodded toward the corner of the landing and a rusty ladder leading to an equally rusty ceiling trapdoor. "We keep going."

It was obvious at first glance that the trapdoor hadn't been opened in years; equally obvious that it wasn't going to be opened now without creating considerable noise in the process. But Bronski was ahead of the problem, waiting until the Bhurtala two floors below were in the process of breaking down the next door before forcing the trap up against its protesting hinges. A minute later both men were on the roof.

"Now what?" Cavanagh asked, shivering in the cool night air as he looked around them. The entire block of buildings had been constructed under a single roof, and aside from a couple dozen vent pipes poking up like defoliated shrubs, the rooftop stretched flat and open. No cover, no place to hide, and on all sides a sheer four-story drop to the streets below.

"We find another stairway and get the hell out of here," Bronski said, peering across the roof. "Looks like another trapdoor over there." He started off in that direction—

And suddenly, from behind them, came the high-pitched screech of tearing metal.

Cavanagh spun around. The trapdoor they'd just come through had vanished, along with about half the metal framing that had attached it to the tarred-wood roofing material. Even as he watched, a huge Bhurtist hand came up through the opening and began ripping away at the rest of the framing.

"Damn!" Bronski bit out, jamming his gun back under his jacket. "Come on."

He headed off, but not in the direction of the trapdoor he'd pointed out. "What about the other stairs?" Cavanagh called, running after him. "We'll never get it open in time," Bronski called back over his shoulder.

Cavanagh frowned. Near as he could tell, they were headed at a dead run straight toward one edge of the roof. "So what are we doing?"

"This," Bronski said. Still running, he dropped into a half crouch and jumped—

And caught hold of a tendril loop that hung a meter down from the main mesh of the Parra vine spanning the sky overhead.

"Don't just stand there," the brigadier grunted, hauling himself up with some effort onto the tendril. "Come on."

Grimacing, Cavanagh backed up a few steps, eyeing the vertical distance dubiously. But a quick survey showed that this was the only tendril over their roof that came even marginally within reach. If the alternative was to wait here for the Bhurtala . . . Taking a deep breath, he ran forward and jumped.

He made it, just barely, getting his left hand and about half of his right on the tendril. "Use your momentum," Bronski instructed, catching his right wrist and pulling the hand into a more secure grip. "Swing your legs, arch your back, and pull. Come on, you must have seen gymnasts do this a hundred times."

"I'm not a gymnast," Cavanagh gritted, swinging his legs as instructed and trying to remember exactly how the professionals did this. It always looked so smooth and quick and graceful that he'd never really noticed the technique.

"No, you're going to be lunch," Bronski shot back. "Come *on.*"

Swallowing a curse, Cavanagh swung his knees up, arching his back and tugging with his arms—

And suddenly he was there, teetering precariously on his chest on top of the vine, pumping his legs hard to try to maintain his balance. Bronski caught him under the right armpit and hauled, and a few seconds later he was up. "About time," the brigadier grunted. "Here they come."

Cavanagh looked behind him. The entire metal framing of the trapdoor was gone, along with sizable chunks of the wood around it, and one of the Bhurtala was fighting to squeeze his massive shoulders through the freshly enlarged opening. "Can we get rid of this tendril somehow?" he asked as he and Bronski pulled themselves up onto the main Parra mesh.

"Take too long to cut it," Bronski said, pulling out his flechette pistol and aiming at the tendril. "Let's try this instead."

He fired three times. But the steel darts merely embedded themselves in the vine's tough outer surface without cutting it. "That should do it,"

Bronski said, putting the gun away again and carefully pulling himself to his feet. "Let's go."

Cavanagh followed suit, wondering what all that had been about. Was Bronski hoping the embedded darts would cut into the hands of the Bhurtala when they tried to grab hold of it? "Where to?" he asked.

"Let's start by getting away from here," Bronski said. "After that we'll figure out how to get down."

They set off. From the ground the tendrils of the Parra vine's intertwined mesh looked fairly thin, even delicate. In fact they were reasonably thick and not delicate at all, most of them measuring a good six to ten centimeters in diameter, with the main supports twice that thick. Slightly flattened on top, they were quite adequate for a human being to walk along. And on a clear, sunny day, at ground level, Cavanagh wouldn't have thought twice about doing so.

At night, five stories above the streets of Puerto Simone Island, it was terrifying.

And they hadn't even gotten yet to where they were five stories over the streets.

"Don't look down," Bronski kept saying as Cavanagh inched with painstaking care along the mesh. "Stick to the main support vines—they're thicker, and they have those outrigger branches coming off the sides you can use if you start losing your balance. And *don't look down.*"

It was stupid advice. Cavanagh *had* to look down if he wanted to see where he was going. Too tense even to swear, he kept going, fixing his eyes on the vine and trying hard to keep the rooftop below in hazy unfocus where he could almost forget how far down it was.

They were nearly to the edge of the roof, with the deep chasm of the street gaping ahead and below, when a triumphant roar came from behind them.

"Keep moving," Bronski ordered, pausing and turning carefully around to look.

"They're on the roof?" Cavanagh demanded, too shaky to risk his balance by turning himself.

"The first one is," Bronski said grimly, pulling out his flechette pistol. "Here he comes toward the tendril." The brigadier looked around them— "Hold it, Cavanagh—sit down right where you are. Sit down *now.*"

There was an urgency in his voice that demanded instant obedience. Carefully, Cavanagh lowered himself into a squat; then, clenching his teeth, he let his legs slip off both sides of the vine, dropping down to land on his rear and stiffly outstretched hands. The jolt of the landing ran straight up his spine as his hands scrabbled for handholds on the short outrigger branches—

And without warning he was suddenly enveloped by a screaming swarm of small brown grooma.

"Bronski!" he shouted, ducking his head to his chest as the grooma darted across and past him, their claws tearing through his jacket into his arms and shoulders. One of the creatures slammed with exquisite pain into his right biceps, all but paralyzing that arm. Cavanagh squeezed his legs tightly around the vine, locking his ankles beneath it, hoping desperately he wouldn't roll over and wind up hanging upside down.

And then, as suddenly as they had appeared, the creatures were gone. "What in the name of—?"

"I'll be damned," Bronski said. "It worked."

Frowning, Cavanagh turned his head. The herd of grooma had gathered on the vine mesh directly above where all three Bhurtala were now standing, screaming and clawing viciously at the lead Bhurt as he struggled against their attacks to pull himself up by the hanging vine loop.

The hanging vine loop that Bronski had fired three flechettes into, cutting into the Parra vine with sharp-edged metal, and sparking precisely this reaction from the vine and its grooma symbionts. "That's not going to hold them for long," Cavanagh said.

"I know," Bronski said, already clambering carefully back to his feet. "Maybe it'll be long enough."

Grimacing, Cavanagh eased one leg up—

And dropped abruptly back into a sitting position as something tore through the outrigger branches and went whizzing past his ear.

"Watch it!" Bronski snapped, flailing his arms for balance. "Stay down!"

Cavanagh dropped his torso to the vine, wrapping his arms around it and looking back. The two Bhurtala still on the roof, not content to wait for their climbing partner to clear away the enraged grooma, were running across the rooftop toward the two humans, jagged pieces of something clutched in their huge hands. Even as Cavanagh watched, one of them hurled one of the pieces upward.

This one came closer, ricocheting off the vine just behind where Cavanagh was sitting. "They're trying to knock us off," Bronski snarled. "Using pieces from the trapdoor."

"What do we do?"

"You just hang on." Dropping into a crouch on the vine, Bronski swung his flechette pistol around and began firing.

For all the effect, he might as well have been throwing snowballs. The jagged missiles kept coming, swishing through the leaves or bouncing painfully off his legs or arms. One piece caught Bronski square on the chest, and he flailed madly for a heart-stopping minute before he managed to regain his balance.

And then, as abruptly as it had started, the barrage was over. Cautiously, Cavanagh leaned his head around the vine he was clinging to and looked down.

One of the Bhurtala was loping back toward the ruined stairway entrance. The second was crouched down below them, digging with his hands at the edge of the roof.

"He's ripping out pieces of wood," Bronski said quietly. "Getting more stuff to throw at us."

And even if he didn't succeed, the Bhurt heading back to the stairway was bound to find more ammunition. And then the two of them would resume the aerial attack, keeping the two humans pinned down until their friend hanging from the vine cleared away the grooma and climbed up.

At which point he and Bronski would be dead.

Cavanagh swallowed, his mouth chalk dry, his pulse racing painfully in his throat. The aliens' scenario was vacuum clear, as inevitable and unstoppable as an incoming tide. And it left them with exactly one option. "Then we have to go right now," he said to Bronski, his voice shaking with dread. "And we have to run."

"I know," Bronski said. Had probably known, in fact, long before Cavanagh had. "You think you're up to it?"

From beneath them came the sudden crack of breaking wood. "Do I have a choice?" Cavanagh snarled back, unlocking his ankles from around the vine and shoving himself to his feet again. "Come on."

He set off along the vine, his careful jogging pace quickly and inexplicably accelerating into a flat-out run as adrenaline or fatigued recklessness or sheer hubris flooded into him. Time seemed to slow to a crawl, his vision tunneling in to block out everything except the vine ahead, the strange madness ruthlessly crowding out any attempt by his rational mind to pause and think any of this through. Beneath his feet the rooftop dropped abruptly away to the lights and insectlike scurrying of pedestrians in the street below; behind him the sudden howling of their pursuers was grimly satisfying proof that they'd been caught off guard. A fresh pair of wooden chunks went spinning past, too late and far too wide of the mark. Cavanagh kept running, dimly noticing that his cheeks were hurting—

"Hold it," a panting voice called. "Cavanagh—hold it."

Cavanagh jerked, coming suddenly aware again of Bronski running beside him. Suddenly aware, too, that the ache in his cheeks was due to a wide, almost feral grin laminated across his face. "What?"

"I said stop, damn it," Bronski growled, coming to a teetering halt and jabbing a finger downward. "Look—we're here."

Cavanagh frowned, looking down. The street he'd last noticed himself running over was gone. In its place, barely two meters beneath his feet, was another roof. "Oh."

"Oh?" Bronski puffed, easing into a crouch and sitting down on the vine. "Is that all you can say, oh? I yelled for you to stop a whole building ago."

"You what?" Cavanagh blinked, sitting down on the vine and looking behind them. The brigadier was right: the rooftop directly behind them— a small roof, just beyond a narrow, dark alleyway—was indeed not the one they'd left from. That particular roof was one building farther back. "I'll be damned."

"I thought for a minute you were going to run all the way to the spaceport," Bronski grunted. Getting a grip on one of the tendrils, he slid off the vine, hanging for a second before dropping the rest of the way. "Damnedest switchover I ever saw. I didn't know you Brits did this ber-serker rage thing."

"Must be the Scandinavian blood in the family line," Cavanagh said, still not believing it as he followed the brigadier down onto the roof. "I don't think that's ever happened to me before."

"Well, don't lose the cutting edge just yet," Bronski warned, working at the edge of a shiny square in the roof with a folding knife. "In case you hadn't noticed, the Bhurtala aren't just sitting there waiting for us to come back."

Cavanagh looked around again. The grooma were still gathered around the damaged tendril, their chattering clearly audible over the city noise coming from below. But the Bhurtala themselves were nowhere in sight. "They must have gone back down to street level."

"Brilliant deduction, Holmes." There was a soft click, and Bronski pulled up the trapdoor. "If we're lucky, maybe they left before they saw which building we wound up on. Let's go."

No one was waiting for them as they emerged from the stairway onto a deserted side street. "Any idea where we are?" Cavanagh asked, looking around. Two blocks ahead he could see one of the more brightly lit major arteries, though even at their distance it was clear that the earlier crush of pedestrian traffic still hadn't resumed.

"Bokamba's place is about a block that way, I think," Bronski said, pointing in a direction roughly parallel to the main street. "The Puerto

Simone street system is an inhumane joke, but I think if we go this way, we'll hit a tram line that'll get us to the spaceport."

"I hope it's not far," Cavanagh said, rubbing his sleeve at the sticky sweat around his neck. His berserker rage, as Bronski called it, had worn off on the walk down the stairway, leaving him a throbbing collection of sore joints, exhausted muscles, and aching bruises where the grooma and the Bhurtala's wooden missiles had struck him. "I don't think I could walk more than another—"

And from behind them came an all-too-familiar roar.

Cavanagh spun around. A block away, in the gloom of the side street, stood the dark figure of a Bhurt, its arms raised in triumph. It howled again, this time in a call of summons.

"Come on," Bronski snapped, slapping Cavanagh's shoulder for emphasis and taking off in the opposite direction.

"We can't outrun them," Cavanagh protested as he broke into a sprint, his aches and exhaustion pushed to the background by a fresh surge of adrenaline.

"You're welcome to surrender," Bronski shot back.

Cavanagh bit off a curse, glancing back over his shoulder. The Bhurt's summons had been answered: all three of the aliens were visible now, running side by side, their short, thick legs pumping rhythmically against the paving stones. In a straight run Bhurtist strength and stamina would eventually win out over almost any human opponent. The recommended counterstrategy, Cavanagh remembered reading, was to use the aliens' greater mass and inertia against them, changing direction as often as possible to limit the pursuers' ability to build up speed. In the middle of a city, though, with changes of direction defined by the layout of the streets, that wasn't going to be easy to do. Cavanagh glanced over his shoulder again—

His pounding heart seemed to freeze. Behind the three Bhurtala, moving silently and without lights, the shadowy shape of a groundcar had joined in the chase. This time, clearly, the Mrachanis were going to make sure their quarry didn't slip through their client aliens' fingers. "Bronski —look—"

He never finished the warning. His toe caught the edge of a loose paving stone, and the ground rushed up and slammed hard into his chest and outstretched hands.

For a handful of heartbeats he lay there, his head spinning, his whole body seemingly paralyzed as his lungs struggled to retrieve the air that the impact had knocked out of him. With a supreme effort he pushed up with one arm, half turning over. The Bhurtala were still there, still coming—

And then Bronski was beside him, his hands grabbing under Cavanagh's armpits. "Get up," the brigadier panted, hauling him halfway to his feet. "Get up, damn it."

But there's no reason to, Cavanagh tried to say. *There's no hope.* But his throat was as paralyzed as the rest of him. He tried to raise an arm, to point at the oncoming Bhurtala and the groundcar pacing along behind them. But the arm, too, was paralyzed, and dropped to his side with the warning undelivered. The aliens were less than half a block away, legs pumping harder as they closed in for the kill. . . .

And suddenly, with a squeal of tires, the groundcar leaped forward, its lights blazing to life. The charging Bhurtala faltered, their silhouettes turning to look behind them—

And with a horrendous crash the vehicle slammed into the three aliens, scattering them like broken dolls through the air to land with sickening thuds on the paving stones. They skidded or rolled across the ground for another second, then lay still.

"See?" Bronski murmured as the groundcar coasted to a stop in front of them. "I told you not to count him out."

The vehicle's lights flicked off, and the driver leaned his head out the side window. "You all right, sir?"

Cavanagh smiled tightly. "I'm fine, Kolchin," he croaked, wobbling toward the groundcar. His muscles and joints still ached, and his chest now felt as if it were a single massive bruise. But suddenly none of it mattered. "I'm just fine."

Piltariab was waiting for them just inside the door to Bokamba's house. "Ah—Moo Sab Plex," he said to Kolchin, a puff of chlorinated coffee mingling with the scent of burned bread. "I'm highly relieved to see you back."

"I told you I'd have no trouble," Kolchin said as the Avuire stood to the side to let the three humans in. "But thank you for your concern. Have our guests behaved themselves?"

"They have created nu further truble," Mitliriab said darkly from an open doorway at the end of the entrance hall. Cavanagh sniffed, caught the same unidentified odor that he'd noticed on their earlier walk from the docks. "Is this the human yu spuke uf, Mu Sab Plex?"

"Yes," Kolchin said, touching Bronski's shoulder. "This is Assistant Commonwealth Liaison Petr Bronski."

Mitliriab's gaze shifted to Bronski. "I salute yu, Liaisun Brunski," he said. "I have a crime tu repurt tu the Human Cummunwealth. Wuld yu cume inside."

He stepped out of the doorway. Silently, Bronski led the way into the room.

It was a conversation room, small but neatly furnished. To the right of the doorway, lying unconscious amid a scattered agglomeration of kindling that had probably once been a side table, was another Bhurt. In the center of the room stood the third Avuire, Brislimab, exuding the same unidentified aroma as Mitliriab.

Sitting on the floor at his feet, huddling like a frightened hamster beneath the Avuire's glare, was a Mrachani.

"Well, well," Bronski said conversationally. "What have we here?"

"It is a Mrachani," Mitliriab said. "As a representative uf the Human Cummunwealth, I hereby infurm yu uf his use uf diargulates against the Avuire citizen Piltariab."

"What are diargulates?" Cavanagh murmured.

"Fragrance exhilarants," Bronski said, his voice suddenly gone very cold. "A subtle Avuirlian equivalent of hard narcotics. You have a cross-star license to dispense drugs, Mrachani?"

"This is all a terrible mistake," the Mrachani moaned. His tone was that of a helpless, terrified child, and despite himself Cavanagh felt a stirring of sympathy deep within him.

"Really," Bronski said. If he was feeling any of the same sympathy, it didn't show. "Let me guess. A group of big, nasty Bhurtala kidnapped you and brought you to Granparra. Then, when Piltariab showed up with a message from Lord Cavanagh, they forced you to mix up a concoction that would eat into his brain, making him so eager to come back and smell it again that he'd kidnap Cavanagh if necessary and bring him here. But instead of Cavanagh, Piltariab brought two other Avuirli, who recognized the smell of diargulates, pounded your jailer into the floor, and jumped to the totally unwarranted conclusion that you were actually the one calling the shots. Am I close?"

The Mrachani seemed to shrink farther into himself. "I am so afraid. Please, Liaison Bronski, you must believe me."

"It is nut an unwarranted cunclusiun, Liaisun Brunski," Mitliriab insisted. "We have seen the chemical vials. They are marked with Mrach symbuls."

"Oh, I believe you," Bronski assured him. "That was what we humans call sarcasm. I'm sure that when we check over the groundcar Kolchin borrowed, we'll be able to connect it to the Mrachanis, too."

"What then du yu plan tu du?" Mitliriab persisted.

"Well, I'm only an assistant liaison," Bronski said. "I don't personally have any police power. Let me talk to someone on the Myrmidon Platform, see what kind of deal I can work out."

Mitliriab's aroma turned peppermint pine. "I du nut wish any deals wurked uut," he growled. "This was an illegal actiun, and an attack against an Avuirlian citizen—"

"Lord Cavanagh?"

Cavanagh turned to find Kolchin's head poking around the corner of the entrance hallway. "Yes?"

"Would you and Liaison Bronski step this way a moment?" Kolchin said. "There's something back here I think you ought to see."

"Certainly," Bronski said. "You Avuirli stay here, please, and keep an eye on the Mrachani and Bhurt. Don't worry—we'll make this right."

They followed Kolchin to what looked to be a small storage area at the back of the house. "I noticed this when I came through here on my way to borrow the Mrachani's getaway groundcar, but I didn't have time for a close look," he said, walking over to a crate whose markings indicated it contained Bhurtist foodstuffs. Lying on top of the crate was a small, flat metal box. "I came back and checked just now," he continued, picking up the box and handing it to Cavanagh.

Cavanagh turned the box over in his hands. To all outward appearances it was just a standard commercial card carrier. "I take it you haven't tried opening it?" he asked, handing the box to Bronski.

"No, I thought I'd let Bronski take care of that part," Kolchin said. "Under the circumstances I suspect it's designed to go bang if the wrong person opens it."

"Or at least erase everything on the cards inside," Bronski said. For a moment he peered closely at the edge of the box, angling it toward the light. Then, with a shrug, he handed it back to Kolchin—

And suddenly the brigadier's flechette pistol was in his hand, pointed at Cavanagh's chest. "I'll take your gun, Kolchin," he said quietly. "Yours too, Cavanagh. Pull them out—two fingers only, please—and set them down on the floor. Then step back against the wall."

Cavanagh looked at Kolchin, found the bodyguard looking back at him, and shook his head. "I thought we'd moved beyond this phase," he said to Bronski, pulling his flechette pistol out as instructed and lowering it to the floor.

"Maybe you did," Bronski said, waiting until the two of them were standing against the storage-room wall before crouching down and retrieving their weapons. "I didn't. Like I told you on Mra-mig, I can't afford to trust you to keep your mouths shut."

Cavanagh felt his stomach muscles tighten. "What does that mean?"

"That part's up to you," Bronski said. "Cooperate, and you'll sit out the war with Taurin Lee and your man Hill for company. Don't cooperate, and we may have to arrange a more permanent kind of silence."

Cavanagh glanced at Kolchin. Back on Mra-mig, the young bodyguard had managed to get the drop on Bronski. If he could do so again . . .

"And if I were you, I wouldn't count on Kolchin pulling any more rabbits out of his hat," Bronski continued, as if reading Cavanagh's train of thought. "He got lucky on Mra-mig. He won't get lucky again."

"Peacekeeper commandos make their own luck, Brigadier," Kolchin said softly. "That was my drill instructor's favorite saying."

"Really," Bronski said. "*My* DI's favorite was that luck scales directly to experience . . . and for the record I had three times as many years in the commandos as you did. I suggest you think about that."

"So what happens now?" Cavanagh asked.

"Three things," Bronski said. "One: you finally get that other cuff attached to Kolchin's wrist. Two: I whistle up some Peacekeepers from the Myrmidon Platform to pick up the Mrachani and any Bhurtala who are still worth picking up. And three"—his mouth tightened—"we head back to my ship and try to open that box."

"As it happened, it was all pretty straightforward," Kolchin said. "Bhurtala might be fast in the long stretch, but they can't change direction worth anything. I just pulled over one of those garbage bins in front of him; and when he came leaping over it, I ducked under him and headed out the other end of the alley." He smiled tightly. "Just in time to almost run square into the other two as they came around the corner."

"That must have been thrilling," Cavanagh said, trying hard to keep his mind on Kolchin's story instead of on the flat box Bronski was working on two meters away from where he and Kolchin sat wristcuffed to wall mounts. The almost certainly booby-trapped flat box . . .

"It was a boost to the heart, all right," Kolchin said. "And I thought I was in for some fancy footwork to get past them. But they kept going into the alley, following the Bhurt I'd just ducked out on. They must have been wired for sound and gotten orders to follow you two instead of me."

"Though that doesn't mean they wouldn't have stomped you if it hadn't meant going out of their way," Bronski put in.

"You just concentrate on that box," Cavanagh told him. "Kolchin can handle the story without footnotes."

"Don't get testy," Bronski said. "I'm already past the tricky stuff."

"Anyway, I knew I wasn't going to catch up with them," Kolchin continued before Cavanagh could reply. "Even if I did, I didn't have anything to stop them with. I figured that whoever had set the trap was probably inside Bokamba's house, so I headed there."

Cavanagh nodded. "And ran straight into another Bhurt and a Mrachani."

"Actually, the Bhurt had already been run over," Kolchin said. "Piltariab's new friends had just finished taking him down and were lining up to have a go at the Mrachani." He shook his head. "Three Avuirli against a Bhurt. I wish I'd been in time to see that one."

"Be thankful you weren't," Bronski said, straightening up from his work and flexing his fingers. "That exotic scent the Avuirli had—you could still smell it when we got back—is the aromotional cue of Avuirlian *fulkumu* rage, probably the coldest anger you'll ever see anywhere. They knew the Mrachani had used diargulates on Piltariab and were ready to take him apart in retribution. Him and anyone who got in their way."

"Interesting," Kolchin murmured. "I'm rather surprised they stopped when I asked them to."

"I doubt they cared one way or the other what you wanted," Bronski told him dryly. "It was probably Piltariab who got them to stop after you suggested it. I'm not sure he even knows now what all the fuss was about. The point is that if you ever smell that cue again, make exhaust the other direction."

"We appreciate the biology lesson," Cavanagh said icily, nodding toward the box. "Now, would you kindly get on with your job?"

"I'm done," Bronski said mildly. Reaching to the box, he touched the release—

And the box popped open.

Cavanagh exhaled a long breath. "Was it booby-trapped?"

"Six ways from April," Bronski confirmed, peering into the box and pulling out three cards. "Let's see what we've got here. . . ."

He slid one of the cards into his plate and spent a few minutes scrolling through various parts. "Interesting reading?" Cavanagh asked.

"Somewhat," Bronski said, pulling the card out and replacing it with the second. "That one was a list of dossiers on about fifty retired Peacekeeper officers of your acquaintance, along with complete data on their current homes. And I mean *complete* data: climate and terrain profiles, macro- and microcultural information listings, city and sector maps—the whole list. Must be a whole lot of Mrachanis scattered around the Commonwealth waiting for you to show up. Probably with a lot of Bhurtala to keep them company."

"I'd wondered how they managed to pinpoint Granparra," Kolchin murmured. "I guess they didn't."

"No, this group was just the lucky one," Bronski said, studying his plate. "Or not, depending on your point of view. Well, well. This one looks like a complete breakdown of CavTronics Industries, including listings for all manufacturing plants, R-and-D stations, sales outlets, and transport vessels. Plus dossiers on all your top management personnel."

Cavanagh swallowed hard. If he and Kolchin had followed their original plan of going directly home to Avon . . . "They must want me pretty bad."

"It's starting to look that way," Bronski agreed, inserting the third card into his plate. "You know, Cavanagh, I didn't put much stock in that Mrach conspiracy theory you spun for me on the way from Phormbi to Mra-mig. That whole idea of a quiet Mrach war against the rest of the universe sounded too much like a Yycroman smoke screen. But I'll admit it's starting to look more and more like the little furballs are sneakier than they like to appear. . . ."

He trailed off, his forehead wrinkling as he frowned at the plate. "What is it?" Cavanagh asked.

"It's some kind of update," Bronski said, his voice suddenly tight. "Projected timetables for two operations. *Mirnacheem-hyeea* One and *Mirnacheem-hyeea* Two."

A cold knot formed in Cavanagh's stomach. "That's the Mrach name for the Conquerors," he said. "Or at least that's where we got the name Conquerors from."

"Yeah, I know," Bronski said, still frowning.

"Where are they supposed to take place?" Kolchin asked.

"The locations are coded," Bronski said. "Looks like they both have the same jump-off point, though, somewhere in Mrach space. Wait a second."

For a minute he was silent, doing something with the plate's keys. "Yes," he said at last. "Still don't have the endpoints; but if I'm reading this right, I've got a transit time from jump-off to end point for *Mirnacheem-hyeea* One. Assuming we're talking standard stardrive speed and not skitters . . . the end point has to be in either Mrach or Yycroman space."

Cavanagh looked at Kolchin. "I'll be damned. They're going to attack the Yycromae."

"No, *they're* not," Kolchin said. "It's the *Mirnacheem-hyeea* operation, remember? They're going to get the Conquerors to attack the Yycromae for them."

"How on Earth are they going to do that?" Cavanagh objected. "How could they even be in contact with the Conquerors?"

"There was a Mrach ship at the Conqueror base when Quinn and his bunch rescued your son Pheylan," Bronski said thoughtfully. "It was damaged, but it was there."

"Any sign of live Mrachanis?" Kolchin asked.

"They didn't see any," Bronski said. "But that might not have been necessary. We know the Conquerors have learned English; the

Mrachanis might have planted data aboard that identified the Yycromae as a threat and persuaded them to launch an attack."

"With a complete timetable included?" Kolchin asked.

Bronski grimaced. "Yeah, there's that," he conceded.

"There's another possibility," Cavanagh said slowly. "The term *Mirnacheem-hyeea* also applies to humans—it was what the Mrachanis first called us after the Peacekeepers made contact with them. Maybe they've found a way to manipulate the Peacekeepers into attacking the Yycromae."

Bronski stroked his lip thoughtfully. "Could be. Wouldn't take all that hard a push, either."

"Not after all the paranoia they've cultivated toward the Yycromae over the years," Cavanagh said. "And not with the access to Peacekeeper information sources the Mrachanis seem to have."

"That last part's been changed, anyway," Bronski said. "I've put through an order cutting the Mrachanis out of all Peacekeeper information lines."

Cavanagh frowned. "I thought you didn't put any stock in my theories."

"I didn't," Bronski said. "That was their punishment for kidnapping and drugging that journalist, Ezer Sholom."

He closed the plate and leaned back in his seat, regarding his prisoners with an unreadable expression. "Well, gentlemen, I've got a problem here," he said. "I can get Myrmidon to send skitters to Earth and Edo with the alert; but what we really need right now is more information. For that someone's going to have to go to Mra and do some snooping. As head of NorCoord Intelligence for Mrach space, that's my job. The problem is what to do with you two."

"I thought you were planning to drop us into a deep hole somewhere," Cavanagh said.

"Oh, I am," Bronski said. "The problem is timing. If I'm reading this right, the jump-off time for the Conquerors One operation is only about forty-nine hours away. This ship is skitter-class, which helps, but from here to Mra and back to Edo will still eat up better than sixteen hours. Figure another twenty-five for Edo to get ships wherever the hell they'll have to go to stop this, and I'm left with only eight hours for actual snooping. That's not a lot of time. If I have to stop first and drop you two off on Mra-ect, I'll have even less. I could leave you here on the Myrmidon Platform; but they haven't got a secure quarantine area, and leaving you with anyone who doesn't know what you know kind of defeats the whole purpose of the quarantine."

"You could let us go," Cavanagh suggested. "I've already given my word we won't say anything."

"And that you won't be coerced into saying anything?" Bronski shook his head. "You know I can't risk that. Not with all these Mrachanis and Bhurtala looking for you. We already saw with Sholom what they're willing to do for information; and we can*not* let them get even a hint that CIRCE doesn't exist. No, what I really want is to keep you with me. But I can't do that and watch my back at the same time." He folded his arms across his chest. "The ball's on your side of the net, Lord Cavanagh. Convince me you can be trusted."

Cavanagh lowered his eyes, suddenly misted with tears. Yes, there was indeed something he could say. The ultimate, unbreakable vow . . . "I swear on the soul of my beloved wife, Sara," he said quietly, the words aching in his throat. "We won't try to escape."

He looked up to find Bronski gazing back at him, something that might be sympathy behind the brigadier's eyes. "I guess that's what I wanted to hear," he said. His wrist flicked; automatically, Cavanagh opened his hand to catch the wristcuff key. "Get yourselves unlocked, then join me in the control room," Bronski told him, shoving the Mrach card carrier into a storage locker and standing up. "I'm going to get the prelaunch started."

Cavanagh hesitated. "Brigadier?"

Bronski paused at the door. "What?"

"I don't know if it's occurred to you," Cavanagh said, "but it's possible the Mrachanis already learned about CIRCE from Ezer Sholom before we found him. If they are in contact with the Conquerors, and if they tell them CIRCE doesn't exist . . ."

"Then we're in trouble," Bronski agreed. "Let's go to Mra and see if we can find out."

14

The landing field was small but crowded, with hundreds of Zhirrzh working busily in and around the twenty-odd ships of various sizes and configurations preparing for their turn to lift into the sky. Loading vehicles wove their way through the crowds, bringing supplies and armaments and fuel to the ships; floaters carried crew members, technics, and at least one overelaborately dressed Zhirrzh who appeared to be a Dhaa'rr-clan leader on an inspection tour. Over and through everything fluttered the usual cloud of Elders, flickering in and out like dusk-glow insects as they brought messages to and from everyone in sight.

Casually, methodically, Thrr't-rokik wove in and out of the ships along with them, giving each person he passed a quick but careful look, fighting against a growing taste of hopelessness. The long trail had led here, to that transport sitting out in the parking area; but he'd been searching for nearly twenty hunbeats now and had found no sign of the two Zhirrzh. Perhaps they hadn't come onto the landing field, or perhaps they had already left on a spaceship or another transport.

Or perhaps they had never been there at all. Perhaps they weren't even the ones using that particular transport anymore. He and Thrr-tulkoj might be on the wrong trail entirely—

And then, suddenly, there they were, walking up a landing ramp into the next ship over, warrior-style travel bags slung over their shoulders.

Thrr't-rokik was inside the entry hatchway in the flick of a beat, easing his face out through the ceramic hull for a closer look. It was them, all right: the two Zhirrzh he'd seen delivering Thrr-pifix-a's stolen *fsss* organ to her house on that fateful latearc six fullarcs ago.

The taller of the two spotted Thrr't-rokik as they reached the top of the ramp. "You—Elder—go tell the ship commander his passengers are here," he ordered.

"Right away," Thrr't-rokik said, feeling a sudden surge of anticipation. The perfect opportunity to find out who they were. "May I have your names?"

"The ship commander knows who we are," the other Zhirrzh said. "Just tell him we're here."

"Right away," Thrr't-rokik said again, swallowing his disappointment as he dropped into the grayworld. It hadn't worked, but at least now he could go tell Thrr-tulkoj that their search had struck ore.

But not yet. Clearly, the two Zhirrzh had assumed he was one of the ship's communicators. If their message to the ship commander didn't get delivered, they would realize he wasn't, and that could lead to trouble.

Besides, delivering the message might give him another opportunity to get their names. Rising again to the edge of the lightworld, he headed toward the front of the ship.

The control area was easy to find, filling the back half of the first hexagon and looking just as control areas always did in warrior documentaries. Inside were twelve Zhirrzh, busily working at consoles or conversing among themselves, preparing the ship for flight.

Thrr't-rokik looked around at them, wishing fleetingly that his son Thrr-mezaz had chosen to become a ship warrior instead of a ground warrior. He was supposed to find the ship commander, but the insignia threads these Zhirrzh were wearing on their uniforms were well-nigh incomprehensible to him. Still, it stood to reason that the ship commander ought to have the most elaborate set of threads—

One of the warriors glanced up, saw him loitering up there. "Yes, what is it?" he demanded.

Probably not the ship commander, but he would do. "Message from the entry hatchway," Thrr't-rokik told him. "The passengers have arrived."

The Zhirrzh frowned. "What passengers?"

"I don't know," Thrr't-rokik said. "They didn't give me their names."

"It's all right, Third, Speaker Cvv-panav sent them," another Zhirrzh spoke up from across the room. An older Zhirrzh, this one, his tone measured and firm. "There were two of them?"

"Yes, Ship Commander," Thrr't-rokik said, gambling on his identity. "They didn't give me their names."

"That's all right," the ship commander said. "Speaker Cvv-panav didn't give me their names, either. But I know who they are. Tell them they'll be in Stateroom Four, Hexagon Two—I'll check in on them after liftoff."

Thrr't-rokik grimaced to himself. Another failure. "Right away," he said.

"What?" the ship commander barked.

Thrr't-rokik froze, his mind racing. What in the eighteen worlds had he—? "I mean, I obey, Ship Commander," he stammered.

"That's better," the other growled. "What's your name, Elder?"

"Ah—Cvv't-rokik," Thrr't-rokik said, improvising a Dhaa'rr name. "Dhaa'rr."

"The Dhaa'rr part I know, thank you," the ship commander said, flicking his tongue contemptuously. "You wouldn't be aboard this ship otherwise. So you're one of the Speaker for Dhaa'rr's family. I might have known. Let me tell you something, Cvv't-rokik: on a warrior ship, even a lowly supply ship like the *Willing Servant,* family influence only goes so far. You forget proper warrior discipline and protocol again, and you'll be back in your shrine, drifting on the wind and waiting for the excitement of watching the next sunset. Understood?"

"Yes, Ship Commander," Thrr't-rokik said humbly.

"Good. Now get going."

"I obey, Ship Commander," Thrr't-rokik said, and vanished, embarrassment and self-disgust mixing on his tongue at his blunder. *That* much about warriors he *did* know.

He flicked to the entry hatchway again. The two passengers were waiting inside, their travel bags dropped on the deck at their feet, their expressions beginning to show signs of impatience. "The ship commander bids you welcome," he told them. "You'll be quartered in Stateroom Four, Hexagon Two, and he'll speak with you later."

"Fine," the taller Zhirrzh said. "Which way?"

Thrr't-rokik hadn't the faintest idea, but fortunately he'd anticipated the question. The beat his message was delivered, he dropped deep into the grayworld. With good luck the two passengers would assume he'd merely dashed off on other business and hadn't heard their question.

But whether they assumed that or not, he had no time to waste. He'd found them, and he was not going to let them get away from him.

He flicked back to Thrr-tulkoj, standing unobtrusively among the bustling activity and pretending to check a stack of containers against a list board some careless inspector had left lying around. "I've found them," he murmured to the young protector.

"Where?" Thrr-tulkoj murmured back, still checking the numbers.

"Two ships over," Thrr't-rokik told him, pointing to his right. "They've just gone aboard as passengers on a ship named the *Willing Servant.* Small ship, only four hexagons."

"Probably a supply ship," Thrr-tulkoj said. "Any idea where it's headed?"

"No," Thrr't-rokik said. "I talked to them, but—"

"You talked to them?" Thrr-tulkoj cut him off. "Right up where they could see you?"

"It's all right, they didn't recognize me," Thrr't-rokik assured him. "The problem is that I wasn't able to find out their names."

Thrr-tulkoj flicked his tongue. "We absolutely need to get those names. Any idea how soon they'll be lifting?"

"No, but I got the feeling it'll be soon," Thrr't-rokik told him. "The control area was very busy."

Thrr-tulkoj nodded grimly. "Well, there's nothing for it, then. I'll just have to go aboard."

"Aboard a Dhaa'rr warship? You can't be serious."

"It's a Zhirrzh warship," Thrr-tulkoj corrected him. "Warrior Command is unified, remember?"

"Trust me, this one's all Dhaa'rr," Thrr't-rokik insisted. "You think Speaker Cvv-panav would trust his agents to just any ship?"

"They're the Speaker for Dhaa'rr's personal agents?" Thrr-tulkoj frowned. "They said that?"

"Not in so many words, but he's the one who sent them here," Thrr't-rokik said. "The ship commander implied he'd spoken personally with the Speaker about them."

Thrr-tulkoj flicked his tongue savagely. "I knew the Speaker was involved in this. I *knew* it."

"The ship commander didn't know their names, either," Thrr't-rokik said. "So far as we know, no one in this entire landing area may know their names."

"Are you suggesting we give up?"

"No," Thrr't-rokik said, flicking his tongue in a negative. A decidedly nervous negative. "I'm suggesting that our best chance now is to somehow stow away my *fsss* cutting on that ship."

Thrr-tulkoj's midlight pupils contracted to slits. "Are you insane?" he hissed.

"Probably," Thrr't-rokik conceded. "But it's the only way. *Someone* in the eighteen worlds has to know who these two Zhirrzh are. One of us has to be there when that person calls them by name, and I'm the only one who can do that."

Thrr-tulkoj's tongue stabbed out in impotent frustration. "It's wrong," he said flatly. "It's just plain wrong. I'm the protector here. I'm the one who's been trained; I'm the one who's supposed to take these risks."

"You can't take this one," Thrr't-rokik said. "Not unless you want to enlist as a Dhaa'rr warrior. Besides, I'm an Elder. What can they do to me? Come on, we're wasting time."

The hatchway on the third hexagon of the *Willing Servant* was standing open, with a loader stacked with shipping containers pushed up against a protruding conveyor ramp. Two Zhirrzh were by the conveyor, laboriously transferring the containers from the loader onto the ramp. "Take a look inside the containers on the loader," Thrr-tulkoj murmured as he walked toward the ship. "Find out what's in them. Don't let anyone see you."

"Right." Thrr't-rokik flicked out to the containers, wove in and out of them, flicked back. "The four on the bottom contain packaged food," he told Thrr-tulkoj. "The two on top nearest the ship are optronic modules and parts. The two rear ones are medical supplies."

Thrr-tulkoj nodded. "Looks like they're going into a war zone."

"What out there isn't a war zone?" Thrr't-rokik countered, fighting back the growing rattle of nervousness. After all, what *could* they do to him? "How are you going to get my cutting aboard?"

"I've got an idea." Thrr-tulkoj hesitated. "I'm going to have to take the cutting out of its box, though. It'll be completely unprotected. Can you handle that?"

Thrr't-rokik snorted. "It's not as if it's overly protected now," he reminded the protector.

"It can be damaged," Thrr-tulkoj reminded him. "It can decay, get attacked by animals or insects, maybe even get crushed or burned. Whatever happens to it, you'll feel everything."

Thrr't-rokik had already thought about the possibilities. Hearing them listed aloud wasn't helping. "Let's get on with it."

"All right," Thrr-tulkoj said. "But if you change your mind at any point—"

"Let's get on with it."

Thrr-tulkoj lowered his list board to his waist and under its cover dipped the fingers of his left hand into his waist pouch. Thrr't-rokik heard the click as he opened the small box; felt a flood of warmth and a vaguely unpleasant pressure as the protector picked up the thin sliver that was his *fsss* cutting. The pressure changed, becoming decidedly oppressive, as he maneuvered the cutting to a secure but hidden grip at the juncture of finger and thumb. "Here we go," Thrr-tulkoj murmured. "Stay out of sight."

He picked up his pace, striding confidently up to the loader. "Good fullarc," he said briskly to the two Zhirrzh. "I've come for a final cargo check."

"You're a little late," one of the workers said, the last word coming out as a grunt as he and his partner lifted one of the optronics containers off the loader. "We're nearly finished."

"Besides, it's already been checked once," the other added.

"I know that," Thrr-tulkoj said in a patient tone tinged with just the right edge of official exasperation. "That's why it's called the *final* check. Shut off that conveyor and let me up." Without waiting for them to comply, he reached up, grabbed hold of the railing, and swung himself up toward the hatchway—

And with a startled curse dropped back to the ground, the palm of his right hand welling with blood.

"What happened?" one of the Zhirrzh yelped.

"What do you think?" Thrr-tulkoj snapped back. "I cut my hand. Shut it *off*, blast it."

They had already set the container hastily back down again, and now one of them grabbed for the control switch. "How bad is it?" he asked anxiously as the conveyor slowed to a stop.

"Bad enough," Thrr-tulkoj said, wincing dramatically as he peered at the blood. "I caught it on the flange edge. I *told* you to shut it down."

"You didn't give us a chance," one of the workers objected. But to Thrr't-rokik the words sounded automatic, with no real conviction behind them. Someone had gotten injured at their workstation, and no matter whose fault it was, it was going to reflect badly on them. "Let me call an Elder and get a healer over here."

"Don't bother the healers," Thrr-tulkoj said, peering briefly at his list board and then setting it down on the optronics container. "I can handle this. Get that end container open."

The two Zhirrzh exchanged startled glances. "Open a container? But—"

"There are medical supplies in there," Thrr-tulkoj cut him off impatiently. "All I need is a small length of pressure bandage. Now quit arguing and get it open before I bleed myself to Eldership."

The Zhirrzh looked at each other again, then silently moved to the indicated container. Twenty beats later they had it open.

"There—that one," Thrr-tulkoj said, peering into the container and flicking his tongue at a bandage roll tucked into one edge. "Get it out of the sealer and give it to me."

"This is supposed to be for the war effort," one of the Zhirrzh said, glancing around nervously as he pulled the roll out of its plastic sealer and handed it to Thrr-tulkoj.

"What do you think all the rest of us are doing?" Thrr-tulkoj countered, carefully unrolling the end of the bandage and rerolling it around his hand. "It's all war effort these fullarcs, my friend, every bit of it."

He finished the wrapping and tore off the bandage, pressing the loose end against his hand to secure it. "There," he said, holding the hand up for inspection. "Good as new." A short length of the bandage hung loose from the roll; shifting the roll to his bandaged right hand, he smoothed it back into place with his left hand.

And as he did so, he slid the palmed *fsss* cutting neatly inside the roll.

"All right," he said, handing the roll back to the Zhirrzh holding the plastic sealer. "Seal it up, put it back, close the container, and let's get back to work."

"Well," Thrr-tulkoj said. "Unless there's something else . . ."

"No, I don't think so," Thrr't-rokik told him, looking around. They were near the main entrance to the landing area, at the very limit of Thrr't-rokik's anchorline, temporarily out of earshot of any of the workers. "I'm all set; and the longer you wait, the better the chance someone's going to ask what you're doing here."

"I suppose so," Thrr-tulkoj said. "I just—well, you know—"

"You got us here," Thrr't-rokik reminded him. "I couldn't have done any of that. This next part's up to me."

"I know," Thrr-tulkoj sighed. "I just feel so . . . useless."

"The last part will again be yours," Thrr't-rokik reminded him. "Just make sure you're waiting in Cliffside Dales when I get those names."

"Understood," Thrr-tulkoj nodded. "It'll take me about a fullarc and a half to get back; but once I'm there, I won't leave."

"Good." Thrr't-rokik hesitated. "And if you happen to go by Thrr-pifix-a's house on your way back, give her my love. And tell her not to lose hope."

"I'll make sure to go by there," Thrr-tulkoj promised. "Good luck to you."

"And to you."

Thrr-tulkoj turned and walked away. Thrr't-rokik waited until he was safely past the predator fence, then flicked back to the *Willing Servant*. For a few beats he circled the ship, noting that the hatchways and other external openings had been sealed and all support vehicles had been moved out of the way. Liftoff could be only a few hunbeats away.

And then, to his surprise, one of the hatchways opened up again.

A beat later he was inside, flicking through the ship as he searched for the two passengers, a horrible suspicion chewing into him. Stateroom Four, Hexagon Two, the ship commander had said—

There they were, walking down a corridor with the ship commander, their travel bags again slung over their shoulders. "—very sorry about this," the ship commander was saying as Thrr't-rokik eased unobtrusively into a half-concealed position in the ceiling behind them. "But the orders came directly from Warrior Command, and there's nothing I can do about it."

"Your apologies are not required, Ship Commander," the taller of the Zhirrzh assured him. "The Mrachani contact mission is of extreme importance to the war effort. If Warrior Command has chosen the *Willing Servant* to take supplies to them, then you must obey not only willingly but eagerly."

"Personally, I think it's merely the Overclan Prime playing politics with the Dhaa'rr again," the ship commander grumbled. "I wouldn't put it past him to divert a Dhaa'rr warship at the last beat just for the fun of it."

"A warrior warship, Ship Commander," the taller Zhirrzh corrected him mildly. "We're all unified under Warrior Command."

"Of course," the ship commander said, flicking his tongue sardonically. "I sometimes forget."

"At any rate, don't worry about us," the shorter Zhirrzh said. "We can get other transportation. You just be careful in this rendezvous with the Mrachanis."

"We will," the ship commander promised. "Farewell, and good luck to you."

They reached the ramp, and the two Zhirrzh headed down.

And suddenly the whole carefully contrived scheme had been burned to ashes.

Thrr't-rokik followed the two Zhirrzh as they walked across the landing area, trying unsuccessfully to listen to their quiet conversation over the noise of the landing area. They reached the length of his anchorline, and he watched helplessly as they continued on past it. Heading to their transport, perhaps, or else to one of the service buildings beyond the predator fence. And from there to another ship, and another world, and a convenient fading into oblivion.

He'd lost them.

He sighed deep within himself, too emotionally drained even to be angry. He'd lost, and that was all there was to it. Thrr-tulkoj was long gone; and even if he hadn't been, the ship and its cargo hatchways were all sealed. The *Willing Servant* was headed for a rendezvous with the alien Mrachanis, and Thrr't-rokik's *fsss* cutting was going with them.

He could abandon the whole idea, of course. Flick back to his main *fsss* at the Thrr-family shrine, and mark down these last few fullarcs to experience and memory and wasted time. His cutting was trapped, but considering how it was situated, there was probably an even chance it would simply fall out unnoticed the next time someone unrolled part of the pressure bandage. And there was certainly no reason anymore for him to stay with the ship.

On the other side, it seemed a shame to waste all of Thrr-tulkoj's heroic efforts, not to mention the blood he'd spilled a few hunbeats ago. Anyway, what else did Thrr't-rokik have to do?

He flicked back to the *Willing Servant;* and he had just decided that the first step would be to give himself a grand tour of the ship when an Elder suddenly appeared in front of him. "You," the other snapped. "Yes, you. Are you connected with the *Willing Servant?*"

"Ah . . . yes," Thrr't-rokik stammered, realizing only after he'd said it that it probably would have been smarter and safer to identify himself instead as one of the landing-area Elders. "What I mean is—"

"Yes, I know—you're not really with the ship, you're one of that shovelful of observers the Overclan Seating loaded us with," the other Elder said impatiently. "You and the rest of your pyramid are to report to the Elder briefing room in Hexagon Two immediately. What's your name?"

Thrr't-rokik was ready this time. "Cvv't-rokik; Dhaa'rr," he said. "What's all this about?"

"It's about war, of course," the Elder growled. "More specifically, it's about observing. You want to observe the contact mission's conversations with the Mrachanis, you have to be able to understand what they're talking about."

"Ah," Thrr't-rokik said, nodding his understanding. "Human-Conqueror language lessons."

"Very good," the Elder said sarcastically. "At least you're not stupid, just ignorant. Hopefully, that's something we can fix over the next few fullarcs." The Elder jabbed imperiously with his tongue. "Well, don't just float there, get going. And hope the language instructor doesn't give you a reprimand for tardiness."

"I obey," Thrr't-rokik said, flicking past him.

And hope too, he added to himself, that no one would take the trouble to count the Elders present and compare it with the number of *fsss* cuttings on this observer pyramid. If they did, he was going to be in trouble. If they didn't, he might just be able to pull this off.

Either way, it was definitely going to be an interesting voyage.

"Sir?"

Parlimin Jacy VanDiver looked up impatiently from his perusal of the latest batch of Peacekeeper troop movements. How was he ever going to keep up with all this if he kept getting interrupted every five minutes? "What is it, Peters?" he snapped.

"Sorry to bother you, sir," the young aide said, stammering slightly.

"But a priority message just came for you by skitter from Mr. McPhee." He started to offer the plate, hesitated. "Shall I summarize it for you, sir?"

The kid was learning, anyway. Slowly, like a brain-damaged slug, but learning. "Make it quick," VanDiver said, dropping his attention back to the Peacekeeper report. McPhee was a time waster, too, always sending reports whether he had anything to say or not. Odds were this was one of those.

"Yes, sir," Peters said. "Mr. McPhee reports that he's tracked Assistant Commonwealth Liaison Petr Bronski to Puerto Simone Island on Granparra. There he observed Bronski with two men, tentatively identified as Lord Stewart Cavanagh and—"

VanDiver snapped his eyes up again, the troop movements abruptly forgotten. "Cavanagh?"

"Yes, sir," Peters said, sounding even more nervous. "Lord Cavanagh and a Mr. Mitri Kolchin—"

"Give me that," VanDiver cut him off, gesturing for the plate.

"Yes, sir," Peters said, hastily stepping forward and handing it to him.

Quickly, VanDiver skimmed the report. It was Cavanagh and Kolchin, all right; the brief long-range video McPhee had included with the report left no doubt about it. Acting all chummy, too, the three of them heading into a small spaceship together. According to McPhee, they were heading next for Mra; McPhee planned to follow.

"I knew it," he said, glaring up at Peters. "Bronski's in this with Cavanagh. In it up to his neck."

"Yes, sir," Peters said. "Speaking of Bronski, sir, I've finished that background report you requested."

"And?"

Peters shrugged fractionally. "Nothing of particular interest. A native of Ukraine, he's apparently been working for various diplomatic and conciliation services since leaving school. According to his file, he joined the Commonwealth diplomatic service in 2282 and has spent the past twenty-one years working his way up to his present position."

"Military service?"

"None listed." Peters hesitated. "Though one thing that struck me as odd, sir. He's listed as joining the Unified Centaurian Civil Diplomatic Corps midway through the Pawolian war. He served with them for twelve years, with assignments that took him all over the Commonwealth and several alien worlds."

"What of it?"

"Well, sir, I did some checking," Peters said. "Apparently the CiDi

Corps has always been strictly for Centaurian citizens. No non-Centaurians were ever allowed in."

"Again, what of it?" VanDiver asked. "Bronski probably had dual citizenship during that period. That wasn't uncommon."

"Yes, sir, I realize that," Peters nodded. "But I did some checking, and about two months before he entered the CiDi Corps, the Ukraine government instituted a one hundred percent military training program for all Ukrainian citizens aged nineteen through twenty-five. The Pawoles had been driving the Commonwealth forces back, and Ukraine wanted their citizens ready to fight in case there was an invasion of Earth."

"Other nations and colonies did that, too," VanDiver said. "If you have a point, get to it."

Peters seemed to brace himself. "The point, sir, is that there's no record that Bronski ever participated in the program, even though he was within the age bracket. The only way for him to have gotten out of it would have been to renounce his Ukrainian citizenship; but there's also no record of him doing that."

"Sounds like someone in high places was doing a little path-greasing for him," VanDiver said, feeling his lip twist in contempt. If there was one thing he hated about the upper crust, it was precisely this casual buying and selling of favors. "Was his family close with any of the NorCoord leaders at that time?"

"There's no mention of anything like that," Peters said. "I could do a little digging, though."

"Get to it," VanDiver ordered. "But first give the Edo Central spaceport a call and have my ship prepared for departure."

"Yes, sir," Peters said with a nod. "Are you going back to Earth?"

"No," VanDiver said. "I'm going to Mra."

Peters blinked. "Mra?"

VanDiver gestured to Peters's plate. "According to McPhee, Bronski and Cavanagh are going to Mra. Whatever they're up to, I want to catch them red-handed at it."

"But, sir . . . ," Peters floundered. "Aren't you needed in Parliament?"

"What for?" VanDiver retorted. "Parliament hasn't got any real business at the moment. Peacekeeper Command is running the show—all they need us for is to clear away the legal underbrush and dispense little inspirational homilies to the masses. They hardly need me there for that."

"Yes, sir," Peters said. "But shouldn't you at least requisition a Peacekeeper warship? You never know where the Zhirrzh will attack next."

"The Zhirrzh can't attack anywhere without giving a couple hours' notice that they're coming," VanDiver said. "Anyway, if this unknown guardian angel of Bronski's is still active in Ukrainian politics, requisitioning a Peacekeeper ship for Mra would be a sure way of tipping him off. I have no intention of standing by while someone slathers official paint over this thing."

"But what about your own personal safety?" Peters persisted. "Only this past week there was a directive from NorCoord Military Intelligence cautioning parliamentary personnel in any dealings with the Mrachanis."

"Military Intelligence is always issuing directives like that," VanDiver growled. "They haven't got anything new on the Zhirrzh, so this is how they try to convince us they're earning their budget."

He waved a hand impatiently. "What am I arguing this with you for, anyway? Get that call in to the spaceport, then get a message out on the next skitter to Mra telling McPhee I'm on my way."

Peters still didn't look happy, but he nevertheless nodded. "Yes, sir," he said. Turning, he left the office.

Idiot, VanDiver thought after the other. That was all he seemed to be surrounded by these days. Idiots like Peters, who submitted incomplete reports and then had the temerity to argue decisions with him. Idiots like McPhee, who apparently hadn't even been able to locate Bronski on Puerto Simone Island until he was ready to leave the place. Five minutes more, and he'd have missed them completely.

Still, sometimes two half-wits could add together to do something right. VanDiver still didn't have all the pieces, but he had enough of them.

He ran the video portion of McPhee's report again. Cavanagh was in the lead as they headed into Bronski's ship, with Kolchin behind him and Bronski bringing up the rear. Definitely looking all chummy. Kolchin even had his hands clasped casually behind his back. . . .

VanDiver jabbed the freeze button, frowning suddenly at the image. Kolchin's hands behind his back . . . and a brief glint of metal.

Wristcuffs?

For a minute he fiddled with the plate's enlargement/enhancement controls, trying to get a clear view of that section of the image. But McPhee had already pushed his equipment to the limit in getting the video, and none of the enhancements did any good. More sophisticated equipment might be able to glean something out of the tape; but that would take time, and time wasn't something VanDiver had to spare at the moment.

Besides, it didn't really matter. Cavanagh and Bronski were up to something—that much was a given. If Kolchin was in wristcuffs, it meant only that he wasn't voluntarily going along with the scheme. Or else the wristcuffs were just for show. Either way, they could sort it out at the trial.

Lord Stewart Cavanagh on trial. What a lovely thought.

Smiling tightly, VanDiver pulled out his phone. There were a hundred trifling matters to be disposed of before he could leave for Mra.

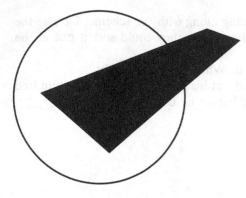

15 "As you can see, Commander, they really didn't leave us much to study," Engineer Lieutenant Alex Williams commented as the group entered the last hexagon of the abandoned Zhirrzh base. Like most of the rest of the rooms, this one had been pretty much stripped down to the walls. "The good news is the buildings themselves," Williams continued. "The analysis team says the material is very similar to the ceramic the Conquerors use in their warship hulls. Thinner, of course."

"That could be useful," Pheylan agreed, looking around and trying to ignore the eerie sensation tingling through him. It had been barely fifteen days since Aric and Quinn and the Copperheads had pulled him out of this place, unconscious, with a dose of Zhirrzh tongue poison in his bloodstream. Hardly enough time even for his metabolism to recover from the poison and the alien food his captors had fed him; and yet, here he was, back on the same world.

Facing once again the memories of his imprisonment. And the memories of the crushing Peacekeeper defeat that had put him there.

"Commander?"

Pheylan snapped out of the painful musings, focusing on the third member of their party. Colonel Helene Pemberton, if he'd gotten the introductions right, a fiftyish woman with dark hair, piercing gray eyes, and a slight Confederate accent. The colonel had been waiting with Williams when Pheylan had landed and had tagged silently along with them during the tour. "I'm sorry, Colonel," he said. "Did you say something?"

"Not yet," she said, her eyes narrowed slightly as she studied him. "As long as I have your attention, though, did you ever see any of this area while you were here?"

"No," Pheylan said, shaking his head. "I saw my cell room—that was the room with the big glass cylinder in the middle—and some of the areas outside. They never showed me anything else."

"I see," she said. "Carry on, Lieutenant."

"That's about it, actually," the engineer said, waving around the room. "Except for the impressions in the ground where the pyramid and domes you mentioned were sitting. And, of course, the fence."

"Yes, Thrr-gilag mentioned an outer fence," Pheylan said. "Where exactly is it?"

"About half a klick out," Williams said, waving a hand in a general sweep around them. "It's made of a fine mesh, extends a couple of meters up and another couple underground. Basically the same design of fence that was around that other pyramid your brother looked at while he and the Copperheads were out looking for you."

"You never saw the fence here?" Pemberton asked.

"No," Pheylan said. "Though there was a path leading from the landing field away through the trees. I assume it led there."

"Yes, it does," Williams confirmed. "You want to go take a look?"

"Sure," Pheylan said, though he couldn't imagine what good it would do. He wasn't exactly a materials expert, after all.

For that matter he wasn't anything that could make much of a difference to this investigation. He'd been sent here to catch what other, inexperienced eyes might miss, Admiral Rudzinski had said; but from what he'd seen so far, there was precious little left for anyone to look at, experienced or otherwise.

They headed out onto the landing field. The sky had clouded up while they'd been inside, and the stiff breeze had turned chilly. "Unfortunately, the Zhirrzh had plenty of time to pack up everything and get it out of here," Williams commented as he led the way toward the path, the red dust scrunching underfoot. "About ninety hours, I understand, before the Peacekeeper assault force could get here."

"Yes, we worried about that time lag on the way back," Pheylan agreed. "There was some discussion about whether we ought to go to Dorcas instead of heading directly to Edo. Peacekeeper warships starting from there could have lopped about thirty-five hours off the turnaround time."

"Why didn't you?"

"We decided it was too big a gamble," Pheylan said, forcing down the hard lump that had suddenly formed in his throat. Melinda had been on Dorcas when the Zhirrzh had attacked. "There hadn't been any warships there when we'd left, and no guarantee that would have changed. Besides, we were low enough on fuel that if we diverted to Dorcas, we wouldn't have had enough to continue on to Edo."

"Good thing you didn't stop," Pemberton said soberly. "You wouldn't have found anything at Dorcas but Zhirrzh and Zhirrzh warships."

"Yes," Pheylan murmured, Melinda's face hovering before his eyes. "A good thing, indeed."

They reached the path, and Williams led the way onto it. Pheylan followed, his chest aching with the memory of how he'd manipulated his captors into triggering the magnets of his obedience suit at this spot. Slammed flat on his face on the ground, he'd used the distraction to covertly pick up one of the sharp pieces of flint that were still scattered around the edges of the path.

A piece of flint that he'd successfully smuggled back to his cell . . . and that had been suddenly discovered hours later by the Zhirrzh. He still didn't know how they'd pulled that one off.

The trees were pretty much as Pheylan remembered them: tall gray-green objects, which didn't look anything like the trees he'd grown up with but which obviously filled that same ecological niche. Walking along a path surrounded by them, however, he realized for the first time that they also put out a distinctive and not entirely pleasant odor. "Interesting aroma," he commented. "Smells like an annoyed Avuire."

"Actually, it's more like an Avuire greeting friends after a long absence," Pemberton corrected absently. "Annoyed Avuirli smell entirely different."

"Ah," Pheylan said, stifling a smile. He'd meant the comment to be more facetious than anything else. He considered pointing that out, decided the colonel probably wouldn't appreciate it, and kept silent.

A few minutes later they emerged from the trees. Five meters ahead, stretching out to both sides in front of them, was the fence.

"That's it," Williams said. "What do you think?"

"Impressive," Pheylan said, looking up and down the fence as he stepped toward it for a closer look. "Goes all around the encampment, you said?"

"Right," the engineer said. "Obviously a defense of some sort."

"Obviously," Pheylan agreed. The strands that made up the mesh were slender, composed of a silvery yet vaguely translucent material that reminded him of glass. "Was it electrified?"

"Nope," Williams said, poking at one of the mesh strands with the tip of a knife. "The material's not even conductive. Some kind of high-tensile ceramic material, really strong. We're still doing measurements on it."

Pheylan looked along the fence, shading his eyes with one hand as the sun winked out of the clouds. "What kind of supports does it have?"

"None that we've been able to find," Williams said. "Apparently, the engineering design of the mesh plus the section underground is enough to hold it upright. Oh, and there's no gate, either, at least none we could find. Looks like the Zhirrzh don't go in for evening strolls."

"The question, of course," Pemberton spoke up, "is what the Zhirrzh were expecting it to protect them against. Certainly not any kind of weapons attack."

"Thrr-gilag implied it was here to keep animals out of the compound," Pheylan said, fingering the mesh. The strands were very smooth.

"That's a pretty tight mesh for keeping out tigers," Williams commented. "You'd think they were terrified of squirrels, too."

"Maybe they're not the ones it was here to protect," Pheylan said, letting his hand drop to his side. "Maybe it was to guard the pyramid."

"Why do you say that?" Pemberton asked.

"Well, we know the pyramid was very important to them," Pheylan said. "Three Zhirrzh came bounding out of the domes and pointed nasty-looking sticks at me when I tried to get too close to it. And it was right after that incident that Svv-selic was replaced as interrogation spokesman by Thrr-gilag."

"What do you think the pyramid's significance is?" Pemberton asked.

"I really don't know," Pheylan said. "I came up with all sorts of crazy ideas, but, of course, I never got close enough to see those sausage slices Aric told me were in the niches in the one the Copperheads found."

"Which doesn't necessarily mean this pyramid had the same sausage slices," Pemberton pointed out. "Or that it even had the same purpose. The Zhirrzh may simply like pyramids."

Pheylan shrugged. "Maybe. On the other hand, they build their ships and buildings out of hexagons."

"So why use pyramids for these other structures?" Pemberton asked.

How the hell should I know? With an effort Pheylan bit down on the retort. Wild hunches and educated guesses were why he was there, after all. "Historical reasons, maybe," he suggested. "Maybe there's a long tradition behind the pyramid design for these things and they want to stay with it. Or maybe they're deliberately designed to look different from other kinds of structures."

"For what reason?" Pemberton asked.

"A warning to strangers to stay away, maybe," Pheylan said. "A warning to other Zhirrzh, even—there could easily be subtle markings on the pyramids we humans wouldn't immediately pick up on."

"Perhaps," Pemberton said. "Anything else?"

Pheylan grimaced. Wild hunches . . . "Or else the shape is purely functional," he said. "Maybe the pyramids are electronic devices. Or weapons."

"What kind of weapons?" Pemberton asked.

Pheylan glanced at Williams. The engineer seemed to have dropped out of this part of the conversation. "Well, I suppose it sounds crazy now, but for a while I wondered if it could be a component for a CIRCE-type weapon."

"Why do you think that sounds crazy?"

"Because I know now this was just a base and not a whole Zhirrzh colony world," Pheylan said. "Not worth bringing in huge amounts of ordnance to protect. Also because they didn't use any exotic weaponry against the Copperhead rescue team, and because they cut and ran instead of waiting to fight the follow-up Peacekeeper force. Finally, because they apparently haven't used anything like CIRCE against the Commonwealth."

"I see," Pemberton said. "Were you aware that each of the Zhirrzh occupation forces has set up at least four of these same pyramids in or around their beachheads?"

Pheylan frowned. "No, I wasn't," he said slowly. "The same kind of pyramid?"

"They look the same on long-range scans," the colonel said. "Beyond that we don't know."

Pheylan stroked the smooth strands of the fence. "Could they have some religious significance, then?" he suggested. "Like a temple or shrine or something?"

"That's a possibility," Pemberton agreed. "Did you ever see any of the Zhirrzh worship or meditate at the pyramid here?"

Pheylan searched his memory. "As far as I can remember, I never even saw any of them go near it," he said. "Except for the guards in the domes, of course."

"I see," Pemberton said, her voice noncommittal. "Well, keep thinking. Perhaps something will come to you."

"Perhaps," Pheylan said. "You're a psychologist, aren't you, Colonel?"

She smiled faintly, the first smile he'd yet seen from her. "Cognitive analyst, actually," she corrected. "My particular specialty is the gleaning of little bits of information from damaged or reluctant minds."

"And which one does mine qualify as?"

She shrugged. "The techniques are basically the same. I'm here to help you dredge up anything you might have seen or heard that could help us in our defense against the Zhirrzh." She cocked her head to the side. "Does my presence or profession bother you?"

Pheylan shook his head. "Melinda took a unit of psychology when she was in med school," he said, a lump again forming in his throat at the reminder of the danger his sister was in. "She spent the entire term break afterward practicing it on my brother and me. Just about drove us crazy."

"You're worried about her, aren't you?" Pemberton asked quietly.

Pheylan looked out at the alien landscape beyond the fence. "I asked to be assigned to whatever force will be going to Dorcas," he said. "They sent me here instead."

"I'm sure Admiral Rudzinski had his reasons," Pemberton said. "There may be something of vital significance here that no one but you would recognize."

"Yes," Pheylan murmured. "Maybe."

He took a deep breath of the pungent air, turned back to face the two of them. "If I do, we're not going to dig it out standing here chatting. Let's get back to the complex."

He spent the rest of the day in the Zhirrzh building complex, watching as Williams's analysis team carried out tests on the ceramic walls, or just wandering around the building and grounds, looking and remembering. When night fell, he returned to the team's laboratory ship, spending a couple more hours dictating his thoughts and impressions into a recorder before retiring to one of the bunks for a fitful night's sleep.

He spent the second day lounging on a cot inside his old prison cell, gazing out through the glass wall and describing for three of the techs the various pieces of Zhirrzh equipment that had been set up around the room. At Colonel Pemberton's suggestion he spent the night there as well. Another night of restive sleep, as it turned out, but without the nightmares he'd been expecting.

Without the nightmares; but with a lot of thinking, particularly in the quiet of the early-morning hours. And by the time the camp began to come alive again, he had come to some unpleasant conclusions.

"Good morning, Commander," Colonel Pemberton greeted him as he entered the main analysis room aboard the laboratory ship. "How did you sleep?"

"Not too badly," Pheylan told her. "I wonder if I could have a private word with you, Colonel."

"Certainly," she said, waving a hand toward a small office that opened off the analysis room. "This way."

He waited until the door had closed behind them. "I'd like to know, Colonel, what exactly I'm doing here," he said. "The truth, I mean."

"Is that all?" she said, frowning. "I thought Admiral Rudzinski laid that out for you back on Edo."

"He gave me the official reason," Pheylan said. "I'm asking for the real reason."

Her eyes flicked thoughtfully across his face. "Can you at least give me a hint?" she asked.

So she was going to play dumb. Pheylan had rather expected she would. "Sure," he said. "To put it in a nutshell, there's nothing here for me to do. The engineers and techs have the analysis part well under control, I've already described at the Edo debriefings everything I saw or did here, and there are no artifacts, tools, or even unexplained skid marks for me to look at."

"Don't you think you're being a little hasty in your judgment?" Pemberton suggested mildly. "You've only been here two days."

"Two days has been enough," Pheylan said. "More than enough, in fact. I'm wasting my time, pure and simple."

"So what would you like me to do about it?" Pemberton lifted an eyebrow. "I presume you *do* want me to do something about it."

"Yes," Pheylan acknowledged. "I'd like to request a reassignment back to Edo and back into the war."

Pemberton shook her head. "I wish I could help you, Commander," she said. "But I don't think I can."

"Why not? You're the senior officer here, aren't you?"

"I'm a tech officer, Commander," she explained patiently. "This is a tech group. I don't have any command authority outside this unit. I certainly can't cut reassignment orders."

"Then let me go back to Edo on the skitter with your next report," Pheylan persisted. "I can talk to someone in Admiral Rudzinski's office—"

"Commander." Pemberton held up a hand. "I understand your eagerness to get back into action, and the irritation of feeling like you're wasting your time. But we all have a part to play in this war, and every part is equally important. Even if it's not the part you would have chosen for yourself."

"Really," Pheylan said. He hadn't intended to bring this up quite yet, but she'd pushed him into it. "And your part, I take it, is to determine whether or not the Zhirrzh did more to me in those three weeks than just lock me up in a giant test tube?"

Her expression didn't even twitch. "What do you mean?"

"I mean the reason you're here is to see if I've been brainwashed," he said bluntly. "And the reason *I'm* here is so that if I suddenly go crazy, it'll be in some nice, safe, out-of-the-way place where I can't do any serious damage."

Pemberton cocked an eyebrow. "That's an interesting allegation," she said. "A bit on the paranoid side, though."

"As the old saying goes, even paranoids have enemies," Pheylan countered. "I'd like an honest answer, Colonel."

For a long moment she studied his face. "All right," she said. "You're right. So what now?"

So the unpleasant conclusion he'd come to in those dark predawn hours had been right, after all. He'd hoped he'd been wrong. "I guess you set up your hoops and I jump through them," he told her. "Just show me what I have to do to prove I'm not dangerous."

Pemberton pursed her lips. "Unfortunately, Commander, it's not quite that easy," she said. "Delving the human mind is tricky enough when dealing with well-established, well-documented human psychoses. The possible indoctrination by an alien species is something well outside standard medical experience."

Pheylan stared at her, a sinking feeling forming in his stomach. "Are you saying," he said slowly, "that there *is* no way for me to prove I haven't been brainwashed?"

"I didn't say that," Pemberton cautioned. "I've studied your file carefully, and I'm sure—"

There was a quiet beep from the wall chatterbox beside the door, and the display came on to reveal Lieutenant Williams. "Colonel Pemberton?"

"Yes, Lieutenant, what is it?" Pemberton asked, stepping over in front of the chatterbox.

"Colonel, we've just made audio contact with a Moray-class battle fueler that meshed into the system about half an hour ago," Williams reported. "The pilot won't give us either his assignment-authorization number or his ship's ID code. All he'll say is that he has to speak with Commander Cavanagh."

"Really," Pemberton said, throwing a frown at Pheylan. "Is he armed?"

"Only minimally," Williams said. "A pair of Melara-Vickers shredder-guns and five medium-range Shrike XV missiles. Nothing we can't handle if we have to."

"Does this pilot at least have a name?"

"He says his name's Max," Williams said dryly. "That's all he'll give me. It's sort of like being hailed by a pet dog."

"I'm glad you find this amusing." Pemberton looked at Pheylan. "Feel free at any time to jump into this conversation, Commander."

Pheylan cleared his throat. "I think there's a good chance that that's the fueler my brother Aric used to come looking for me."

"And Max?"

"Actually, the lieutenant's comment wasn't that far off," Pheylan said. "Max is a parasentient computer."

"I thought parasentients were always supposed to identify themselves."

"CavTronics parasentients are programmed only to do so in response to a direct question," Pheylan explained. "My father's always hated the way other companies' parasentients seemed so smug about themselves."

"I see," Pemberton said. "So what's this all about?"

"I don't know," Pheylan admitted. "At the time I left Edo, Aric was planning to take the fueler and go look for our father."

"Maybe he found him," Williams suggested. "Could be that the two of them are aboard and just letting Max do the talking."

"Let's find out," Pemberton said, gesturing Pheylan over to the chatterbox. "Pipe the comm channel down here."

"Yes, Colonel." The display image split, one half still showing Williams, the other blank to signify an audio-only signal. "Channel open."

Pheylan stepped up to the chatterbox. "Max?"

"Yes, Commander Cavanagh," Max's smooth electronic voice came promptly. "A pleasure to speak with you again. Are you well?"

"I'm fine, Max," Pheylan said. "Are you alone?"

"Yes."

So much for his brother and father's being aboard. "What are you doing here?"

"I would prefer to discuss the matter privately, as it pertains to personal family matters," Max said. "Would it be permissible for me to land?"

Pheylan looked at Pemberton. "Colonel?"

She was gazing back at him. A thoughtful, measuring gaze. "You have a very interesting family, Commander Cavanagh," she said. "One might almost say notorious. Go ahead and let him land. I'm rather curious to hear what they've done now."

". . . and so I concluded it would be best to come here and speak with you," Max said. "I hope I have not acted improperly."

"No, not at all," Pheylan assured him, rubbing at the bridge of his nose and trying to sift through this mess. "And you're absolutely sure this Mr. X you mentioned was really NorCoord Military Intelligence?"

"I examined the ID card closely," Max said, "and I have a visual copy in my files for comparison. It was genuine."

Pemberton shifted her position on one of the fueler control room's jump seats. "Yet you won't tell us his name."

"As I stated before, Colonel Pemberton, he made it very clear that I was not to tell anyone else about him," Max said. "I'm sorry."

And whoever he was, he was very interested in finding Aric and their father. What could NorCoord Intelligence possibly want with them? "Could this be some kind of delayed fallout from their borrowing of Masefield's Copperhead unit?"

"I don't know, Commander," Max said. "Legally, though, my understanding is that the inquiry board's decision should have ended the matter. Also, if the borrowing, as you put it, of the Copperheads was the issue, shouldn't this fueler have been impounded as evidence?"

"Probably," Pheylan conceded. "Legal minutiae aren't my specialty. And you have no idea where Aric might have gone?"

"Not with any significant probability," Max said. "I assume he had already left Edo from the fact that I was unable to locate a register for his phone after I spoke with the Intelligence officer. I unfortunately have no data on when precisely he departed."

"The Edo spaceports have listings for all traffic in or out of the planet," Pheylan said. "Did you think to contact them?"

"Yes," Max said. "However, I was able to obtain only the public list, which includes commercial, merchant, and passenger transport. Diplomatic and military craft are on a separate list, which was not available to me."

"Of course," Pheylan murmured, an unpleasant feeling tugging at him. First their father; now Aric. Where in the Commonwealth had the two of them disappeared to? And could the Peacekeepers be involved? "Well, let's start there and—"

"Shh!" Pemberton hissed.

She was staring into space, her head cocked slightly to one side, an expression of intense concentration on her face. "What is it?" Pheylan whispered.

"Didn't you hear it?" Pemberton whispered back. "Like a small explosion."

"No," Pheylan said, feeling his heartbeat pick up its pace. "Max?"

"I've activated my external microphones," the computer said. "Analysis of reverberations is inconclusive."

And then, audible even in the interior of the fueler, Pheylan heard it. A cracking noise, crisp and remote, sounding like a distant thunderclap.

Except that there hadn't been any thunderclouds in the sky when he and Pemberton had entered the fueler twenty minutes earlier. He looked at Pemberton . . . and on the colonel's face he could see the reflection of his own sudden thought.

The Zhirrzh had returned.

They were out of the fueler and into the lift cage in ten seconds flat. "Get us down, Max," Pheylan ordered, shading his eyes as he scanned the sky. But he could see nothing up there except scattered clouds. "Can you tell where that came from?"

"Inconclusive," Max said as the lift cage started down. "But the highest probability is that the sound originated in or near the building complex."

"He's right," Pemberton said grimly, pointing toward the Zhirrzh structure. "Look—you can see smoke rising from the far side of the closest hexagon."

Pheylan nodded. "I see it. Max, are you picking up any spacecraft? Or aircraft of any sort?"

"None at all," Max assured him.

From the direction of the complex came another sharp crack, this one dragging out into almost a ripping sound, with another puff of the smoke drifting up to swirl away in the breeze. "Then it must be a booby trap," Pemberton concluded.

They reached the ground and headed at a dead run toward the Zhirrzh complex. Between the thuds of their footsteps, Pheylan could hear excited voices coming from the complex, and he braced himself for the gruesome sight of broken, bleeding bodies. He reached the first hexagon, rounded it—

And faltered to a confused stop. There in front of him, as he'd expected and feared, a meter-wide, jagged-edged gap had been blown into the smooth ceramic of the wall. Grouped around the hole were piles of equipment and a dozen or more of Williams's engineers and techs.

But none of them were lying bloodied on the ground or gazing at the hole in horror or bewilderment. Instead they were all on their feet, chattering enthusiastically to each other. And smiling.

Beside Pheylan, Pemberton skidded to a halt of her own. "What the hell?" she panted. "Williams?"

Williams's head popped into sight; he'd been kneeling beside one of the equipment piles. "Hey—Colonel," he called, snagging a rag and wiping his hands as he jogged over to them. His own grin was even wider than those of his techs. "Break out the champagne, Colonel. We did it."

"Did what?" Pemberton demanded.

"What do you think?" Williams said triumphantly, waving his rag toward the hole. "We found a way to break up Zhirrzh ceramic."

"It's real tricky stuff," Williams said as Pheylan and Pemberton joined the techs grouped around the ring of equipment by the wall. "Incredibly tough, incredibly resilient, able to handle kinetic impacts and shock waves and even flash-heating from lasers—"

"We know all that," Pheylan interrupted. The memory of those invulnerable hulls, and of the men and women from the *Kinshasa* who had died because of them . . . "Just tell us what you did."

"Well, where brute force fails, you turn to chemistry," Williams said. "We'd already used a meson microscope to map out the atomic structure, so it was mostly a matter of coming up with some kind of catalytic glop that would displace enough atoms to put a strain on critical molecular bonds." He gestured to a pair of tanks with hoses attached to stopcocks. "The stuff doesn't do metal a whole lot of good, either, but fortunately you can make it up as a binary—half the chemical in one bottle, the other half in the other, and they combine on contact to make the catalyst."

"And that's it?" Pemberton asked. "You spray the stuff on the wall and it just falls apart?"

"No, actually, that's just the first step," Williams told her. "The catalyst starts the ceramic crystallizing along irregular planes, which is what we want. But it's only a temporary effect, and as soon as the energy from the reaction has dissipated, the molecular bonds reform. Usually right around the intruding molecules of the catalyst, incidentally, which maybe helps explain why shrapnel attacks don't seem to do much good against the stuff. So before that can happen, you have to give it a good, sharp rap."

"With what, an explosive?" Pemberton frowned, looking around them.

"Oddly enough, no," Williams said, waving at a hornlike metal tube connected to a bank of electronics cabinets. "It turns out that the most effective kick is a fast, precisely modulated series of ultrasonic blasts. In creating those crystallization planes, the catalyst apparently sets up a whole new set of natural frequencies in the ceramic, and when you kick all those resonances in the right order in rapid succession, the stuff just gives up. *Then* it falls apart."

Pemberton shook her head. "Amazing," she said. "Congratulations are indeed in order, Lieutenant."

"I see just two small flies in the ointment," Pheylan said. "Fly number one: how do you know this same technique will work against Zhirrzh warship hulls? You said yourself the ceramics weren't exactly the same."

"We'll have to check that, of course," Williams agreed. "But I've got a copy of the full analysis Command made of the hull fragments they found at the site of the *Jutland* battle. Now that we know the approach to take, it ought to be pretty straightforward to figure out how to modify the catalyst to handle the other ceramic."

"Okay," Pheylan said. "Then fly number two: how in the world do you expect to use ultrasonics against a Zhirrzh warship in the vacuum of space?"

"That one's going to be trickier," Williams admitted. "I don't know yet. I've got a couple of ideas; unfortunately, it's going to take a lot more computing power than we've got here to sort them through. We'll have to send all the data back to Edo and let them run with it."

"Maybe not," Pheylan said, an idea slowly beginning to form in the back of his mind. "How much computing power do you need?"

"Oh, we'd need at least—" Williams broke off, his eyes widening slightly. "That's right, you've got a parasentient out there, don't you? What type and specs?"

"He's a CavTronics Carthage-Ivy-Gamma," Pheylan said, searching his memory. "With Class Seven decision-making capabilities, I think, and eight-point-something megamyncs of compressed memory."

"That should do it," Williams said, suddenly looking doubtful. "I don't know, though—we're talking a civilian computer here. Command probably wouldn't like us loading military secrets onto it."

"On the other hand, if the technique works, it won't be a military secret for long," Pemberton pointed out. "We'll *want* the technique to be as widely disseminated as possible."

"Point," Williams conceded, still looking doubtful. But the chance to test his theories was apparently too strong to resist. "All right," he said, wiping his hands again and pulling a pair of cards from a recorder. "Why don't you go to your fueler and get these loaded up. I'll go to the ship and get the hull stats and join you."

"I'll come with you, Commander," Pemberton added as Pheylan took the cards. "I'm rather curious to see how this works out."

Pheylan threw her a sideways look. Could she suspect what he was thinking? But there was no hint of any suspicion in her expression. "Of course, Colonel," he told her. "Come on."

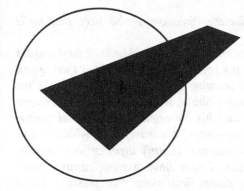

 16 Commander Cavanagh and Colonel Pemberton reappear around the corner of the building 16.85 minutes after their departure from camera range, accompanied by an officer I identify as Lieutenant Williams. I magnify the image, studying their faces and comparing with my human-expression algorithms. While there is a moderate degree of tension in all three expressions, I judge the level to be far below that which should be engendered by the devastation of an enemy trap. I also note that Commander Cavanagh holds two cards in his left hand.

Lieutenant Williams alters direction toward the expedition headquarters ship and enters by the starboard midship hatch. Commander Cavanagh and Colonel Pemberton continue toward me. I analyze their expressions again, calculate a probability of 0.93 that there is no urgency in opening communications with them. I therefore wait until they reach the base of the fueler and Commander Cavanagh speaks.

"Got a job for you, Max. Some heavy-duty data extrapolation and chemical-design manipulation. Think you can handle it?"

I note that there is the same moderate level of tension in his voice that I perceived earlier in his expression. "It sounds most interesting, Commander. I'll do my best."

They enter the lift cage. I activate the mechanism, bringing it to the hatch 22.82 seconds later. After 27.44 seconds more they are both again in the control room. Commander Cavanagh spends 1.04 seconds examining the labels on the cards, then chooses one and inserts it into the transfer slot. "Okay, here's the first batch of data. Take a look."

The reader requires 0.23 second to collect all the data and reassemble it into standard format. 0.18 second into the process I note via the fueler's external cameras that Lieutenant Williams has reemerged from the expedi-

tion ship and has turned in the fueler's direction. I also note that he is carrying a card in his hand.

The reader finishes its formatting, and I spend an additional 0.04 second sorting and collating the data into my preferred arrangement. I then spend 2.66 seconds examining it. Most interesting to me is the data on the ultrasonic blast profiles of 20.88 minutes earlier, which I now recognize were produced by Lieutenant Williams and his colleagues. My external microphones had detected only limited fragments of the waveforms, which had in turn left me unable to properly analyze and identify them or their source. With this new data in my possession I now have a significantly refined understanding of the microphones' design limitations. "Interesting. Have you the active sensor data as well?"

"Right here."

Commander Cavanagh inserts the second card. As promised, it is the active sensor data from the experiments, recording the complete dynamics of the ceramic wall's structural failure. "What level of extrapolation do you wish, Commander?"

"For now, just look the data over and get a feel for the process. Lieutenant Williams will be bringing you the main challenge."

"I understand."

I perform a brief preliminary examination, studying both the macroscopic and microscopic effects, creating an active first-approximation stress-point map, producing a similar map of molecular energy levels within both the ceramic and the induced crystallization planes, calculating energy-transfer profiles between each of the ultrasound frequencies and the crystallization planes, and extrapolating possible new resonance frequencies based on this analysis.

The examination process requires 3.67 minutes, during which time I also lower the lift cage for Lieutenant Williams and bring him up. "I've performed an initial examination, Commander. Are you ready to provide further data and instructions?"

Lieutenant Williams's expression changes. From the algorithms I calculate a probability of 0.68 that he is not entirely happy. I calculate an additional probability of 0.92 that this emotion relates to the project I am currently working on. "Or should that question be directed toward Lieutenant Williams?"

Lieutenant Williams's lip twitches in a gesture I interpret as mild distaste. "I'm still not sure I like this. But here goes."

He inserts his card into the transfer slot. "I trust Commander Cavanagh has explained that everything we're giving you is privileged military information and not to be divulged to anyone but properly designated Peacekeeper personnel."

"I was not so informed, but I am now." *I spend 0.04 second examining the relevant sections of Commonwealth law and Peacekeeper regulations.* "I also understand the requirements and limitations your order places on me."

He nods, his expression altering slightly. "I hope so. All right. What I'm giving you now is everything Peacekeeper Command's got on Zhirrzh warship-hull material. The bottom-line questions are, one, can we use the same technique on them that we did on the wall over there; and two, how does the technique have to be modified."

Commander Cavanagh takes a step behind Lieutenant Williams toward the doorway. "And, three, how do we go about using ultrasound against the hulls in space."

Lieutenant Williams again nods. "Right."

Commander Cavanagh takes two more steps, the last one bringing him to a position directly in front of the doorway. "While you're working on that, Max, why don't you put some of the results of your first analysis on the displays. I'm sure Lieutenant Williams would find them interesting."

"Of course."

I choose the microscopic sensor data, the stress-point analysis, and the energy-transfer map and bring them up on three of the control room's displays. Synchronizing their timings, I begin to play them. The reader finishes collecting the incoming data from the card, and I spend 0.03 second again arranging it in a more convenient form.

I begin my analysis, starting with a chemical/structural comparison routine. As I do so, Commander Cavanagh quietly exits the room.

I continue both the presentation and the analysis, studying the faces of the two Peacekeeper officers still in the control room. The algorithms indicate Lieutenant Williams to be intensely absorbed in the presentation, the size of his pupils and his slow blink rate allowing me to calculate a probability of 0.96 that he has both a high degree of interest and an equally high degree of understanding of the material. I similarly compute a probability of 0.78 that Colonel Pemberton has a high degree of interest; however, I also calculate a probability of 0.64 that she has little actual comprehension.

I also compute a probability of 0.93 that neither has noticed Commander Cavanagh has left the control room. Examining the correlation between his actions and his suggestion that I display this data, I estimate a probability of 0.80 that this result was deliberately intended.

The stress-point and energy analyses conclude, and I replace them with false-color schematics created from the meson microscope study of the ceramic. I also continue with my analysis of the Zhirrzh hull-ceramic data, as well as following Commander Cavanagh's movements on my internal monitors as he retraces his path back to the hatchway.

I estimate a probability of 0.80 that he intends to leave the fueler, but that conclusion is proved erroneous. He opens the emergency locker beside the hatchway and extracts a survival pack. *I recompute, estimating a probability of 0.60 that he is hungry and seeking a ration bar.*

This conclusion is also proved erroneous. From the survival pack he withdraws a flechette pistol.

He conceals the flechette pistol beneath his tunic and returns the survival pack to the locker. He looks at the entryway camera, his expression changing. I compare algorithms, compute a probability of 0.67 that he knows I have observed his actions and is wondering what conclusions I am drawing. But he does not speak to me; he merely retraces his path back to the control room.

He reenters the room 68.54 seconds after leaving it. I watch the other two officers' expressions as he enters the doorway behind them, compute a probability of 0.85 that his absence has gone unnoticed by both of them. "Interesting stuff, Max. Anything yet on the actual hull material?"

I spend 0.45 second examining the results of my chemical/structural comparison and begin a first-approximation extrapolation of the catalytic/ultrasound technique. "I've done a comparison of the two ceramics, Commander. They are chemically similar, though with differences in certain admixture ratios."

Lieutenant Williams waves his right hand, his expression one of impatience. "We know all that. What we need to know is whether or not the catalytic/ultrasound method can be adapted to work against it."

"I understand that, Lieutenant. My analysis of that question is as yet incomplete."

Lieutenant Williams mutters something under his breath. I replay the sound, enhancing the volume, and discover it to be a vulgarity in common usage on Kalevala twenty years previously. "How long is it going to take?"

Commander Cavanagh moves around behind him, passing him and continuing on to a point at Colonel Pemberton's side. "Take it easy, Lieutenant. Max is a parasentient computer, not God."

"Right." *Lieutenant Williams steps to the transfer slot and withdraws the card.* "Unfortunately, I don't have time to sit around watching his gears spin—I've got work to do. Where are the cards I gave you?"

Commander Cavanagh hands him the two cards that he brought aboard. "I'll stick around and let you know when he's got some answers."

"Fine." *Lieutenant Williams turns to look at Colonel Pemberton, lifting his eyebrows in a questioning gesture.* "You coming, Colonel?"

For 0.73 second Colonel Pemberton looks at Commander Cavanagh, her head tilted 5.97 degrees off vertical to the right. "No, go on ahead. I'll stay here."

"Okay. See you later." *Lieutenant Williams turns and leaves the control room.*

Commander Cavanagh walks around the room to the number-two jump seat and pulls it out. "There's no particular reason you have to stay, you know."

Colonel Pemberton's face alters to an expression indicating thoughtfulness and a certain degree of distrust. "I like your company. Besides, you might get lonely." *She looks around, simultaneously waving her right hand in a gesture that encompasses the control room and, by inference, the entire fueler.* "Here in this big ship all alone."

I finish my extrapolation of the catalytic/ultrasound technique against the Zhirrzh hull material. "I have a preliminary result, Commander. I compute a probability of 0.92 that Lieutenant Williams's technique can be used successfully against Zhirrzh warship-hull material. It will actually require only minor modification."

"Great." *Commander Cavanagh takes a deep breath. The low-level tension that has been in his face changes, altering into an expression of firm resolve.* "Print out everything you've got onto some cards. The raw data, your analyses and extrapolations—everything."

He pauses 1.05 seconds, during which time his lips tighten together and then relax. "And then get the fueler prepped to fly."

I begin printing out onto the cards as ordered and activate the fueler's electronics self-test. I also examine Colonel Pemberton's face, finding a slight hardening of her expression but no overt surprise. "You going somewhere?"

"As a matter of fact, I am."

"Without saying good-bye?"

Commander Cavanagh's mouth tightens for 0.24 second. "You've already said you're not going to let me leave anytime soon. That you don't even know how I can prove I'm safe for the Peacekeepers to use."

"And you think going AWOL is going to help your case?"

I finish writing onto the cards and eject them into the holder. Commander Cavanagh glances over, then returns his attention to Colonel Pemberton. "I don't have time to waste playing psych games, Colonel. We've got a way here—maybe—to hit back at the Zhirrzh. I intend to give it a try."

Colonel Pemberton's eyes narrow. "What about Peacekeeper Command?"

"What about them? They'll get their copy of the results—that's who the cards are for. Go ahead, take them."

Moving slowly, Colonel Pemberton steps to the holder and takes the cards, her expression and body language indicating caution. "Then what is all this supposed to prove? You're not planning to take this fueler up against a Zhirrzh warship, are you?"

An edge of amusement enters Commander Cavanagh's expression. "Hardly. I'm not trying to prove anything, either. Max, how long before we're ready to lift?"

I examine the progress of the preflight checklist. "All critical components have been checked and cleared. It'll take three minutes to pressurize the Icefire pumps once you authorize it."

Commander Cavanagh nods. "Pressurize the pumps."

Colonel Pemberton shakes her head slowly. "This isn't the way, Commander. All it'll do is wreck your career and make you a fugitive."

"My career is hardly the important issue here. Max, let me know when the pumps are pressurized."

"Yes, Commander."

Colonel Pemberton half reaches a hand out toward Commander Cavanagh. "Commander—Pheylan—listen to me." *Her voice is soft and quietly pleading. I analyze her expression and tonal pattern, compute a probability of 0.87 that her concern is genuine.* "I understand how much you want to get out of here, and I sympathize with you. But whatever it is you've got planned, believe me, it isn't going to accomplish anything."

Commander Cavanagh smiles. With the underlying tightness of his expression, the smile carries no significant degree of humor. "We'll find out."

For 3.66 seconds neither of them speak. I study Colonel Pemberton's expression, noting several changes of emotion that culminate in shocked understanding. "You're taking the information to your sister on Dorcas. Aren't you?"

Commander Cavanagh nods. His expression indicates mild surprise at her comment. "Very good, Colonel—full marks for inspired guesswork. It's almost time—better get moving. And be careful with those cards on your way out."

Colonel Pemberton doesn't move, but her expression and voice take on a degree of scorn. "So that's all this is? You think your sister is entitled to this information before anyone else in the Commonwealth gets it?"

A faint flush of blood flows briefly into Commander Cavanagh's cheeks. From his expression I calculate a probability of 0.92 that the flush is due to anger and not embarrassment. "Let me tell you something, Colonel Pemberton. I checked the records before I left Edo to come here. There's been one attack—one—on the Zhirrzh blockade ships around Dorcas. And that was over ten days ago. There haven't even been any surveillance ships sent into the system since then to find out what's going on there. The fact of the matter is that Peacekeeper Command's written them off."

He points to the cards in Colonel Pemberton's hand. "Maybe there's a chance they can use this technique. It's worth the risk of one life to give them that chance."

Colonel Pemberton draws herself up to her full height, adding 1.98 centimeters to her normal posture. "And if I refuse to let you?"

Commander Cavanagh reaches beneath his tunic and takes hold of the hidden flechette pistol. Midway through his action Colonel Pemberton's expression changes, and I calculate a probability of 0.83 that she has suddenly perceived the protrusion of the weapon beneath the material. She makes no move to interfere, however, as he draws the flechette pistol from concealment. "You don't have a choice, Colonel."

Colonel Pemberton nods toward the flechette pistol. Her expression indicates a mixture of caution and scorn, but not fear. "And you expect me to believe you'd really use that on me?"

Commander Cavanagh smiles again. Unlike the previous smile, this one has a degree of actual humor associated with it. "Of course I would. I'm a desperate man."

"I see." *There is still no fear in Colonel Pemberton's voice.* "What you really mean is that now that I've been physically threatened, I'm off the legal hot seat for letting you go?"

"Something like that. Max, what about those pumps?"

"Approximately one minute remaining, Commander."

"Just enough time for Colonel Pemberton to get to the ground. Goodbye, Colonel."

Another series of emotions passes across Colonel Pemberton's face. After 1.44 seconds she turns and walks to the command-room doorway. There she pauses 0.61 second, then turns back to face Commander Cavanagh. "For what it's worth, Commander, I admire your family loyalty. As a matter of fact, if you *weren't* willing to risk your career for your sister, I might consider it evidence of Zhirrzh tampering. Off the record, good luck; on the record, I'll see you at your court-martial."

Commander Cavanagh throws her a salute. "I hope so, Colonel."

Colonel Pemberton again turns, this time leaving the room. Commander Cavanagh waits 3.02 seconds, then returns the flechette pistol to its hiding place beneath his tunic. "Watch her, Max. Make sure she leaves, and that she doesn't mess with anything on her way out."

I am already monitoring Colonel Pemberton's movements. "Yes, Commander."

Commander Cavanagh stands up from his jump seat, opens the side access slits and pulls out the restraint straps, then sits down again. "And once she's down, make sure she gets far enough back from the ship to be safe. As soon as she is, get us out of here."

Colonel Pemberton reaches the hatch and enters the lift cage. I start it down the side of the fueler. "I must agree with the colonel, Commander, that this is an unreasonable risk for you to take. A surveillance ship from Edo could transmit the data via laser to the Dorcas Peacekeepers."

Commander Cavanagh begins strapping himself to the jump seat for lift. "Except that I can't trust Edo to necessarily follow through." *He pauses 0.92 second.* "Besides, even if Williams's technique flames out, you've got a supply of fuel aboard that they probably desperately need. That alone would make the trip worthwhile."

Colonel Pemberton reaches the ground. Leaving the lift cage, she heads at a brisk jog away from the fueler. I begin bringing the lift cage back up. "I understand."

"Good." *Commander Cavanagh completes the strapping-in procedure.* "I'm ready. Where's Colonel Pemberton?"

Colonel Pemberton is still moving away. The lift cage is in position, and I rotate it securely into its storage compartment. "She is fifty-two meters from the base of the fueler, moving northeast. Established unprotected safety distance is sixty meters."

"Let her get at least seventy—I don't want to take any chance of hurting her. Or anyone else, for that matter."

I scan the area with my external cameras. There is no one else nearby. "I trust you also understand that there is a significant probability that Melinda Cavanagh will not have survived the Zhirrzh attack."

Commander Cavanagh's jaw muscles tighten noticeably. The algorithms indicate dread. "I know that, Max. But she and Aric got me out of this place. I have to try to help them."

I spend 0.02 second considering this comment, then spend another 0.04 second reviewing the previous conversation. At no time was Aric Cavanagh's name even mentioned. "Where does Aric fit into this?"

Commander Cavanagh smiles, some of his dread masked behind forced humor. "Oh, come on, Max. Where else do you think he and Dad have disappeared to?"

I spend an additional 0.05 second examining this statement. Commander Cavanagh's inference is obvious, but I can detect no logical pathway to such a conclusion. "Are you suggesting they're also on Dorcas?"

"With Melinda in danger there? Where else would they go?"

"I presume the question is rhetorical. The conclusion is nevertheless extravagant conjecture."

Commander Cavanagh shakes his head, his expression indicating complete certainty. "I know my family, Max. They got me out from under the Zhirrzh; now they've gone to get Melinda out. I'll bet you my pension they're there."

"I don't gamble, Commander." *I spend 0.06 second reviewing*

Peacekeeper regulations. "Besides which, if you're convicted at a court-martial, you'll no longer have a pension."

Commander Cavanagh's expression puckers oddly. "And they say parasentients don't have a sense of humor. Is Pemberton clear yet?"

Colonel Pemberton is 82.74 meters from the fueler. "Yes."

"Then let's get moving." *Commander Cavanagh takes a deep breath and settles himself inside his restraint straps.* "My family's waiting for me."

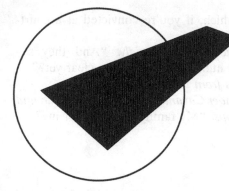

17 Nearly two fullarcs had passed since her last visit when the Human named Doctor-Cavan-a finally returned again to the metal room. "You're back," Prr't-zevisti said, speaking the Human words carefully. "I was become worried."

"I was a little worried myself," Doctor-Cavan-a said, closing the door behind her.

For a few beats Prr't-zevisti studied her face. An alien face, its display of emotions dark to his understanding. Even so, there was something about it that disturbed him. "You were gone a long time," he said, trying hard to wring some meaning from that face. "Has something happen?"

"My commander thinks you are lying to me," Doctor-Cavan-a said. "He thinks you can talk from here to your commander."

Prr't-zevisti stared at her, the very bluntness of the accusation startling him into silence. "I do not lie to you," he protested. "Why does your commander think I do?"

"Your commander attacked a place they shouldn't have known about."

"Why shouldn't they have know about the place?" Prr't-zevisti asked. "Is it hid from the Elders?"

Doctor-Cavan-a turned her head back and forth to the side. "Sorry. I meant to say they shouldn't have known the (something) of the place."

Prr't-zevisti flicked his tongue in perplexity. "I don't know that word, the one before 'of the place.' "

"It means the purpose or possible purpose."

Significance: purpose or possible purpose. Prr't-zevisti tucked the word and its definition away in his ever-increasing Human vocabulary. "Why does your commander think Zhirrzh activeness at the place has significance? Commander Thrr-mezaz sees much, and is curious about all."

"That is possible," Doctor-Cavan-a said. "But my commander does not think we can take that risk."

"The risk is that the war continue," Prr't-zevisti snapped. "Does he not accept that truth?"

"He does not yet accept that it is truth," Doctor-Cavan-a said. "He sees that the truth might be different: that you are a spy."

For a handful of beats Prr't-zevisti gazed at her alien face. "What about you, Doctor-Cavan-a? What do you accept?"

Again Doctor-Cavan-a turned her head back and forth to the side. "I do not know," she said. "We will think more. It is possible we will yet accept that you do not lie."

Prr't-zevisti flicked his tongue, this time in exasperation. The Humans and Zhirrzh were poised for wholesale slaughter of each other; and here was their only way out, blocked by the paranoid fears of a minor Human warrior commander. What in the eighteen worlds did he think was up here that was worth spying on, anyway? "How can I prove my truth?" he demanded.

"I do not know any way," Doctor-Cavan-a said, her voice quiet. "I am sorry."

For a few beats the metal room was silent. The metal prison. "Then what do we do?" Prr't-zevisti asked at last. "How can we stop the war?"

"I do not know any way," Doctor-Cavan-a said again. "We must try to think of a way."

She turned around and pushed the door open just far enough for her to slip through. "You go?" Prr't-zevisti asked.

"I must go," Doctor-Cavan-a said. "My commander has ordered me to stay away from you until he decides."

"But—"

"I am sorry, Prr't-zevisti. Farewell for now."

She slipped out through the opening, swinging the door shut behind her. It closed with a muffled boom.

And Prr't-zevisti was once again alone.

"The fools," he murmured aloud. "The irresponsible fools."

The words echoed through his mind and faded into silence. So it was over. His own people had abandoned him here; and now the Humans themselves had rejected the truth.

Which made them doubly fools, because with that rejection they had resigned themselves to their own destruction. The Zhirrzh warriors would win this war, just as they always won. And it would serve the Humans right.

He flicked his tongue in disgust. It would serve them right . . . but he knew perfectly well that he couldn't just sit by and let that happen. Not if there was any way to stop it. He'd been a warrior once, a warrior of the proud and noble Dhaa'rr clan. True warriors made war only in self-defense.

Which meant he would just have to find a way to convince Doctor-Cavan-a and her Human commander that he was telling the truth.

And hope that until then neither the Humans nor the Zhirrzh did anything that would inflame the war so much that nothing he could do would stop it.

Bronski shook his head. "I don't know, Cavanagh. It seems to me that if it was this easy, someone at Command would have come up with it by now."

"There's a good chance someone has," Lord Cavanagh said, running his eye over the numbers one more time. With access to Bronski's ship computer he'd finally been able to nail down the idea that had been floating nebulously around his mind during all those days stuck on Granparra. "On the other hand, maybe not. Peacekeeper Command may be concentrating on high heat-capacity materials. If they're even experimenting with ablative coatings at all."

"Oh, you can bet they're concentrating on pretty much everything," Bronski assured him, flipping through the graphs on the display again and stopping at a sharply rising hyperbolic curve. "These philo-plant leaves really behave like this?"

"Trust me," Cavanagh assured him. "The R-and-D group that first tested them thought they'd found the ideal circuit-board material: tough yet flexible, and with a better semimagnetic profile than even sloanmetal."

"Not to mention free," Bronski murmured.

"Right," Cavanagh said. "The Palisades Alps were practically covered with the things. Anyway, the team thought they had their bonuses already in the bank on this one. They had fifteen hundred boards made up and flown to Avon for further tests."

He smiled tightly at the memory. "And then someone tried laser-welding components onto them; and bingo: vapor defocusing."

"Yeah," Bronski muttered. "You realize, of course, that defocusing a welding laser is a far cry from doing the same to those big war lasers the Zhirrzh use."

"Of course," Cavanagh said. "These self-cohesion curves might easily break down under that sort of flash-heating. But I think it's at least an avenue worth exploring further."

"I suppose," Bronski agreed grudgingly. "Sure, get it written up and we'll send it out on the next skitter headed for Earth or Edo."

"Brigadier?" Kolchin's voice called. "Nearly time to mesh in."

"Thanks," Bronski said, brushing past Cavanagh and heading up into the control room.

Cavanagh filed away his calculations and followed, arriving just as Bronski was replacing Kolchin in the pilot's seat. "I hope we'll be exercising a certain amount of discretion," he commented, sitting down behind the brigadier.

"I wasn't planning on charging in with shredders blazing and making wholesale arrests, if that's what you mean," Bronski said. "Don't worry, I know how to sneak into places."

"The ship has a false ID signal?" Kolchin asked.

"You'd be amazed at the assortment of ID signals it has," Bronski replied. "Here we go."

From somewhere beneath them came the rattle of multiple relays snapping open. The blackness outside the canopy became a brief illusion of a tunnel; and then the stars flowed back into their proper places surrounding the planet ahead. "Looks like we're about a half hour out," Bronski said, giving his displays a quick survey.

"What do we do about passports?" Cavanagh asked. "Or were you planning on leaving us on the ship while you snoop around?"

"Tempting thought," Bronski said. "But knowing you, you'd probably steal it. Here."

He tossed a pair of dark-green passports—Arcadian issue?—back over his headrest. Cavanagh caught them and opened them up.

They were Arcadian, all right, made out to a father-and-son merchandising team of Baccar and Gil Fortunori. Cavanagh's and Kolchin's photos and thumbprints were already imprinted beneath the tamper proofing. "Impressive," Cavanagh said, handing Kolchin his passport. "Who do you get to be?"

"Jan-michael Marchand," Bronski said. "Your pilot and cultural facilitator." He threw Cavanagh a look over the back of his chair. "Which means I do all the talking while you two stand in the background grinning like harmless innocents. Got it?"

"I think we can handle the roles," Cavanagh said, sliding his new passport into his jacket.

"Good," Bronski said, turning back to his board. "I tucked some background info on your characters into the backs of the passports. I suggest you get to know yourselves."

The Prime gazed down into the carrier box that Speaker Cvv-panav had just dropped unceremoniously onto his desk. "All right," he said, looking up again. "It's a *fsss* organ. So?"

"It's not just any *fsss* organ, Overclan Prime," the Speaker for Dhaa'rr bit out. "It's Prr't-zevisti's *fsss* organ. You remember Prr't-zevisti?"

"It would be hard to forget him," the Prime said dryly. "Certainly not after all the Dhaa'rr petitions I've received calling for Commander Thrr-mezaz's removal. I was under the impression that the Dhaa'rr clan was preparing final rites for him."

Cvv-panav smiled. "You hide your disappointment well, Overclan Prime. I'm sure you would have preferred to have the evidence destroyed in the ceremony of fire. Tell me, did you and Thrr-gilag make the arrangements together to take an illegal cutting of this *fsss*? Or was your role merely to assist in burying the crime after its commission?"

With the ease of many cyclics of practice, the Prime kept his gaze steady and his tail spinning serenely. "That's a very serious allegation, Speaker Cvv-panav. Have you any proof that Searcher Thrr-gilag was involved in any illegal acts?"

"I have proof that some of the semiliquid material from the interior of this *fsss* was removed by needle," Cvv-panav said. "I can also prove that Thrr-gilag visited the Prr-family shrine shortly before the tampering was discovered."

"I see," the Prime nodded. "And for how many cyclics before Thrr-gilag's visit had the *fsss* been resting unexamined in its niche?"

"That's irrelevant."

"Is it?" the Prime countered. "Seems to me it's the first question a jurist would ask."

For a long beat Cvv-panav gazed at him, a mixture of speculation and irritation on his face. "This is the key, Overclan Prime," he said softly. "The key to bringing you down."

"Undoubtedly," the Prime said with a sigh. "And I wish you good luck when you've taken over the burden of running the eighteen worlds. For right now, though, that's still my job. If you'll excuse me, I have a great deal of work to do."

Cvv-panav flicked his tongue in contempt. "Mock me while you can, Overclan Prime. But I will see you toppled. And perhaps the entire Overclan system along with you." With a haughty, sweeping gesture straight out of Dhaa'rr history records he turned and stalked away—

"Speaker Cvv-panav?" the Prime called.

The other paused at the door. "Yes?"

The Prime flicked his tongue at his desk. "You forgot Prr't-zevisti's *fsss*."

Cvv-panav smiled tightly. "You may keep it for now, Overclan Prime. Study it; contemplate it. Therein lies the embryo of your destruction."

Turning again, he pulled the door open and stepped through, closing it with a resounding thud behind him.

"I didn't think Zhirrzh talked like that anymore," the wry voice of the Fifteenth said from behind the Prime's shoulder.

"Say what you like about him, Speaker Cvv-panav does have a flair for the dramatic," the Fourth agreed, appearing just in front of the door. "Reminds me of the Speaker for Dhaa'rr when I was Overclan Prime."

"I imagine that's exactly the style he's trying for," the Prime said, carefully closing the box lid over Prr't-zevisti's *fsss*. "How many Elders are there outside?"

"The Eighteenth is watching," the Fourth said. "I believe I missed your explanation as to why you think the Speaker will have Elders waiting for him."

"They're witnesses," the Prime said. "Cvv-panav will want to have someone who can attest that he brought Prr't-zevisti's *fsss* organ into my private chambers but didn't have it when he left five hunbeats later, thereby proving he left it with me."

"To what end?"

"To the end of blaming the Prime for any damage that might occur to it, of course," the Eighteenth said, appearing in front of the desk. "You were right, Overclan Prime: there were five of them, waiting just outside the shadow region. At the Speaker's request they performed a rather complete examination of his person and clothing."

"Incredible," the Fourth murmured. "Does he really think you foolish or desperate enough to destroy evidence left in your possession?"

"I'm sure he doesn't," the Prime said grimly, opening the secure drawer of his desk and placing the box inside. "It's more likely he plans to discreetly steal the *fsss* back and destroy it himself."

"That would certainly fit the Speaker's slash-tongue style," the Fifteenth agreed. "As well as providing a certain symmetry to the way we trapped and blackmailed him over the theft of Thrr-pifix-a's *fsss*."

"Indeed." The Eighteenth nodded agreement. "You'll want a triple guard on your chambers from now on."

The Prime flicked his tongue in irritation. There was a war for survival under way, with Zhirrzh beachheads under constant threat and an assault fleet poised for a make-or-break attack on the Human-Conqueror surveillance installations on Phormbi. He didn't have time for this political nonsense. "A guard won't be enough," he told the Elders. "Cvv-panav's got something else under his tongue. Do we still have a secure pathway to Dorcas?"

"Reasonably secure," the Eighteenth said.

"Open it," the Prime instructed. "I want to speak to Searcher Thrr-gilag."

"From here in your chambers?" the Eighteenth asked, frowning. "That's not recommended."

"We don't have a choice," the Prime said. "In this case—"

"The Eighteenth is right," the Fifteenth put in. "This chamber is supposed to be inaccessible to all Elders. That deception must be maintained."

"I'm aware of that, thank you," the Prime said. "However, in this case—"

"The secret nearly escaped once before," the Fifteenth continued as if he hadn't spoken. "During the term of the Twenty-second."

"I remember," the Fourth rumbled. "The Twenty-second opened a pathway from here, and an Elder eavesdropping at the other end noted the exact time and checked on when he was supposed to have been in his chambers—"

"I'm aware of the risks," the Prime said sharply, cutting through the growing discussion. "But in this case it's a chance we have to take. Cvv-panav has allies all over Unity City, physicals and Elders both. I can't afford the risk that one of them might overhear this conversation. Now open the pathway."

"As you wish," the Eighteenth growled, still not sounding convinced. He flicked away. The beats ticked by; and then he was back. "The pathway is open, Overclan Prime," he said. "You may begin."

"Thank you," the Prime said. "Searcher Thrr-gilag, this is the Overclan Prime. Are you alone?"

The Eighteenth nodded and vanished, returning a few beats later. " 'My brother, Commander Thrr-mezaz, and Searcher Klnn-dawan-a are here with me,' " he quoted. " 'Shall I ask them to leave?' "

The Prime flicked his tongue. More witnesses, should this ever make it to the jurist level. But on the other side, Thrr-mezaz and Klnn-dawan-a could hardly be more involved in this than they already were. "No, they may stay," he said. "This concerns them, as well. But make sure no one else is listening."

The delay this time was nearly double the previous interval. " 'We're ready,' " the Eighteenth quoted when he finally returned. " 'Thrr-mezaz has sent all the Elders to inspect the beachhead perimeter.' "

And if any of them had lingered behind . . . but there was no way to totally eliminate that risk. "First of all, I want to know if you've made any progress on your Human-Conqueror studies."

" 'I'm afraid it's going slowly,' " the reply came half a hunbeat later.

" 'The facilities here are limited, and an organism's biochemistry is an immensely complex system.' "

"There's nothing even preliminary you can tell me?"

" 'Nothing relating to my theory of Human aggression. We've established a baseline, though, and compared it to the similar readings from the first Human prisoner, Pheylan Cavanagh. That gives us a start.' "

The typical maddening pace of searcher studies. "Keep at it," the Prime ordered, trying to keep the frustration out of his voice. "I want any information you get as soon as you get it. Not a tentharc later; right away. Is that clear?"

" 'Very clear, Overclan Prime.' "

"Good," the Prime said. "Now, what about the other matter? The one that also concerns Searcher Klnn-dawan-a's presence there?"

" 'Again, we've made no progress,' " the cautious answer came. " 'The climate and other factors aren't yet right.' "

The Prime grimaced. Translation: they hadn't yet been able to get Prr't-zevisti's new cutting within range of the Human-Conqueror mountain stronghold. Perhaps hadn't even tried. "You may not be able to wait for the climate to be right," he warned. "Matters are coming to a crisis here. Possibly there, as well."

The Eighteenth nodded and vanished. "What did you mean by that?" the Fourth asked.

"I mean that Speaker Cvv-panav isn't just going to wait around and hope I'll make a mistake," the Prime said grimly. "He has to make another move; and the odds are that move will involve Thrr-gilag."

"Yes, of course," the Fourth murmured. "Thrr-gilag has the evidence of *fsss* tampering that Cvv-panav wants, after all. Shouldn't you warn him?"

"I just did," the Prime said. "Even with a supposedly secure pathway I don't want to risk being any clearer than that."

The Eighteenth returned. " 'We understand, Overclan Prime,' " he quoted. " 'We'll do our best.' "

"Make certain you do," the Prime said. "Keep me informed as to your progress. Farewell, and good luck." He nodded to the Eighteenth. "Deliver that, and unless there's more from their end, you may release the pathway."

"Yes, Overclan Prime." The Eighteenth vanished.

For a merciful wonder, the other two Elders kept quiet. Reaching across his desk to his reader, the Prime keyed for the latest warrior update. The eight beachheads they held in Human-Conqueror territory were still holding firm under enemy pressure, though three of them just barely. The diplomatic group on Mra was settling in for the long term; a

Dhaa'rr ship was on its way there with extra supplies for them. The ships for the quick-strike assault on the Human-Conqueror surveillance bases on Phormbi were assembled and on their way to the attack, and Warrior Command was busily trying to gather a force together for the planned thrust into the Human-Conqueror homeworld.

Assuming, of course, that the Mrachanis made good on their promise to sneak those warships past the Human-Conqueror detectors.

The Eighteenth returned. "No further messages from Thrr-gilag," he reported.

"Thank you," the Prime said. "That'll be all."

"I daresay." The Eighteenth paused. "If I may comment, Overclan Prime, you seemed unduly interested in Thrr-gilag's Human-Conqueror biochemical studies. I would have thought such subtleties had already been overtaken by events."

"Only if you trust the Mrachanis," the Prime said sourly. "I'm not sure I do."

"You're worried about the Phormbi attack?" the Fourth asked.

"I'm worried about all of it," the Prime said with a tired sigh. "Everything the Mrachanis say seems perfectly reasonable at first look. Even at second look. But whenever I start really thinking things through . . ." He flicked his tongue in a negative.

For a few beats the room was silent. "There's no point in worrying excessively about it," the Eighteenth said. "The decisions have been made, and the events are in motion. What will happen will happen."

"And whatever does happen, it is always safe to put your trust in Warrior Command," the Fourth added. "Whether the Mrachanis are being honest or deceitful, the Zhirrzh warriors will be capable of handling it."

"I hope so," the Prime said, turning back to his reader. "I truly hope so."

The Elder vanished, and for perhaps twenty beats the only sound in the room was the spattering of the cold, windswept rain lashing against the office windows in the latearc darkness. "I don't know about you," Thrr-gilag said at last. "But to me that sounded like an order."

"It was," Thrr-mezaz said heavily. "Something's happening back on Oaccanv. Or else is about to happen."

"Maybe someone's discovered our tampering," Klnn-dawan-a said. "Maybe they're on their way here."

And Thrr-gilag knew exactly what that would mean, both to them and to their families. He didn't doubt that his brother knew, too. "We'll just have to beat them to the slash, then," he said. "One way or another, we have got to get Prr't-zevisti's cutting up into the Human stronghold."

"What, in this?" Thrr-mezaz retorted, flicking his tongue toward the downpour outside the window. "Not a chance. The storm extends all the way to the mountains. We try climbing in this, and we'll be raised to Eldership in twenty hunbeats."

"The rain has to stop sometime," Klnn-dawan-a said. "How soon after that could you start climbing?"

"At least a fullarc," Thrr-mezaz told her. "The storm has high winds trailing behind it. Even if it didn't, wet rock is notoriously dangerous to climb."

The room fell silent again. Thrr-gilag stared out the window at the sheets of rain shimmering in the lights of the village, a hundred plans flickering through his mind, each more far-fetched than the previous one. Launching an aerial attack on the Humans? Dangerous, and probably illegal without specific orders from Warrior Command. Firing the *fsss* container into the mountains via catapult? Unlikely they could put something together that would have even half the range they would need. Lashing the container to an animal and sending it into the mountains? Too ridiculous even to think about. Returning the Human prisoner Sergeant Janovetz to his people with the cutting planted somewhere on him?

The flow of schemes paused in midtaste. Sergeant Janovetz . . .

He looked back at the others. Thrr-mezaz was still gazing at the floor in contemplation of his own; but Klnn-dawan-a, clearly sensing the change in Thrr-gilag's manner, was looking back at him with guarded hope. "You have an idea?" she asked.

"Yes," he said as Thrr-mezaz also looked up at him. "I don't like it, but I think it's our best chance. Possibly even our only chance. Certainly if we want to get the cutting up there as quickly as possible."

"Sounds terrific," Thrr-mezaz said. "You want to skip the dramatics and spit it out?" He looked over at Klnn-dawan-a. "He was always doing this when we were children," he added in explanation. "I hoped he'd grow out of it."

"He hasn't yet," Klnn-dawan-a said, trying to keep her voice light but not succeeding very well. "Go ahead, Thrr-gilag."

"We do exactly what the Humans did with Sergeant Janovetz," Thrr-gilag said. "We send someone into the Human stronghold on some pretext and send Prr't-zevisti's *fsss* cutting in with him."

"Brilliant," Thrr-mezaz said. "There are just two small problems: how do we keep the Human-Conquerors from shooting down his transport, and how do we get him out again?"

"For the first, I presume we do it the same way the Human commander did," Thrr-gilag said. "We send an unarmed vehicle, and we send
it in flying slow and steady. For the second—" He grimaced. "We don't
get him out. Like Sergeant Janovetz, the courier would have to stay there
as a prisoner."

"I was afraid you'd say that," Thrr-mezaz said. "Unfortunately, I can't
afford to lose any of my warriors."

"I know," Thrr-gilag said. "That's why the courier has to be me."

He'd expected a reaction of some kind. The complete lack of one
showed that both of the others had already arrived at the same conclusion. "It'll be dangerous, Thrr-gilag," Thrr-mezaz warned. "These are
the Human-Conquerors. We don't know what they'll do to you."

"Believe me, my brother, if I thought I was walking straight to my
Eldership, I wouldn't be volunteering," Thrr-gilag assured him. "I don't
believe they'll hurt me."

"What about your theory?" Thrr-mezaz reminded him. "You'll be facing a whole group of Human-Conquerors up there, not just single individuals."

"Yet a whole group of them let Klnn-dawan-a and your warriors go
unharmed at the underground room," he pointed out. "There's clearly
more to these Humans than just reflex biochemical reactions."

"You could still wind up a prisoner until the end of the war," Thrr-
mezaz persisted. "Or be raised to Eldership if and when Warrior Command gives me the order to attack the stronghold in force."

Thrr-gilag felt his tail twitch. "I know that. It's a risk I'm going to have
to take."

Thrr-mezaz hissed with frustration, looking over at Klnn-dawan-a.
"Aren't you going to say anything, Klnn-dawan-a?" he demanded.

"What would I say?" Klnn-dawan-a said, her voice soft and filled with
distant dread. "You can see he's made up his mind. Besides, you know as
well as he does that it's the only way."

"I don't accept that," Thrr-mezaz growled. "Not yet."

"You've got the rest of the latearc to come up with an alternative,"
Thrr-gilag said. "But if we haven't come up with anything else by
premidarc, I think we'll have to go with this plan. In fact, it might be
pushing it to wait even that long—we don't know what's happening on
Oaccanv that has the Overclan Prime worried enough to call us like this."

"We're waiting until premidarc whether the Prime likes it or not,"
Thrr-mezaz said firmly. "I'm not going to try sending a transport into
enemy territory in the dark. Not even a slow, unarmed one."

"We need the time for preparation, anyway," Thrr-gilag agreed. "Can you have someone get some supplies together for me? Especially some food—I don't know if I'm really ready to try Human cuisine just yet."

"I'll take care of it," Thrr-mezaz promised in a resigned tone. "We'll also need to come up with a good excuse for why you're doing this."

"Perhaps you can be taking information back to the Human-Conquerors about Sergeant Janovetz," Klnn-dawan-a suggested quietly. "Proof that he's alive and well. That might also help in their treatment of you."

"Good idea," Thrr-gilag said. "Thrr-mezaz?"

"I'll take care of that, too," his brother said.

"All right, then." Thrr-gilag got to his feet, trying to keep his tail motion steady. He didn't like this any better than the others did. Far less than they did, actually—he could still feel the residual stiffness in his neck where Pheylan Cavanagh had gripped him during the Human's escape. The Humans were aliens, with the fundamental unpredictability that that implied.

But it had to be done. That was the summation line: it had to be done. "If you'll excuse me, then, I'd better go get some rest. It's going to be a very busy fullarc."

"I'll come with you," Klnn-dawan-a said, standing up and stepping to his side. "At least walk with you to your quarters."

And to say their last farewell before his arrival at the Thrr-family shrine? But that wasn't something Thrr-gilag really wanted to think about. He doubted Klnn-dawan-a wanted to, either. "Certainly," he said. "Sleep well, Thrr-mezaz. I'll see you in the premidarc."

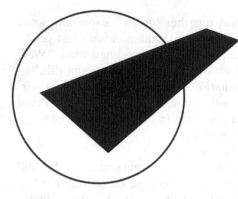

18 "All right, easy now," Aric said, standing well back out of the way as the four bulky Yycroman males hefted the NorCoord 110 mm cannon and swung it up onto their shoulders. The sheer size of the cannon implied a weight somewhere on the far side of two hundred kilograms, and Aric wanted to be ready to run if the Yycromae lost their grip on the thing.

Fortunately, they didn't. Grunting strange alien sounds in unison, they heaved the cannon up and shoulder-pressed it into place beneath the stubby airfoil wing of the freighter towering above them. The other two males waiting there on the makeshift scaffold were ready, and with half a dozen brief showers of sparks the cannon was spot-welded into place.

"Great," Aric said, breathing a little easier as he cautiously approached from the side and peered up at the welds. They wouldn't handle any really serious stress, of course, but they'd be more than adequate to hold the cannon in place for the twenty minutes it would take the adhesive to cure. "Okay, now you need to connect the cables—those ones coming out of the wing—to those input slots there."

One of the Yycromae on the scaffold grunted, and they set to work. "Who's got the mu-plus shield?" Aric asked, looking around.

[Here,] another Yycroma said, stepping forward with the soft metallic material in his hand.

"Toss it up to them," Aric instructed. "You, up there—make sure you get a double layer wrapped around every exposed part of the cables before you seal it."

A movement to Aric's right caught the corner of his eye, and he turned as a Yycroman female stepped up to him, the tooled half cloak of a midlevel government official rippling as she walked. [Aric Cavanagh,] she greeted him, her black eyes studying the operation going on above their heads. [Have you progress to report?]

"I should have some soon," Aric told her. "As soon as the cables and mu-plus magnetic shield are in place, they can run the control module through its paces. The shield should fix the phase-interference problems."

[And then?]

Aric gestured upward. "A little armor-plate conduit over the cables, and this one will be finished. Then we just have to go back and correct the three that were done wrong and make sure the workers add this step to the procedure from now on."

The female was still gazing upward. [Will your assistance be needed further?] she asked.

Aric frowned at her, a strange feeling in the pit of his stomach. "What do you mean?"

[You have been of great service to the Yycromae,] she said. [I ask again: will your assistance be needed further?]

Aric braced himself. An ominous-sounding question, made downright sinister by the cold Yycroman delivery. "Not really," he conceded. "I could certainly be of further help, but I'm not really necessary. Your people should be able to handle everything from here on."

[Thank you,] she said, lowering her gaze at last to him. [Please come with me.]

With the requisite two males marching behind as guards, the female led the way out of the underground hangar, back through the maze of corridors, and up the stairway into the government building where he'd been taken when he'd first arrived on Phormbi three days ago. Two hallways later the female stopped beside a door, this one guarded by four males. [The ci Yyatoor awaits you,] she said. [Farewell, Aric Cavanagh.]

She turned and left, the escort leaving with her. One of the guards swung open the door; swallowing, Aric went inside.

The room was large and ornate, lavishly stocked with both furniture and museum-class art objects. Seated in a carved chair in the center, dressed to the hilt in her ceremonial helmet and tooled cloak, was Klyveress ci Yyatoor. Seated in a pair of human-sized chairs facing her, their heads turned to look in Aric's direction, were two young men. [He is here, as I promised,] Klyveress said, gesturing toward him. [Aric Cavanagh, these human males have come to Phormbi seeking you.]

"Really," Aric said, stepping forward as both men got to their feet. Offhand, he couldn't remember ever seeing either of them before. "What can I do for you?"

"My name's Daschka; Commonwealth Diplomatic Service," one of them identified himself, offering a shimmery ID card for inspection. "This is my associate, Cho Ming. You've led us quite a chase, Mr. Cavanagh."

"I was unaware I'd been leading anyone on any chases," Aric said, glancing casually at the ID and handing it back. Giving the card a long, suspicious examination might be taken as an insult, and he didn't have the expertise to spot a forgery anyway. Besides, Klyveress had undoubtedly already had the two men checked out.

"A figure of speech only," Cho Ming assured him. "Actually, Mr. Cavanagh, we were becoming worried about you."

Aric lifted his eyebrows. "Really. You personally, or the whole Commonwealth diplomatic service?"

Daschka's expression didn't even twitch. "But we've found you, and you're safe, and that's what really matters, isn't it?"

"I've always thought so," Aric said. "If that's all, I trust you'll excuse me . . . ?"

Daschka held up a finger. "Not quite, Mr. Cavanagh. Actually, we're here to bring you back to Edo."

Aric glanced at Klyveress, but the impassive crocodilian face wasn't giving anything away. "Why?"

"Purely routine," Cho Ming said. "Some administrative details of the inquiry got buried, and you left Edo before the bureaucrats noticed their files were incomplete. Bureaucrats get upset over things like that."

"I'm terribly sorry for the bureaucrats," Aric said, eyeing them with sudden suspicion. Daschka's ID card had listed his current service post as the Mra colony world of Mra-ect, which if Aric remembered correctly was also where Admiral Rudzinski had said Petr Bronski was based.

Only he knew now that Bronski wasn't a Commonwealth diplomat at all, but a senior officer in NorCoord Military Intelligence. Were Daschka and Cho Ming two of his operatives?

"We knew you'd understand," Daschka said. "If you'll come with us, we have a ship waiting."

"Why can't I just fill out the forms here?" Aric asked. "You brought everything with you, didn't you?"

"I'm afraid it's a little more complicated than that," Cho Ming said apologetically. "The fact is that we have to go back to Edo. It won't take long, I assure you."

"But I'm needed here," Aric protested. "I'm doing important work for the Yycromae, work vital to the war effort against the Conquerors." He looked at Klyveress. "The ci Yyatoor can vouch for that."

Klyveress shifted position on her chair. [I am told your work here is finished,] she said. [You may leave with your fellow humans.]

"But—" *I don't want to leave with them!* But there was no point in saying the words. Whatever pressure Daschka had brought to bear, diplomatic or otherwise, Klyveress had clearly caved in to it.

[Your service has been greatly appreciated, Aric Cavanagh,] Klyveress said gravely. [The Yycroman people will not soon forget.]

"No, of course not," Aric murmured. He'd served his purpose and now was being cold-bloodedly thrown to the wolves. "I won't forget either."

A groundcar and Yycroman driver were waiting outside the building to drive the three humans back to the spaceport. The trip was reasonably short, and very quiet.

Daschka's ship turned out to be a slightly run-down-looking old Wolfgant schooner-class spacecraft with the name *Happenstance* etched in curly script at the bow. They arrived to find Aric's luggage stacked neatly at the foot of the boarding ramp, and the Yycroman spaceport workers just finishing up the preflight servicing. "You've got to hand it to the Yycromae," Cho Ming commented as they helped carry the luggage up the ramp. "On straight-line efficiency they'll beat anyone hands down."

"That's one of the things that makes them dangerous," Daschka said sourly as he sealed the hatchway behind them. "Efficiency combined with sheer bonehead stubbornness is a bad combination."

"Yeah." Cho Ming threw a speculative look at Aric. "Speaking of stubbornness, you notice anything funny about this scenario? We show up and ask for Cavanagh, and the ci Yyatoor just gives him up. No blustering about sovereign rights, no demand for papers or procedures— nothing. She just gives him up."

"I noticed," Daschka agreed, giving Aric a speculative look of his own. "You wear out your welcome, Cavanagh?"

"Not that I know of," Aric said. "Maybe she just gets nervous with NorCoord Military Intelligence people around."

Daschka smiled tightly. "Bright boy," he acknowledged. "What did she do, show you Bronski's signature on her copy of that statement of understanding your father ramrodded through? Where *is* the honorable Lord Cavanagh, by the way?"

Aric shook his head. "I don't know."

Daschka grunted. "Neither did the ci Yyatoor. Or so she claimed."

"Maybe that's why she gave us this one," Cho Ming suggested. "A bone to keep us happy while she keeps Lord Cavanagh under wraps somewhere."

"As far as I know, he's not here," Aric said. He hesitated— "If you find out differently, I'd be very interested in knowing it."

"I'll bet you would," Daschka said. "Well, let's see if we can find out. Stow your stuff in number-three cabin, then come up to the flight deck."

The flight deck was something of a surprise to Aric when he arrived. The forward part, with the wraparound canopy and piloting/navigational control boards, was about the right size for a schooner-class ship. But the aft section, which normally included only the engineering and life-support monitors, had been expanded to nearly four times the usual size and equipped with a dizzying array of electronic equipment. "Welcome to NorCoord Intelligence, Mobile," Cho Ming said from the depths of one of the three seats in the aft section. "Your first visit, I take it?"

"Yes," Aric said, looking around. About half the equipment he vaguely recognized, or at least could take a guess at its function. The rest he didn't have a clue about.

"Probably your last, too," Daschka called back from the pilot's station. "Needless to say, it all comes under the Official Secrets Regulations. Sit down and strap in—we've got clearance to lift. And don't touch anything."

Aric chose the chair closest to Cho Ming. "Have you found out anything?"

"Only that the Yycromae are suddenly running around like beavers at a bark sale," Cho Ming said, frowning at the displays around him as his fingers danced across one of three keyboards arranged around his seat. "A lot of communications traffic zipping back and forth around the planet—probably ten times the amount a place with Phormbi's population ought to have. Most of it encoded, too—looks like government codes. Something's got them stirred up, but good."

With a lurch the ship started forward. "Maybe your leaving here spooked them," Aric suggested.

"We only spook people when we arrive, Cavanagh," Daschka called back dryly. "Not when we leave."

"Lots of vehicle movement, too," Cho Ming said. "Mostly up by . . . hmm."

"What?" Aric asked.

Cho Ming was peering at one of his displays. "Daschka, remember that big refitting area the Yycromae had set up over at the Northern Wooded Steppes?"

"Where we found Lord Cavanagh when we were here last? Sure."

"The Yycromae seem to be emptying it."

The ship lifted off the ground and angled upward. "You sure?" Daschka asked.

"Pretty sure," Cho Ming said. "It's over the horizon, but I'm getting enough secondary leakage bouncing off the ionosphere for an eighty-count signature ID. I'd say there are at least fifty ships either gearing up for lift or already on the move."

Daschka swore, a brittle Russian curse. "So much for Yycroman guarantees. I'll bet ten against five they're off to attack the Mrachanis."

"Looks like it," Cho Ming agreed. "Anything we can do about it?"

"Not really," Daschka conceded. "We can send a message skitter on ahead with a warning, but there's not a lot the Mrachanis can do to get ready for them."

"What about Peacekeeper forces?" Aric asked, a cold rage aching in his throat. A rage, and a deep shame. He'd seen those guarantees, too. His father had signed them. He himself had helped arm those ships.

And now the Yycromae were heading out to continue a war that had lain dormant for a quarter century.

"As far as I know, there's nothing between here and the Myrmidon Platform at Granparra," Cho Ming said. "Certainly nothing that could get here in time to intercept that assault fleet."

"If the assault hasn't already started," Daschka pointed out. "For all we know, this could be the second wave. Might explain why the ci Yyatoor was so anxious to get us out of here. Check the wake-trail detector—see if you can pick up anything farther out."

"Right," Cho Ming said, swiveling to face one of his other keyboards. "I hope we've got Yycroman freighter tachyon trails on file. If we don't, this is going to be a little tricky . . ."

He trailed off. Aric glanced over at him, paused for a closer look. The man's face had gone suddenly tight. "What is it?" he asked.

Cho Ming took a deep breath. "Daschka, I think we can scratch the Mrachani-attack theory. We've got . . . looks like ten or eleven ships incoming." He turned to look in Daschka's direction. "Conqueror ships."

There was a long, brittle silence. Aric looked forward, too, seeing only the top of Daschka's head above his headrest against the darkening sky as the schooner headed for space. "You sure?" Daschka asked at last.

"Positive," Cho Ming said. "Unless someone loaded us the wrong baseline back at Edo."

The top of Daschka's head nodded slowly. "ETA?"

"About ninety minutes," Cho Ming said. "Wait a minute. I'm picking up something else now. Slightly different vector but still incoming . . . good God."

"What is it?" Daschka demanded.

"I don't know," Cho Ming said, frowning at the display. "We've got nothing like it in the baseline file. Looks big, though. Huge. I've got to get a copy of this."

"You think it's a new type of Conqueror ship?" Aric asked, his mouth suddenly dry.

"I hope not," Cho Ming said as he keyed his board. "If they've got something that big, we're in very serious trouble."

"Maybe it's a Yycroman warship," Daschka put in. "We found out a month or so ago that they still have a couple stashed away."

Aric gazed at the wake-trail, a sudden thought belatedly occurring to him. A Conqueror invasion force ninety minutes out from Phormbi meant the Yycromae must have detected them nearly half an hour ago. "So that's why the ci Yyatoor let you take me," he murmured, half to himself. "She knew they were coming and wanted us out of here before they arrived."

"Afraid she's going to be disappointed on that last," Daschka grunted. "Cho Ming, we've got seventy or eighty minutes to get someplace where we can watch without getting trampled. See what you can find."

"We're not leaving?" Aric asked.

"And miss the chance to see what happens when a Yycroman warship takes on the Zhirrzh?" Daschka snorted. "You must be kidding."

"We know what'll happen," Aric retorted. "The Yycromae will get cut to ribbons."

"All the more reason to stay and watch," Cho Ming said. "If the Yycromae lose, there may not be anyone left here to report on the battle."

"That's a cheery thought," Aric growled. "And you think the Conquerors will just let us make our recordings and leave?"

"With luck they'll never even know we were here," Cho Ming assured him. "This ship can be rigged for sensor-stealthing that's just a hair short of what Peacekeeper watchships get."

Aric grimaced. "So we're just going to sit out here and watch the Yycromae get slaughtered."

"If you'd rather join in the fight, we can take you back to the ground," Daschka offered, turning half around to look at Aric over the edge of his chair back.

Aric looked away, anger and frustration and guilt all tugging at him. Anger at Daschka's and Cho Ming's coolly detached attitude toward the coming slaughter. Guilt at the way he'd been so prematurely quick to misjudge both Klyveress's character and her motives in letting the two Intelligence agents take him away.

And frustration at his inability to make the proper and honorable decision.

Because it was obvious what that decision should be. The Yycromae weren't ready to face the Conquerors—not by a long shot. His two hands would be of only limited help in their race against the clock, but offering that help was still the right thing for him to do. Pheylan would certainly have done so if he'd been there. Melinda was apparently trapped on Dorcas because she'd made a similar decision. How could he do less? Because he was afraid. That was the bottom line: he was afraid. He'd already risked his life once to rescue his brother, and that time he'd gotten away with it. Risking himself again—not for family but for virtual strangers—would be tempting fate in a way he somehow couldn't bring himself to do.

Yet down deep he knew that it was what he *should* do. And hadn't his parents always taught him that personal comfort or safety should never interfere with doing the right thing?

"Hold everything," Cho Ming said suddenly, peering at his displays and keying a switch. "Got some small asteroid fragments in low planetary polar orbit—probably leftovers from some mining operation. What do you think?"

"Not bad," Daschka agreed. "None of them are big enough to hide behind, but skulking along in the middle of the group ought to do nicely. How far away are they?"

"About five minutes at full throttle," Cho Ming said. "Or we can take fifty and do a minimum-fuel course. Your choice."

"Never spend fuel if you don't have to," Daschka admonished him. "Especially heading into a situation like this. Minimum-fuel it is." There was a lurch, and Aric found himself being pressed into his seat by acceleration. "Offer withdrawn, Cavanagh. You're stuck here for the duration."

"I'd gathered as much," Aric murmured. So that was that. The decision had been made, its weight and guilt taken away from him.

But still he had hesitated. And somehow he knew that that hesitation would haunt him for the rest of his life.

The Mrachani receptionist's iridescent hair stiffened briefly before laying down again across his neck and shoulders. "I'm afraid you were misinformed, Monsieur Marchand," he said apologetically. "Ambassador-Chief Valloittaja is on meditation-retreat and will not be seeing visitors for the foreseeable future."

"Oh," Bronski said, his face and shoulders sagging slightly in a nicely underplayed gesture of disappointment. "I'm of course pleased for the Ambassador-Chief, but . . . There can be no exceptions?"

"None at all," the Mrachani said, his voice rich with regret and commiseration. "I'm very sorry for your disappointment."

"But our work was done specifically for him," Bronski persisted, gesturing to Cavanagh. "At the Ambassador-Chief's own request, Signor Fortunori has been developing a business plan for his family. We have nurtured this plan through to its birth and are eagerly anxious to present it to him. This is most frustrating to us."

"I understand both your eagerness and your frustration," the Mrachani said, his fur stiffening again. "Perhaps a meeting with one of the Ambassador-Chief's kinsmen would serve your purpose."

"It would not substitute, but it might be useful," Bronski agreed reluctantly. "Can you tell me how to locate one of them?"

"Certainly." The Mrachani busied himself at his terminal, and a card popped out of the slot beside Bronski's hand. "I have listed the names and contact information for three of the Ambassador-Chief's closest kinsmen," he said as Bronski took the card. "I trust one of them will be able to assist you."

"Only if he can persuade the Ambassador-Chief to see us," Bronski sighed, motioning Cavanagh and Kolchin toward the door. "Thank you for your concern, and may your family flourish."

The three of them left the building and headed back out into the street again. "I hope you realize what a chance you were taking in there," Cavanagh murmured to Bronski as they headed down the walkway toward where they'd parked their rented groundcar.

"It wasn't all that big a chance," the brigadier assured him. "I supervise Mrach operations, but I haven't personally been here on Mra in several years. Besides, distinguishing between humans is as hard for most Mrachanis as distinguishing between them is for us. Most of them aren't up to the challenge."

"So what did all this prove?" Kolchin asked.

"Ambassador-Chief Valloittaja is easily the leading Mrach expert on dealing with alien races," Bronski said. "If he's suddenly and mysteriously missing, I'd say we've found our thread to whatever this game is they're playing."

"Why is it necessarily mysterious?" Cavanagh asked. "I thought meditation-retreats were pretty standard among the Mrach elite."

"They are," Bronski said. "But they're strictly a yearly ritual. Valloittaja had his three months ago."

"I see," Cavanagh said. "So what now? We tug on the thread and see where the seam unravels?"

"I'd like to avoid anything quite that obvious," Bronski said. "Nine times out of ten, when you start tugging on threads they either break or you find out they're tied to something with a lot of teeth at the other end. No, let's try tracking along the thread first. We'll start with these three kinsmen and try to get some idea where Valloittaja might have gone."

"Just a second," Cavanagh said, touching Bronski's shoulder as a display in the window they were passing caught his eye. The sign, in ten languages, announced it to be a visitor information center. "Wait here; I'll be right back."

He was back with them two minutes later. "Did you ask them where Valloittaja was?" Bronski asked, a touch of sarcasm in his voice.

"No, we didn't get around to that," Cavanagh told him. "It occurred to me that whatever the Mrachanis are up to, their plan might require large tracts of isolated territory." He held up his new collection of cards. "So I picked up some travel-and-vacation brochures."

Bronski smiled tightly as he took the cards. "Not bad," he said approvingly. "Not bad at all. Kolchin, you're driving. Let's get back to the ship."

They had left the capital's central district and were in sight of the spaceport tower when Bronski looked up from his plate. "You did it, Cavanagh," he said with a grim satisfaction. "Here it is: *Puvkit Tru Kai*—the Garden Of The Mad Stonewright. Two months ago it was a public park and recreational area."

"Suddenly closed for renovation?" Kolchin asked.

"Nothing so obvious," Bronski said. "It's still listed. Only it's listed at the wrong place."

Cavanagh blinked. "Come again?"

"They've changed its location," Bronski said. "Or, rather, its alleged location. What they're calling the Garden now is a fairly minor group of rock formations about two hundred kilometers farther north. Close enough to the real one that most people looking at the brochure won't even notice the difference; far enough away that any visitors will be safely out of the way of whatever's happening there."

"So what's our next move?" Cavanagh asked.

"We take a closer look at the real Garden, of course," Bronski said, fiddling with the controls of his plate. "Let's see. We'll take the ship over to Douvremrom—that's about three hours away if we go suborbital. Then another three hours by rented aircar, and we'll be there."

Cavanagh frowned over the brigadier's shoulder. Three hours by aircar was a pretty healthy distance. "Aren't there any closer spaceports?"

"Of course there are," Bronski said, turning off his plate and sliding it back inside his jacket. "The Garden's got one of its own, in fact. What's convenient about Douvremrom is that it's listed on this other card as the home of one of Valloittaja's kinsmen."

"Ah." Cavanagh nodded understanding. "Which means that if anyone's bothering to track our movements, they should conclude we're going there to see him."

"Oh, they'll be tracking us, all right," Bronski said. "If not now, then the minute we cross whatever invisible circle they've drawn around the Garden and their little Conquerors Without Reason project."

And there would be Bhurtala waiting for them in the darkness. . . .

"What do we do then?" he asked, suppressing a shiver.

"We'll go with standard procedure," Bronski said. "We find out what we can and get the hell out."

"Always nice to have a plan," Cavanagh murmured.

"Don't worry about it," Bronski soothed him. "In a pinch I've still got that fake red card I used on you back in Mig-Ka City. It would take a pretty high-level Mrachani not to be intimidated by that."

Cavanagh grimaced. "High-level Mrachanis like Valloittaja, for instance?"

"Well, yes," Bronski conceded. "There is that."

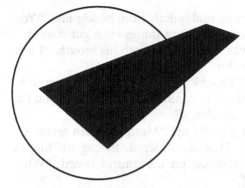

19

Most of the Yycroman freighters had reached their prescribed positions well within that first hour. With their drives cut they were drifting now, the nearer ones discernible only by the gaps they made in the starfield beyond, the farther ones not even that visible. A handful of drive trails still blazed as last-minute additions to the defense force scrambled to get to their places. Beneath the drive trails Phormbi's nightside had become an unrelieved black as the scattered clusters of Yycroman settlements shut down lights and power sources to deny the enemy such obvious targeting indicators.

The battle lines were drawn. And the Conquerors were on their way.

"Looks like they're about ready out there," Daschka commented over his shoulder. "Are we?"

"As ready as we can be," Cho Ming said. "Power output is at minimum, sensor-stealthing is fully operational, and I've got all sensors and recorders running."

"Conquerors' ETA?"

"Anytime now," Cho Ming said. "We'll get about ten seconds' warning when they start their mesh-in, but that's about it. A ship this size just hasn't got enough hull for a wake-trail detector that'll work on close-in targets."

The flight deck fell silent again. Seated in the copilot seat where he would have a better view of the approaching battle, Aric gazed out the canopy, listening to his heart pounding in his ears. There was a gentle thud against the side of the ship, and he jerked violently against his restraints before realizing that the *Happenstance* had merely brushed against one of the slowly rotating asteroid fragments they were nestled up against.

"Take it easy, Cavanagh," Daschka said quietly from beside him. "You don't want to burn out all that tension before things even get started."

"Sorry." Aric exhaled, the breath vibrating through his mouth. "I was hoping to be a little calmer than this."

"A little calmer might be nice," Daschka agreed. "But don't overdo it. A certain amount of tension's normal in combat situations. It's good for you—keeps your senses and reflexes sharp."

"Okay—here we go," Cho Ming spoke up. "Mesh-in in ten seconds."

"Double-check the recorders," Daschka ordered, flexing his fingers once and resting them in ready position on his control board. "What about that big unidentified ship?"

"It's still coming," Cho Ming said. "And still unidentified. Two, one—"

And suddenly they were there, meshing in in rapid succession: the conglomerations of thick milky-white hexagons that were the unique design of Conqueror warships.

"I make the count six," Daschka said, peering out the canopy and adjusting its magnification. "Regrouping into probably a battle formation. Where are the rest?"

"They meshed in a hair too soon," Cho Ming said. "I make five ships about fifteen thousand klicks back."

Daschka grunted. "Backup."

Aric grimaced. As if they really needed more than six ships against the Yycromae.

The Conqueror ships finished their maneuvering, and for a long moment nothing happened. Almost as if, Aric thought, both sides were sizing up their opponents. Then, abruptly, drive trails blazed as a dozen Yycroman freighters surged toward the enemy.

"Yycromae ships engaging," Cho Ming reported tightly. "Looks like they're firing shredder-burst guns."

"They're old Celadonese models," Aric said. "I saw a lot of them in the conversion hangar."

"Probably the easiest things they could get their hands on," Daschka said. "Not much use against Zhirrzh hulls, though."

From one of the Conqueror ships a laser beam lanced out, its path dimly marked by ionized upper-atmosphere atoms and vaporized shredder-burst projectiles. One of the Yycroman freighters flashed brilliantly, its drive trail suddenly waggling like the tail feathers of a wounded bird. Two more lasers fired from different hexagons of the same ship, and with two more flashes the drive trail flicked out.

As if that were the signal everyone had been waiting for, the other Conqueror ships opened fire, and for a handful of agonizing heartbeats the black of space flared as the Yycroman freighters flamed into instant death pyres for their crews. Another dozen drive trails appeared as a second group of ships joined the battle, and then another group, and then another. The Conquerors' lasers flashed in response, systematically tracking and destroying the defenders.

And then, as quickly as it had begun, the last of the drive trails was cut off, and it was over.

Supreme Commander Prm-jevev flicked his tongue in perplexity, gazing at each of the displays in turn. "You're absolutely certain?" he demanded again of the cloud of Elders hovering around him.

"There's no doubt at all, Supreme Commander," one of them said again. "Within range of our anchorlines, that's all that's out there."

Another Elder appeared, joining the group. " 'What's going on?' " he demanded. " 'Supreme Commander Prm-jevev, report.' "

Prm-jevev flicked his tongue in annoyance. He'd forgotten what it was like to be at this end of the battle-communication pathway, taking valuable time to describe what was happening to the rest of Warrior Command. "We've just repulsed an attack by a group of small spacecraft," he said. "Extremely small, with virtually no weaponry at all. There are many others in the area, with equally weak weaponry."

The Elder nodded and vanished. "Check the area again," Prm-jevev ordered, looking up at the other Elders. "Order the other warships to spread out a little. This makes no sense at all."

The Elder reappeared. "Speaker Cvv-panav: 'What are you waiting for? Destroy them and launch your ground attack.' "

Prm-jevev flicked his tongue in contempt. That was the Speaker for Dhaa'rr, all right, his slash-tongue attitude blazingly obvious even without the Elder's identification. "I'm waiting, Speaker, because these are clearly not the Human-Conqueror warships we were led to expect," he said tartly. "I have no interest in laying a world waste just for the exercise of it."

The Elder nodded and was gone. "Supreme Commander?" one of the warriors called across the command/monitor room. "Messages are coming in via direct link from the other warships. Their commanders want to know when we will attack."

"When I give the order," Prm-jevev growled. "Until then they are to fire only in defense of themselves."

The Elder was back. "Speaker Cvv-panav: 'Your principles are admirable, Supreme Commander. But they have no place in warfare. If the Human-Conquerors plan a trap, you are merely playing into their snare.' "

A second Elder flicked in. "The Overclan Prime: 'Have you determined there are no warships waiting on the surface or hidden behind the planet itself?' "

"There's nothing on the surface our telescopes can detect," Prm-jevev said, deciding that Speaker Cvv-panav's comment wasn't worth a reply. "As to the horizon, the answer is also no. I dropped part of my force a distance behind me, in a position where they could see the parts of the planetary far side, which we cannot."

The Elder vanished. "More incoming spacecraft, Supreme Commander," a warrior called.

Prm-jevev nodded. "Repulse their attack," he ordered.

"I obey."

The warriors and Elders set about their work . . . and the Supreme Commander settled down to watch. And to try to figure out what exactly was going on here.

With an effort Aric forced moisture into his mouth. His hands, he noticed suddenly, were gripped rigidly around his restraint straps. "They haven't got a chance," he whispered. "Not a chance."

"It's not looking good," Daschka admitted. "Were shredder-bursts all they had?"

Aric took a deep breath. The Conqueror ships were just sitting there, waiting with arrogant patience for the Yycromae to decide which of them would be next to sacrifice themselves. "No," he said, forcing his mind to unfreeze from the horror he'd just witnessed. "No, they also had some Nadezhdan space-to-space missiles—Deathknell XIIs, I think they were —and some NorCoord 110 mm cannon. They had some weapons of their own design, too."

"They were using some pretty good stuff back when we first ran into them," Daschka said. "Let's hope they've still—there they go."

A new group of drive trails had appeared, perhaps fifty of them this time, driving with suicidal directness toward the Conqueror ships. "Opening up with the 110 mm cannon," Cho Ming reported. "Looks like . . . well, I'll be damned."

"What?" Daschka asked.

"That first assault wave wasn't as useless as I thought," Cho Ming said, sounding impressed. "This group's doing some bull's-eye targeting on the laser ports that fired on the last group."

Aric stared out the canopy as the Conqueror ships belatedly began returning fire. "They sacrificed themselves just to pinpoint the laser ports?"

"Looks that way," Daschka agreed. "I told you this would be a battle worth recording."

The exchange this time lasted a little longer. But only a little, and in the end the Yycroman offensive was once again quashed with little trouble. "Any damage to the Conquerors?" Daschka asked.

"Hard to tell," Cho Ming said. "But it looks like they had ten or fifteen of their lasers put out of commission."

The words were barely out of his mouth when another group of Yycroman drive trails blazed to life. "Third wave away," Cho Ming announced. "Directing more cannon fire against the laser ports." The Conqueror lasers fired in reply, and once again the night was lit by vaporized Yycroman freighters—

"Fourth wave!" Cho Ming barked. "Cutting in behind the third. I'm getting missile-arming signals . . . there they go."

Aric squinted out the canopy. The drive trails themselves were almost lost in the sputtering flashes; but he could occasionally catch glimpses of faint secondary trails as the Deathknell missiles shot outward from the Yycroman defenders. The lasers shifted direction toward this new threat, and smaller flashes began to appear where they found their targets. Aric gripped his restraints. . . .

And suddenly a flash of acrid blue-white light blossomed on the side of one of the Conqueror ships.

"Got one!" Aric blurted, slamming his fist down on the edge of the control board, the recoil bouncing him up against his restraints.

"Steady," Daschka advised him. "Let's see if it did any damage before you break out the champagne. Cho Ming?"

"Can't tell yet," the other said. "Too much after-scintillation. It's sure as hell gotten them riled up, though."

Aric nodded silently, his elation of a few seconds earlier crushed back down to reality. The Conqueror ships were blazing with laser fire now, the Yycroman defenders flashing to plasma and shrapnel all around them. In the midst of the slaughter two more of the Deathknells got through, and two more blue-white fireballs briefly silhouetted the sharp hexagonal edges of the Conqueror ships. But if the blasts caused any damage, it wasn't obvious from where Aric sat.

Or even from where Cho Ming sat. "I don't read any damage from the Deathknell blasts," the Intelligence man reported with a sigh. "If there is any, it must be negligible."

"So much for the missiles," Daschka said. "So much for the Yycromae, too. You got any more good news?"

"Plenty," Cho Ming said. "Those five ships we thought might be hanging back? They've kicked into gear and are on their way."

Aric shook his head in horrified disbelief. "How many ships do they think they *need* to take this place?"

"Maybe they're not planning to take it," Daschka suggested darkly. "Maybe Phormbi's going to be a special sort of object lesson."

Aric gazed out at the laser flashes, a cold chill running through him. That other incoming ship, with a wake-trail like nothing Cho Ming had ever seen . . . "You suppose that's what that unidentified ship is for?" he asked. "Something to—I don't know—burn off the planet, maybe?"

"I still say it's Yycroman," Daschka insisted. But the stubbornness had an edge of uncertainty to it now.

"We'll find out soon enough," Cho Ming said grimly. "ETA's something around fifteen minutes."

"About the same time those other five warships will get here?" Daschka asked.

"Just about."

And at the rate these first six ships were going, Aric knew, fifteen minutes would be all they would need to eliminate the rest of the Yycroman defenders, leaving the planet wide-open before them. "Are we still going to stay?" he asked, though he knew what the answer would be.

"As long as we can." Daschka threw him a gruffly sympathetic glance. "There's no reason you have to watch this, though. If it gets too bad, you can go back to your cabin. Cho Ming, what's this going on now?"

With an effort Aric focused his attention back on the carnage of the battle zone. Amid the flashing lasers the current wave of Yycroman ships was rapidly dwindling, but now another fifty or so drive trails had appeared behind them. Again he could half imagine he saw missile trails lancing out ahead of them—

"Cho Ming?" Daschka repeated.

"You got me," the other said, sounding puzzled. "They're firing something, all right, but I can't get anything on it. Almost reads like some kind of stealthed missiles—"

"There!" Aric snapped, pointing out the canopy. On one of the Conqueror ships a splash of white light had appeared.

He paused, frowning, finger still pointed. The white flash wasn't expanding as an explosion ought to. Or fading away, either, for that matter. "What is that?"

"Whatever it is, they've landed six more of them," Daschka said, frowning. "Four more on the port hexagon of that ship, and one each on the two ships to starboard. Come on, Cho Ming, look alive."

"I'm working on it, I'm working on it," Cho Ming growled. "The albedo's incredibly high—maybe they're some kind of targeting markers. Let me try this . . ."

His voice trailed off into the soft clicking of keys. Aric gazed out the canopy, catching sight of three more white explosions as they appeared against the lead ship and froze in place. If they were targeting markers, there ought to be missiles firing in right behind them. But so far, nothing.

And then, from behind him, came a sound that sounded suspiciously like a strangled-off laugh. "I don't believe it," Cho Ming said. "Daschka, get this: it's paint."

"It's *what*?"

"Good old-fashioned white paint," Cho Ming said. "Well, not *that* old-fashioned—it's pretty high-tech stuff, really. Quick-dry, adhesion coefficient right off the scale, and an albedo of just a hair below one. And every one of those paintballs is dead center on top of a Conqueror laser port."

Daschka turned back around, shaking his head slowly. "I'll be damned."

"I don't get it," Aric said. "Are they trying to seal over the laser ports?"

"Basically," Cho Ming said. "But they've added a nice touch. Albedo measures reflectivity, on a scale of zero to one, which means that paint is a nearly perfect light reflector. If the Zhirrzh fire that particular laser—you see?"

"Got it," Aric nodded, finally understanding. "The beam reflects straight back into the mechanism."

"Which probably won't hurt it any," Cho Ming said. "But it should keep it out of the fight for a while."

Another blue-white flash erupted against one of the Conqueror ships, followed immediately by two more. "More Deathknells?" Daschka asked.

"Some of them are," Cho Ming said. "Others are more of those stealthed missiles—pretty potent warhead on those things. Looks like they're concentrating on the connecting edge between the first two hexagons."

"Any damage?" Daschka asked.

"Hard to tell," Cho Ming said. "And getting harder. There's a lot of debris between us and them."

The remnants of the Yycroman ships, and of the Yycromae who had flown them. "Have you seen any escape pods or suits?" Aric asked.

"I haven't noticed anything," Cho Ming said. "Doesn't mean they're not out there. Okay, I'm starting to get something from that last salvo of Deathknells . . . looks like we've got a few pieces of Zhirrzh hull floating around. They're small, but they're there."

"Which may not mean anything," Daschka grunted. "The ships that took out the *Jutland* had a few pieces cracked off of them too without—"

"He's pulling back," Aric interrupted excitedly, pointing at one of the Conqueror ships. "Look—he's pulling back."

"He's pulling around, anyway," Daschka agreed cautiously. "Whether he's actually pulling out, we'll have to—"

He broke off as the ship, with a flicker from its aft surfaces, abruptly meshed out.

"One down," Cho Ming announced, a note of grim satisfaction in his voice.

Aric looked out at the five remaining Conqueror ships, their lasers still methodically blasting the Yycroman freighters into fiery dust. In the distance behind them he could see the faint drive trails of the other five enemy ships as they hurried to join the battle. "It's not going to work," he murmured. "They just don't have the firepower."

"No, they don't," Daschka said quietly. "Strange, isn't it? I've spent really my entire career working to make sure the Yycromae never became a military threat to the Commonwealth. Almost wish now we hadn't done such a good job."

Aric grimaced. The Klyveress ci Yyatoor and her people had worked so hard in this crash-defense program of theirs. Aric had seen that effort up close; had met and actually started to get to know a few of them. It had been an eye-opening experience, severely eroding the unflattering stereotype of Yycromae that he'd grown up believing.

And all of it for nothing. Very soon now Klyveress and all the rest would probably be dead.

"Here it comes," Cho Ming snapped. "The big ship's starting its mesh-in. Five seconds."

Aric peered out of the canopy, hands clenched helplessly around his restraints, hoping but no longer really believing it was a Yycroman warship come to help. The seconds counted down—

And then suddenly there it was, appearing above and behind the Conqueror battle force.

And from beside him he heard Daschka's stunned curse.

"All right, Omicron Four," the voice of Fighter Commander Schweighofer came in Quinn's ear. "Cut in behind Kappa Two: Pattern Charlie."

"Acknowledged," Clipper's voice replied. There was a soft click as he keyed back to the group's private frequency—"Paladin, take point; Maestro, you're on high cover," he ordered. "Let's go."

Quinn drew the Corvine back up slightly, letting the rest of the squadron shoot past beneath him as they moved into backup behind Samurai's group, the flare of their kickthrusters bright against the dark bulk of the planet beneath them.

From the seat behind Quinn came an obviously disgusted grunt. "Too slow," Bokamba muttered. "Much too slow."

"Probably the wind sheer," Quinn said. He twitched his lip three times —left, right, left—and the Corvine's vector map appeared superimposed across his vision. Smack in the middle was a narrow stream of high-speed wind slicing through the upper atmosphere directly across the Copperheads' approach path. "Schweighofer's got us cutting straight through the jet stream."

"That's only because he couldn't find a hurricane or thunderstorm to run you through," Bokamba retorted. "Or were you expecting the Zhirrzh to be thoughtful enough to provide good weather for our attack?"

"I'm not complaining or excusing," Quinn said mildly. "Just explaining."

Bokamba grunted again. "I know."

Quinn twitched his lip again and the display vanished. "Considering we've been running these tests for three days straight, I think they're handling it pretty well," he said. "Especially Samurai and Dreamer."

"Yes," Bokamba murmured. "Dreamer and Con Lady make a good team. Remarkably good Copperheads."

"For women, you mean?"

There was the faint squeak of leatherene from behind him, and Quinn could imagine Bokamba shifting uncomfortably in his seat. "I make no apologies for my cultural views of women in combat," the older man said gruffly. "Though were the full truth known, I imagine it would be you of NorCoord who would be in the true minority on this subject."

Quinn thought back to all the people over the years with whom he'd had discussions about the philosophy of warfare. "You could be right," he conceded. "I think the NorCoord nations have always seen this as a matter of individual rights and responsibilities."

"You've also always had a tendency to elevate personal rights over what is best for society as a whole," Bokamba pointed out.

There was a brief moment of turbulence as Quinn guided the Corvine through the jet stream. "Can't argue that one, either," he agreed. "Though we wouldn't be the first culture to overshoot that direction."

"True," Bokamba said. "I think what disturbs me the most is the cynicism with which NorCoord's leaders exploit such cultural differences for their own ends."

Quinn grimaced. Here it came again: Bokamba's obsession with what he considered to be NorCoord's manipulative domination of the rest of the Commonwealth. The two of them had been around this same track dozens of times back when Bokamba had been his wing commander. "You have any particular examples in mind?"

"They're flying in front of you right now," Bokamba said. "Dreamer and Con Lady, along with Hawk and his female tail, Adept. You know as well as I do that female Copperheads are extremely rare—rare enough to be highly visible. Yet we have three of them aboard an expeditionary force that will soon be heading into enemy territory. Haven't you wondered why?"

A thick cloud bank loomed ahead, swallowing up the rest of the attack force. Quinn squinted, enhancing the Corvine's sensor-penetration settings, and dived in after them. "I assumed we just needed them to make up a full complement."

"What, they couldn't trade two Corvines from Earth-defense duty?" Bokamba scoffed. "You know better than that. The women were specifically and deliberately assigned to the *Trafalgar*. They had to be."

"Clipper, I've got a make on Target Three," the voice of Paladin's tail, Dazzler, came in Quinn's ear. "Tally three buildings and twelve aircraft defenders."

An echo feed of Paladin's view came over Quinn's Mindlink, superimposed on the skyscape outside the Corvine's canopy. "Tally that," Clipper acknowledged. "Let's go in, Copperheads."

The group swerved toward the target zone. Keying for extended long-range scan, Quinn gave the area around him a quick search. No enemy bogies were visible as yet, but he didn't doubt Schweighofer had something devious waiting for them. Fighter commanders didn't achieve that lofty position without learning how to spin the low inside curve. "So what's your theory as to why they were assigned here?" he asked Bokamba.

"Understand, this is just my personal feeling," the other cautioned. "I have no proof of any sort. But I believe that Peacekeeper Command has decided to make them into martyrs. That they've decided having women sacrifice their lives in battle over a Zhirrzh world will create outrage and guilt among the nations and states of the Commonwealth, thus stiffening their resolve to resist the invasion."

An oddly queasy sensation settled in Quinn's stomach. "That seems rather cold-blooded," he said carefully.

"It's extremely cold-blooded," Bokamba said. "But war is a cold-blooded business. You've been involved with politics recently, working for Lord Stewart Cavanagh. Do you deny the NorCoord Parliament might do something like that?"

Quinn chewed at his lip. "Well . . ."

"All Copperheads, this is Schweighofer," the fighter commander's voice cut in suddenly. "The exercise is aborted; repeat, the exercise is aborted. All fighters will return to the *Pelican* immediately."

"Acknowledged," Samurai's voice said. "All Copperheads, come around on your own, then re-form into units. Flash it."

Quinn swung the Corvine up into a steep climb, throwing in the kick-thrusters and driving hard for the sky. Behind him, he sensed the click as Bokamba shifted them to the overcommand frequency. "Commander Schweighofer, this is Bokamba. Is this part of the exercise?"

"Negative, Bokamba," Schweighofer said tightly. "Just get your people up here. Fast."

The *Pelican* was an Arcturus-class fuel carrier that Schweighofer and his team had been using as their operational base during the past three days of combat exercises. Quinn docked the Corvine at his assigned external connector alongside the rest of Clipper's Copperheads, and three minutes later they were all on the *Pelican*'s bridge. Samurai and the rest of Kappa Two were already gathered around Schweighofer, floating in front of the command chair, with Dreamer and her unit just arriving. Captain Irdani, the *Pelican*'s commander, was at the sensor station, talking with quiet intensity with the officer manning the post.

"We've got enemy contact, Copperheads," Schweighofer announced without preamble. "It's pretty far out—right on the edge of our wake-trail detectors—but there doesn't seem to be any doubt that it's them. Best guess is that we're looking at eleven Zhirrzh ships; the vector indicates their target is Phormbi."

A faint murmur rippled briefly through the room. "What in blazes would they want with Phormbi?" Clipper asked.

"Maybe they're tired of tangling with Peacekeepers," Con Lady said dryly. "Could be they're looking for someone who doesn't fight back as well."

"Or perhaps they're looking for someone to make an alliance with," Samurai suggested, his voice dark. "The Yycromae have been waiting for years for just this sort of chance at us."

"You could be right," Schweighofer agreed. "Last I heard all the Pacification forces had been withdrawn from Yycroman space. It'd be a perfect time for a backroom deal."

"Have you sent word to Commodore Montgomery yet?" Bokamba asked.

Schweighofer shook his head. "The fleet's already on its way. Apparently still trying to shake the wrinkles out of the Wolf Pack. Should be here anytime."

"Commander Schweighofer?" Irdani called, pushing off the wall and floating back toward his command chair. "Wolf Pack's about to mesh in."

"Yes, sir," Schweighofer said, moving out of the captain's way.

"Put it on main," Irdani ordered as he maneuvered himself into the seat.

The view shifted, pointing now toward the spot in space where the sensor officer was predicting the Wolf Pack would mesh in. There was a movement to Quinn's right, and he turned to see Dreamer float up beside him. "I don't know about you, Maestro," she said quietly, gazing at the display, "but this Wolf Pack thing has got to be the loopiest idea Command's ever come up with."

"It's a perfectly reasonable solution to the ship-dispersal problem," Bokamba disagreed from Quinn's other side. "You can't launch a successful blitz attack when microsecond differences in mesh-in time and vector scatter your fleet across thousands of square kilometers of space."

"Oh, I agree that's a problem," Dreamer said. "I just think the Wolf Pack is a loopy way to solve it."

And with a flicker of light, there it was. "The Wolf Pack," someone murmured, "has landed."

Quinn gazed at the display. At the multikilometer-long, multikilometer-wide framework of metal and composite and empty space, looking more like a collection of giant window frames welded together than like anything that had any business being part of a war fleet.

And at the other fourteen warships of the *Trafalgar* fleet, each nestled snugly inside one of the frames. Like one big, close-knit family, all set to mesh together.

Dreamer thought it was loopy. Bokamba thought it was brilliant. Personally, Quinn thought they were both right.

"Signal the *Trafalgar*," Irdani ordered his comm officer. "Do not disengage fleet from Wolf Pack; repeat, do *not* disengage fleet from Wolf Pack."

Quinn gazed at the monstrosity filling the display, wondering if the message would get to Montgomery before the ships started snapping their tether lines and breaking out above and beneath the framework. So far the disengagement procedure had been mired in a tangle of minor problems, which was why Montgomery still had the fleet flying back and forth practicing it. He hoped this wouldn't be the time they finally got it right. . . .

"*Pelican*, this is Montgomery," the commodore's voice boomed irritably from the bridge speaker. "Schweighofer?"

"Here, Commodore," Schweighofer said. "Captain Irdani's people have just picked up the wake-trail of what appears to be a Zhirrzh fleet."

There was a long pause. "Confirmed," Montgomery's voice acknowledged, the irritation gone. "We read Phormbi as their probable target."

"That was our projection, too, sir," Schweighofer said. "I thought you'd want to know about this before you disengaged the fleet from the Wolf Pack. In case you wanted to check it out."

"I would, and we will," Montgomery rumbled. "Captain Irdani?"

"Sir?"

"How fast can you get the *Pelican* to its slot in the Wolf Pack?" Montgomery asked. "No—belay that; it'll take too long. Schweighofer, get your Copperheads back in their fighters and flash it back over here. You and your command team can borrow one of the *Pelican*'s shuttles. We're meshing out in fifteen minutes."

"Yes, sir," Schweighofer said, pushing off the command chair toward the door. "You heard the man, Copperheads. Flash it."

Quinn had the Corvine secured in his *Trafalgar* fighter bay in twelve and a half minutes. Exactly two and a half minutes later he felt the lurch as the *Trafalgar* and, presumably, the entire Wolf Pack meshed out.

Five minutes after that, as he and Bokamba were heading down the furrow toward the dayroom, the call came for him to report to the bridge.

The other fighter commanders were there already, both those from the *Axehead* and *Adamant* attack fighter wings as well as the three commanders of the *Trafalgar*'s Copperhead contingent, gathered together in the command ring around Montgomery, Schweighofer, and Fleet Exec Germaine. Germaine looked over as Quinn arrived, motioned him to stay back. Quinn nodded and waited where he was, watching the bridge crew as they went through the procedure for securing from mesh-out and wondering what Montgomery wanted with him.

The meeting broke up a few minutes later, and as the fighter commanders headed back across the bridge, Germaine motioned him to approach. "Lieutenant Quinn," Montgomery said gravely as he reached the command ring. "Good of you to join us. I have a question for you, and I'd like a straight answer."

"Of course, sir," Quinn said.

"I mean a *straight* answer," Montgomery repeated, his eyes boring into Quinn's face. "I don't care what anyone else has told you to say or not to say. I don't care whether they've invoked the Official Secrets Regulations, your own personal honor, or God Himself. I want the truth."

The other two senior officers were also staring unblinkingly at him. Not with any obvious animosity, but not with any friendliness, either. "I understand, sir," Quinn said.

"All right." Montgomery paused. "You've been working closely with

Lord Stewart Cavanagh for several years now, ever since you resigned the Peacekeepers to become his head of security. Question: is he still involved in NorCoord politics? Specifically, has he recently been authorized by the NorCoord Parliament or Peacekeeper Command to act in any sort of diplomatic capacity?"

It was about the last subject Quinn would ever have guessed this summons was going to be about. "I don't know, sir," he said. "As far as I know, Lord Cavanagh's a completely private citizen now."

"I see." Montgomery gazed hard at him. "You're absolutely sure he has no links to the NorCoord government?"

"No, sir, I can't be absolutely sure about that," Quinn said, beginning to sweat a little. What was all this about? "Lord Cavanagh doesn't confide all of his activities to me."

"Yet he chose you to lead the rescue mission for his son," Montgomery persisted.

"Actually, sir, I volunteered," Quinn said. "May I ask what this has to do with me?"

"It has nothing specific to do with you, Lieutenant," Montgomery said. "It has to do with this unscheduled detour we're taking from our assigned mission, and how we're going to deal with the Yycromae when we mesh in at Phormbi. Whether we treat them as victims, potential enemies"—his lip twitched—"or allies."

Allies? The Yycromae? "I'm afraid you've lost me, sir," Quinn said.

Germaine stirred. "Perhaps, Commodore, we should go ahead and show him the communiqué."

"I suppose we'll have to," Montgomery said reluctantly, reaching over to his command chair and pulling a plate emblazoned with the Peacekeeper insignia from a slot in one of the armrests. "You understand, Lieutenant, that this is strictly confidential."

"Yes, sir."

"All right." Montgomery keyed up a page on the plate and handed it to him.

It was a Secret-One message, routed through Edo ten days previously, and addressed to all senior Peacekeeper officers and all command-rank officers with forces stationed within thirty light-years of Yycroman space.

Describing a rearmament agreement between Peacekeeper Command and the Yycromae.

"As you see," Montgomery said, "Lord Cavanagh's name is mentioned as being on both the guarantee of Yycroman intent and the statement of Peacekeeper understanding. The question boils down to whether these are properly authorized documents, or whether they're something else entirely."

"Such as part of some private business scheme of Lord Cavanagh's," Germaine put in. "Or even something the Yycromae might have obtained under duress."

Quinn looked back down at the plate. "According to this a senior NorCoord Military Intelligence officer also signed the documents," he pointed out.

"Unfortunately, the officer isn't identified," Montgomery growled. "I understand there are security considerations involved; but, unfortunately, it also leaves me accepting this sudden de facto alliance with the Yycromae on blind faith. I don't like that."

For a brief moment it occurred to Quinn to remind the commodore that that was exactly how he and the rest of the lower ranks usually had to accept their orders. But he resisted the temptation. "Were copies of the actual documents included with this?" he asked instead.

"Yes," Montgomery said. "With the Intelligence officer's name blanked out, of course."

"May I see them?"

Montgomery's forehead creased slightly. "Why?"

"I may at least be able to tell you whether Lord Cavanagh's signature was obtained under duress."

The commodore glanced at Germaine, and Quinn caught the fleet exec's microscopic shrug. "It's a rather severe violation of military protocol," Montgomery commented, taking the plate back from Quinn. "But having come this far already, I suppose that hardly matters." He keyed the plate to a new position and handed it back.

It took Quinn nearly five minutes to wade through the three pages of thick legal wordage. But when he was done, he was convinced. "Lord Cavanagh was not coerced into signing either document, Commodore," he told Montgomery, handing him back the plate. "Furthermore, if there was any fraud or deceit on the part of the Yycromae, he was unaware of it. To the best of his knowledge both documents were written and signed in good faith."

"Amazing," Germaine murmured. "Just like that?"

"Just like that," Quinn assured him. "There are special ways Lord Cavanagh will write a contract or document to indicate whether or not he's in full voluntary agreement. Particular phrasings, key words—that sort of thing." He nodded toward the plate. "All the proper cues are there."

"I see," Montgomery said. He gazed at the plate another few seconds; then—reluctantly, Quinn thought—he closed it and returned it to its slot in the armrest. "Then I suppose that's settled. We go in as allies, until and unless matters indicate otherwise. Thank you, Lieutenant: dismissed." He turned to Germaine—

"One other matter, Commodore, if I may," Quinn spoke up. "The last I heard, my new tail man still hadn't arrived."

Montgomery looked at Schweighofer, lifted his eyebrows. "That's correct, sir," the fighter commander confirmed. "He was promised for two days ago, but he hasn't shown up yet. I don't know what's happened to him."

"Some snarled order somewhere," Montgomery nodded. "I suppose that means you'll be sitting this one out, Lieutenant."

Quinn grimaced. "With all due respect, Commodore, I'd rather not. Not to seem immodest, but against eleven Zhirrzh warships, you're going to need me."

"We're going to need the Eighth Fleet, too," Montgomery countered dryly. "We'll just have to make do without them."

"You know the regulations, Lieutenant," Schweighofer put in. "We haven't got any spare Copperheads, and you can't fly combat without a tail. No exceptions."

"I understand the regulations, sir," Quinn said. "But in this case—"

"You've been dismissed, Lieutenant," Germaine cut him off sharply. "Return to your quarters."

Quinn didn't move. "You're going to need every resource you've got, Commodore," he said firmly. "Furthermore, you *do* have a spare Copperhead aboard."

Germaine lifted a half-beckoning hand toward the Marine guards at the door. "If I have to have you physically removed—"

"At ease, Tom," Montgomery said mildly. "I presume, Lieutenant, that you're referring to Tac Coordinator Bokamba."

"Reserve Wing Commander Bokamba, sir, yes," Quinn said. "He could fly tail for me."

"Bokamba's been retired from active duty for five years," Schweighofer reminded him. "Retired for good and proper reasons, I might add. Furthermore, he was a pilot, not a tail man."

"He can handle the job," Quinn insisted. "And I think he'd like to get back in the cockpit."

"That's not the point," Montgomery said. "Using resources is one thing. Wasting those resources is quite another."

"You won't be wasting them, sir," Quinn assured him. He hesitated— "Please."

For a moment Montgomery just gazed at him. Then, with a sigh, he shook his head. "Commander Schweighofer, you'll inform Tac Coordinator Bokamba that he's been reassigned as Lieutenant Quinn's tail man."

Schweighofer cleared his throat. "Sir, if I may remind you of the reason why Bokamba was retired from active duty—"

"I'm aware of the reason, Commander," Montgomery said. "I'm also aware of Lieutenant Quinn's reputation as a pilot. And he's right: we can't afford to let him sit this one out. Tac Coordinator Bokamba is to be reassigned as ordered, effective immediately."

He looked at Quinn. "And you, Lieutenant Quinn, will get off my bridge. Now."

"Yes, sir," Quinn said, straightening to full attention. "Thank you, Commodore."

Montgomery's lip twitched. "Thank me when you and Bokamba come back alive," he said quietly. "Not before."

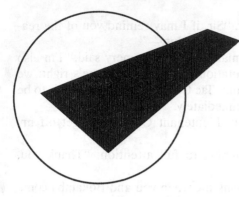

20 It was unbelievable, Aric thought in that first breathtaking second. Completely and totally unbelievable. Like something out of a lavishly budgeted thriller, created by a lunatic designer on a huge production stage with no regard for the rules of scale or even the laws of physics. Appearing from nowhere amid the flashing lasers and exploding missiles, it might even have been some fever dream from a dark and distant mythology: a vast, ghostly Flying Dutchman, blown up to the scale of the Greek Titans, with an ominous hint of the Norse Valkyrie thrown in. Such a thing couldn't possibly exist.

Yet there it was, drifting from its mesh-in point toward the raging battle, utterly dwarfing the Conqueror warships. And nestled within the gaps of the delicate-looking framework, pinned there like some grotesque butterfly collection, was what appeared to be an entire Peacekeeper fleet.

A fleet that, like a slowly awakening giant, was beginning to show signs of movement . . .

"I don't believe it," Cho Ming whispered, his voice somewhere between stunned and reverent. "What in God's name *is* that?"

"You got me," Daschka said, shaking his head. "But I'd lay you odds it has something to do with that Lupis Project that's been drifting in and out of the Intelligence reports for the past six months. Let's get some IDs on these guys—that carrier first."

From behind Aric came a renewed tapping of keys. "It reads out as the *Trafalgar*," Cho Ming said. "Rigel-class attack carrier. Thirteen other ships with it. Just a second; I'm getting small explosions now at the *Trafalgar*'s bow and stern. Looks like they're popping their tethers to that outer framework."

"What are the Zhirrzh doing?"

"Nothing yet," Cho Ming said. "They're probably as flabbergasted by it as we are."

"That won't last long." Daschka pointed out the canopy toward the Peacekeeper ships. "Look—you can see the flares."

"The *Trafalgar*'s launching its fighters."

"Alert all warships!" Supreme Commander Prm-jevev barked, staring in a mix of fascination and horror at the huge space vehicle that had suddenly appeared from the tunnel-line behind the Zhirrzh force. Awesome, terrifying, impossibly huge, like something out of ancient legend.

The Elder he'd sent to report to Warrior Command flicked back in. "Speaker Cvv-panav: 'It's a trap!' " he quoted. " 'Exactly as I warned you.' " His voice was harsh with the Speaker's anger, as if Prm-jevev had gotten himself into this predicament solely to spite him.

A second Elder appeared before Prm-jevev could respond. "The Overclan Prime: 'It does indeed appear to be a trap,' " he said. Unlike Cvv-panav's, his tone was calm, even matter-of-fact. " 'Can you handle it?' "

"Supreme Commander, they're launching their fighter warcraft," one of the warriors called.

And with that the fascinated horror seemed to dissolve from beneath the Supreme Commander's tongue. "Understood," he said, smiling grimly. The thing out there was merely a weapon of war, and he knew how to deal with weapons of war. "All warships: attack and defend at will."

A handful of Elders vanished, scattering to the other warships to relay his order. The Elders who'd come from Oaccanv remained where they were, still waiting for his reply. "To the Overclan Prime: I'll do my best," he said. "To the Speaker for Dhaa'rr—"

He looked at the displays, and at the fire trails that marked the Human-Conqueror fighter warcraft streaking toward his warships. Cvv-panav had been right about its being a trap, and no doubt would now be working to parlay that serendipitous guess to his own political advantage. That was how the Speaker worked; and Prm-jevev saw no need to help him. "To the Speaker for Dhaa'rr: no reply."

"All systems checks complete," Bokamba said briskly from the seat behind Quinn. "Straight green."

"Acknowledged," Quinn said, hunching his shoulders forward and resettling himself one last time against the contoured seat. He'd just felt the lurch a few seconds ago as the Wolf Pack meshed in. Any minute now they should be getting the order to launch.

Assuming there was still something here to fight. With a half-hour lead on them, the Zhirrzh fleet might well have already finished this particular slaughter and moved on.

And then an image flicked into view in front of his eyes, fed through his Mindlink and superimposed on the scorched and heat-stressed composite of the launch tube outside the Corvine's canopy. An image obviously being fed from the *Trafalgar*'s external cameras.

There was indeed still something there to fight.

"I make it five Zhirrzh ships," Bokamba said. "No, make that ten; five more are coming in from outsystem. Drives are firing toward us—must be decelerating."

"Someone's putting up a pretty good fight against them," Quinn said, pulling up a vector map and an ID overlay. The small ships buzzing around the Zhirrzh warships—and being methodically blasted to dust— read out as Yycroman freighters, passenger shuttles, asteroid miners, and zero-gee construction drudgeships. Brave, foolish, or just plain desperate, the Yycromae were taking on the Conqueror juggernaut.

Not surprisingly, they were losing.

"This is it, Copperheads," Schweighofer's voice came tautly in Quinn's ear. "Go to Level X and launch at will. Warrior's luck to you all."

Schweighofer's last words were nearly swallowed up in the rumble of drives that suddenly reverberated from the rest of the launch tubes around him. Bracing himself, Quinn keyed the drive, joining in the mad rush. The Corvine leaped forward like a hungry predator, the acceleration shoving him back into the seat cushions as the fighter skimmed on superconducting magnetic bearings down the launch tube toward space. "Maestro?" he heard Bokamba call over the roar. "We were ordered to X."

Level X: the full Mindlink integration between the Copperheads and their fighters. The moment Quinn had been dreading ever since making the deal with the hearing board that had gotten Clipper and the others out from under their court-martial.

"Maestro?" Bokamba called again.

"Go ahead," Quinn called back. "I'll be right with you—"

And then the Corvine cleared the tube rim and they were in space, driving hard away from the *Trafalgar*. The rest of the Corvines and Catbirds were burning space beside him, an advancing battle line of the most awesome warriors and fighting machines the Commonwealth had ever produced.

And it was time for those warriors to go to work. All of them. Taking a deep breath, Quinn shifted his Mindlink to Level X.

And abruptly, all around him, the universe changed.

His vision changed, expanding from its usual boundaries to a full 360-degree wraparound, with only experience, kinesthetic awareness, and a hazy orange circle to indicate which way was forward. The dark and muted colors of the scene in front of him became a rainbow of vibrant color, with all spacecraft within his immediate strike zone turning a bright red, while those farther away shaded into yellow and green and finally blue for the most distant.

His hearing changed, the other Copperheads and command orders no longer voices in his ear but words and images in his mind. The vector overlay he'd called up earlier likewise became audible, pitches and tones in the background meshing with the visual color cues to give him complete information on where every ship out there was, and exactly what each ship's vector was relative to him.

And he himself changed. He was no longer Adam Quinn, Copperhead, piloting a Corvine Tactical Superiority attack fighter. He *was* that Corvine attack fighter.

His skin was the Corvine's hull, with the controlled heat of the drive's fury at his back and the faint brushing of friction with the tenuous medium of Phormbi's magnetosphere on his face and chest. His sense of smell was the Corvine's systems monitors, the steady almond aroma indicating all systems were primed and ready. His sense of taste was the damage monitors, the tang of cinnamon signaling that the Corvine was as yet uninjured. His stance—for even in this strange disembodied mental image he could still envision himself as having a physical stance—was the manifestation of the fighter's medical monitors as they in turn watched over his physiological status. He seemed to himself to be standing firm and alert and strong, his body twisted slightly into a taut martial-arts stance, his hands held ready for combat—a composite indicator that showed his oxygen, blood sugar, and adrenaline levels to be at optimal levels.

But perhaps the most traumatic change of all—the most exhilarating and at the same time the most terrifying aspect of the Mindlink—was the fact that in this world within his own mind he was no longer alone.

Bokamba was there, close by his illusory side, his thoughts and emotions and sensations swirling around and within Quinn's own. Quinn could sense his alertness and ordered thoughts as he settled into the role of tail man; could feel his quiet exultation in what was probably his last chance to fly a combat mission as a Copperhead; could also feel the tinge of private uncertainty as to whether he would be able to handle the job. There was uneasiness of another sort, as well: an uneasy concern about Quinn's own state of mind, triggered by Quinn's delay in going to Level X when Schweighofer had given the order, and underlined by his knowledge of why Quinn had left the Copperheads in the first place. Clipper and the other Copperheads of the Omicron Four unit were there, too, a level below the experiential peak where he and Bokamba stood; spread out a level beneath that were the Copperheads of Samurai's Kappa Two and Dreamer's Sigma Five. And a level below that were Schweighofer and the other non-Copperhead signals from the *Trafalgar*—

Human Peacekeepers, we welcome you. Displayed as images and sensations in his mind, it took Quinn a fraction of a second to realize the words coming in along the *Trafalgar*'s comm feed had been spoken in Yycroman. *Your assistance is most desperately needed.*

Our target is number three, Clipper's voice came in Quinn's mind. One of the Zhirrzh ships, edging from green to yellow now as the Copperheads approached it, flashed briefly red as Clipper marked it for them. For another instant it was superimposed by an overview of Clipper's proposed attack plan: a split-wedge thrust, with Quinn and Shrike veering to starboard into an over/under scissor, Paladin and Harlequin doing the mirror to port, while Clipper did a straight-in run. *Go for laser ports,* Clipper continued. *Try to knock them out so the line ships' missiles can get through. Tails, watch for any signs of hull damage or weakness they can exploit.*

Bokamba and the other three tails acknowledged. The target had shaded from yellow to red now; and as Quinn began easing toward starboard in preparation for the split, he saw one edge of the ship brighten and the opposite edge dim, the pitches of the sound coming from those edges similarly rising and falling. *He's swinging around toward us,* Bokamba confirmed. A group of orange diamonds appeared on the edges of the hexagons—*Laser ports,* Bokamba identified them—which the Zhirrzh were obviously trying to bring into range.

We're glad we're in time to help. That was Commodore Montgomery, talking to the Yycromae. *What can you tell us about the enemy?*

Clipper's signal sparked; and with a wrenching move that momentarily staggered his imaginary combat stance as the gee forces drained some of the blood away from his brain, Quinn threw the Corvine into a ninety-degree turn to starboard. One of the orange diamonds Bokamba had marked flared suddenly; reflexively, he ducked, the Corvine twitching simultaneously, as the white vector line of a laser blast shot past him. There was a flicker of warmth on his left arm, but the taste of cinnamon remained steady. An orange cross appeared on the laser port as Bokamba got a targeting lock on it, and even as he twisted the Corvine into his scissor, Quinn threw a left-handed punch from his imaginary stance, sending a burst of 55 mm cannon shells directly into the port. The

Corvine scissored beneath the hexagon before he could see what if any damage he'd inflicted.

There was another flicker from the hull above him, and another laser pulse flashed past. Again it missed, but not by nearly as great a margin. A sudden warmth ran across his right shin, and for a second the cinnamon taste in his mouth was mixed with oregano as the ionized gases in the laser's wake momentarily scrambled the Corvine's aft-starboard sensors. The oregano faded as Bokamba reconfigured the pathways and connections and brought the sensors back on-line—

And then, at the back of Quinn's consciousness, two images abruptly winked out. One of Samurai's Corvines had been hit, the two Copperheads aboard killed. For them warrior's luck had run out.

You took out the laser lens with that last shot, Bokamba informed him.

With another dizzying turn Quinn swung the Corvine back around again. *What's the opening's size?* The last image of the laser port as they'd swung beneath the ship appeared in front of him, the details scrubbed and measurements marked. Yes: it was just the right size. *Is the laser itself still functional?*

We won't know until and unless it fires again, Bokamba said dryly.

Which meant that what Quinn was planning was going to be a huge gamble. But definitely a worthwhile one. If the laser had been put out of commission, the opening was just big enough to drop one of their four Vejovis missiles into, bypassing the whole problem of the invulnerable hull and depositing a warhead directly into the interior of the Zhirrzh ship.

If the laser *hadn't* been put out of commission, on the other hand, he was about to give the Zhirrzh the easiest shot they would ever have.

He had the Corvine almost in position now, swinging around in a tight arc ready to come into line with the laser port and drive down its throat. A green targeting cross flicked into place in front of Quinn's eyes, Bokamba's confirmation that the Vejovis missiles were ready to launch. Quinn turned his head slightly, moving the cross onto the port—

Maestro: signal from Schweighofer, Clipper's voice came in his mind. *The Cascadia has gotten snarled in the Wolf Pack. You and Shrike break off and go help shoot them loose.*

Not now, Quinn told him. A quick status update flicked between them—

Acknowledged, Clipper agreed. One melded-consciousness level below, Quinn could sense his giving the order to Harlequin instead as he brought the Corvine up almost into line—

And again twitched away as a laser pulse shot past him.

Still active, Bokamba reported, as if Quinn needed to be told. *But I see now that without the lens there's a 0.74-second optic precursor.*

A replay of the laser shot flicked into view, along with a graph of the intensity from the light-leakage precursor Bokamba had identified. Three quarters of a second wasn't a lot of warning, but it would have to do. *Watch it closely. Here we go.*

He swung up toward the laser port; and as he did so, the mental sensations that were Harlequin and his tail, Savile, flashed and vanished. Another Corvine, this time one from his own unit, had run out of warrior's luck.

Later, he knew, he would be able to feel the pain and loss of these deaths of his comrades. But not yet. For the moment the Mindlink connection rode supreme, suppressing all emotion and all thought except what was necessary for survival and the completion of his job.

He was in line with the laser port now, the green targeting cross dead center on the hole. In his imaginary stance he prepared a right-hand punch. . . .

Concentrating on the target, he completely missed the brief flare from the next laser port to starboard. Bokamba's warning flicked into his mind; firing the missile, he threw the Corvine into a flat dive. The laser beam flashed over his head—

And suddenly the whole of his lower back flared with heat, the sharp tang of pineapple and the stench of burned toast flooding in on him as the Corvine bucked violently. The dorsal stabilizer and engine had been hit, and hit badly.

He fought to bring the fighter back under control, feeling Bokamba in the back of his mind as the other worked furiously to reroute the electronics and create a compensation profile for the remaining engines. The Vejovis missile was nearly to the target port now, he saw, burning with the single-mindedness of its scorpion namesake toward its target. Almost there—

Bokamba, his full attention occupied by the dead engine, didn't spot the optic precursor. But Quinn did, and with a rush of adrenaline that brought his imaginary combat stance even tighter, he threw full power to the drive. He was already driving up toward the edge of this particular Zhirrzh hexagon; if he could get to that edge and roll the Corvine over the top—

He almost made it. But with one dead engine the Corvine was just a hair too slow . . . and suddenly beneath him came the flicker of the laser, and the secondary and much brighter flash as the Vejovis missile in its path detonated.

The fading heat on Quinn's back was abruptly joined by an unpleasant prickling on both shins, accompanied by a flood of oregano and garlic. The shrapnel from the missile had raked across the Corvine's aft underside, delivering another blow to the aft sensors and penetrating into the backup power cells. But at least there was no more engine damage. He kept the Corvine curving over the hexagon, balancing forward and side thrusters, flying on reflex as he split his attention between watching for more Zhirrzh laser ports and monitoring Bokamba's repair work.

Maestro?

We're all right, Clipper, Quinn assured him.

Break off your attack, Clipper ordered. *Go help Shrike free the* Cascadia *from the Wolf Pack.*

Quinn grimaced. A necessary task, and Bokamba could certainly use a breather while he got the Corvine put back together. But it was embarrassing to have taken a hit so early in the battle. *Acknowledged.*

Hitting the steering thrusters again, he sent the Corvine spiraling away from the Zhirrzh ship. Ahead and to port, a cluster of missiles from the *Galileo* was sweeping across his vector, and he sent a quick ID pulse toward them to prevent them from locking on to him. In the distance he could see the *Cascadia* still trapped in its section of the Wolf Pack frame, with Shrike's Corvine and a pair of Axeheads flying around the bow and both flanks blasting away at the snarled tether lines.

Bokamba paused in his repair work long enough to pull up a sensor map of the *Cascadia*. The stern tethers were still securely fastened; shifting his vector slightly, Quinn headed for that part of the ship.

And then another image flicked into view, a picture coming from Dreamer's Mindlink feed. Four small craft had emerged from hatches in the aft hexagons of the Zhirrzh warship her Sigma Five group was harassing. Ignoring the Copperheads, the four craft were dropping rapidly toward the planet's surface.

Laser bombers, Bokamba identified them. *They carry heavy lasers for short-range atmospheric assaults. The Zhirrzh used them in the surface attacks on Dorcas, Massif, and Pasdoufat.*

Which meant the aliens hadn't come there just to reconnoiter or to clear out orbital defenses. They were serious about taking Phormbi, or at least about doing serious damage to it. *Clipper?*

I see them, Maestro, Clipper replied. *Dreamer's already signaled* Trafalgar *for new orders. You already have yours.*

But they may need help, Bokamba protested.

Quinn frowned. There'd been a strange surge of emotion in those words. And in Bokamba's sense, for that matter. Both disturbingly out of character for a Copperhead at full Level X Mindlink.

You have your orders, Clipper repeated firmly. *The* Cascadia*'s a sitting duck where she is, and the battle's drifting that direction.*

Acknowledged, Quinn said. At his lowest melded-consciousness level, he heard Schweighofer give the order for Sigma Five to attack the Zhirrzh laser bombers. The scene and Dreamer's combat stance shifted as she and three of her fighters broke off and dropped planetward in pursuit, 55 mm cannon blazing away furiously. One of the laser bombers seemed to shatter under that blistering hail, exploding into a cloud of secondary shrapnel that momentarily rocked the others flying beside it. The attack focus shifted to the second Zhirrzh—

And then, behind them, the warship they'd just left rolled leisurely over and sent a stuttering barrage of laser blasts directly into the fighters.

They're hit! someone's thought came, rolling through Quinn's mind like a deep wave racing across the ocean toward shore. They'd been hit, all right, and with a cold feeling in his chest Quinn fought to sort through the dizzying chaos of images and thoughts that Sigma Five had suddenly become. He singled out Hawk and his tail, Adept, in their Catbird, their combat stances abandoned as they struggled to remain on their feet amid the smells and tastes of two lost engines, severe electronics damage, and hull-integrity failure. Cooker and Faker were a little better off, with near-total engine failure but at least retaining hull integrity and a small degree of firepower capability. There was no sign at all of Cossack and Glitter, nor were there any readings from their fighter. Already dead.

And it looked very much as if Dreamer and Con Lady were soon going to be joining them.

Quinn focused on the two women, his mind flicking unwillingly to that brief conversation he'd had with them in the dayroom back on the *Trafalgar*. Then they'd casually walked past the other Copperheads' doubts and Samurai's outright and bitter hostility to welcome him back into the ranks of the Copperheads.

Now they sat trapped in the blackened husk of a shattered Corvine, their combat stances transformed into the faintly twitching sprawls of unconsciousness, the sense around them a chilling emptiness completely devoid of either smell or taste. The entire Corvine was dead, only the Mindlink and their self-powered combat suits keeping them alive.

And that not for much longer. Only until the Zhirrzh ship found the range and opened fire again. Or until gravity and air friction turned the Corvine's nose downward and sent it spinning to a fiery crash on the planetary surface.

We have to do something, Maestro. We have to do *something.*

Quinn jerked in his seat, a sudden shock running through him. Again Bokamba's words and sense had come to him riding a surge of emotion.

But this time it was more than just a distraught attitude. There was a new intensity behind it, an impatient and all-consuming drive to take action to rescue Dreamer and Con Lady from the death looming over them.

An intensity that utterly defied the emotion-suppressing grip of the Mindlink.

Quinn didn't ask why Bokamba felt that way. With the Mindlink bringing the cores of their beings together, he didn't have to. Dreamer and Con Lady were women; and in the cultural matrix that formed the underpinning of Bokamba's soul, women were to be honored and respected and protected. No matter whether they were helpless children or trained warriors.

No matter what.

Quinn could ignore Bokamba's unspoken plea, of course. He was the Corvine's pilot, in ultimate command, and there was nothing Bokamba could do to alter or override that. They had their orders, and it was his duty to obey them.

But then, long ago, it had also been his duty to listen to the senior Peacekeeper officers who had assured him that there were absolutely no problems with the Copperhead screening procedures. He'd defied direct orders then by going to Lord Cavanagh and the NorCoord Parliament, and had ultimately paid the price for his perceived betrayal. But it had been something he'd felt he had to do.

Just as fulfilling his own sense of responsibility toward the dying women out there was clearly something Bokamba had to do.

And Quinn came to a decision. *Rig for attack,* he ordered Bokamba, swinging the Corvine in another gut-wrenching turn away from the Wolf Pack and the *Cascadia* and toward the Zhirrzh ship still spitting laser blasts toward the helpless Copperheads. It was most likely a useless gesture, he knew, all the more so given that he wasn't sure he agreed with Bokamba's point of view or even understood it.

But perhaps that didn't matter. What mattered was that Bokamba was a friend.

And friendship was something he most certainly understood.

The Zhirrzh ship's lasers flashed, sending a withering blaze of fire squarely into the group of fighters chasing after the remaining three laser bombers. "Did they get them?" Daschka called over his shoulder.

"They got 'em, but good," Cho Ming said grimly. "Three fighters seriously damaged, one vaporized outright."

Daschka shook his head. "Someone wasn't paying enough attention, I guess. Damn."

"Can't we do something?" Aric asked anxiously, gazing out at the damaged fighters. One of them in particular: speeding along on its last vector, clearly out of control, it was skimming perilously close to Phormbi's atmosphere.

"Like what?" Daschka asked. "Go charging out there and pull them out?"

Aric hissed helplessly between his teeth. No, of course there wasn't anything they could do. Not without revealing their presence to the Conqueror warships and getting themselves blown to bits along with everyone else.

"Besides, we don't have to," Daschka continued, pointing out the canopy. "Looks like there's someone already rushing to their defense."

Aric looked. Angling away from the huge transport frame, almost invisible amid the flashes of laser fire and the brighter explosions of Peacekeeper missiles, was the flare of a single fighter heading toward the damaged ships. "I wonder what he thinks he's doing," he said.

"Maybe trying to distract the Zhirrzh ship," Daschka suggested doubtfully. "I presume he doesn't think he can pluck all three of those wrecks out from under their snouts."

"Well, whatever he's thinking, he's apparently thinking it on his own," Cho Ming put in. "Here, take a listen."

From the speaker on Daschka's console came a sudden cacophony of voices, snatches of conversation picked up as the Peacekeepers' comm lasers swept past the *Happenstance*'s hiding place. From the midst of the clamor came a single voice as Cho Ming did a select-and-enhance: "—mmediately. Repeat: Maestro, return to—"

The voice cut off as the comm laser swept past. "Maestro," Daschka repeated, throwing Aric a frown. "Isn't that your friend Adam Quinn's tag name?"

"Yes," Aric murmured, staring out the canopy and abruptly feeling physically ill. Quinn was *here;* and if Quinn, then probably Clipper and the rest of the Omicron Four force, too. The men who'd risked their lives and careers to help him rescue his brother from the Conquerors.

And suddenly it was no longer a matter of sitting by and reluctantly watching aliens he respected being slaughtered by the enemy. Now he was watching the slaughter of friends.

"Take it easy, Cavanagh," Daschka said quietly. "Don't get sick on me now. Quinn's good—you know that. He'll make it through."

"I know," Aric said mechanically. Not believing it for a moment.

Another shock wave rippled through the command/monitor room as yet another Human-Conqueror missile slipped in past the Zhirrzh defenses to vent its explosive fury against the outer hull. Another shock wave to rattle the optronics, shatter fluid-main connectors, and throw the warriors and technics around like children's clothwork dolls.

And Supreme Commander Prm-jevev, gripping his couch supports to keep from being shaken off, was no longer smiling. Grimly or otherwise.

"Tell Ship Commander Dkll-kumvit I don't care what else gets through," he snapped to the Elder hovering nervously in front of him. "He and the *Imperative* are to concentrate on clearing the way for those heavy air-assault craft."

"I obey," the Elder said, and vanished.

Prm-jevev turned his attention back to the monitors, a bitter taste beneath his tongue. Three of the Human-Conqueror warships had already been disabled in the handful of hunbeats since their part of the battle had begun, one of them burned virtually beyond recognition. The small fighter warcraft were being systematically destroyed as they continued to dart in and out of the fight, distracting his warriors, or worse, occasionally managing to knock out one of the Zhirrzh fleet's lasers. His initial reluctance to attack the poorly armed Yycroman civilian spacecraft had long since vanished, and the fleet was busily burning them out of the sky as well. To all outward appearances the Zhirrzh were winning.

But they weren't. Behind their virtually invulnerable hulls the mighty warships were slowly being pounded and shaken and battered into useless hulks. Already the secondary effects of the missile attacks had knocked out more lasers than the fighter warcraft had, and with every lost laser the odds of a given missile getting through rose that much more. It was a race to see which side would disable the other first . . . and deep within him Prm-jevev suspected the Zhirrzh were going to lose it.

But he couldn't pull back. Not yet. Not while there was still a chance of driving away the defenders and knocking out this center of Human-Conqueror power. And, if extraordinary good luck was with them, perhaps even eliminating the threat of the Human-Conquerors' terrifying CIRCE weapon.

And certainly not while five hundred cyclics of former Supreme Warrior Commanders were watching over his shoulder from the eighteen worlds.

An Elder popped into view. "Message from the *Imperative*," he said. "Ship Commander Dkll-kumvit reports strong harassment from the Yycroman spacecraft, and that his systems are continuing to fail under Human-Conqueror bombardment. He states he cannot guarantee survival of the assault craft."

Prm-jevev cursed under his breath. Those Yycromae were incredible, the way they threw themselves to their deaths for such little gain. What in the eighteen worlds were they protecting down there, anyway? "Understood," he growled. "Message to the *Exonerator:* have them move immediately to the *Imperative's* support. Those heavy air-assault craft have got to get through."

"I obey," the Elder said, and vanished.

"Helm!" Prm-jevev called across the room. "Shift course: twenty angles right, twelve angles beneath. Communicator: order our three air-assault craft to prepare for launch on my command."

"I obey."

Prm-jevev swore again, thoughtfully, as he studied the displays. Somewhere out there, there had to be a hole in the Human-Conqueror and Yycroman defense forces. Not big, certainly, but maybe big enough to slip the assault craft through before they could respond. . . .

And then, suddenly, he heard a muffled gasp from behind him.

He spun around on his couch to find himself looking at an Elder. An Elder who was himself staring to the side in rigid and obvious horror. Prm-jevev opened his mouth to demand an explanation—

"Supreme Commander Prm-jevev!" one of the warriors shouted.

Prm-jevev spun back again. It was one of the warriors at the display console, and he was jabbing his tongue at one of the displays that showed the curve of the planetary horizon ahead of them.

And in the center of that display . . .

The Supreme Commander cursed again. And this time he meant it.

Another laser pulse flashed past, the beam slashing down toward the Corvine. Quinn twitched away—too late—and there was another burst of vaporized metal from the aft starboard flank. He felt the sudden heat on his thigh; a moment later the smell of freshly cut grass joined in the potpourri of aromas swirling through his head. *That one took out the stardrive,* Bokamba confirmed. *No way for me to fix it.*

Which meant that in the increasingly likely event that they were the only two Peacekeepers to survive this battle, there would be no way for them to escape from the system. *Understood,* Quinn said, trying hard to hide his growing frustration from his tail man. The area around Dreamer and Con Lady was starting to ripple visibly, the sign that their Corvine was getting into dangerously thick air. Even if he and Bokamba could get there without being vaporized, it was going to be problematic whether they could get a tether hooked on to the crippled fighter in time to haul it to safety.

Another laser flashed toward him. Quinn twitched again; but this time the beam didn't make it all the way, instead throwing a brilliant splash of vaporized metal from one of the Yycroman ships still buzzing around.

Apparently the Zhirrzh had decided to concentrate on the closer Yyc-romae instead of on him.

He frowned. Preoccupied with the endangered Copperheads out there and the slow disintegration of his own Corvine beneath him, he hadn't been paying much attention to the Yycroman ships except when one of them happened to enter his immediate strike zone. But with little to do now but fly evasive maneuvers . . .

He pulled up a vector map first, switching the usual audio/visual cues into an overlay that could be distracting in the heat of combat but that at the moment wouldn't bother him. A high-speed replay of the past five minutes came next, drawing on both the Corvine's and the *Trafalgar's* recorders. Some of the Yycromae, he could see, were attacking the Zhirrzh ships directly, using shredder-bursts, cannon, missiles, and something that looked like white paint. A few others were hanging back performing long-range spotting duty for the attackers; fewer still were skimming right over the enemy ships' hulls, carrying out the dangerous task of close-in spotting.

But the vast majority of them were being vaporized by the Zhirrzh. And for the first time since the battle had begun, Quinn saw why.

They were running interference for the Peacekeeper forces. Moving in groups between the waves of fighters and the Zhirrzh warships, trying to block or confuse whatever sensors the enemy was using, helping the Corvines and Axeheads to get across the kill zone into combat range. Flying directly in front of missile clusters, diving suicidally straight into the Zhirrzh lasers and taking the blasts that would otherwise detonate the missiles too far from their targets.

And even sacrificing their lives to run a moving screen between Zhirrzh firepower and a lone Corvine on a quixotic rescue mission.

Quinn keyed for verbal comm. "Yycroman defense forces," he said, the sound of his physical voice a startling intrusion into the mental images and effortless communication of the Mindlink. "This is Corvine Three Omicron Four."

The answer came immediately. "This is Savazzci mey Yyamsepk," the Yycroman words came, already translated, along the Mindlink. "What are your orders?"

"I want you to quit protecting me and do your job," Quinn told him, focusing on the Zhirrzh laser bombers still heading toward atmosphere. Adept had gotten their Catbird moving again, and she and Hawk were attempting to pursue, but with only a single working engine their effort was clearly futile. Cooker and Faker were trying, too, but most of their sporadic bursts of 55 mm cannon shells were going wide. "Those laser bombers are getting away."

In the distance off to starboard the Zhirrzh ship seemed suddenly to have become fully aware of Quinn's presence, and the space around them began to shimmer with the ionization afterglow of laser shots. Most skimmed harmlessly past as Quinn kept the fighter dipping and swerving in a semirandom evasion pattern. One caught one of Savazzci's screening ships, turning it into a blazing fireball.

"We are doing our job," the stiff-sounding retort came. "We aren't swift enough to catch them. We protect you in the hope that you can do so."

Quinn grimaced, dropping an extrapolation overlay on top of the vector map. The Corvine's dead dorsal engine plus the hefty lead the laser bombers had on them . . .

We can do it, Bokamba told him. *A drop-J curve through the atmosphere will get us to an intercept point.*

Quinn studied the curve that had appeared on his extrapolation overlay. It was a tricky maneuver, all right, a modified version of the approach he'd used when he and Aric Cavanagh had dived down from near orbit to snatch Pheylan from his Zhirrzh captors.

But in that situation he'd been flying an undamaged fighter through skies unpunctuated by heavy fire. Here pulling such a stunt would be begging for gradient instabilities or turbulent control loss. There was probably no better than a fifty percent chance that they would make it to the rendezvous point ahead of the Zhirrzh.

What *was* certain was that committing themselves to the attempt would mean abandoning any chance of rescuing Dreamer and Con Lady.

Bokamba knew that, too, and for a moment his sense was tangled in an agony of indecision and guilt. But only for a moment. *We have no choice,* the tail said, his mental tone heavy but determined. *Let's do it.*

Right, Quinn acknowledged as an updated version of the drop-J curve appeared on the overlay. Bracing himself for another ninety-degree turn, he prepared to flip the Corvine over—

And then, without warning, a double blaze of blue-white fire flashed into sight over the planet's horizon directly ahead.

Incoming spacecraft! Bokamba snapped out the warning. New vectors appeared on Quinn's overlay: the two spacecraft were coming up incredibly fast over the curve of the planet, skimming the top of the atmosphere, the extrapolation indicating an ETA to the main battle of barely five minutes. Quinn keyed in full magnification—

And felt his breath catch in his throat. To the unaided eye the approaching spacecraft were little more than dark blotches against the ragged-edged corona of their drive trails, but as the Corvine's optics edited out the glare, he could see the splashes of lights across their dark surfaces and the strangely curved edges glowing with an eerie luminescence. Images from the military history texts; images that supposedly no longer existed.

Yycroman Vindicator-class warships.

Quinn found his voice again. "Savazzci, this is Three Omicron Four."

"They have come," the Yycroma's reply came through the Mindlink into Quinn's mind. Not with any trace of joy or relief, but with the grim satisfaction of a Yycroman male who has seen the time for vengeance finally at hand. "Now shall we see."

The lights on one of the Vindicators dimmed, and the slender blue beams of particle-beam weapons lanced out toward the three Zhirrzh laser bombers diving ever deeper into the atmosphere. But too far ahead: the beams sliced through the air ahead of them for a clean miss—

And then, abruptly, the blue lines were sheathed with an explosive and expanding swirl of furious white turbulence. The beams, flash-ionizing the tenuous upper atmosphere, had created an instant hurricane.

The Zhirrzh laser bombers were caught flat-footed. Their mad race planetward floundered as the shock wave of superheated air slammed across their bows. Before they could recover, the second Vindicator fired, this shot sizzling past their starboard flank.

Charging toward the main battle like a pair of enraged bears, the warships were already out of range for a third shot. But it didn't matter. They'd slowed the laser bombers' descent just enough . . . and Quinn, whose years with Lord Cavanagh had taught him how to appreciate a dramatic entrance, also knew a cue when he saw one.

He had the Corvine in a vertical dive even before the second Yycroman shot had been fired; was scorching the fighter's hull with friction before the laser bombers finished their bouncing. By the time they'd settled down and were again throwing power to their drives, he'd started into his main curve.

Before they could do anything else, he was right on top of them.

" 'We have no idea,' " the Elder quoted, stumbling over the words in his haste to get them out. " 'But the description doesn't sound like that of any Human-Conqueror warship we've yet seen.' "

"I could have told you that," Supreme Commander Prm-jevev snarled under his breath as he gazed at the patches of blue-white flame charging toward him. Yycroman, without a doubt. And armed with weapons the like of which he also had never seen.

And apparently left deliberately out of the battle until this exact beat. Why?

The answer was obvious. The Human-Conquerors and their Yycroman allies weren't fooled by the impervious Zhirrzh hulls—not a bit. They knew perfectly well how much internal shock damage their missiles were causing . . . and everything they'd done up until this point had clearly been for the sole purpose of softening their defenses so that these two ships could get in close.

Close enough to use their blue-beamed weapon. An unidentified, hitherto unseen weapon.

CIRCE?

There was a faint flash of distant light on one of the telescope displays. The heavy air-assault craft, their crews dazed or stunned, being destroyed by the single Human-Conqueror fighter warcraft that had followed them down. More good warriors being prematurely raised to Eldership.

Another Elder appeared. " 'Supreme Commander, this is Speaker Cvv-panav,' " he said. " 'These are nothing more than part of the Yycroman war fleet the Mrachanis warned us about. Hold your territory, and they'll break over you.' "

Prm-jevev flicked his tongue in vicious contempt. Here he was in the boiling cauldron of combat, facing Eldership for himself and every one of his warriors and technics, and all Speaker Cvv-panav could do was waste his time with pretentious political banalities. "It may not be that easy, Speaker," he bit out. "Not if that weapon is what I think it might be."

" 'Don't be ridiculous,' " the Speaker's scoffing reply came back a few beats later. " 'Hold your courage, Supreme Commander—this is no time to fall apart on us.' "

Prm-jevev flicked his tongue savagely. It was also no time to face a weapon like CIRCE. Not here, with a fleet that had already been battered halfway to uselessness. Certainly not on the Human-Conquerors' terms and timing.

But how could he call a retreat? Especially when none of the Elders who would be judging his actions even knew of CIRCE's existence?

Another Elder appeared. " 'Supreme Commander Prm-jevev, this is the Overclan Prime,' " he said. " 'You are hereby ordered to withdraw.' "

Prm-jevev felt his midlight pupils narrow in surprise. What in the eighteen worlds—?

And then he got it. The Overclan Prime had listened between the words and understood the full scope of Prm-jevev's suspicions and fears. By ordering Prm-jevev to retreat from what looked to be an imminent victory, he was taking on himself the public scorn and political repercussions that would follow this defeat.

On the telescope display, the last of the heavy air-assault craft flashed into vapor . . . and with it went their last reason to stay. "I obey, Overclan Prime," he acknowledged. Taking a deep breath, he looked up at the Elders grouped around him. "Supreme Commander Prm-jevev to all ships," he called. "Break off your attacks and retreat."

The laser bombers saw the Corvine coming, of course. But there was absolutely nothing they could do about it. At close-combat range the faint flickers of light that preceded each laser shot were easily visible, and even with one dead engine Quinn was able to avoid their shots with ease. Between the 55 mm cannon and one of his three remaining missiles, it was over in seconds.

Weaving around the expanding clouds of debris, he turned the Corvine's nose upward again . . . and for the first time since the Vindicators' sudden appearance, he turned his attention back to the main battle.

To find that it was over.

He stared in disbelief. There was the *Trafalgar*, looking half-dead but still limping gamely along. There was the fleet, or at least what was left of it. There were the two Vindicators, their drive coronas now flaming violently in the opposite direction as they attempted to brake from their mad charge.

But the Zhirrzh ships had turned and were driving away from the planet. Even as he watched, they meshed out and were gone.

What in the world? Bokamba said, clearly as surprised as Quinn was.

I don't know, Quinn said. *They just gave up.*

But they were winning, Bokamba protested.

I know.

Well, let Montgomery and the others figure it out, Bokamba said. *We've got to get back to Dreamer and Con Lady.*

Right. Quinn curved the Corvine back around, searching for the women's fighter.

To find it little more than a blur, its shape all but smothered by the roiling air turbulence around it. Like a sleek metal meteoroid, it was heading toward a spectacular and fiery death.

He threw full power to the engines, feeling Bokamba's sudden surge of guilt as both men were slammed back into their seats. A flood of warmth hit his face and chest, the intensity increasing as air friction began heating the Corvine's already overstressed hull toward the danger point. Behind him he could sense Bokamba trying furiously to coax more power out of the engines, all the time fully and bitterly aware that they weren't going to make it. . . .

And then, suddenly, a spurt of maneuvering flame erupted barely a klick from the women's Corvine. A shadowy ship, visible only through the air turbulence sheathing it, was closing fast on the stricken fighter.

It's a sensor-stealthed ship, Bokamba said, his relief bubbling almost visibly. *Probably one of the* Trafalgar*'s watchships.*

Quinn held his breath, ignoring the heat now burningly hot on his skin. The chase ship was nearly to the fighter . . . the two masses of turbulence merged . . .

And abruptly the shape and texture changed as the chase ship curved upward back toward space, the wounded Corvine safely aboard.

"I guess that's that," Quinn said aloud, easing up on the throttle and lifting the Corvine's nose away from the planet below. The battle was over, and with it any need to stay at Level X. Bracing himself, he disengaged.

With a breathtaking suddenness, the brilliant colors were gone. The colors, and the aromas, and the sensations, and the other presences in his mind. He was all alone again, suspended precariously in the center of a vast, uncaring universe that had once again become dark and dreary.

A universe from which several of his friends and comrades in arms had now been taken. Forever.

For a long, agonizing moment he fought the old silent battle within himself: whether to stay here, or to go back to Level X for just a few minutes more. But down deep, he knew what the final outcome of that battle had to be. Level X was a glorious existence, a dazzling universe where life was neat and ordered and there were no emotional knives to cut and twist into a person's gut. But it wasn't reality; and a long time ago he'd decided where it was he had to live his life.

And so, with a hollowness in his soul, and with silent tears streaming across his cheeks, he turned the Corvine to follow the rescue ship back across the dark of space toward the battered fleet. And wished he'd been one of the ones who had died.

The teeth-aching screech of metal on metal ground to a halt, and there was a distant clang as the forward cargo hatch slammed shut. "That's got 'er," Cho Ming called out.

"Right," Daschka said, easing the throttle back and pulling up toward space. "There you go, Cavanagh. Happy?"

"Yes," Aric murmured. "Thank you."

Daschka shrugged. "I never said I wasn't willing to help out," he said. "I just didn't want to get vaporized in the process."

Aric smiled. "I guess that's understandable."

"Bet your sweet assets," Daschka agreed. "Well, let's get over to the *Trafalgar.* We've got some damaged goods here to deliver. And I suspect we're going to want to have a long talk with Commodore Montgomery."

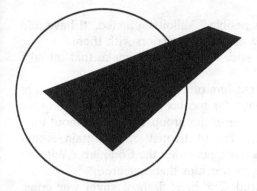

21

Valloittaja's fur had been gradually stiffening throughout Nzz-oonaz's description of the battle, a gesture or reaction the searcher had found both disturbing and strangely distracting. Now, abruptly, the fur snapped flat again. "So, then, what you are saying is that you have failed us," the Mrachani said.

"I'm sorry," Nzz-oonaz said automatically before catching himself. There was no need for him to apologize to the Mrachanis. In fact, if anything, the apologies and explanations should be traveling the other direction. "But if there's any blame to be placed here, I believe there's enough for all of us to share."

Valloittaja seemed to shrink into himself. "Of what use is blame?" he asked, his voice low and edged with fear and pain. "The Zhirrzh strength has been tried and has failed . . . and the Mrachanis now face extinction at the hands of our oppressors."

"That will not happen," Gll-borgiv put in, flicking his tongue for emphasis. "We will not allow it."

"And you and the Conquerors Without Reason are both wrong if you think that Zhirrzh strength has failed," Svv-selic added with equal firmness.

"Do you truly believe that?" Valloittaja's voice was still soft, but suddenly there was an undertone to it that sent a chill of shame through Nzz-oonaz. "You, who were driven out before them? You, who by your own admission wavered in your determination when first faced with the Yycroman line of defense?"

"I don't entirely understand that part myself," Nzz-oonaz admitted. "There was something about the defenders being nonwarrior craft instead of warships—"

"The Yycromae are a warrior people," Valloittaja hissed. "I have told you that again and again. There are no nonwarriors with them."

"We understand," Gll-borgiv said. "And we won't make that mistake again. In fact—"

"If I may speak," Nzz-oonaz cut him off, throwing a warning glare at both him and Svv-selic. He'd been far too lax lately in maintaining his rights and responsibilities as speaker of this group, and it was about time he reasserted that authority. "The fact of the matter, Valloittaja, is that your information did not lead us to expect either the Conqueror Without Reason fleet or the two Yycroman warships that appeared."

"I know," Valloittaja murmured. The brief flash of anger was gone, and once again he seemed to shrink in his seat. A vulnerable, helpless creature facing a future full of fear and hopelessness. "And that is why I can see only extinction for myself and my people. For the universe is filled with the unexpected; and if Zhirrzh strength and resolution cannot face even so small a test, how can you hope to endure a truly difficult challenge?"

"And what is this challenge?" Nzz-oonaz asked, resisting the temptation to again defend his people and their character.

"What else but the proposed attack on the planet Earth?" Valloittaja said. "That is the center of their power and influence. More important, it is undoubtedly the place where the weapon CIRCE is being assembled."

From the edges of his eyes Nzz-oonaz saw Gll-borgiv's and Svv-selic's tails speed up; felt his own tail twitch despite his best efforts to control it. "An attack on Earth would hardly be merely another challenge," he said to Valloittaja. "Your information as well as our own indicates that Earth is defended by awesome weaponry. And with their tunnel-line detectors, they would have eighty hunbeats of advance warning that our warships were coming."

"There is a way around that," Valloittaja said, sounding almost pathetically eager. "We have a way, if only you'll agree to help and protect us."

"We will listen to your ideas," Nzz-oonaz said with a nod. "But not right now."

There was an uncomfortable shuffling from the two searchers flanking him. Nzz-oonaz felt it himself: the sense of frantic urgency filling the air, tugging at him to agree to whatever the Mrachanis wanted. If they didn't attack Earth as quickly as possible, all could be lost.

But he had his instructions from the Overclan Prime himself, and he was determined to obey them. "We must first wait until Warrior Command has had a chance to assess the damage to the strike force," he told Valloittaja, "and to fully evaluate the warriors' performance in that battle. Only then will we discuss what further actions are to be taken."

"But that will take time," Valloittaja objected. "Time that neither you nor we can afford to waste."

"We do not consider such evaluations to be a waste of time," Nzz-oonaz said firmly. "Regardless, that is how it will be."

For a few beats Valloittaja looked in turn at each of the three searchers, his eyes large and liquid and with a pain and disappointment behind them that made Nzz-oonaz ache with shame for what his people were doing to these helpless victims of Conqueror Without Reason tyranny. But he had his instructions, and for a change both Svv-selic and Gll-borgiv remembered their places and also remained silent, and finally Valloittaja sighed. "If that is how it will be, then that is how it will be," he said, the forlorn resignation in his voice making Nzz-oonaz ache even more. "May I at least beg your leaders to perform their evaluation with the utmost speed?"

"They will," Nzz-oonaz promised, fighting against the urge to back down on this. It was not a decision he had any power to change. "We understand the dangers as well as you do."

The Mrachani smiled wanly. "I doubt that, Searcher Nzz-oonaz," he said softly. "I doubt that very much."

Turning, he walked out of the conference room. "Searcher Nzz-oonaz?" the soft voice of an Elder said in Nzz-oonaz's ear. "There's a private pathway waiting for you aboard the *Closed Mouth*."

Nzz-oonaz flicked his tongue silently in acknowledgment. "I need to go back to the ship for a few hunbeats," he said to Svv-selic and Gll-borgiv, playing their usual game wherever Elders were concerned. "You two go on back to our rooms, and I'll join you there soon."

An Elder was waiting for him in the room aboard the *Closed Mouth* where they held all their communications with Oaccanv. "Who is it?" Nzz-oonaz asked as he sealed the door behind him. "The Overclan Prime?"

"No," the Elder said darkly. "It's Searcher Thrr-gilag; Kee'rr."

Nzz-oonaz felt his midlight pupils narrow. Thrr-gilag? "Open the pathway," he ordered. "Thrr-gilag, this is a pleasant surprise."

The Elder didn't move. "May I remind you, Searcher, that this mission has an extremely high warrior security classification," he said. "You aren't supposed to be speaking with anyone except the Overclan Prime and Warrior Command."

"I understand that," Nzz-oonaz said. "But Thrr-gilag was once part of this study group, and I consider him to be one still. Besides, the fact that the Elders coordinating our communications have allowed him this contact implies the Overclan Prime has given him permission to speak with me. Please open the pathway."

"I obey," the Elder growled, his voice still deep with disapproval, and vanished.

He returned a few beats later. " 'For me, as well, Nzz-oonaz,' " he quoted Thrr-gilag's reply. " 'How are your discussions with the Mrachanis going?' "

"They're certainly interesting," Nzz-oonaz said. "Beyond that it's hard to say. Where are you, anyway? I thought you were supposed to come to Mra with us."

" 'That got changed at the last beat. I'm on Dorcas with my brother, Thrr-mezaz, and Klnn-dawan-a. We were sent here to study a Human prisoner and two Mrachanis who came claiming to be ambassadors.' "

"That's a relief," Nzz-oonaz said. "I was afraid you'd been staked out in a stream somewhere for the savagefish."

" 'You'd be surprised,' " the wry answer came back. " 'I know you're probably not supposed to be talking to me at all, so I'll keep this brief. Do you happen to have the metabolic data from the two Mrachanis we brought back to Oaccanv from Base World Twelve?' "

"The ones who warned us about the Human-Conquerors and then died?" Nzz-oonaz asked, swiveling a reader toward him and keying it on. "I think so. Why?"

He had the proper data located by the time the Elder returned. " 'I've got some metabolic baselines now for these two Mrachanis, and they don't seem to fit. But I don't have the original data to compare it with, so I thought maybe I was just remembering it wrong.' "

"Well, I've got the original data in front of me," Nzz-oonaz told him. "Go ahead and read me your numbers, and I'll read you these, and then we'll both have a set of each."

" 'Sounds good. Okay: oxygen metabolic usage: twelve-point-seven per hunbeat . . .' "

It took several hunbeats to get all the numbers transferred back and forth. And when they were finished, it was clear to Nzz-oonaz that Thrr-gilag's memory wasn't the problem. "You're right, this makes no sense at all," he said, flicking his tongue thoughtfully as he gazed at the parallel columns of numbers. "It almost looks like those other two Mrachanis were from an entirely different subspecies."

" 'You've seen a lot more Mrachanis than I have. Is that possible?' "

"Probably not," Nzz-oonaz had to concede. "I haven't seen any evidence of separate species or subspecies. None of their information lists mention such a thing, either."

He frowned as the Elder headed off with his message, gazing at the numbers again. There was a pattern there—he could almost taste it. But where was it?

" 'There's one other possibility,' " Thrr-gilag's answer came back a hunbeat later, " 'though I almost hesitate to bring it up. Klnn-dawan-a just pointed out to me that the Base World Mrachanis' metabolic rate would be consistent with some kind of slow poisoning.' "

Nzz-oonaz's tail twitched. There it was—the pattern he hadn't quite seen. "Klnn-dawan-a's a genius," he said, motioning the Elder to follow as he headed toward the study group's analysis room. "She's absolutely right. I don't know why none of us saw it before."

He had the analyzer going by the time the Elder returned. " 'I'll bet it's because the Mrachanis there haven't let you do any real examinations. I know ours here tried everything to get out of letting us look at them.' "

"You're half-right," Nzz-oonaz said as he keyed in the numbers Thrr-gilag had given him. "They've agreed to let us examine them, but somehow it's never happened."

" 'Without your even noticing, I'll bet. You know, I'm starting to get a really uneasy sense about these aliens.' "

"Welcome to the group," Nzz-oonaz said grimly. "The numbers are starting to come up. It's a toxin pattern, all right. And if the extrapolations are correct, the initial metabolic poisoning occurred just about a fullarc before they reached Base World Twelve."

" 'That would be right after they were captured by the Cakk'rr warship?' "

"Right," Nzz-oonaz confirmed. "And I'm not suggesting the Cakk'rr had anything to do with it."

The pause this time was longer, and Nzz-oonaz could visualize Thrr-gilag reluctantly coming to the same uncomfortable conclusion he himself had already reached. " 'Are you saying the Mrachanis poisoned themselves? Why would they do something like that?' "

"To achieve precisely the result they got," Nzz-oonaz said. "They were in a coma most of the way back to Oaccanv, woke up just long enough to deliver a warning about the Human-Conquerors to the Overclan Seating, and then died."

He threw a glance around the analysis room. "Sacrificing themselves so that we wouldn't have any other way to learn about them except to send a ship here."

" 'You think it's a trap, then?' " the reply came back. " 'That they're working with the Humans?' "

"I don't know," Nzz-oonaz said, flicking his tongue in a negative. "It could be. Personally, I'd guess they're doing this entirely on their own. Maybe they're telling the truth about being under Human-Conqueror domination and thought this was the only way to get us to talk to them."

" 'Maybe. Either way, we'd better alert Warrior Command and the Overclan Prime about it.' "

"Absolutely." Nzz-oonaz glanced at his armwatch. "I'll do it—I'm due to speak with the Prime in another twenty hunbeats anyway. Don't worry, though; I don't think they really trust the Mrachanis either. Certainly not after the events at Phormbi this postmidarc."

The Elder flicked his tongue. "You shouldn't refer to the Phormbi battle, Searcher Nzz-oonaz," he said.

"Yes, you're right." Nzz-oonaz nodded. These former warriors could be a pain under the tongue sometimes, what with their rambling reminiscences and generally obsolete suggestions on how things had been done back in their fullarc. Occasionally, though, listening to them could help keep you out of trouble. "Send everything but that last sentence."

"I obey," the Elder said, and vanished.

He was back a few beats later. " 'All right. I'll let you get back to whatever you were doing, Nzz-oonaz. Thanks for the information.' "

"No problem," Nzz-oonaz assured him. "Thank *you* and Klnn-dawan-a for figuring out this metabolism thing. Farewell."

" 'Farewell.' "

And that was that, Nzz-oonaz said to himself: possibly the last stitch in the edgework on this proposed attack on Earth. Warrior Command, already leery, would undoubtedly insist on more evidence of Mrachani trustworthiness before risking their warships on such a mission.

Which might save them from a second ambush. Or might spook the Mrachanis into calling down the Human-Conquerors on them if they were in fact working for the enemy. Or might irreparably damage a potentially useful alliance if they weren't.

Or might do nothing at all except give the Human-Conquerors the time they needed to finish assembling CIRCE.

Nzz-oonaz grimaced, a sour taste under his tongue. Fortunately, he supposed, none of these potentially disastrous decisions were his to make. In this case he was little more than the communicator.

He looked at his armwatch again. Never mind the schedule; this one was important enough to interrupt Warrior Command. "Elder?"

"No," Commodore Montgomery said firmly. "Absolutely not."

"I'd respectfully request you reconsider, sir," Daschka said. His tone was quiet and respectful, but Montgomery wasn't fooled: the man had the full quota of arrogant self-confidence that seemed to come standard issue with NorCoord Military Intelligence operatives. "This is our chance to find out where this Zhirrzh raiding party came from."

Montgomery snorted. "Trust me, Mr. Daschka, we know exactly where they come from. In fact, we were supposed to be delivering this same sort of message to one of their worlds. Now I presume that delivery will be put on indefinite hold."

"What I mean is that this is our opportunity to learn whether or not the Zhirrzh and Mrachanis have put together some kind of deal," Daschka said. "Coincidentally or otherwise, they're currently headed off on a vector that will keep them out of range of every other Peacekeeper tachyon detector in these two sectors. If we let them get out of our range, too, we'll lose them."

One of the command ring displays flicked on: the damage report on the *Antelope* was finally in. "You have a ship, Mr. Daschka," Montgomery reminded the other tartly, running his eyes down the list. Not good, but it could be a lot worse. "If you want to go chasing after Zhirrzh warships, be my guest."

"We intend to," Daschka said patiently. "But chasing them down is only half the problem. If that fleet is headed for some cozy hideaway, they're going to be very unhappy when someone from our side shows up to take a look. I'd like to have enough firepower along so that we'll have half a chance of meshing in, seeing what's going on, and meshing back out again before we're blown to atoms."

"So ask the Yycromae," Montgomery growled, scrolling down the list and making a note on his plate. Good; the *Antelope*'s life support was still functional. Maybe the techs could get their spare scrubber system over to the *Galileo* before the jury-rig there fell apart completely. "They seem to have firepower to spare at the moment."

"I'd rather not," Daschka said stiffly. "I don't altogether trust the Yycromae."

Carefully, Montgomery laid down his plate. "Look," he said, fixing Daschka with his best command-rank glare. "My task force has been demolished. You understand? Demolished. The only ship I would trust to fly right now is the fuel carrier *Pelican*, and that only because we left it back at the practice area when we charged in on this ridiculous rescue mission. I'm not going with you; I'm not assigning a ship to go with you; I'm not *letting* a ship go with you."

He leveled a finger. "And let me also point out that it's been your colleagues in NorCoord Intelligence who've been running around making sub-rosa armament agreements with the Yycromae. If you don't trust them, that's hardly a sterling endorsement for either you *or* your treaties."

"Commodore?" the comm-duty officer called. "There's a call coming in for a Mr. Daschka. Is he there with you?"

"Ensign, this is not Mr. Daschka's private answering service," Montgomery snapped. "Whoever it is can just file it."

"Yes, sir," the officer said. "Uh . . . it's the Klyveress ci Yyatoor, sir: Twelfth Counsel to the Yycroman Hierarch. She'd like to speak with Mr. Daschka."

Montgomery glowered at Daschka, stomach tightening with the unpleasant feeling of having just been had. "Thank you," he growled, punching for the channel and beckoning Daschka forward. "I believe it's for you."

Daschka moved to his side as the display lit up to reveal a crocodilian Yycroman face. "This is Daschka, ci Yyatoor," he said. "How can I serve you?"

[A skitter from Granparra has just arrived,] Klyveress said. [I presume the Peacekeeper forces detected it.]

Daschka glanced at Montgomery, a questioning look on his face. Montgomery shrugged in response. He'd been far too busy lately to notice any skitters, but he wasn't really surprised to hear that one had sneaked in. Come hell or high water, the mail always seemed to make it through.

[It contained an encrypted message for you,] the ci Yyatoor continued. [Would you like me to transmit it?]

"Yes, thank you," Daschka nodded, pulling out a card and sliding it into the transfer slot. "Go ahead."

The slot beeped, and he removed the card. [Commodore Lord Montgomery,] Klyveress said, the long snout shifting to point at him. [Allow me to present my gratitude for your unselfish and sacrificial aid in our time of critical need. The Yycroman Hierarchy and the Yycroman people will not soon forget.]

"You're welcome," Montgomery said, bowing his head toward the display and trying furiously to remember the proper protocol for dealing with Yycroman leaders. "May I also say that our sacrifices would have been considerably greater without the assistance and similar sacrifices of your people. We thank you in turn."

Klyveress inclined her head in acceptance. [It is to our mutual advantage to have your battle force repaired as quickly as possible, Commodore Lord Montgomery,] she said. [To that end I am placing our repair facilities at your complete disposal. I would beg you to take advantage of them.]

"You won't have to offer twice," Montgomery said. "I accept, again with thanks. With your permission I'll transfer this channel over to my fleet exec, who's coordinating our repair efforts."

[I will await with anticipation my conversation with him,] Klyveress said gravely. [I bid you farewell for now.]

Montgomery keyed for hold. "Transfer this to Captain Germaine," he called to the comm officer. "Tell him it's the Yycromae with an offer of assistance. And tell him to take everything they'll give him."

"Yes, sir."

Montgomery looked back to Daschka, who was frowning thoughtfully at his plate. "If that's all, then, we're very busy here," he told the other. "I'd appreciate your getting off my ship as soon as your partner finishes your refueling. And be sure you take that civilian Aric Cavanagh with you."

"We were planning to, Commodore," Daschka said, reversing the plate and offering it to him. "But before I go, you might find this interesting."

Grimacing, Montgomery took the plate and skimmed through the message. A senior NorCoord Intelligence officer—he noticed that, as with his copy of the Yycroman agreements, Daschka had discreetly screened off the officer's name—had found indications that two major Mrachani operations were imminent. The first—

"You'll notice that the first operation—*Mirnacheem-hyeea* One—was scheduled for today," Daschka pointed out. "As you may know, *Mirnacheem-hyeea* means *Conquerors Without Reason;* and on Day Zero we've just had a Conqueror attack on Phormbi. Coincidence?"

Montgomery shrugged noncommittally. "Why Phormbi?"

"Because this is where the Yycromae have been working to rebuild their space forces," Daschka said. "There's no particular reason why the Zhirrzh would have known about that. But we know for a fact that the Mrachanis did."

"Mm," Montgomery grunted, skimming over the rest of the message. The Intelligence officer had subsequently headed off to Mra to do some snooping around, taking Lord Stewart Cavanagh with him—"Lord *Cavanagh?*" he demanded, glaring up at Daschka again. "He's involved in this, too?"

"You'd be surprised at the things he's involved in," Daschka said ruefully. "I don't even think *I* know all of it."

Montgomery nodded, a sour taste in his mouth. It was becoming increasingly and annoyingly difficult to swing a dead cat around this war without hitting something Lord Cavanagh had had a hand in, from secret Yycroman agreements to former employees who had their own individualistic idea of how orders were supposed to be carried out. And *that* whole thing was just one more headache he didn't need right now.

He paused, a sudden idea occurring to him. Maybe this was his chance to kill two birds with one stone. Or at least chase one of the birds out of his hair for a while. "Tell you what," he said to Daschka. "I can't spare you any capital ships; but what I *can* do is let you have a single fighter and a pilot. You can put it in your forward hold where it'll be ready to launch if you run into trouble. It'll be better than nothing, anyway."

Daschka pursed his lips. "I suppose so," he conceded. "Very well, I accept. I don't suppose this fighter will be in anything close to mint condition."

"No, but it's not as bad as some we've got aboard," Montgomery assured him. "You'll have a few hours; perhaps you can make some running repairs. Oh, and I won't be able to spare you a tail man, either—we need him aboard."

"This sounds better all the time," Daschka said dryly. "Is the pilot at least conscious?"

"Conscious, in perfect health, and one of the best," Montgomery assured him. "I'll have the orders cut immediately, and he'll be in the hangar bay by the time you're ready to leave."

"We'll be expecting him," Daschka said. "May I ask his name?"

"Certainly," Montgomery said. "Copperhead Lieutenant Adam Quinn. Former—and also probably future—employee of Lord Stewart Cavanagh."

Daschka shook his head. "Why," he said, "am I not surprised?"

Speaker Cvv-panav sipped at his cup of aged Minsinc wine. "Interesting," he said. "Tell me this, Searcher Gll-borgiv: do you still trust him?"

The Elder nodded and vanished. Cvv-panav sipped again at his wine, savoring the delicate aroma of the glycerol and flavorings, and touched another key on his reader. There was a beat, and then the listing came up.

The Elder returned. " 'Implicitly, Speaker Cvv-panav,' " he quoted Gll-borgiv's words. " 'Everything Valloittaja told us about Phormbi and the Yycromae was subsequently proved to be correct.' "

"Except for the part about the Human-Conqueror attack," Cvv-panav pointed out. "Did he have anything to say about that?"

The Elder vanished, and the Speaker turned his attention back to the listing. All right. The first five warships were already in position, less than two tentharcs from their respective rendezvous points. Six others would be in position in another fullarc, plus the three from the Phormbi attack force if he decided they were still reasonably battle capable. The follow-up forces would be more complicated; still, if he started breaking into the various colony-world fleets before they were reassembled . . .

The Elder reappeared. " 'He has repeatedly warned us the Yycromae are allies of the Conquerors Without Reason. I don't consider the unexpected appearance of that attack force to be in any way a failure of Mrach intelligence.' "

And perhaps you're just too easy to please, Cvv-panav thought contemptuously. But that didn't matter. He, Speaker Cvv-panav, was the one making the decisions here, and he was safely detached from whatever warm, fuzzy image of themselves the Mrachanis had been weaving around the young fools of the contact team. Of course the Mrachanis were fallible. They were possibly even untrustworthy.

But the opportunity was just too good to pass up. "Has he given you any more details about this supposed plan they have for slipping our warships in through Human-Conqueror space?"

The Elder nodded and vanished. *All right,* Cvv-panav said to himself, studying his reader. Follow-up forces. Four warships from the Dharanv defense forces—no problem; they were all under the authority of the Dhaa'rr Leadership Council, which answered solely to him. Three more warships, commanded and crewed exclusively by Dhaa'rr, had been recalled from the Etsiji and Chigin encirclement forces and were on their way to bolster the various Zhirrzh beachheads. They would have to be diverted without Warrior Command noticing. . . .

The Elder flicked back. " 'Searcher Nzz-oonaz wouldn't listen to him, but I myself have had two further private discussions with him. He informs me the technique is very workable and is in fact similar to the one the enemy used at Phormbi. Eight to ten Mrach spacecraft will be attached to each Zhirrzh warship and will literally tow them through the tunnel-line. Without their own tunnel drives operating, our warships will not create the distinctive supraluminal trail markings that the Conquerors Without Reason use to identify approaching spacecraft. They will detect only the Mrachani craft.' "

"Yes," the Speaker murmured. He would have to take the Mrachani's word for that, but it sounded reasonable enough. "And he still feels he can guarantee complete surprise?"

" 'Without a doubt,' " the confident reply came. " 'All the ships would converge on Earth along different vectors. There would thus not be any large groups of ships coming in from a single direction to arouse suspicion.' "

Cvv-panav smiled cynically. And it might also help conceal the Mrachanis' role from vengeful Human-Conqueror survivors. But that was all right. Enlightened self-interest was, after all, the summation line for all thinking creatures. He'd have been far more suspicious if this Valloittaja *hadn't* taken careful steps to protect his own neck.

And it meant Mrachani ships would be right there with the Zhirrzh warships for this attack. After Phormbi that was something he would have insisted on even if their transport method hadn't required it. "Very well, then, Searcher Gll-borgiv," he said. "Inform Valloittaja that despite the failure at Phormbi, our private agreement remains in force. The Dhaa'rr clan will assist them in this attack on Earth."

He held up a finger as the Elder began to nod. "And remind him, Searcher Gll-borgiv," he added darkly, "that this is still to be kept a private matter between him and you. *No* one else must hear anything about this."

He waved the Elder permission to leave, then turned back to his reader. Yes, it would be tricky; but with a first-strike force of fourteen warships and a follow-up force of at least ten more, he had enough firepower here to turn the Mrachanis' so-called Conquerors Two operation into a devastating and decisive strike at the very throat of the Human-Conqueror race.

And with that victory would come his final political triumph over those of the Zhirrzh who had set themselves in opposition to him and the Dhaa'rr clan. From the lowliest Elder all the way up to the Overclan Prime himself.

So let the nornin-hearted of Warrior Command count their wounds and list their new Elders and debate this or that or the other. What mattered now was courage and resolve and action; and as it had so many times in the past, the Dhaa'rr clan would show the way.

"There it is," Bronski said, pointing out the window of their rented aircar toward the horizon. "*Puvkit Tru Kai,* the Garden Of The Mad Stonewright. Interesting formations, the odd bit of unusual plant life, and a fortress carved into solid rock you could hide a battalion in."

"So what now?" Cavanagh asked, shading his eyes as he peered out at the distant rock formations. "We just fly over and knock?"

"I don't think that would be a good idea," Kolchin said tightly. "That aircar making a dropline toward us would probably object."

"Where?" Bronski asked.

"Coming straight out of the sun."

"I see him," Bronski nodded. "Let's set down and see if he's interested in talking."

He keyed for landing, and as the computer eased off the aft jets and eased in the underside jets, the aircar dropped smoothly to the ground with only a gentle bump to announce its arrival. A moment later the other aircraft landed fifty meters away, its nose pointed at the rental's side. "At least they're learning some basic tactics," Bronski grunted as he popped the catch and let the gull-wing door swing up. "Okay, it's show time. You two better stay here. Kolchin?"

"I'm ready," the bodyguard assured him, his flechette pistol lying unobtrusively across his lap. "What's the cue if you want me to open fire?"

"Standard commando flash-hand signal," Bronski told him, climbing out. "Go for the antenna cluster first—extra company will be high on our list of things to avoid. Oh, and try to give me time to hit the ground first."

He headed off across the uneven ground toward the other aircar. He'd covered about half the distance when its gull-wings swung open and two Mrachanis got out of the left-hand side.

Out of the right-hand side squeezed a Bhurt.

"Uh-oh," Cavanagh muttered as the alien lumbered around the nose of the aircar toward Bronski.

"Don't panic," Kolchin murmured. "If they were going to shoot first, they wouldn't have sent him out the far side."

Bronski hardly even glanced at the Bhurt as the alien came to a stop beside him. For a few minutes he talked earnestly with the Mrachanis, his posture one of authority and confidence, the wallet folder containing his forged red card prominent in his hand. One of the Mrachanis took the wallet at one point and examined the card closely before almost reluctantly handing it back. Bronski returned it to his jacket, and with a crisp nod he turned and walked back toward the aircar. The Bhurt and Mrachanis got back into their vehicle and, in a cloud of dust, lifted into the air.

"How did it go?" Cavanagh asked as Bronski climbed back into the pilot's seat.

"A little mixed," Bronski shrugged. "I told them we'd been hired to look over their outside security arrangements."

"And they bought that?" Kolchin asked.

"They bought the red card, anyway," Bronski said. "But I don't think they were very happy about doing it."

"Sounds like our clock is ticking down," Kolchin said. "Maybe we should go in for our look and get out."

"Patience," Bronski said, gazing thoughtfully at the rock formations in the distance. "They seemed marginally less nervous about our presence here when I let on that we had no idea about what was going on inside the rim fortress. I imagine they'll be watching us, so let's be good little boys and stay out here at the perimeter for a while. Maybe by the time they get bored, we'll have spotted a back door into that fortress."

"Meanwhile, they'll be burning up the lines to the capital to check out your red card," Cavanagh pointed out.

"Let 'em," Bronski grunted. "The authorizing signature's the name of a Mrachani who happens to be on meditation-retreat at the moment. Take them hours to even locate him."

He started to key in the drive; paused. "Two other things," he said. "The Mrachanis told me to shut down all my radars and radios, which tells me that whatever's going on in there is highly sensitive to electromagnetic radiation. Both of you ought to keep that in mind if we need to create a diversion on our way out."

He half turned in his seat to face the others. "Final point, then. If I read that card right on Granparra, the Conquerors One operation starts sometime today. May have already started, for that matter. The bad news is that if it's a straight military operation, it means someone in Yycroman space is going to get pounded; the good news is that the fact that we're the only humans in sight implies the operation doesn't involve Peacekeeper forces. So we're out of it."

Cavanagh felt a hard knot in his stomach. The mental image of the gravely dignified Klyveress ci Yyatoor dying amid the wreckage of one of her worlds was an oddly distressing one. "Isn't there any way to stop it?"

"Not a chance," Bronski said flatly. "If it's a long-term campaign, we might be able to cut it short, but probably not. My point is that we need to consider Conquerors One to be a done deal, and to concentrate all our efforts on figuring out Conquerors Two. That's the one we might still have a chance of stopping. Understood?"

Cavanagh nodded. "Understood."

"All right." Turning back around, Bronski keyed in the drive. "The game starts here. Let's play."

22 "The sentries at Post Two first spotted it about half an hour ago," Takara told Holloway as the two of them climbed carefully down the sloping and treacherously tanglevined ground just outside the encampment's northern perimeter. "They thought at first that it was chasing something, or else that it had been injured. Nightbear Raille brought it down, took one look, and called it in."

The animal was lying half–propped up against a tree, one of its sharp-edged horns wedged into a leaf cluster. Three men—two Peacekeepers and a civilian—were standing in a silent group around it. "Okay, let's have it," Holloway said. "Doctor?"

"Nightbear was right, Colonel," the doctor said. "It's halucine disease."

"Terrific," Holloway said. "All right, give me the bottom line."

"It's bad enough," the doctor said. "But it's not as bad as it could be. The halucine virus is waterborne, but it's easily neutralized or filtered. Even if any gets through, it has only a mild effect on most humans." His lips compressed briefly as he gestured down toward the dead razorhorn. "Where it's going to hurt is the game animals."

Holloway shifted his attention to the tall black-haired civilian hunter. "Any chance of tracking it back to where it picked up the virus, Nightbear? Maybe we can wipe out this batch before it spreads."

"We can try, Colonel," Nightbear said, shaking his head. "But I don't think it'll help. The scent's already in the air."

"What scent?" Takara asked.

"The altered scent of a sick razorhorn," the doctor explained. "In individual animals, it attracts predators and warns other razorhorns away. But if you get enough of them giving off the same diseased smell, it'll drive everything out of the affected area. Predator and prey both."

And the wind was blowing hard from the northeast, sending the aroma straight across the civilian bivouac area. "How soon before that happens?"

"It's already happening," Nightbear said. "The hunters have already noticed a decline in their take."

"The trappers, too," the doctor added. "I checked their numbers for the past five days. It's not too bad so far, but it's definitely there. And definitely going to get worse."

Holloway grimaced. "How long before the epidemic runs its course?"

"The last halucine outbreak in this section of the continent drove the razorhorns out of about an eight-thousand-square-kilometer area for four months," the doctor said. "The virus itself disappeared after about two, but it took another two for the animals to wander their way back again."

Holloway chewed at the inside of his cheek. Four months. And it was only three months until the beginning of winter. "All right," he said. "Nightbear, you go to the leaders of the hunting and trapping teams and get them working double time—we need to take whatever we can before the game heads off for greener pastures. Doctor, I want you to try to analyze the altered scent from this animal, see if you can come up with some way to neutralize it or cover it up. And get some teams out to the nearby streams and find out where the contamination's coming from. We might as well kill off as much of the virus as we can find."

"Yes, sir," the doctor said. "Come on, gentlemen, let's get this animal up to the encampment."

Holloway gestured to Takara, and together they headed back up the slope. "This isn't going to help," Takara commented in a low voice as they climbed. "And I think you know it. Sooner or later we're going to have no choice but to pull up stakes and get out of here."

"You have no idea what you're saying, Fuji," Holloway said. "Move twenty-five thousand civilians at least fifty kilometers across mountainous territory? And under enemy observation and probable enemy fire?"

"I didn't say I liked the idea," Takara said soberly. "I hate to think how many people we're going to lose along the way. But the longer we postpone it, the bigger the risk that we'll hit winter without a food supply built up. We do that, and we'll be guaranteeing slow starvation for all of us."

Holloway looked up at the sentry post above them, part of the perimeter of the refuge they'd worked so hard to put together. "I should have insisted they all leave," he said. "Even if we'd had to throw them bodily onto the ships."

"There wasn't enough space on the ships for all of them, Cass," Takara said. "Even if every flight here before the Zhirrzh hit had gone out full. We'd still have had at least ten thousand left."

Holloway's comm buzzed. "Ten to one it's more good news," he said sourly, pulling out the comm and flicking it on. "Holloway."

"Crane, sir," Crane's voice came. "Spotter One just picked up an aerial explosion southwest of the base."

Holloway threw a frown at Takara. As far as they'd seen, the Zhirrzh didn't use explosives. "What kind of explosion?"

"Gasperi's running an analysis on the blast spectrum," Crane said. "But all indications are that it was either a missile or a spacecraft."

A cold chill ran up Holloway's back. A spacecraft? "Get that analysis done fast," he ordered. "We'll be right there."

"Commander Cavanagh?"

Pheylan started awake. "Yes, Max?"

"We've reached the Dorcas system, Commander," the computer said. "We'll be meshing in in approximately ten minutes."

"Thank you," Pheylan said, unstrapping his sleep webbing and rubbing at his eyes. "Do we have any idea where the Peacekeepers might have holed up?"

"We have no definite information," Max said. "However, I have a general focus area based on the vectors of the supply flights I observed while Dr. Cavanagh and I were waiting for Commander Masefield's Copperhead unit to arrive."

A display came on, showing the area around the main village. "There are numerous possible bivouac sites in the mountains to the east," Max went on. "If we can get within visual range of them, the Peacekeepers should be able to do the rest."

"Let's hope they're on their toes," Pheylan said, retrieving the survival pack he'd prepared from its locker and strapping it on. "And that the Zhirrzh aren't on theirs. You sure this mesh-in plan is going to work?"

"The theory itself is perfectly sound," Max said. "The distances themselves can be calculated precisely, and Dorcas's average atmospheric density at our chosen mesh-in altitude is well within safety margins. However, as is generally the case with real-world situations, there are likely to be variables the theory does not take into account."

"Translation: we're throwing dice on this," Pheylan said.

"Our odds are considerably better than that," Max assured him, sounding almost huffy. "I wouldn't have agreed to it if I thought it was overly dangerous."

"Loaded dice, then," Pheylan corrected dryly, pulling out a jump seat and beginning to strap himself in. "It's still a damn sight safer than meshing in where we'd have to run the gauntlet of Zhirrzh ships."

"We can still abort and go elsewhere," Max reminded him. "We have sufficient fuel to go anywhere in the Commonwealth."

"Convince me my family's safely off Dorcas and you've got a deal." Pheylan checked his restraints and nodded. "Ready. Give me a count-down."

The minutes passed, and soon it was time. Pheylan braced himself, watching the displays as Max's countdown ran to zero—

He was prepared for the standard jolt that always seemed to accompany mesh-in while riding in a small craft. He was not prepared for the thunderous blast that slammed the fueler back like a toy and threw him hard against his restraints. "Max!" he shouted over the sudden pummeling.

"Under control," Max called back. On the status board a dozen warning lights flashed red; returned to green or amber as Max rerouted systems or shut them down. "A quantum hysteresis in the core caused mesh-in to be eighty point six meters lower into the atmosphere than planned. The turbulence itself is due to conduction resonance with the planetary magnetic field and is normal for this procedure."

"Terrific," Pheylan muttered, getting a grip on his restraints with one hand and keying for a sensor scan of the area with the other. The whole object of this exercise had been to mesh in beneath the Zhirrzh blockade ships. If that hadn't worked, the ride was likely to get a whole lot rougher.

He stiffened. There was one now, above and east of him: the distinctive linked-hexagon configuration of a Zhirrzh ship. "Got one," he snapped.

"I have it," Max confirmed. "Bearing one-one-two by six-four-one, distance four hundred eighty-two kilometers."

Pheylan braced himself. This wasn't going to be fun, but with an enemy ship this close they had no choice. "Drop us," he ordered. "Straight down and in."

"Acknowledged."

For an agonizing heartbeat nothing happened. Pheylan stared at the distant Zhirrzh warship, waiting for the flashes of laser light that would mean he'd been spotted and was under attack. The linked hexagons weren't much more than a bumpy blur at this distance, but he could imagine it rotating lazily around to bring its weapons to bear. . . .

Then, with a jolt that again crushed him against his restraints, the fueler fired a burst directly along their vector, slowing them down and interrupting the rhythm of the resonant turbulence.

And with its forward momentum cut abruptly in half, the fueler plunged down toward the ground six hundred klicks below.

Pheylan swallowed hard. *I meant to do that,* he reminded himself tautly, his full attention still on the Zhirrzh ship. So far it hadn't reacted, but any surprise at his maneuver wouldn't last long. The fueler had to be hidden behind a thick shield of atmosphere before they recovered and started firing.

The trick being to get to safety under that shield without building up so much downward speed that they couldn't stop at all.

They were starting to get into real atmosphere now, and he could hear the faint friction whine beginning to build up along the outer hull. The Zhirrzh ship still hadn't reacted, and for the first time Pheylan risked taking a look at the displays showing the view beneath them.

It wasn't encouraging. There was a solid floor of clouds below, completely masking the terrain. Worse, straight ahead along their flight path he could see the telltale swirl of a massive tropical hurricane. The weather would be churning down there. "Max, do you know where we are?"

"I have a rough idea," the computer said. "Based on the elapsed time since our last visit, coupled with Dorcas's listed rotational data, I believe us to be approximately nine thousand four hundred kilometers southwest of the mountains where we expect to find the Peacekeeper forces."

Pheylan glanced at the vector-data display, did a quick mental calculation. "We're going to need some more forward momentum," he said.

"Confirmed," Max said. "But the atmosphere above us is still too thin for proper laser protection. I'd prefer to wait until we were no higher than sixty kilometers before leveling into horizontal flight."

Pheylan pursed his lips. Flying this crate like an aircar would burn fuel at a prodigious rate, which would mean dipping into the supply he'd been hoping to deliver to Colonel Holloway. But less fuel was better than no fuel at all, which was what they'd get if he was shot down. "Fine," he said. "But no lower than sixty klicks."

"Yes, Commander."

The screeching from the outer hull was still increasing, and Pheylan could now feel a slight rise in temperature of the air around him. Still the Zhirrzh ship falling rapidly away above him hadn't reacted. Could they have missed seeing him entirely? "Max, can we get any readings on that Zhirrzh ship up there?" he asked.

"He's out of the range of the fueler's passive sensors," Max said. "Shall I try the active sensors?"

Pheylan felt his stomach tighten, remembering how the Zhirrzh ships after the *Jutland* battle had used the honeycomb escape pods' emergency radio beacons to lock in their lasers. The active sensors used similar electromagnetic wavelengths. "Better not," he said. "No other enemy ships or vehicles out there?"

"None that I can detect."

Pheylan began to breathe a little easier. Maybe—just maybe—they'd gotten away with this.

They reached the sixty-klick mark, and Pheylan began to feel pressure against his chest as Max used the edge-effect airfoils to ease the fueler into more or less horizontal flight. "We've leveled off at fifteen kilometers," Max reported a few minutes later. "What speed shall I maintain?"

Pheylan took a quick look at the displays. The combination of the curving descent plus their original insertion vector had cut the distance to the Peacekeeper mountains to a little over five thousand klicks. A long four and a half hours away if they kept it subsonic; but considering that the fueler hadn't been designed for extended atmospheric flight, going supersonic would probably be begging for trouble. "Keep it below Mach 1, but as close as you can without getting into turbulence problems," he told the computer. "And drop our altitude another five klicks—edge-effect airfoils work better in denser air."

"Acknowledged."

Pheylan spent the first hour watching the external displays, shifting his attention from one to the next, waiting tensely for signs of the pursuit or intercept. He had no idea whether the Zhirrzh presence here was confined to a relatively small beachhead or whether they'd spread out over half the hemisphere by now; but wherever they were, eventually they'd have to show up. The closer he was able to get to the Peacekeeper enclave, the better his chances of getting air or ground support from them.

Assuming, of course, that the Zhirrzh hadn't already destroyed them.

No enemy aircraft showed up during the second hour either, but much of Pheylan's attention during that time was distracted by the necessity of getting the fueler past an impressively long line of thunderstorm cells. Possibly part of the same system that included the hurricane he'd spotted on their way in, the storms lay scattered across his path like nature's own aerial land mines. The fueler could have lifted over them, but with their fuel level already dropping faster than Pheylan liked, he opted instead to let Max thread them between the thunderheads. Fortunately, the computer was up to the task, and they made it with little more than occasional buffeting to mark their passage.

After that the flight settled down into something almost routine. It was becoming clear that the Zhirrzh hadn't overextended themselves there—though, to be fair, Pheylan could remember nothing in the Dorcas catalog that would offer any military incentives for an invader. If they were still confined to the areas the Commonwealth colonists had carved out—and if that blockade ship up there really hadn't spotted him—there was a fair chance he could at least get into communication range of the Peacekeepers before he was spotted.

They were about an hour and a little under eleven hundred klicks out from their target mountains when the first signs of trouble appeared.

It started as a faint sizzling sound, like meat on an open-fire grill in the distance, accompanied by a slight drooping of the fueler's starboard side. "Max?" Pheylan asked, frowning at the status board. The whole line of lights under the AIRFOIL heading had begun to flicker uncertainly between green and red.

"The airfoils are losing charge capacity," Max said. "I'm attempting to degauss and restart them, one at a time."

The fueler dipped again, this time to port, this time noticeably deeper. "How long does the procedure take?"

"In a maintenance shop it would normally take three hours," Max said. "There are shortcuts, though, for emergencies. None of them recommended, I might add, but under the circumstances I don't think we have many other options."

"Not many, no," Pheylan agreed tightly, checking the location display. They were still well out of the line-of-sight range they'd need to signal Holloway with either the fueler's laser or radio. And considering how and where they'd meshed in, there was a good chance the Peacekeepers didn't even know they were there. "We need to find a way to signal Holloway before we go down. What's the best in-atmosphere range we can get out of our Shrike missiles?"

"That number isn't listed in the specifications," Max said. "From this altitude, launched at optimum angle, I estimate they have a range of approximately six hundred eighty kilometers."

Pheylan grimaced. Not nearly far enough to be seen from mountains a thousand klicks away. "How much farther can we get before the airfoils fail completely?"

"Unknown," Max said. "I estimate a probability of point five that we can go another two to three hundred kilometers before we have to put down. But we'll be losing altitude before then."

And a lower altitude would also limit the missiles' range. "Activate two of the missiles," he ordered. "Fire the first at optimum angle when you can't hold this altitude any more. Fire the second at your best guess for farthest range after that point. Fuse them both for above-ground detonation—we want something they'll be able to see."

"Understood."

The screeching and jostling continued to worsen as the flight began to take on the characteristics of an entertainment-park thrill ride. Pheylan split his attention between the displays and the status board, the back of his mind working out contingency plans depending on how far they got and whether it appeared likely that the Peacekeepers might see either of his distress missiles.

And then, with 850 klicks to go, a new sound interjected itself into the growing cacophony: the distinctive bubbling hiss of a missile being launched. "First Shrike is away," Max announced. "I'd like to try decreasing our altitude. That may help with the airfoil reactivation."

"Go ahead," Pheylan said. "Try not to hit anything."

The fueler took on a downward pitch as they dropped toward the ground. "It doesn't look from here like it's helping," Pheylan said, watching the status board.

"Not from here, either," Max admitted. "I don't think there's anything more I can do, Commander. I can nurse them along a little farther; but when they go, they'll go."

And without at least some airfoil capability it would be all but impossible to land the fueler without splattering it all over the landscape. "Understood," Pheylan said. "Fire that second missile and start looking for a place to set down."

"I have a possible location directly ahead," Max said as the second bubbling hiss briefly sounded. A flashing circle appeared on one of the displays, the range finder marking it as forty klicks away. "It looks like a fire clearing on the side of a low hill," the computer went on. "Plenty of visibility if you choose to wait for rescue; conversely, the immediate route toward the northeast appears reasonable if you instead choose to begin walking."

"What, no restaurant?"

"Excuse me?"

"Never mind," Pheylan sighed. Sometimes the parameters that a parasentient computer decided to focus on could get a little strange. "Just concentrate on getting us down in one piece. The nonessentials we can sort out later."

"It was just barely in range of our spotters," Crane said, tapping a spot with his finger as Holloway and Takara joined him at the map table. "But it was definitely a Peacekeeper missile. Gasperi says either a Sperling or an old Shrike."

"Any idea where it came from?" Holloway said.

"Southwest somewhere," Crane said. "He says that if it was a Sperling, it could have made maybe eight hundred klicks. The Shrike could only have gone six or seven."

"Six to eight hundred klicks," Takara muttered. "Well, that certainly narrows it down."

"Sorry, sir, it's the best we can do," Crane apologized.

"I know." Takara looked at Holloway. "So are we going to go take a look?"

"We don't have much choice," Holloway said, running his fingers through his hair. "Stray missiles are usually either misfires or distress signals. Either way, it says there's a Peacekeeper out there who needs help. Crane, what's vehicle status?"

"We've got an aircar and cargo carrier on standby," Crane said. "I also took the liberty of telling Duggen to pull together a team."

"Sounds good," Holloway said. "Go ahead and confirm the orders."

"Yes, sir."

"You think we should send Bethmann with them?" Takara suggested.

Holloway shook his head. "I'm not going to risk our only combat-capable Corvine. Not even if that was Admiral Rudzinski stuck out there." He rubbed a finger across his lower lip. "I wonder how he got in past the Zhirrzh warships."

"Sensor-stealthing, probably," Takara said. "Or else he just meshed in beneath them while they were all looking in the other direction."

"Pretty sloppy work on their part," Holloway said, a nebulous thought beginning to form in the back of his mind. If the Zhirrzh warships really weren't paying attention up there . . . "Let's hope he's brought some spare supplies or fuel with him."

"And that we can get to it before the Zhirrzh do," Takara added. "Exploding a missile in front of God and everybody kind of ruins the whole point of sneaking in."

"Maybe," Holloway said. "Have the Zhirrzh at the village reacted yet?"

Takara peered at the status display. "No one's reported any troop or vehicle movements," Takara said. "Why, you think they might not have noticed the blast?"

"Or else didn't understand its significance," Holloway said. "In fact, I'd put it more strongly: if I were their commander, I'd wonder if a useless explosion like that was an enemy trick to distract his attention while we hit him from another side."

"Possibly," Takara conceded. "Or he might think it was an accident."
"Either way, it keeps his attention here instead of wherever the
downed ship is," Holloway said. "And if we're lucky he won't know otherwise until Duggen's team heads out."

Takara nodded. "At which point it becomes a race."

"Right," Holloway said grimly. "Let's just make damn sure we win it."

"Here," the Elder said, jabbing his tongue at a point on the map. "This
is where the spacecraft came down."

"Rough country," Thrr-mezaz commented, eyeing the aerial photos of
the region. "You're sure it didn't crash?"

The Elder nodded and vanished. "What about that second explosion?"
Thrr-mezaz asked Klnn-vavgi.

"Again, no damage," Klnn-vavgi said. "At least none the Elders were
able to see. We could get a closer look if you'd let me send a Stingbird
over."

"No Stingbirds," Thrr-mezaz said firmly, gazing at the map and trying
to think. The *Requisite* had tracked two separate explosive missiles from
the Human-Conqueror spacecraft, both fired roughly this direction. No
apparent damage from either missile, which implied they weren't meant
as attacks. Signals?

The Elder returned. "The technics say they cannot be absolutely certain the spacecraft landed safely," he reported. "Their orbit had nearly
carried them out of view of the area by the time the spacecraft landed."

And they would continue to be out of view of the area for another
tentharc. "Understood," Thrr-mezaz said.

"I take it, then, you don't think the explosives were a precursor to an
attack?" Klnn-vavgi asked.

"I think it more likely they were a signal," Thrr-mezaz told him. "The
Human-Conquerors in the mountains couldn't possibly have seen his
spacecraft come in. Knowing he was going down, he had to find some
way to alert them to his presence."

"All right, I'll accept that," Klnn-vavgi said. "But we still need to check
it out, don't we?"

Thrr-mezaz flicked his tongue thoughtfully, trying to put himself in the
enemy commander's place. A Human-Conqueror spacecraft was down,
and he'd undoubtedly be sending a rescue team as soon as he had one
put together. If he saw Stingbirds heading that direction, of course, he'd
put it together even faster. Possibly even send his Copperhead warriors
along for extra protection.

But if he saw the Zhirrzh sitting here, apparently oblivious to it all, he
might not be in quite so much of a hurry. . . .

"Message to Ship Commander Phmm-klof," he said, beckoning to the Elder. "I'd like him to send a transport to pick up any survivors from the Human-Conqueror spacecraft and bring them here to me."

"I obey." The Elder vanished.

"I wouldn't expect much if I were you," Klnn-vavgi warned. "It sounds like Phmm-klof's in a major snit over having to sit there and watch that spacecraft come in without being able to stop it. I doubt he's in a favor-granting mood."

"We'll see if we can change that," Thrr-mezaz said.

Behind them the door opened and Thrr-gilag came in. "I got your message," he told his brother, breathing hard. "What's this about a Human spacecraft?"

"It came down right here," Thrr-mezaz said, indicating the spot on the map. "About seven hundred thirteen thoustrides away."

"Survivors?"

The Elder from the *Requisite* reappeared. Thrr-mezaz motioned him to wait. "We think so," he told Thrr-gilag. "I've asked Ship Commander Phmm-klof to send a transport for a closer look."

Thrr-gilag nodded, his tail spinning with barely restrained excitement as he looked at the map. "What about pictures?"

"We don't have any here," Klnn-vavgi said. "I imagine the *Requisite* has some, but they're currently out of direct-link laser range."

"Yes," Thrr-gilag said, his mind clearly already elsewhere. "Thrr-mezaz, we need to get a survivor from that spacecraft. My whole theory of Human aggression hinges on there being measurable metabolic changes when two or more Humans are in close proximity. We don't have any of that sort of data."

"I know," Thrr-mezaz said, watching the Elder out of the corner of his eye. "And I know how vitally important it is to the war effort. Didn't you tell me the Overclan Prime himself said that?"

"Yes, he did," Thrr-gilag confirmed, frowning slightly at his brother. Thrr-mezaz blinked twice, the old childhood signal they'd used when trying to con their parents into doing something, and Thrr-gilag's face cleared. "Yes, he said that this was our single best chance of finding a weakness we could exploit," he said, clearly on track now. "Maybe even turn the whole war around."

"We can hope so." Thrr-mezaz looked at the Elder, still waiting to deliver Ship Commander Phmm-klof's reply. "What did the ship commander say?"

"A beat, if you please, Commander," the Elder muttered, and vanished again.

"Nicely done," Klnn-vavgi murmured approvingly. "The Ghuu'rr clan absolutely adores the Overclan Prime."

"It was true, too," Thrr-gilag said.

"All the better."

The Elder reappeared. "Ship Commander Phmm-klof has ordered a transport and warrior team to be prepared," he announced. "They'll leave orbit as soon as possible."

"Good," Thrr-mezaz said. "Warn them to stay out of sight of the Human-Conqueror stronghold."

"I obey."

He vanished. "You'd better go prepare for new visitors, Second," Thrr-mezaz said to Klnn-vavgi. "With good luck we'll have them back here within a tentharc."

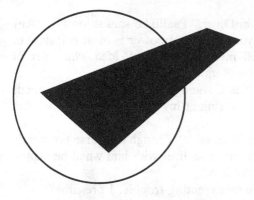

 23

It was a pleasure, Parlimin Jacy VanDiver thought as he accepted a second glass of cherry claretee, to finally find someone who knew how to treat a NorCoord Parlimin with the proper deference and honor. A far cry from those pompous idiots back in Parliament itself, who whispered about him behind his back in the offices and private meeting nooks. A far cry even from the members of his own staff, who might fear him, but whose devotion was as thin and bendable as their monthly pay chits.

But here it was different, as different as fog from sunshine. And with all the frustrations and heavy responsibilities of his office, as welcome as a breath of fresh air.

"I trust the beverage is to your liking," Paallikko said as the Mrachani who'd delivered the second glass scuttled respectfully away with the dregs of the first.

"It's quite adequate," VanDiver said, sipping at the claretee and the icy tangyslush that floated on top of it. "Any word yet on Bronski or Cavanagh?"

"Not yet, I'm afraid," Paallikko said, his voice laced with genuine regret. He peered briefly at the terminal on the low table beside him and shook his head. "They're still searching the hotel records. I apologize greatly for the delay."

"Quite all right," VanDiver assured him, waving a hand in dismissal. One could afford to be magnanimous when those around were clearly trying so hard to please. "Actually, I should be the one to apologize to you. One of my agents was supposed to be keeping tabs on Cavanagh, but like an idiot managed to lose him. I appreciate your efforts here—this matter is hardly your concern."

"On the contrary, Parlimin VanDiver," Paallikko said smoothly. "Any matter that troubles a man of your rank and power is most certainly of concern to the Mrachanis. Tell me, have you any idea what sort of scheme Lord Cavanagh might be planning?"

"All I know is that if it involves Cavanagh, it's something that needs looking into," VanDiver said, glowering at his drink. "You have no idea what the man is like."

"Actually, I believe I do," Paallikko said. "Though of course not nearly as well as you do. I had occasion to cross lives with him when he visited Mra-mig a little over three weeks ago."

"Really," VanDiver said. "He was creating trouble, I presume?"

"A little," the Mrachani said, his voice almost purring. "Though not so much as he'd perhaps hoped."

VanDiver grunted. "That's Cavanagh, all right. Mra-mig was where he bumped into Bronski, too, wasn't it?"

"Yes, it was," Paallikko murmured. "We are most grateful to you for bringing Liaison Bronski's presence here to our attention, Parlimin VanDiver."

He glanced again at his terminal. "Ah—the hotel search has been completed," he said. "No information on either Liaison Bronski or Lord Cavanagh. They're beginning a search now of vehicle rentals."

VanDiver nodded, glancing surreptitiously at his watch. Paallikko noticed the movement. "I'm sorry this is taking so long, Parlimin," he apologized. "If you'd prefer to return to your hotel, I could phone you when we locate them."

"Thank you," VanDiver said, inclining his head to the other. "Unfortunately, I won't have time to properly appreciate your hospitality. My duties back on Earth require me to return as soon as I have Cavanagh in hand. If it's all right with you, I'll just wait here until you locate him, then go wherever he is and pick him up."

"I would be honored by your presence," Paallikko said. "I'm quite sure it won't be much longer."

"The transport's rolled to a stop now," Kolchin said, his elbows braced on the edges of the aircar's window as he pressed the binoculars to his eyes. "Forward and cargo ramps are coming down."

"Do we need to get a little closer?" Cavanagh asked.

"We shouldn't even be this close," Bronski said. "If anyone's still keeping tabs on us, they're probably already wondering."

"They're starting to disembark now," Kolchin reported. "Three . . . four . . . five . . . five in the first group, all Mrachanis. The hover carriers are on the move—looks like they're forming a line over at the cargo ramp."

There was a sudden whooshing sound from above them. "Lose 'em, Kolchin," Bronski snapped, glancing up. "We've got company."

Kolchin dropped the binoculars out of sight into his lap, just as an aircar swooped past overhead and settled into a parallel course to their left. "I think that's the same one as before," Cavanagh said.

"You're right," Bronski agreed. "Same two Mrachanis; but their Bhurt's not with them anymore. What's that they're holding up to the window?"

"Looks like a plate," Cavanagh said, taking the binoculars from Kolchin and peering through them. It was indeed a plate, with a hastily scrawled message on its display:

Emergency—attempted breakout at western entrance.
Follow us quickly.

"Attempted breakout?" Kolchin frowned as Cavanagh relayed the message. "Who's in there to break out?"

"I don't know," Bronski said, waggling their wings in acknowledgment. "But it's going to look suspicious if we don't go along."

The Mrachanis pulled away, heading toward the western edge of the ring cliffs. Bronski fell into formation behind them; and as he did so, Kolchin abruptly grabbed the binoculars out of Cavanagh's hands. "What is it?" Bronski demanded.

"Zhirrzh," Kolchin said tightly, the binoculars again pressed to the window. "Three of them, coming down the cargo ramp."

A chill ran up Cavanagh's back. Somehow, even with all the evidence they'd already seen of Mrach duplicity, he'd never really believed they would make a private bargain with the Conquerors.

"Any dignitary-type Mrachanis on the scene?" Bronski asked. "Or anything that looks ceremonial?"

"Not that I can see." Kolchin lowered the binoculars. "They're out of sight now."

"Then this isn't the first batch to come in," Bronski concluded. "Probably a supply run or a personnel change. And the fact that they're on a Mrach transport means they've set up a rendezvous point for cargo transfers. Saves them the problem of trying to sneak Zhirrzh ships in and out of the system."

"Yes," Cavanagh murmured. "I suppose that establishes who's playing the title role in the *Mirnacheem-hyeea* One and Two operations."

"Not the Peacekeepers," Bronski agreed. "Kolchin, how's our backtrack look?"

"Three aircars in the distance," Kolchin said, looking out the rear windows. "Could just be more perimeter observers."

"I don't think they'd stay observers for long if we made a break for it," Bronski grunted. "Let's see if we can bluff this through."

"Should one of us stay with the aircar?" Cavanagh suggested. "Kolchin, maybe?"

"It'd be an instant tip-off that we know they're conning us," Bronski said. "We'll stand a better chance if they think we're walking in stupid."

The Mrach aircar put down beside the rim cliffs next to an inward cleft in the rock, at the end of which was an open doorway. The door itself, Cavanagh noted, had been camouflaged to look like the rock around it— a secret entrance, apparently, left over from the days when the facility served as a working fortress. The two Mrachanis were waiting beside it as the three humans joined them. "Four of the visitors' food animals have escaped," one of the Mrachanis said, his voice trembling with agitation. "They have claws and predatory teeth, and they are loose inside the fortress."

"Are all other exits covered?" Bronski asked, brushing past him and looking into the doorway. Up close now, Cavanagh could see that it led into a dimly lit tunnel of indeterminate length. Neither Bronski nor Kolchin had made any move to draw their flechette pistols; he took the cue and left his own weapon in concealment.

"All are covered," the Mrachani said, his body trembling along with his voice now as he jabbed a finger anxiously toward the doorway. "Please—you must find them before they harm someone, or before the visitors learn they are gone."

Come into my parlor, said the spider to the fly, the ominous old line flicked through Cavanagh's mind. Secret exits from fortresses, he remembered reading once, were nearly always booby-trapped to keep the enemy from coming in that way. He had no idea what the ancient Mrachanis had used for their security, and had no interest in finding out.

He looked at Bronski, hoping that the brigadier would decline the invitation and they could make a run for it. But— "Sure," Bronski grunted, waving a hand toward the doorway. "Show us where they were kept."

"All right," the first Mrachani said, stepping to the doorway and visibly bracing himself. "Follow me." Together, they stepped inside—

And taking a long step around behind them, Bronski got a grip on the stone-covered door and pulled his full weight against it. It swung ponderously past him and slammed with a thud, cutting off the Mrachanis' startled expressions. An instant later the thud was echoed by two sharper cracks as Kolchin fired a pair of precisely placed flechettes into the slender crack between door and frame, jamming the door closed.

"Changed my mind," the brigadier grunted. "That should slow them down a little. We'll take their aircar—Kolchin, you're on shotgun duty." He turned—

And froze.

Cavanagh spun around. Glowering at them from ten meters away, apparently materialized out of thin air, were six Bhurtala.

For a long moment no one moved or spoke. "Gentlemen, you have a choice to make," a disembodied Mrachani voice said. "You may surrender and become our guests for a while; or you may die here and now. Which do you choose?"

There was another short silence. One of the Bhurtala rumbled something impatient sounding under his breath and took half a step forward. "Gentlemen?" the Mrachani voice prompted. "I should perhaps mention that we've just received word of the fate of their companions on Granparra, and they're all rather upset with you. I would say they're looking for an excuse to make the decision for you."

"Such a gracious and congenial invitation," Bronski called, his voice thick with sarcasm. "How could we refuse?"

"Lay your weapons aside," the Mrachani instructed, "and step back."

"Do as he says," Bronski said, pulling out his flechette pistol and dropping it onto the ground in front of him.

Cavanagh and Kolchin followed suit. The overanxious Bhurt stepped forward and collected the weapons, glaring balefully the whole time. Then, brushing past them, he went to the camouflaged door and pulled the wedged flechettes out of the crack with his bare fingers.

"Excellent," the disembodied voice said; and to Cavanagh's surprise a section of rock beside the line of Bhurtala swung open to reveal a Mrachani in a small rough-hewn alcove. A camouflaged sentry hole, probably also how the Bhurtala had made their magical appearance. "Welcome to the Garden Of The Mad Stonewright," the Mrachani continued, stepping out of the sentry hole and swinging the door closed behind him. "Lord Cavanagh, Liaison Bronski, and Bodyguard Kolchin, I presume?"

"Yes," Bronski said, inclining his head slightly. "Ambassador-Chief Valloittaja, I presume?"

"Correct," Valloittaja said, returning the ritual nod. "Please—inside. Before any of our other guests see you."

"I congratulate you all on your ingenuity and persistence," he continued as they started down the tunnel Cavanagh had glimpsed earlier. "Also on your forged credentials. You very nearly succeeded."

"Fortunes of war," Bronski said. "What gave us away?"

"An old acquaintance of Lord Cavanagh's alerted us to your presence on Mra," Valloittaja said, his eyes glittering sardonically as he looked at Cavanagh. "Once we knew you were here, the rest was quite straightforward."

"More straightforward than your *Mirnacheem-hyeea* operations, anyway," Bronski said. "I imagine it's going to be quite a challenge to persuade the Zhirrzh to launch an all-out attack on a major Commonwealth world. What are you going to do, try to convince them you can sneak their warships in past the wake-trail detectors?"

Cavanagh stared at him in amazement. But Valloittaja merely gave the brigadier the Mrach equivalent of a smile. "You are amazingly insightful, Liaison Bronski," he said approvingly. "Very impressive indeed. Your conjectures are correct; it is merely your tense that is flawed."

"Meaning?" Bronski prompted.

"Meaning that I do not need to persuade the Zhirrzh to launch the *Mirnacheem-hyeea* Two attack," Valloittaja said, "because I have already done so. Here we are."

He gestured to an open door on their left. An old wooden door, Cavanagh noted, fitted out with an only slightly more modern mechanical lock behind riveted metal plates. "Go on in," Valloittaja said. "Unless you wish the Bhurtala to assist you."

Silently, Cavanagh stepped inside. It was a single square-shaped room, relatively small, apparently carved directly out of the rock of the cliffs. Carved into the wall at about knee height was a deep groove that had once held a Mrach ribbon candle, though the lighting now was being provided by a primitive incandescent electric-light rectangle set into the center of the ceiling, probably part of the same upgrade that had included the door lock. The furniture consisted of three Bhurtist military cots: liquid-filled floater-bag mattresses resting on bolted and wire-strung metal frames.

"I apologize for the accommodations," Valloittaja said as the others followed Cavanagh inside. "I'm afraid you caught us unprepared for extra visitors."

"Don't worry about it," Bronski assured him, looking around. "So when and where does the *Mirnacheem-hyeea* Two attack take place?"

Valloittaja smiled. "The *when* is as soon as the attack force can be assembled. The *where* . . . but you must forgive me if I choose to keep some matters secret. Good day, gentlemen."

He stepped back and gestured. One of the Bhurtala reached into the room and pulled the door closed.

It took nearly half an hour for Pheylan to get through a job he suspected a qualified tech could have knocked off in five minutes. But at last he was finished. "Okay, Max, I'm down to the cable," he informed the computer. "You ready?"

"I'm ready," Max said. "But again I urge you to reconsider. Once I'm disconnected from the fueler, I'll have access only to my internal audio and visual sensors, which are extremely limited. If you instead leave me connected, I'll be able to give you a more timely warning of approaching aircraft."

"Except that if those aircraft are Zhirrzh, I won't have time to get you out," Pheylan pointed out. "We're going to need you to work out the details of that sonic hull-cracking technique Williams came up with. Here we go."

Carefully, he cut through the final cable. Just as carefully, he lifted the meter-long silver cylinder out of the interlock chamber. "Still with me?" he asked, balancing the cylinder on the floor as he snagged the carrying case he'd rigged out of a pair of backpacks.

"I'm here," Max's voice came from the speaker in the cylinder. "Or at least most of me."

"Sorry," Pheylan apologized. "I wish I could bring your peripherals and libraries along, but I can't handle all that alone. Next time we do this, I'll bring along a couple of pack animals."

"I would hope so," Max said. "Incidentally, I'm not nearly as fragile as you seem to think. My casing and component placement have been designed to withstand reasonably severe mistreatment."

"Glad to hear it," Pheylan said, stuffing the cylinder into the carrying case and fastening it securely in place. "Let's hope we don't wind up pushing the design specs."

Hoisting the cylinder onto his back, he settled the straps in place and picked up his own survival pack. Heavy and awkward—he hoped he wouldn't have to walk all the way to the Peacekeeper base. "Let's make tracks."

Max had set them down on a small knoll that jutted up through the tree-covered landscape around it. The knoll itself was free of both trees and large bushes, but there was a fair amount of ankle-high vegetation underfoot consisting of interlocking vines that threatened to tangle his feet with each step. Pheylan had picked his way through perhaps thirty meters of the stuff and was nearing the edge of the knoll when he heard the distant sound. "Max?"

"Approaching air vehicle," the computer said. "Only one, I believe, though with only my internal sensors I can't be certain."

"Never mind how many," Pheylan said, throwing a quick look around the sky as he picked up his pace. Nothing visible yet. "Is it ours or theirs?"

"I can't tell," Max said. "But from the drive pitch I'd say it's more likely a space vehicle than an aircraft."

Pheylan swore under his breath, kicking into a flat-out run toward the edge of the knoll. The only people in this system who had spacecraft to spare for a rescue search were the Zhirrzh. "What direction is it coming from?" he asked, scanning the sky again. A few more steps and he'd be to the edge of the knoll and the partial cover of the trees.

And then, suddenly, one of the vines caught his ankle, pitching him forward toward the ground. He threw out his arms, his hands hitting the ground—

And with a crash and flurry of tearing leaves and vines they went straight through the layer of interlocked vegetation and into empty space.

Two meters sooner than he'd expected to, he'd found the edge of the knoll.

The next few seconds were a disoriented tangle of movement and pain as he rolled and tumbled down the slope, slamming into rocks and stiff plant stalks with the repetitive impact of Max's cylinder pounding against his back. He fought unsuccessfully for balance, hands scrabbling for a grip on the plants as they rushed past, legs flailing as they tried for enough friction to at least slow down his mad slide. Something hit his head hard enough for him to see stars—

He awoke slowly, vaguely aware that someone was softly calling his name. "Commander Cavanagh? Commander Cavanagh?"

"I'm here, Max," he said, his voice sounding distant and slurred in his ears. His left leg was throbbing strangely; absently, he reached down to rub it.

And gasped in pain, coming fully awake in an instant as a stab of agony ripped through the leg.

"Keep your voice down, please," Max said. "Is it broken?"

"Oh, yes, definitely," Pheylan managed, clenching his teeth hard together. Gasping in pain was undignified enough without adding flat-out screaming to it.

He paused, listening, the throbbing in his leg abruptly pushed into the background of his thoughts.

The sound of the incoming aircraft, which had sparked his disastrous rush toward cover, had stopped.

"Are they here?" he whispered.

"Yes," Max confirmed. "I've counted five separate voices; there may be more."

Pheylan grimaced. "Not human voices."

"No."

Carefully, Pheylan turned his torso and head to look above him. He was about two thirds of the way down the slope, wrapped around the tree trunk that had probably been responsible for breaking his leg. Behind him the false ground cover hung a couple of meters off the end of the knoll, giving him partial concealment from the view of anyone up there. Aside from that, though, he was about as exposed as he could possibly be.

"Can you move at all?" Max asked. "Two meters downslope is a large bush that would provide you with concealment."

Gingerly, Pheylan tried it. He got about five centimeters before conceding defeat. "I can't do it," he panted, wiping at the sweat dripping into his eyes. "The pain's too much."

"Can you tell how bad the break is?"

"No," Pheylan said. "Bad enough."

For a minute Max was silent. Pheylan could hear the voices himself now, chattering quietly away above him on the knoll.

And, no, they weren't human.

"I don't think you have any choice, Commander," Max said at last. "Whatever the Zhirrzh do here, the probability is high that the Peacekeepers will assume all survivors have been captured and won't come themselves to search. Even if you could get to your survival pack, the medical pack would be of limited help with a broken leg."

Pheylan hadn't even missed the survival pack yet. He looked around, but wherever it had ended up, it was out of his immediate sight. "You're suggesting I surrender."

"I see no other alternatives. I'm sorry."

Pheylan sighed. So much for his big grandstand scheme to come here and help his sister. And to wind up a Zhirrzh prisoner again on top of it. If he lived through this, he was never going to live it down. "I'm sorry, too, Max," he said.

He took a deep breath. "Hey!" he shouted. "Down here!"

Parlimin VanDiver was halfway through his third glass of claretee when the word finally came through. "Ah," Paallikko said, looking at the terminal at his side. "At last. Yes, Parlimin VanDiver, Lord Cavanagh and Liaison Bronski were indeed here on Mra. Unfortunately, that is no longer true. It appears they both left five hours ago for Mra-mig."

VanDiver swallowed a curse. That figured. Once again, regular as nuclear clockwork, Cavanagh had found a way to waste some of his precious time. "Where on Mra-mig were they going?"

"The information does not say," Paallikko said, his voice heavy with regret and an echo of VanDiver's own irritation. At least he understood that a NorCoord Parlimin didn't have this kind of time to squander. "We only know their destination from the fact that the servicer who refueled their spacecraft happened to overhear them discussing it."

VanDiver tapped at his glass with a fingernail. "What about a skitter? Can we send a message ahead asking them to hold him?"

"The scheduled message skitter has already left," Paallikko said. "I could of course send a diplomatic skitter, but I'm afraid it would be of only limited benefit. Liaison Bronski's ship is courier-class, which means the skitter would still arrive at Mra-mig behind him."

"That figures," VanDiver growled. A courier-class ship: twice as fast as a normal stardrive, at five times the cost. Undoubtedly at government expense, too. Just one more irritation, plus one more charge to add to the mental list he was preparing for the prosecutor general.

"Shall I order your ship to be refueled?" Paallikko asked. "A courtesy, of course, with no cost to the NorCoord Parliament."

"Yes, thank you," VanDiver said. If Cavanagh was gone, there was no sense hanging around Mra anymore. "I'd also like you to send that diplomatic skitter on ahead, just in case they're planning to stay on Mra-mig for a while. At my personal expense, of course."

"The skitter will be prepared," Paallikko said, tapping keys on his terminal. "But at Mrach expense. I insist."

No doubt about it, these Mrachanis knew how to treat visiting dignitaries. "Again, I thank you," VanDiver said, setting down his glass and climbing to his feet. "And for your hospitality, as well. I'm in your debt."

"Not at all," Paallikko assured him, standing up as well. "It is always a pleasure to deal with men like you. A very great pleasure, indeed."

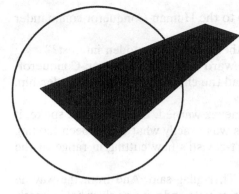

24

The Human-Conqueror prisoner Srgent-janovetz straightened up, turning his head back and forth to the side. "What can you tell me?" Thrr-mezaz asked him. The optronic speaker on his shoulder gave the translation, and Srgent-janovetz replied. "The left leg's definitely broken," the Zhirrzh words came from the translator link in Thrr-mezaz's ear slits. "Was he unconscious when you found him?"

"I'm told he was conscious then, but that he lost consciousness when they moved him into the transport," Thrr-mezaz said. "Can you heal him?"

Srgent-janovetz looked down at the injured Human-Conqueror as he spoke. "No," the translation came. "I'm not that skilled a healer."

"Mm." Thrr-mezaz looked over at Thrr-gilag. "What do you think? Should we turn him over to our own healers, or ask the Human-Conqueror commander to send us one of theirs?"

But Thrr-gilag wasn't looking at him. He was instead staring intently into the unconscious alien's face. "Thrr-gilag?" Thrr-mezaz said, slapping at his brother's spinning tail. "You want to join in this conversation?"

"Sorry," Thrr-gilag said without looking up. "I was just . . . I might be wrong, Thrr-mezaz, but I think this is Pheylan Cavanagh."

Srgent-janovetz's face turned back up as the translation came through. "Did you say Pheylan Cavanagh?" he asked.

"Yes," Thrr-mezaz said. "Do you know of him?"

Srgent-janovetz seemed to hesitate before he spoke again. "I know one of his family," the translation came. "His sister."

Thrr-gilag looked at Thrr-mezaz. "I need him to be healed, Thrr-mezaz," he said. "I'm willing to go to the Human-Conqueror commander to ask for a healer for him."

Thrr-mezaz frowned at his brother. "Why the sudden interest?"

Thrr-gilag flicked his tongue toward the injured Human-Conqueror. "Back on Base World Twelve he had the chance to raise me to Eldership. Yet he didn't. I want to know why."

"It could be dangerous," Thrr-mezaz warned. But even as he spoke, it suddenly occurred to him that this was exactly what they'd been looking for: the perfect excuse to get Prr't-zevisti's new cutting in range of the Human-Conqueror stronghold.

"I'm willing to take that risk," Thrr-gilag said. And from the way he was blinking at Thrr-mezaz in their private code, it was clear he'd already realized that. Which meant this conversation was as much for the listening Elders' benefit as it was for his.

"I don't like it," Thrr-mezaz said, putting some reluctance into his voice. "But you're probably right. You—Srgent-janovetz—would your commander be willing to send a healer here?"

Srgent-janovetz nodded. "Yes, I think so," the translation came in Thrr-mezaz's ear. "Especially if you tell the commander who it is."

Thrr-mezaz looked questioningly at Thrr-gilag, but his brother flicked his tongue in a negative. Perhaps Pheylan Cavanagh was a member of an important family or clan. That might explain, in fact, why they'd gone to such effort to rescue him from Base World 12.

And might imply they would go to equal effort to rescue him now.

It was not a situation Thrr-mezaz would welcome, considering the shape of his ground defenses. But he would slice that rope when he reached it. "I'll have a transport prepared," he said. "In the meantime, Srgent-janovetz, do what you can for him."

The storage cavern appeared to be deserted, but as Melinda stepped to the door of the electronics-reconfiguration chamber, she gave the area a last casual sweep just to be sure. No one was visible. Gripping the handle, she swung the heavy metal door open and slipped inside. "Prr't-zevisti?" she called, pulling the door closed behind her. "Are you awake?"

The ghostly form appeared in front of her; involuntarily, Melinda flinched, shying back to bump against the door. She was never going to get used to this. "I do not sleep, Doctor-Cavan-a," the Elder said in that thin, distant voice of his.

"No, of course not," Melinda said. "I'm sorry."

"You need not to be sorry," the Elder assured her. "What has your commander to tell me?"

"He didn't send me," Melinda said. "Actually, I'm not even supposed to be here."

Prr't-zevisti's expression changed. "Why do you risk defying your commander?"

"Because I believe you're telling the truth about not being a spy," Melinda said. "The problem is convincing Colonel Holloway of that. I came here hoping you'd come up with a way to do that."

The insubstantial tongue flicked out. "I have not found an idea. Why does he not believe?"

"I don't know," Melinda said with a sigh. "Maybe he's afraid to. He's the one responsible for the lives of all these people, both the warriors and the civilians. That's a heavy burden, and he takes it very seriously."

"And yet you do not?"

Melinda shrugged. "I'm a healer, and because of that I often have responsibility for people's lives. But I don't have the same kind of total responsibility as Colonel Holloway." She smiled wryly. "Besides, I come from a family accustomed to taking calculated risks."

For a long moment Prr't-zevisti seemed to be disgesting that. Or else was working his way through the alien words. "What do you say, then, Doctor-Cavan-a?" he asked. "Do you come here to free me?"

Melinda took a deep breath. That was in fact exactly what she'd been planning to do when she came here today. But now, staring into that translucent alien face, the doubts were beginning to trickle back. She was willing enough to risk her own life on this; but could she unilaterally make that same decision for the others living here under the Zhirrzh threat? If Prr't-zevisti was lying—if his report back to the Zhirrzh commander led to the destruction of this refuge—then she would be directly responsible for the deaths of thousands of people.

But if he wasn't lying—if the war really was an accident of misunderstanding—then inaction on her part would mean condemning those same people to a war neither side really wanted. And not just the Peacekeepers and civilians here, but humans and nonhumans all across the Commonwealth.

And put in those terms, there was only one thing she could do. "Yes," she told Prr't-zevisti, ungluing herself from the door and crossing the room to the shelf where his *fsss* cutting lay in its box. For a moment she stared at it; then, taking another deep breath, she reached out—

And with a gentle creak the door behind her swung open.

She spun around, a surge of blood flooding into her face, her memory flashing back to the day when her mother had caught her stealing one of their dinner steaks to give to a stray dog. Holloway was standing in the doorway gazing at her, his expression unreadable. "Doctor Cavanagh," he nodded, stepping into the chamber and pulling the door half-closed. "I thought I might find you here. Though I could swear I'd told you to stay away."

"Yes, you did," Melinda said, an odd mixture of defiance and guilt twisting through her stomach. No matter what she believed the right course of action to be here, the fact was that she'd been caught in the act of betraying Holloway's trust. And that hurt.

"I see," Holloway said. "Under normal circumstances that would have earned you one hell of a lot of trouble. But we don't have time for that now. A Zhirrzh aircar has landed near Sentry Post Nine. They're asking for a healer to attend to a human prisoner they've just captured."

Melinda blinked. "A prisoner? From where?"

"From a spacecraft that landed southwest of here a few hours ago." Holloway's face tightened. "Which we were too damn slow off our butts to get to first."

"I'm sorry," was all Melinda could think of to say.

"You're going to be sorrier," Holloway said. "According to the Zhirrzh, the prisoner is your brother Pheylan."

Melinda felt her mouth drop open, a horrible lightness suddenly gripping her vision. "Pheylan?" she breathed. "But how—?"

"I don't know the hows or whys," Holloway said. "I only know that he has a broken leg, and that the Zhirrzh are offering to take one of our healers back to treat him."

With an effort Melinda broke the paralysis gripping her. "Of course," she said, starting toward the door. "I'll get my bag."

Holloway caught her arm as she started to pass him. "I want to make sure you understand this before you go, Doctor," he said. "If this was a purely humanitarian gesture, they could as easily have brought your brother here for treatment. The fact that they want you to go to them instead implies they're looking to pick up another hostage."

"I understand," Melinda said, trying to pull away from him.

He didn't let go. "I don't think you do," he said, his voice suddenly grim. "The fact that your brother made it here alive instead of being vaporized on the way down implies that their blockade may have suddenly developed a crack. Maybe more than a crack; maybe it's completely gone. Either way, it's time we gave it a little nudge."

Melinda stared at him. "Are you saying you're going to attack?"

Holloway's eyes flicked over her shoulder to where Prr't-zevisti was hovering, silently watching them. "I'm saying it's time to test their strength," he said. "Without going into details, it's suddenly become very urgent that we do whatever we can to get our civilians out of here. If the

Zhirrzh have diverted their blockade ships to another theater of operations, now's the time for us to get a ship off and go for help."

"But you don't have to attack the ground base for that, do you?" Melinda asked.

Holloway's cheek twitched. "I wish we didn't. But we do. The ground base is undoubtedly acting as targeting spotter for the blockade forces, as well as being a threat to any incoming transports. It has to be neutralized."

"I see," Melinda said quietly. "Never mind that the war might be a mistake?"

"That's for the diplomats to work out," Holloway told her. "If we get off Dorcas, I'll be happy to tell them your theory. But until then I have a job to do."

"And anyone caught in the cross fire has to be considered expendable."

"Would you have me risk twenty-five thousand lives for your three?" he countered. "Or, rather, for their two? You don't have to go."

"Don't be ridiculous," Melinda bit out. "We're wasting time, and I still have to go get my bag."

Holloway let go of her arm and pushed open the door. "I've already had it sent for," he said. "It'll be waiting at Sentry Nine."

"Thank you." Melinda stepped past him into the doorway, then paused and turned around. "Farewell, Prr't-zevisti," she called, looking around for him. "I'll try to come back again soon."

But the pale form was nowhere to be seen, and her words brought no response. Turning back again, she left the chamber. Holloway sealed it behind them, then led the way across the cavern. "Can you at least tell me when you're going to attack?" Melinda asked as they ducked through the blackout curtain into the cool mountain air outside.

"You'll hear us coming," Holloway assured her. "You'd better not mention this to Janovetz or your brother, either. The Zhirrzh will undoubtedly be monitoring you, and I don't want them tipped off."

Holloway led the way around an outcropping of the cliff; and there it was, its milky-white hull gleaming brightly in the afternoon sunshine. A Zhirrzh aircar, surrounded by a semicircle of Peacekeepers, their Oberon assault guns leveled warningly. Standing a few meters in front of the aircar, under the wary eyes of more Peacekeepers, a single Zhirrzh was in the process of emptying the contents of his hip pouch onto the top of one of the rock-filled magnesium crates that had been set up to provide the sentries with some protection.

"Fuji's got your bag and some other supplies over there," Holloway said, nodding toward where Major Takara was standing watch over the whole operation. "Two of the tubes mixed in with the analgesics are phonies; you'll know them by the fake chemical names. They contain a low-yield binary explosive that you should be able to use to break out of whatever building they lock you into. Janovetz will know how to use them."

Melinda grimaced. "I understand. Any other surprises?"

"Yes." Holloway hesitated. "We've put in a vital-signs monitor for you. Among the usual electronics we've added a high-power white-noise radio transmitter."

Melinda stopped. "You've *what?*" she hissed. "Are you out of your mind? That's their idea of the ultimate weapon—what if they catch me with it?"

"They'll never know it's there," Holloway assured her. "The whole casing's metal—their Elders won't be able to even look inside."

"That's so very comforting," Melinda said icily, ashamed and enraged both by this betrayal. She'd given him all this Elderdeath information in good faith, assuming he would use it to help stop this war. Instead he'd taken Prr't-zevisti's gesture of trust and turned it back into a weapon. "Excuse me, please, my brother's waiting for me."

She pulled away from him, stalking off alone across the uneven ground toward the Zhirrzh aircar. Holloway made no move to follow, undoubtedly the smartest thing he could do. That stupid, rigid, military mind of his—

"Doctor-Cavan-a?"

Melinda jerked as if she'd touched a hot electrode, sheer momentum keeping her feet moving. Nothing was visible in the sunlight; but it had been Prr't-zevisti's voice.

Except that the configuration chamber had been sealed behind them . . .

"They have brought me another cutting," the Elder hissed. "It is resting on the box with other items. The box is metal—I cannot return to my *fsss* from there. Can you move it?"

Melinda bit at the inside of her cheek. The Zhirrzh had finished emptying his pouch now and had taken a few steps back toward the aircar. His collection of artifacts was sitting in plain sight on the crate almost directly ahead of her, being ignored by the Peacekeeper squad. It would be easy enough to reach over as she passed and pick it up.

Except that Prr't-zevisti had been listening in the configuration chamber when Holloway was discussing his planned attack on the Zhirrzh base. For that matter, there was an even chance he'd also heard Holloway talking about the Elderdeath weapon he was planting on her. If she helped him get to where he could talk with other Zhirrzh . . .

"I will not tell what I have heard, Doctor-Cavan-a," Prr't-zevisti said. "I give you my promise of honor."

"Why not?" Melinda murmured back, trying to keep her lips from moving. "Your people's lives are at stake."

"Not their lives," Prr't-zevisti corrected her. "They would only be raised to Eldership."

"And that's not important to you?"

"It is very important," Prr't-zevisti said. "But it is more important that the war be ended quickly."

Melinda swallowed. "I would be trusting you with my life, Prr't-zevisti. Do you understand that?"

"With my promise of honor, Doctor-Cavan-a. I will not tell what I have heard."

And so there it was. Fifteen minutes ago she'd been willing to gamble with the lives of everyone up here in the mountains on the words and promise of an alien ghost. Was she equally willing to gamble her own life, right here and now, on those same words and promise? "All right," she said. "Where's the cutting?"

"In the small tube at the end," Prr't-zevisti said. Even with his alien intonations the relief in his voice was unmistakable. "Do you see it?"

"Yes," Melinda said. It was about the same diameter as a marking stylus, and about half its length. Small enough to palm, if she could get to it without anyone noticing. Here was her chance, she thought wryly, to see whether she could make it as a thief if her surgical career ever fell through. A shame Prr't-zevisti couldn't create a diversion—jump out at the Peacekeepers and say boo or something—

And then, just as she reached the line of artifacts, there was a sudden mechanical-sounding screech from the aircar, and a flood of warm air washed over her. The Oberons twitched warningly; but the aircar merely lifted a few centimeters off the ground and then settled back down again.

But for those few seconds all eyes were on the aircar. With the help of the aircar's pilot, Prr't-zevisti had indeed arranged a diversion.

She had the cylinder in her hand before the aircar had completely settled down again, forcing herself to keep her pace steady as she stepped up to the waiting Zhirrzh. "I greet you," she said to him. "I am Melinda Cavanagh. A healer."

"I greet you, Melinda Cavanagh," the alien said in remarkably good English. "I am Thrr-gilag; Kee'rr. I will take you to your brother."

Melinda glanced back at Holloway, standing impassively beside Takara as two Peacekeepers headed toward the aircar with the supplies. "Thank you," she murmured.

Two minutes later they were airborne; and as they lifted over the first line of low peaks, Prr't-zevisti's ghostly form appeared beside Thrr-gilag. They conversed for a few minutes in the Zhirrzh language, and then Thrr-gilag turned to face Melinda. "You do not know me, Melinda Cavanagh," he said, "but I am acquainted with your brother Pheylan Cavanagh. I was the speaker for the alien-studies group who examined him following his capture."

Melinda felt her stomach tighten. "Are you angry with him for escaping?" she asked.

The alien's deadly tongue slashed briefly into the air. "No. I seek merely to understand the roots of Human aggression toward the Zhirrzh."

"We have no aggression toward the Zhirrzh," Melinda said. "Or at least we didn't have until you attacked the *Jutland.*"

"Nor did we have any aggression toward Humans until the *Jutland* attacked our ships," Thrr-gilag countered. His tongue jabbed again, this time curving around to point at Prr't-zevisti hovering beside him. "Perhaps at last we both now understand."

"Perhaps," Melinda said. "The challenge will be to get anyone else to listen to us."

"Do not fear, Melinda Cavanagh," Thrr-gilag assured her. "When we return to the encampment, we will open a pathway to the Overclan Prime. He is wise and honorable, and he will listen."

"I hope so," Melinda said, frowning. There was something wrong here. "But can't Prr't-zevisti do that himself? I thought he'd be able to go directly to his main *fsss* organ once he was out of the configuration chamber and away from all our metal."

Prr't-zevisti murmured something and turned away, fading until he was barely visible. "He has tried," Thrr-gilag said. "But the anchorpoint-sense no longer exists. It appears that his *fsss* has been destroyed."

Melinda looked at Prr't-zevisti, feeling a prickling sensation on her skin. "What will happen to him now? Will he die?"

"I do not know," Thrr-gilag admitted. "I think he will continue to live but will be confined to the small region around this new cutting."

"And the cutting back at the Peacekeeper base," Melinda said. "We'll get it back to you, Prr't-zevisti, after all this is over."

Prr't-zevisti stirred, his image returning to its earlier brightness. "I am shamed by my sadness," he said. "You have risked your honor for me, Doctor-Cavan-a. I am alive, and I am free. What more shall I wish would be selfish."

They were over the last row of foothills now, with the colony in distant sight. Melinda found herself studying the village as they approached, wondering what changes the Zhirrzh had made in the area. She spotted the warehouse where she'd stored the supplies for Pheylan's rescue mission; it seemed incredible that that had been only three and a half weeks ago. The last transmission they'd had before the Peacekeepers had seemingly abandoned them had reported that Pheylan and Aric and the others had all returned safely to Edo and had included a summary of their debriefing.

Yet here Pheylan was, back in Zhirrzh hands. How in the world had that happened?

Abruptly, Thrr-gilag leaned forward, reaching over to touch the pilot on the shoulder. He jabbed his tongue toward the village and said something that sounded agitated. Prr't-zevisti moved into the space between them, and for a minute the three of them conversed in rapid-fire Zhirrzh. "What's wrong?" Melinda asked.

"I do not know," Thrr-gilag said, jabbing his tongue again. "There is a new arrival in the encampment since we departed to seek your assistance. It is a flash-ship bearing the markings of the Speaker for Dhaa'rr."

Melinda squinted out at the white ship parked off to one side of the landing area. "Is that bad?"

"The Speaker for Dhaa'rr is not a friend of the Thrr family," Thrr-gilag said. "I do not believe he will be pleased to find Prr't-zevisti still alive."

Melinda frowned at the ghost. "But I thought Prr't-zevisti was a member of the Dhaa'rr clan."

"He is," Thrr-gilag said. "It is too complicated to explain now, Melinda Cavanagh. We must not reveal that Prr't-zevisti is here until we know the reason for this visit."

"That's going to be a tall order," Melinda said. "Won't the other Elders recognize him?"

Thrr-gilag jabbed his tongue viciously. "Yes. You are right; it is no use. Unless we drop his *fsss* cutting to the ground right here, there will be nowhere he can go that the other Elders cannot also reach."

Melinda's eyes fell on the equipment Holloway's men had loaded aboard. Her bag, the medical supplies and disguised explosives—

And the vital-signs monitor with its metal casing.

"Yes, there is," she told Thrr-gilag, crouching beside the monitor and pulling out her multitool. "We can hide his cutting in here until we know what's going on. Tell the pilot to slow down—I need time to get this open."

She had the back of the monitor open by the time the pilot had begun his descent toward the landing field. Thrr-gilag and Prr't-zevisti had been conversing together the whole time in quiet tones, and now Thrr-gilag handed Melinda the small cylinder containing the cutting. "Make certain he has a small space around him," he told her. "And that the cutting is safely secure in place. Damage to it will hurt him."

"Yes, I know," Melinda said, wedging the cylinder between two circuit boards near one side. There was a lot of metal in there, but the boards themselves were nonmetallic. "How's that, Prr't-zevisti?"

"It is fine," the Elder's voice said from inside the monitor.

"Be quick," Thrr-gilag warned, looking ahead. "Other Elders may look in at us."

Melinda nodded and got to work. She had the monitor sealed and the last screw in place by the time the aircar settled to the ground.

She had expected a group of warriors to be waiting for them as she and Thrr-gilag exited the aircar. To her surprise there was only a single Zhirrzh standing at the foot of the ramp. For a minute he spoke to Thrr-gilag; then, touching a device draped over his shoulder, he turned to Melinda and spoke. "I greet you, Melinda Cavanagh," the translation came from the shoulder device. "I am Second Commander Klnn-vavgi; Dhaa'rr. The seriousness of the situation requires that we dispense with the usual ceremony."

Melinda felt her heart speed up. Seriousness? "Has something happened to Pheylan?"

"Pheylan Cavanagh is not worse," Thrr-gilag said, his voice sounding abruptly strange. "It is my brother, Commander Thrr-mezaz. On the orders of the Overclan Seating, he has been placed under detention."

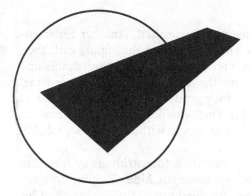

25

The supply cart rolled along the bumpy stone corridor, every turn of its wheels taking Thrr't-rokik farther away from the Mrach spacecraft and the pyramid full of Elders that had been brought there along with the other supplies from the *Willing Servant.* A decidedly mixed blessing, he'd already concluded. On the one side, it would probably be safer to have the box containing his illegal *fsss* cutting moved farther away from the prying eyes of the other Elders of this expedition; on the other side, he wasn't sure exactly where the box was being taken. There'd been something about putting it in the Zhirrzh study group's quarters—

An Elder suddenly appeared in the grayworld in front of him. "There you are," he snapped. "I've been looking all over for you, Cvv't-rokik. Didn't you hear the announcement for all Elders to assemble in the *Closed Mouth*'s command room?"

Thrr't-rokik grimaced. Of course he hadn't heard—the announcement had undoubtedly been made directly to the collection of *fsss* cuttings in the pyramid. "I didn't realize it was to be immediately," he improvised. "I was asked to watch over these supplies and make sure they were properly delivered."

"Asked by whom?" the Elder demanded suspiciously.

"One of the warriors," Thrr't-rokik said. On his way out of the ship he'd overheard something. . "He told me to make sure the supplies arrived all right since the members of the study group were sleeping."

The Elder flicked his tongue, still obviously suspicious. But it apparently wasn't worth the effort of checking up on. "All right, get going," he growled. "But as soon as they're delivered, get yourself back to the ship and the meeting."

"I obey," Thrr't-rokik said.

The Elder flicked his tongue again and vanished. Another Elder appeared nearby, glanced briefly at Thrr't-rokik and the supply cart, then left without speaking. A few beats later a third Elder appeared, this one moving in and out of the boxes on the cart before similarly leaving. Clearly, they were approaching the study group's quarters and the Elders assigned to watch over them; and if Thrr't-rokik didn't want to have to keep explaining his presence here, a strategic withdrawal was probably called for.

Fortunately, with his *fsss* cutting already a thoustride away from the *Closed Mouth,* there was an obvious place to hide. Zipping forward ahead of the wobbly supply cart, he stretched out to the full length of his anchorline, moving out of range of the Elders in the hangar area.

It was more of the same up there: more stone tunnels and more dimly lit stone rooms. Also more deserted. He drifted in and out through the walls without seeing any signs of life or habitation. Apparently, this part of the fortress wasn't being used right now.

Or rather, he corrected himself, not being used very much. From the wall to his right came a faint but distinct thunking sound, followed by something that might have been voices. He moved through the wall to investigate—

And jolted to a stop, dropping reflexively into the safety of the grayworld.

The room was indeed occupied. By three Human-Conquerors.

Cautiously, fighting against the urge to zip away out of there, he moved to one of the upper corners of the room and rose again toward the lightworld. Two of the three Human-Conquerors were seated on low metal couchlike structures placed against one wall, while the third knelt at the door tapping methodically on the end of a long rigid sliver of some black material with a piece of rock. The other end of the sliver had been inserted behind a metal plate set into one side of a wooden door. A lock mechanism, perhaps?

A quiet surge of relief flooded over Thrr't-rokik as the truth suddenly hit him. These Human-Conquerors weren't a prelude to attack, nor were they evidence of Mrach treachery. On the contrary, they were Mrach prisoners.

One of the two seated Human-Conquerors was speaking. Easing a little closer to the lightworld, Thrr't-rokik focused his attention and his freshly obtained knowledge of the Human-Conqueror language and listened.

"I'm surprised they haven't killed us," the alien was saying. "I'd have thought keeping us alive would be dangerous."

The other seated alien moved his head back and forth to the side. "Don't worry, Cavanagh, they'll kill us soon enough," he said. "But not before they use us against the Zhirrzh."

"How?" the first asked.

"No idea," the second answered. "Some way that helps (something) their position here. Maybe they'll tell the Zhirrzh we came to attack them. Maybe even stage a real attack. Kill a couple of them and blame us."

"And our side of the story won't be mentioned?" the first Human-Conqueror said.

"I'm sure we'll be dead before anyone asks us," the second said.

The first made a rude-sounding noise and the conversation ceased.

For perhaps a hunbeat Thrr't-rokik continued to watch, running the words he'd heard through his mind and wondering if he could have misinterpreted them. The warriors on the *Willing Servant* had spoken of the Mrachanis as allies of the Zhirrzh. They wouldn't deliberately attack the study group. Surely these Human-Conquerors were lying.

But if they weren't . . .

He found Searcher Nzz-oonaz asleep in one of the rooms of the study group's quarters. "Searcher Nzz-oonaz?" he said softly, trying to watch in all directions at once for other Elders. If he was caught waking up the group's speaker without orders, they *would* take the effort to check up on him. "Searcher?"

Nzz-oonaz's eyes fluttered open, the lowlight pupils widening a little as the others stayed narrowed to slits. "Um?" he murmured. He focused on Thrr't-rokik's face and frowned—

"I'm not one of your usual Elders," Thrr't-rokik told him. "My name is Thrr't-rokik; Kee'rr. I'm Thrr-gilag's father—I think you and I met once a few cyclics ago."

"Um," Nzz-oonaz murmured again, nodding this time in recognition. He gestured toward the ceiling, flicking his tongue in the universal signal for caution.

Thrr't-rokik nodded back; they'd been warned aboard ship that the Mrachanis were probably monitoring all conversations. While the Elders themselves couldn't be heard, the physicals still had to be careful what they said aloud. "I'm actually not supposed to be here at all," he told Nzz-oonaz, "so I'll ask this quickly. Are you aware that the Mrachanis have taken three Human-Conqueror prisoners and are holding them about four thoustrides north of here?"

Nzz-oonaz's lowlight pupils narrowed, and he flicked his tongue in a negative. "You're sure they haven't told you about them?" Thrr't-rokik persisted. "Because they're there. I saw them, not two hunbeats ago." He hesitated. "And this might not mean anything, but they were speculating that the Mrachanis were planning to raise some Zhirrzh to Eldership and blame it on them. I don't know why—it doesn't make much sense to me."

Nzz-oonaz's expression was suddenly fully awake. Sliding off his couch, he snagged his jumpsuit and put it on. Gesturing Thrr't-rokik to follow, he left the room and headed down the corridor toward the hangar area.

The corridor was bustling with Zhirrzh and Mrachanis—and hidden Elders—as more of the supplies brought from the *Willing Servant* were shifted around. Nzz-oonaz kept going, not stopping to talk, until they'd reached the *Closed Mouth.* Still silently, he led the way inside and back to the rearmost section of the ship, ending up finally in a small room nestled in among the softly humming engines.

"All right," he said after he'd sealed the door behind him. "The technics believe this room should be impossible for the Mrachanis to monitor. Tell me again what you saw and heard."

"I saw three Human-Conqueror prisoners," Thrr't-rokik said. "They're locked in a small room in a part of the fortress that seems to be otherwise deserted. They were talking among themselves about the possibility that the Mrachanis planned to use them against us, and then kill them."

"Any idea how long they'd been there?"

"Long enough for one of them to start trying to damage the door lock," Thrr't-rokik said. "Not long enough for him to make any progress."

"You're sure the door was locked, then?" Nzz-oonaz asked.

"Actually, I didn't check," Thrr't-rokik admitted. "The mechanism was metal—"

"Go check now," Nzz-oonaz ordered. "And while you're there, see if you can find out whether the Human-Conquerors are armed."

"I obey," Thrr't-rokik said automatically, and flicked back along his anchorline. One of the Human-Conquerors was still sitting on the couch, while the other was still working on the door. The third, though, was now walking slowly along one wall, hands and eyes systematically examining a horizontal crack that ran around the entire room. As unobtrusively as possible, Thrr't-rokik completed the checks Nzz-oonaz had asked for, then flicked back to the ship.

Another Elder was in the room with Nzz-oonaz when he returned, and a second was just leaving. "I've ordered the warriors put on full alert," Nzz-oonaz told Thrr't-rokik. "What did you find?"

"It does appear to be a lock," Thrr't-rokik said. "The Human-Conquerors also don't seem to be armed, though two of them are wearing what seem to be holsters that would accommodate small hand weapons."

"That would fit if they were Mrach prisoners," the Elder rumbled thoughtfully. "Warriors merely playing a role, on the other side, would more likely retain their weapons."

"Unless their warriors behave differently than ours would," Nzz-oonaz said. "No, that's wrong. Pheylan Cavanagh was a warrior, and he was carrying a small hand weapon when he was captured."

"Pheylan Cavanagh?" Thrr't-rokik murmured, half to himself, as the name jogged his memory.

"You have something?" Nzz-oonaz asked.

"It may mean nothing," Thrr't-rokik said slowly, "but I heard one of the Human-Conqueror prisoners call one of the others Cavanagh. Could he be related to Pheylan Cavanagh?"

"It's possible," Nzz-oonaz said, frowning. "Cavanagh would be the family name, and they frequently use those alone as identification." He gestured to the other Elder. "Open a pathway to Thrr-gilag on Dorcas. Maybe he knows more about Pheylan Cavanagh's family."

"I obey," the Elder said, and vanished.

"I didn't mean for you to go to this much trouble," Thrr't-rokik said, feeling more than a little awkward.

"It's no trouble," Nzz-oonaz assured him. "Actually, you've got me curious now, too."

Thrr't-rokik grimaced. "I suppose I should also say that I'm not trying to damage any of the diplomatic work you've been doing here. There may be some completely innocent explanation for why the Mrachanis haven't told you about those prisoners."

"Trust me, Thrr't-rokik," Nzz-oonaz said grimly. "To some of us the Mrachanis are looking less and less innocent all the time."

The Elder flicked back. "I'm sorry, Searcher Nzz-oonaz, but normal communications with the ground-warrior beachhead on Dorcas have been suspended. Only pathways going through specifically designated Elders are being allowed."

"What designated Elders?" Nzz-oonaz demanded. "Who ordered this?"

"I don't know," the Elder said. "But I noticed that both of the allowed Elders carry Dhaa'rr-clan names. And the Elder I talked with hinted the order had come down from the Speaker for Dhaa'rr himself."

Thrr't-rokik looked at Nzz-oonaz, found the other looking back at him. "I don't like this, Thrr't-rokik," the young searcher said quietly. "Not at all."

"Perhaps you should speak to the Overclan Prime," Thrr't-rokik suggested, trying to suppress his own apprehension. "He'll know what's going on."

"Maybe," Nzz-oonaz countered. "The problem is that all our direct communication pathways to Warrior Command and the Overclan Prime are under the accuracy-control monitoring of Dhaa'rr Elders."

"I object to your inferences, Searcher Nzz-oonaz," the other Elder said stiffly. "My communicators are all former warriors themselves, completely professional in the performance of their duties. They would not allow clan politics to interfere."

"I'm sure that under most circumstances that would be true," Nzz-oonaz said. "But I'm beginning to wonder whether the circumstances here are normal anymore. Can you guarantee—really and thoroughly guarantee—that none of the Dhaa'rr Elders aboard the *Closed Mouth* would pass the content of a private conversation to Speaker Cvv-panav? Especially if the Speaker was the target of that conversation?"

The Elder flicked his tongue. "No," he conceded. "I cannot positively guarantee that."

Nzz-oonaz looked at Thrr't-rokik, the frustration in his expression suddenly turned to something else. "Wait a beat. Thrr't-rokik, where's your *fsss*?"

"You mean my cutting?" Thrr't-rokik asked cautiously.

"No, your main *fsss*. Is it anywhere near Unity City?"

"Not really," Thrr't-rokik said. "It's at the Thrr-family shrine near Cliffside Dales, about forty-three hundred thoustrides away."

Nzz-oonaz flicked his tongue. "No more than a couple of tentharcs' flight away, though. This could work. Is there anyone there you can trust? I mean *really* trust."

"Yes," Thrr't-rokik said. "Thrr-tulkoj. He was chief protector for the shrine, and a close personal friend of Thrr-gilag's. I've already trusted him with my family's honor, and he hasn't failed me."

Nzz-oonaz flicked his tongue again. "We'll have to risk it. Go tell him to get to somewhere where he can't be easily overheard. As soon as he's in position, come back so I can talk to him. Have you ever done communicator work before?"

"Not really," Thrr't-rokik said.

"You'll pick it up," Nzz-oonaz assured him. "Get going."

"It's really quite simple," the taller of the two Zhirrzh said, his voice quiet and almost courteous. "We've been authorized by the Overclan Seating to search for evidence of criminal activity here. Until that search has been completed, we're in command on Dorcas. You can either accept that and cooperate, or you can join Commander Thrr-mezaz in detention inside the Human-Conqueror transport."

"Most considerate of them to provide it for us," the second Zhirrzh added. He was over in the corner, contemplating the thick-walled metal safe where Prr't-zevisti's *fsss* cutting had been hidden barely a tentharc ago. "A solid metal aircraft means we can isolate him from the Elders, too."

"Your authorization makes no mention of locking him away," Thrr-gilag argued, trying hard to keep his tail calm and knowing full well he wasn't succeeding.

"Our authorization allows us to do our job any way we see fit," the taller Zhirrzh said, his voice hardening. "We see Commander Thrr-mezaz as a troublemaker, and he'll remain out of communication until we've found what we're looking for."

Not *if* they found it; *when* they found it. They knew about the cutting, all right. "But it's dangerous," Thrr-gilag protested. "He's also isolated from his *fsss* in there. If the Humans launch another attack, he could die."

"That's a danger, all right," the taller Zhirrzh nodded. "Let's hope we find what we're looking for quickly."

An Elder appeared. "We've finished searching the transport," he reported. "They haven't found"—he glanced at Thrr-gilag—"anything unusual."

"As expected," the taller Zhirrzh said equably. "Shift those Elders to a search of the ground beneath the route the transport came in on. They may have thrown it outside when they saw our ship."

The Elder grimaced—highly offended, no doubt, by the suggestion that a *fsss* cutting might have been treated with such horrendous disrespect. "I obey," he growled, and vanished.

"Or are we wasting our time?" the second Zhirrzh suggested, eyeing Thrr-gilag. "Have you hidden it somewhere out of the Elders' range?"

"At the Human-Conqueror stronghold, for instance?" the other put in. "Was that the real reason you went there?"

"I went there because the new prisoner needs a healer," Thrr-gilag said, forcing some firmness into his voice. They were drifting uncomfortably close to the truth here. "He needs treatment, and I need him alive if I'm to complete my studies. You've searched the healer; can't you now let her treat him?"

The taller Zhirrzh shrugged. "I don't see why not," he said. "Communicator?"

"I'll need to go with her," Thrr-gilag added as an Elder appeared. "She'll need a translator."

The two Zhirrzh looked at each other, and the shorter shrugged slightly. "Again, why not?" the taller said. "The two Human-Conqueror prisoners are still together. You may take the healer and her equipment across to them."

Pheylan Cavanagh was sleeping when Thrr-gilag and Melinda Cavanagh arrived, his breathing making unpleasant rasping noises. "Glad you're here, Doc," Sergeant Janovetz said as Melinda Cavanagh set her share of equipment down and opened one of the containers. "I've given him a unit of glavamorphine from his survival pack, but he's not doing too good."

"No, he's not," Melinda Cavanagh agreed, feeling gingerly around the discolored flesh. "But I think I can fix him up."

Casually, Thrr-gilag looked around. Hovering above and behind both Humans, keeping back out of their sight, were a pair of watchful Elders. He looked back at Melinda Cavanagh, found her looking sideways at him, and shook his head back and forth in the Human gesture for no. Her head tilted slightly in understanding, and she turned her attention back to her work.

For now Prr't-zevisti and his *fsss* cutting would have to stay hidden in the box.

"Overclan Prime?"

The Prime started awake, jostling his reader onto the floor beside his couch. The last thing he remembered was settling onto the couch to read more of the warrior reports. . . . "Yes, what is it?" he asked, focusing on the Elder hovering in front of him.

It was the Twentieth, his pale face set in unusually grim lines. "There's a pathway just opened up for you from a protector in the Kee'rr town of Cliffside Dales," he said. "I think you should speak with him."

"Now?" the Prime said, glancing at his armwatch. It wasn't a particularly civilized tentharc in the Kee'rr homeland, either. "What's so important that he has to talk to me personally?"

"I don't know," the Twentieth said. "He won't give his message to anyone but you. But he has one of the private recognition codes you arranged with Searcher Nzz-oonaz."

The Prime frowned. What was Nzz-oonaz doing, calling out of the mission's carefully established Elder pathways? Or was this merely a case of some Elder leaking the recognition code? "All right," he sighed. "I suppose I ought to talk with him. Open the pathway."

The Twentieth nodded and vanished. The Prime picked up the reader, checked how much he had yet to read. It was a depressingly large amount. Worse, even with all the time he'd now lost to sleep, he still didn't feel particularly rested.

The Twentieth returned. " 'I greet you, Overclan Prime,' " he quoted,

" 'and apologize for the lateness of this message. My name is Protector Thrr-tulkoj; Kee'rr. I have been asked by Searcher Nzz-oonaz; Flii'rr, to deliver a message to you. The recognition code he gave me is Mistrand over Kylee.' "

The Prime felt his tongue press against the inside of his mouth, his mind dragging itself fully awake. This wasn't just one of the private recognition codes he'd set up. This was the signal that indicated potentially serious trouble with the rest of the mission. "Understood," he said. "I'm listening."

The Twentieth vanished, reappearing a few beats later. " 'Searcher Nzz-oonaz would like you to meet with me out here as quickly as possible.' "

"Why?"

" 'He doesn't want to explain over an open pathway. I don't even know myself. But he assures me it is very important.' "

The Prime frowned. "What do you think?" he asked the Twentieth.

"I don't know what to think," the other said frankly. "I've had the servers double-check the list of Elders on the *Closed Mouth*, and none of them are from shrines anywhere near Cliffside Dales."

"What about from the *Willing Servant*?" the Prime asked. "It had a large contingent of observer Elders aboard, and they should have reached Mra by now."

"Also checked," the Twentieth replied. "Again, none from that part of Kee'rr territory. This could be a trick of some sort."

"Let's find out," the Prime said. "Send this: does he want me to come alone?"

"Good idea," the Twentieth said approvingly, and vanished. Reaching to his reader, the Prime cleared the warrior reports and pulled up the two Elder lists himself. The Twentieth was right: not a single Elder was from that region. What in the eighteen worlds was Nzz-oonaz doing? And how was he doing it?

The wait this time was longer, as if the protector had had to discuss the question with someone else. But after a hunbeat or so the Twentieth returned. " 'Nzz-oonaz urges you not to come alone,' " he quoted. " 'He recommends you bring warriors you can trust.' "

"Interestingly worded," the Prime commented.

"Yes," the Twentieth agreed. "If it's a trap, at least the trapper is avoiding the obvious."

Another Elder appeared: the Fourteenth. "I've done an independent trace of the pathway, Overclan Prime," he reported. "The origination point is indeed in the Kee'rr village of Cliffside Dales."

"Any idea which Elder he's talking to Nzz-oonaz through?"

"Not yet," the Fourteenth said. "They're still trying to track that down."

The Prime nodded, gesturing to the Twentieth. "Very well, I'll come as soon as I can," he dictated. "Where do I meet you?"

The Twentieth vanished. A half dozen of the previous Primes had gathered in the room now, the Prime noticed as he crossed back to his desk, listening with silent intensity. Activating the desk reader, he called up a map and an aerial photo of the Cliffside Dales area and waited.

He didn't have to wait long. " 'I recommend a group of hills at the eastern edge of the Amt'bri River Valley approximately twenty thous-trides west of Cliffside Dales,' " the Twentieth quoted. " 'There's room for transports to land, as well as the privacy Searcher Nzz-oonaz wishes.' "

"There," the Fourth said, dropping down to the Prime's shoulder and jabbing a tongue at the map. "It's certainly got privacy."

"Yet it's not forested," the Twenty-second added. "That implies no easily concealed ambush waiting for you. And on top of hills you'll have good warning of unwanted arrivals after you land."

"Yes," the Prime murmured, studying the photos. It certainly looked like a reasonable place for a legitimate meeting.

And if it *was* a trap, he was rather interested in seeing how the plotters intended springing it. "I'll be there in two tentharcs," he said. "Will you be alone?"

" 'I certainly intend to be,' " the Twentieth brought back the rather dry answer. " 'If I'm not, you'd better assume something's wrong.' "

"Understood," the Prime said. "Tell Searcher Nzz-oonaz I'll look forward to hearing what he has to say." He gestured to the Twentieth. "Relay that, then close the pathway. Twenty-second, alert Commander Oclan-barjak to prepare five transports and ten sectrenes of his most trustworthy warriors. We'll leave as soon as they're ready."

The two Elders vanished. "I hope you know what you're doing, my son," the Twenty-eighth said quietly, moving up beside the Prime.

"I do," the Prime said firmly, opening the storage drawer of his desk and pulling out the packed travel bag he always kept there. "I trust Nzz-oonaz's judgment. Besides, I'll be well protected."

"Even excellent judgment can be manipulated," the Twenty-eighth reminded him. "And if the Speaker for Dhaa'rr is behind this, the goal may not be an overt attack. It might merely be a ploy to draw you out of Unity City for a few tentharcs."

"I don't know what that would gain anyone," the Prime said. "I'll hardly be out of communication with the Overclan Seating or Warrior Command anywhere along the way."

"It may not have anything to do with you at all," the Fourth said darkly. "At least not directly." He jabbed his tongue meaningfully at the desk's secure drawer.

The drawer containing the box that Speaker Cvv-panav had thrust into his face the previous fullarc. With Prr't-zevisti's *fsss* organ inside.

Cvv-panav himself was supposedly back on Dharanv, but of course that didn't mean anything. If this was his scheme, his agents would already be in place inside the Overclan Complex. "You have a point," he agreed, unlocking the drawer and withdrawing the box. "But I think we can fix that."

"How?" the Seventeenth asked. "Where can you hide it that would be more secure than here?"

"In a place where thousands of Elders would be available to witness its theft," the Prime told him, sliding the box into an empty pouch of his travel bag.

"After also witnessing a direct attack on the Overclan Prime himself," the Fourth said, nodding his approval. "Excellent."

"At least not unreasonable," the Seventeenth said doubtfully. "A clever ploy might still succeed."

"What sort of ploy?" the Fourth scoffed. "The Prime will have some of the Overclan's best warriors with him—"

"Whatever's going on, we'll soon know all about it," the Prime cut them off, his tongue flicking impatiently. Never, he swore to himself, never, never, never would he fall into this infuriating habit of second-guessing the decisions of the Overclan Prime when he himself was raised to Eldership. "Seventeenth, go tell Commander Oclan-barjak I'm on my way to the transport hangar."

He set off down the hallway, still seething, the warriors falling into step around him. And tried not to wonder how many of the former Primes back there had promised themselves exactly the same thing.

The relays cracked, a much louder sound down in the forward hold than it was up on the flight deck. Once again, the *Happenstance* had meshed in.

"Here we go again," Quinn said, his voice muffled as he floated in the zero-gee, his arms and head inside the Corvine's starboard sensor access panel.

"Okay, fire it up," Daschka's voice came over the open intercom to the flight deck. "Let's see if they've gone to ground yet."

"Right," Cho Ming's voice answered.

"A little straighter, please," Quinn said.

"Sorry," Aric apologized, shifting the angle of the diagnostic display he was holding so that Quinn could see it better over his shoulder. They'd meshed in perhaps a dozen times already since leaving the *Trafalgar,* returning to normal space to track the movements of the fleeing Zhirrzh warships. A perfectly straightforward pursuit strategy, apparently straight out of the NorCoord Military Intelligence manual.

Except that in this case Aric was starting to wonder if the technique was going to backfire on them. Every time they meshed in and the fleeing Zhirrzh warships didn't, the pursuers fell a few minutes farther behind the prey. Already the warships were right on the edge of Cho Ming's wake-trail detector; another three or four of these stops and they'd be out of range completely.

"Nope," Cho Ming said. "There they are, still chugging along."

"I see them," Daschka growled. Maybe he was starting to wonder if this was such a good idea, too. "Anyone else out there?"

"Actually, this time there is," Cho Ming told him. "Coming in roughly from the direction of Mra-mig."

"Mrachanis?"

"Hang on," Cho Ming said. "It's a strange reading—give me a second to sort it out."

Carefully, Quinn eased his way out of the access panel, steadying himself with a grip on the edge of the access opening as he looked over toward the intercom. The silence from the flight deck grew a little thicker. . . .

"Got it," Cho Ming said. "It's a group of Mrach transports flying in loose formation. Breaks down to ten Hrenn-class heavy-haulers."

"They on an intercept course with the Zhirrzh?" Daschka asked.

"No," Cho Ming said. "Looks like the vector cuts along their back-trail."

"Are they on an intercept with us?" Quinn called.

"Doesn't look like it," Cho Ming replied. "Though if we keep going . . . hold it."

"What?" Daschka asked.

"They've meshed in," Cho Ming said. "Somewhere about four light-years ahead of us."

"Directly ahead?" Quinn called.

"No," Cho Ming said. "About thirty degrees wide of our vector."

"They may not have anything to do with us or the Zhirrzh, actually," Daschka added. "There's a solar system over there. Could be mining ships."

"Maybe," Cho Ming agreed. "Wait a second, we've got another group just meshing out. Two Hrenn haulers this time, heading away from the same area where the other group meshed in."

"Sounds like a mining operation, all right," Daschka concluded. "Let's get back to the focus at hand. Are the Zhirrzh still holding their original course?"

"Pretty much," Cho Ming said. "They've shifted a few degrees . . . I'll be damned."

"What?" Daschka asked.

"You're going to love this one, Daschka," Cho Ming said, his voice suddenly tight. "We chased ten Zhirrzh ships away from Phormbi, right?"

"Right," Daschka said. "Plus the one that had already left ahead of them."

"Right," Cho Ming said. "Well, of those ten I'm only reading seven now. In the thirty-two minutes since our last wake-trail reading three of them have meshed back in."

"Have they, now," Daschka said softly. "Quinn, you might want to step up here."

Cho Ming had finished his preliminary analysis by the time Quinn and Aric reached the flight deck. "All right," he said, running a spot pointer across a large-scale on one of the displays. "Here's my best-guess scenario. Right after we meshed out the last time, three Zhirrzh ships broke away from the pack and headed along this vector, meshing back in again in the cometary halo of this system over here. The rest continued on, hoping we wouldn't notice they'd lost some numbers."

"And the Mrach haulers are running a supply line?" Quinn asked.

"Or else helping with repairs," Daschka said. "Between the *Trafalgar* and the Yycromae, the Zhirrzh lost a brickload of lasers. Quinn, how fast can you put that Corvine back together?"

"Not fast enough," Quinn said. "Two hours, maybe one."

Daschka made a face. "Damn."

"Not fast enough for what?" Aric asked.

"Not fast enough for us to split up," Daschka growled. "We've got two targets, and only one ship to chase them with. Means we have to flip a coin."

"If we're going to follow the main fleet, we need to mesh out right away," Cho Ming warned. "Otherwise, we're going to lose them."

"I know," Daschka said. "Let me think."

For a minute he stared out at the stars outside the canopy. Then, abruptly, he stirred from his musings and reached for his control board. "Okay, decision made," he said, keying in a course change. "Our best chance of finding the Zhirrzh and Mrachanis doing the morris dance together is where our wounded wolves have gone to ground. So that's where we go."

There was another thunk, and the tunnel illusion, and they were once again meshed out. "Okay," Daschka said. "ETA at the rendezvous is about an hour twenty. You two get back down and do whatever you have to to get that Corvine buttoned up. Cho Ming, you'd better go help them."

"I have a question first," Aric said. "How did the Zhirrzh know when we had meshed out and therefore wouldn't be able to spot their course change?"

Daschka shrugged. "Seems pretty obvious. The Mrachanis have wake-trail detectors; the Zhirrzh have instantaneous communication. QED."

"In other words, you're saying that the Mrachanis over at that system have to have a Zhirrzh ship with them," Aric said.

"Or else the Zhirrzh have given them their communication technique," Cho Ming said. "What's your point?"

"Two points," Aric said. "One, that this is enough evidence to implicate the Mrachanis as collaborators without having to go take a look ourselves. We can head back right now and blow the whistle."

Daschka shook his head. "Inference hardly counts as proof."

"Even under martial law?"

"Even then."

Aric grimaced. "All right, then, point number two. If the Mrachanis and Zhirrzh *are* collaborating, then they're onto us. They've seen us here, and they'll see us coming toward them. And they'll be ready for us."

"But they won't know exactly where we're going to mesh in," Cho Ming pointed out. "Not accurately enough for an ambush."

"We don't know that," Aric said. "The Zhirrzh managed a pretty impressive pinpoint mesh-in when Quinn and I were out searching for Pheylan. We don't know everything they can do."

"We're NorCoord Intelligence, Cavanagh," Daschka reminded him. "It's our job to occasionally stick our heads in the lion's mouth."

"It's my job, too," Quinn added quietly. "I'm sorry, Mr. Cavanagh, but I agree with them."

Aric sighed. If he somehow managed to live through all of this, he promised himself, he was never, ever going to leave his nice, safe Cav-Tronics desk again. "It's not Cavanagh when we're flying, Maestro," he reminded Quinn morosely. "It's El Dorado, remember? Come on, let's go get that Corvine buttoned up."

"The Mrach transport craft have met with the five warships of the *Trillsnake* force at Rendezvous One," the Elder reported. "The connections have been successfully completed on two of them; the other three are not yet finished. The Mrachanis estimate two more tentharcs to completion."

Cvv-panav nodded, making another note on his reader. "What about the others?"

"The *Compelling* is nearly to its rendezvous point," another of the group of Elders circling around him said, moving forward. "The ship commander has no knowledge of whether the Mrachanis are there yet."

"They are," a third Elder confirmed. "The *Dhaa'devastator* is there already and is being tethered to its Mrach transport craft."

"Good," Cvv-panav said, making another note. Many cyclics ago he could remember cursing the ancestors for moving the Dhaa'rr homeland away from Oaccanv and the true center of Zhirrzh power. Now, finally, he understood the wisdom of that decision. Only on Dharanv, surrounded exclusively by Dhaa'rr Elders, could such a conversation as this be truly private.

One by one the Elders communicating with the other Dhaa'rr warships made their reports. "That leaves only the warships from the Phormbi attack," he said at last. "What about them?"

"All three have arrived safely at Rendezvous Five," an Elder told him. "Two groups of the transport craft have arrived; the third group is on its way."

"I see," Cvv-panav said, making a final note. That rendezvous point had been set up more or less at the last beat, so it made sense that the Mrachanis were running a little behind.

"But there's a potential complication," the Elder went on. "The Mrachanis have detected a Human-Conqueror spacecraft following the Phormbi warships."

Cvv-panav felt his midlight pupils narrow. "What sort of spacecraft?"

"They claim it is not a warship, but only a small cargo craft," the Elder said.

"Following our warships?" Cvv-panav snorted. "Not likely. Small or not, it's some kind of Human-Conqueror warship."

"The ship commanders agree," the Elder said. "The Mrachanis have stated that eight transport craft will be adequate to pull the *Tireless,* so the ship commanders have ordered the other two craft sent away in hopes of persuading the Human-Conqueror warrior that the rendezvous is merely a Mrach meeting point or mining center."

"A reasonable plan," Cvv-panav said. "Go see if it worked."

"I obey." The Elder vanished.

Cvv-panav glowered down at his reader. The Human-Conquerors were welcome to follow the rest of the Phormbi warships all the way back to Oaccanv if they felt like it. But he did *not* want them poking around his attack forces. Particularly not the warships at Rendezvous Five. He'd gone to considerable trouble to mask what he was doing with those ships from Supreme Commander Prm-jevev; he had no interest in having to dodge Human-Conquerors, too.

The Elder returned. "I'm sorry, Speaker Cvv-panav," he said. "The Mrachanis say the Human-Conqueror craft has altered course toward Rendezvous Five."

With an effort Cvv-panav refrained from cursing. Words weren't going to help now. "Do they say how long it will be until the craft arrives?"

"They estimate less than a tentharc," the Elder said. "Longer if the Human-Conqueror leaves the tunnel-line to use his detector."

That all-but-magic method of detecting spacecraft at the distances between stars. Some fullarc very soon he would have to pry that secret away from the Mrachanis. "Then the solution is obvious," Cvv-panav said. "The work must be completed and the warships moved before the Human-Conqueror arrives."

The Elder stared at him. "In less than a tentharc? But—"

"I don't want arguments," Cvv-panav cut him off. "Nor do I want excuses. We are the Dhaa'rr; and it *will* be done."

The Elder's tongue flicked. "Understood, Speaker Cvv-panav."

He vanished. "And if they fail?" another of the Elders asked quietly.

Cvv-panav focused on him. A very old Elder, this one, who'd been a warrior during the Third Eldership War five hundred cyclics ago. The war where the erosion of Dhaa'rr sovereignty had first begun, surrendered to the idealists of the embryonic Overclan Seating. "They won't fail," he told the Elder. "Because they know that with this victory over the Human-Conquerors the resurgence of the Dhaa'rr clan will begin."

The Elder flicked his tongue. "Perhaps," he said. "We shall see."

26

The meal the Mrachanis had brought in had long since been eaten and the dishes taken away by a silent Mrach server; and now there was nothing much for Cavanagh to do except lie on his cot, his head propped up on one arm, and listen to the silence. And wonder when and how the Mrachanis were going to kill them.

"The walls are getting cooler," Bronski commented. "Must be getting late."

Cavanagh opened his eyes and looked across to the opposite corner of the cell. Similarly stretched out on his cot, Bronski was watching Kolchin work on the door lock, his expression a study in frustration at their forced idleness. "I think you're right," he told the brigadier.

"It's about eleven-thirty," Kolchin said without looking up.

Bronski glared at him from under bushy eyebrows. "How in hell can you know *that*?"

Kolchin shrugged. "It's a sort of time sense. I've always had it."

The brigadier grunted and fell silent. Cavanagh half closed his eyes, sympathizing with the other's irritation but wishing he would accept the inevitable and stop biting heads off at the slightest provocation. It had been Bronski himself, after all, who'd located the pair of elongated wand-lens monitor cameras the Mrachanis had stuck inside opposite corners of the ribbon-candle groove running around the room. The associated microphones had been easy enough to knock out—undoubtedly to the great annoyance of the Mrachanis monitoring them—but the lenses themselves had been made of sturdier stuff, and the simplest way to block their view of Kolchin's work was for Cavanagh and Bronski to move their cots into those corners and stretch out in front of the lenses.

Which they'd now been doing for a good two hours. *They also serve,*

Cavanagh misquoted tiredly to himself, *who only lie and doze.* A movement at the corner of his eye caught his attention, and he opened his eyes all the way—

And caught his breath. It was back. Moving slowly across the ceiling, visible mainly where it passed in front of darker sections of stone, the apparition was back.

"Bronski?" he murmured. "Ceiling."

The brigadier flashed him a look, his simmering annoyance vanishing. Shifting the arm propping up his head, he casually turned his head a few degrees upward.

The apparition didn't seem to notice the movement. Its full attention was apparently on Kolchin, watching as the bodyguard probed his strip of collar stiffener delicately inside the small crack he'd opened in the lock's cover plate.

"Interesting," Bronski murmured. "I take it back, Cavanagh. You're not crazy."

"Thank you," Cavanagh said. It was still drifting across the ceiling, still watching Kolchin. "Some Mrach trick, you think?"

"Not a chance," Bronski said. "Not inside a solid stone room. They couldn't even retrofit those spy-eyes and mikes worth a damn—they sure haven't hidden a holo projector in here. Besides, look at it. Looks just like a Zhirrzh."

The apparition jerked as if it had touched a hot wire, twisted impossibly, and vanished.

"Whoa—nice trick," Bronski said, looking around. "I guess it understands English, too."

Cavanagh frowned at him. "What do you mean? What understands English?"

"Our friend there," Bronski said, nodding toward the spot where the apparition had vanished. "You never got to read your son Pheylan's report on his captivity, but he claimed he saw something just like that when he was trying to escape. Of course, he was poisoned by his interrogator right afterward, so everyone's been putting it down to a fever hallucination—"

"Just a minute," Cavanagh interrupted, half sitting up before he remembered his camera-blocking duties. "You never said anything about him being poisoned."

"I didn't want to worry you," Bronski said. "Anyway, it wasn't all that important. The interrogator used his tongue poison to knock Pheylan out during the escape attempt."

"And you didn't consider that important?" Cavanagh demanded. "It could have killed him."

"Yes, I imagine that's what the Zhirrzh had in mind," Bronski said patiently. "But the Copperheads got there first and were able to neutralize the stuff. He was completely recovered before they even got to Edo."

"You're sure of that?"

"The doctors double-checked just to make sure," Bronski assured him. "The point is that he reported having seen one of those ghost things. Come to think of it, your other son, Aric, reported hearing voices screaming near a pyramid thing they found on an otherwise deserted planet."

"Did he see anything?" Kolchin asked.

"No, he just heard voices," Bronski said thoughtfully. "But right about that same time two Zhirrzh warships apparently changed course from several light-years away and came roaring to the rescue."

Cavanagh's mind was still back on Pheylan's poisoning. "So what does it mean?"

"I don't know," Bronski said, still sounding thoughtful. "We don't know if the voices and the ghosts are even connected. But if they are, maybe we've stumbled on a clue to the Zhirrzh long-range communication system." He shrugged. "Or maybe it's nothing at all. Maybe the Zhirrzh just like ghost stories so much they made them real."

"That's certainly a pleasant thought," Cavanagh said, looking around. The phantom was still gone.

Or rather, it still wasn't visible. But, then, it hadn't been all that visible before; and according to Bronski, Aric had heard voices without seeing anything. Could the ghost still be there listening?

He looked around again, his skin on the back of his neck tingling uncomfortably. The thought of a culture with real ghosts was a distinctly unsettling one.

Yet if Bronski's guess was right, they might be sitting on the secret of the Zhirrzh interstellar communication here. If they could somehow draw it out . . . "Hello?" he called softly. "Can you hear me? My name is Lord Stewart Cavanagh. I'd like to talk to you."

"You're wasting your time," Bronski said. "They're the Conquerors, remember? Mass killers. They're not interested in talking to their victims, just killing them. Like that interrogator who tried to kill your son Pheylan Cavanagh."

Cavanagh frowned at him. Bronski wasn't simply lashing out in frustration—there was a distinctly calculating expression on his face as he looked around. Was he trying to goad the ghost into reappearing?

And then, not half a meter away, it did.

Cavanagh jerked back, bumping the back of his head against the stone wall. His lips moved, forming words, but the breath needed to make actual sounds was frozen in his lungs as all the dark fears of humanity's past flooded in on him. The spectral, alien face stared at him for what seemed forever—

"You father of Pheylan Cavanagh?"

Cavanagh blinked. The words had been English. Mangled, distorted, but still English.

"Go on," Bronski prompted softly. "Answer him."

Cavanagh flicked a glance over—no, *through*—the face in front of him. Bronski was still lying on his cot, but his face and body were tight and alert. To Cavanagh's left Kolchin had paused in his work, his eyes set in the icy expression of a bodyguard facing an unknown but potentially dangerous situation.

He focused again on the transparent face. "Yes," he said, the words finally making it out. "I'm Lord Stewart Cavanagh. Pheylan Cavanagh is my son."

"What's your name?" Bronski put in.

The ghost ignored him. "Thrr-gilag not try kill Pheylan Cavanagh," he said. "Try only stop him leave."

Cavanagh looked at Bronski. "Thrr-gilag was the chief Zhirrzh interrogator," the brigadier said. "He's the one who poisoned Pheylan."

"Not try kill him," the ghost insisted.

"All right," Cavanagh said soothingly. "If you say so."

"You tell me now," the ghost said. "Why Pheylan Cavanagh not raise Thrr-gilag to Eldership?"

Cavanagh looked at Bronski. "Eldership?"

"The Elders are a segment of Zhirrzh society," Bronski told him. "Leaders or something, maybe—Pheylan had the impression they were important. That's all we know."

Had Pheylan's escape ruined this Thrr-gilag's chances for promotion? "Pheylan did what he had to do," he said carefully to the ghost. "Surely if Thrr-gilag had been a prisoner, he would also have tried to escape."

"No," the ghost said, an insubstantial tongue darting out as if for emphasis. "I not speak of escape. I speak of raise to Eldership. Why Pheylan Cavanagh not do that?"

"I don't understand," Cavanagh said. "What did Pheylan do?"

"Not what he do," the ghost said. "What he not do. He not do this." The transparent hands lifted up, closed around his own transparent neck. "Not do this."

Cavanagh shook his head helplessly. Charades had never been his strong point, even within his own family. Trying to figure out the gestures and body language of a totally alien being was going to be well-nigh impossible.

"He's miming strangulation," Kolchin said suddenly. "Or else neck breaking."

"You're right," Bronski agreed. "And Pheylan mentioned that—said he had the interrogator in a neck lock when he hauled him into the Mrach ship. He's asking why Pheylan didn't kill him."

"That can't be," Cavanagh argued. "He just said that—"

And abruptly it hit like a faceful of ice water. Eldership—death—the ghost hovering in front of him—

He took a careful breath. "You're an Elder," he said.

The ghost's head twitched in a not-quite nod. "Yes."

A dense silence seemed to settle into the room. Cavanagh stared at the face before him. "They've conquered death," he heard his voice say. "They've really, truly conquered death."

"Why Pheylan Cavanagh not raise Thrr-gilag to Eldership?"

Cavanagh swallowed hard, trying to gather his wits together. He was asking why Pheylan hadn't killed the interrogator. "I don't know for sure," he said. "Probably because there was no need to. Humans don't kill unless it's absolutely necessary."

"You raise other Zhirrzh to Eldership."

"This war wasn't our idea," Bronski put in. "It was the Zhirrzh who attacked first."

"Not true," the ghost insisted. "Elders say Human-Conquerors attack first."

"Then the Elders are wrong," Bronski said. "We didn't attack first. I know."

The ghost spat something and vanished. Cavanagh waited, but he didn't come back. "Nice job," he said to the brigadier.

"He'll be back," Bronski said, looking around. "We've just shaken his belief in government truthfulness, and he's gone away to think it over. But he'll be back."

Cavanagh eyed him suspiciously. "You seem awfully sure of yourself. What do you know that we don't?"

"I don't actually know anything," Bronski said. He rubbed a sleeve across his forehead, wiping away sweat that had collected despite the coolness of the cell. "I'm following up on the impressions Pheylan had of his captors. He was pretty sure he'd gotten Thrr-gilag thinking about what the Zhirrzh leaders had told them about the *Jutland* attack. He thought there was a good chance he would look into the matter, maybe spread some of his doubts around to the other Zhirrzh." He gestured toward the ceiling. "This Elder seems to know him. I thought it would be worth trying to give him a little push."

"Perhaps," Cavanagh said. "Not that he has any reason to believe three Human-Conquerors."

From the door came a soft click. "Got it," Kolchin said, withdrawing his probe from the lock mechanism. Getting to his feet, he got a set of fingernails between the door and jamb and eased it open a crack—

And was abruptly thrown backward, spinning around toward Cavanagh as the door was slammed violently open. Reflexively, Cavanagh threw up his arms, catching Kolchin as he fell with a crash into him and the cot.

And a Bhurt charged into the cell.

Bronski was off his own cot and into a combat stance even before Kolchin had come to a complete stop. Another two seconds and Kolchin was back on balance as well, poised to receive the attack.

But the attack didn't come. The big alien skidded to a stop a meter inside the cell, and for a long moment stood there glowering at each of the humans in turn. "I am ordered not to hurt you," he rumbled at last, backing into the doorway. "Not yet."

He got a grip on the handle and pulled the door closed behind him. It sealed with a solid-sounding thunk.

"You all right?" Cavanagh asked as Kolchin slowly rose out of his combat stance.

"Just feeling stupid," Kolchin said, an edge of bitterness in his voice. "I would have sworn there weren't any guards out there."

"Bhurtala can be amazingly quiet when they want to be," Bronski said. "Don't let it worry you."

"Yeah," Kolchin said. "Right."

Cavanagh patted his shoulder reassuringly. "Zhirrzh Elder?" he called. "Are you still here?"

There was no answer. "Still chewing it over, I guess," Bronski said, resettling himself on his cot. "Until he decides to come back, we might as well get some rest. At least now we know how to open the door. That's something."

"For all the good that does us with a Bhurt outside," Cavanagh pointed out.

Bronski smiled grimly. "Don't worry. We'll think of something."

With an audible exhaling of breath, Melinda Cavanagh straightened and pushed back a few strands of cranial hair that had dropped down across her face. "Finished," she said.

"That's all it takes?" Thrr-gilag asked, frowning at the skintight immobilization cast she had put on Pheylan Cavanagh's left leg. It looked far more fragile than even the light-ceramic casts the Zhirrzh used for broken bones.

"That's it," she assured him, trying to work a finger under one of the magnet rings on her new obedience suit to rub her side. Mnov-korthe had insisted on the obedience suit; pointedly, he'd given the triggers to two of his warriors, not to Thrr-gilag or Klnn-dawan-a. "The membrane cast immobilizes the leg and also stimulates bone repair."

Amazing technology, indeed. "He'll be all right, then?"

"He should be fine," she said.

"I'm glad," Thrr-gilag said, looking down into that sleeping alien face. He *was* glad, he realized suddenly, and not just because it meant he wouldn't lose a potential research subject. Perhaps now he would finally be able to learn why Pheylan Cavanagh hadn't raised him to Eldership when he'd had the chance back on Study World 12.

To his left the door opened, and he turned to see Second Commander Klnn-vavgi step into the room, flanked by two warriors. "Thrr-gilag," he nodded in greeting.

"Commander Klnn-vavgi," Thrr-gilag said stiffly. "I suppose congratulations are in order on your promotion."

"Thank you," Klnn-vavgi said coolly. "I'm sorry you don't approve. Fortunately, your approval isn't necessary. How's the prisoner?"

"I thought you were Thrr-mezaz's friend," Thrr-gilag bit out. "Thrr-mezaz thought so, too. I guess we were both wrong."

Klnn-vavgi didn't even wince. "This has nothing to do with friendship, Searcher Thrr-gilag," he said. "This has to do with my duty as a warrior. Mnov-korthe has clear authorization from the Overclan Seating. It's my duty to help him carry it out."

"To carry what out?" Thrr-gilag demanded. "He won't even tell me what he's looking for."

"He won't tell me, either," Klnn-vavgi said, crossing the room to gaze briefly into Pheylan Cavanagh's sleeping face. "Only some of the Elders. Though he seems to believe you and Commander Thrr-mezaz already know. How's the prisoner doing?"

Thrr-gilag flicked his tongue. "I'm told he'll recover."

"Excellent," Klnn-vavgi said. "I presume you and Klnn-dawan-a will want to begin your studies on him immediately."

"We'll begin as soon as he's well enough," Thrr-gilag growled. "He *has* had a serious injury, you know."

"So much the better—you can get baseline data for a Human-Conqueror under injury stress. That could be very useful, couldn't it?"

Thrr-gilag glanced at Melinda Cavanagh and Sergeant Janovetz, who of course had no idea what the conversation was about. "Yes. Perhaps."

"Then it's settled," Klnn-vavgi said, also looking at the other two Humans. "You'd best start collecting your equipment together. I've set up a private examination room for you across the landing field. Klnn-dawan-a's already there getting the preparations started. Srgent-janovetz will have to stay here, but I presume you'll be wanting the Human-Conqueror healer to come help you."

Thrr-gilag frowned. That had been a decidedly odd comment. "I suppose we could use her."

"I'm sure you can," Klnn-vavgi said, wandering over to the table where Melinda Cavanagh had laid out her tools and medicines. "Especially with her specialized healer equipment."

Thrr-gilag felt his tongue pressing painfully at the inside of his mouth. Not half a stride away from Klnn-vavgi was the metal box where Prr't-zevisti's *fsss* cutting was hidden. . . . "You're right, of course," he said.

"Good," Klnn-vavgi said, stepping around behind the table and turning to face Thrr-gilag again. "It should be a lot calmer over there, actually. Mnov-korthe and his brother are going to be turning this encampment inside out until they find what they're looking for." He paused, resting one hand on top of the metal box, and locked eyes with Thrr-gilag. "I gather that it has something to do with that missing Elder, Prr't-zevisti."

"Ah," Thrr-gilag murmured.

"They've already spoken at length to Commander Thrr-mezaz," Klnn-vavgi continued, casually rubbing the smooth metal surface with his fingertips. "And I know they're eager to talk to you, too. But I've convinced them that your Human-Conqueror studies must take priority. I hope you and Klnn-dawan-a can obtain some useful results."

"We'll try," Thrr-gilag said, his earlier resentment melting away. Despite their efforts to keep Klnn-vavgi out of this mess, the second commander had clearly figured out enough of it on his own. But instead of turning them in to the Dhaa'rr agents, he had connived to buy them some time.

And in the process had put his own neck on the line along with theirs. "We'll try our best."

"Good," Klnn-vavgi said, his eyes flicking upward to the Elders hovering nearly invisibly overhead. "I'll detail some warriors to carry the prisoner and escort you to the examination room. Good luck."

He left the room. "Is there trouble?" Melinda Cavanagh asked.

"No," Thrr-gilag told her, conscious of the fact that all the Elders up there knew some of the Human language. "We need to move Pheylan Cavanagh to another place for study. A more private place, I'm told. You'll be coming with me."

"And Sergeant Janovetz?"

"He'll stay here."

"I see," Melinda Cavanagh said. "How private will this place be?"

"Reasonably," Thrr-gilag said, hoping she would read between the lines. "There will be warriors outside, of course."

"Yes," she said, stepping over to the table and selecting two of the tubes of medicine. Crossing to Sergeant Janovetz, she handed him the tubes. "Before I forget again, Sergeant, I brought you some of your special rash ointment."

"Thanks, Doc," he said, glancing at them briefly and dropping them casually beside him on his cot. "Use as needed, right?"

Melinda glanced at her watch. "You should probably wait a couple of hours," she said. "And just use a small amount. I know that kind of rash can get distracting, but the prescribed treatment doesn't involve extermination."

The tufts of hair over his eyes lifted a little higher. "None?"

"None," Melinda Cavanagh said firmly. "There are new indications that the rash might actually be benign."

"Benign?" Sergeant Janovetz said, his voice sounding odd. "You're joking."

"Not at all," she assured him.

His shoulders went up and down again. "Well, you're the doctor. Prescription understood."

She nodded and turned to Thrr-gilag. "All right," she said, picking up the box with Prr't-zevisti's cutting in it. "Let's go."

"There," Commander Oclan-barjak said, gesturing out the transport's canopy. "Straight ahead, on top of that hill."

A beat later the dark figure made his location obvious, flashing a light briefly toward the incoming transports. "Is he alone?" the Prime asked.

"Appears to be," Oclan-barjak grunted. "We'll find out soon enough. All right, pilot—signal the others, then put us down."

They were on the ground four hunbeats later. Two hunbeats after that the warriors had been deployed and the shadowy figure brought into the subdued semicircle of light spilling out from the transport's open hatchway. Just inside the semicircle one of the warriors handed him a *kavra* fruit, waiting until he'd sliced it before escorting him the rest of the way. As he approached the light, the Prime could now see that there was an Elder accompanying him.

"I'm the Overclan Prime," the Prime identified himself. "You're Protector Thrr-tulkoj?"

"Yes," the Zhirrzh said, gesturing to the Elder hovering beside him. "This is Thrr't-rokik; Kee'rr. He's the one who brought me the message from Searcher Nzz-oonaz on Mra."

"Thrr't-rokik," the Prime nodded greeting. It was, he suspected, going to be very interesting to hear how this pathway had come to be. But first things first. "Has Nzz-oonaz been informed I'm here?"

"Yes," Thrr't-rokik said. "He said to give you the recognition code 'Pllaa'rr beside the Softly Raging Sea.' "

Another of their private recognition codes. "Very well. Message: this is the Overclan Prime. What is this matter you wish to discuss?"

Thrr't-rokik vanished. The Prime waited, glancing around the hilltops and the warriors in ready position. If it was a trap, the attackers were taking their time about springing it. Or else had been frightened away by the size of the Overclan warrior contingent.

Thrr't-rokik returned. " 'I have had disturbing news, Overclan Prime, which I felt could not be safely trusted to my usual pathways. Were you aware that normal communications with the Zhirrzh ground forces on Dorcas have been suspended?' "

The Prime felt his lowlight pupils contract. "No," he said. "For what reason?"

" 'I've been unable to find out,' " the answer came. " 'But I've heard rumors that indicate the Dhaa'rr clan may be behind it.' "

The Prime grimaced. Yes, he could smell Speaker Cvv-panav's saliva all over this one. Whatever was happening on Dorcas was clearly the most recent thrust in his campaign to catch Thrr-gilag with his illegal cutting and then to link it back to the Prime.

Only this time the Speaker had gone directly to the source. If Thrr-gilag hadn't managed to get rid of the cutting, they were indeed going to be in trouble. "You said normal communications had been cut off," he said to Thrr't-rokik. "What exactly did you mean by that?"

"An Elder aboard the *Closed Mouth* tried to open a pathway," Thrr't-rokik said. "He came back and said—"

"He meant for you to take the question to Nzz-oonaz," Oclan-barjak cut him off gruffly. "Not answer it yourself."

"I'm sorry," Thrr't-rokik said, with no apology in face or voice that the Prime could detect. "I was there when it happened. I thought answering it myself would save time."

"I'm sure it would," the Prime said. "But the form must be followed. Take the question to Nzz-oonaz."

"I obey," Thrr't-rokik said, and vanished.

"Insolent illegit," Oclan-barjak muttered. "Overclan Prime, I have a listing of Overclan-certified Elders in the area. If you'd like, I'll summon one to open a pathway back to Unity City. Then you can dispense with this amateur."

The Prime flicked his tongue in a negative. "Let's see what Nzz-oonaz has to say first."

Thrr't-rokik returned. " 'One of my Elders tried to open a pathway to Thrr-gilag on Dorcas,' " he said. " 'He returned with the information that the only pathways that were being allowed were through Dhaa'rr Elders.' "

"On whose orders?" the Prime asked.

Thrr't-rokik vanished; returned. " 'He had the impression it was the Speaker for Dhaa'rr.' "

Oclan-barjak rumbled something under his breath. "In case any of us hadn't already guessed."

"Still, more overt than his usual style," the Prime said. "He must be very sure of himself. All right, Searcher, I'll deal with it. Was there anything else?"

" 'Yes,' " the answer came a few beats later. " 'Thrr't-rokik has discovered the Mrachanis have taken three Human-Conqueror prisoners and are holding them in the fortress four thoustrides from us. He has also overheard speculation that the Mrachanis may be planning to attack us and blame the Human-Conquerors.' "

The Prime frowned. "Is this true, Thrr't-rokik?"

"To the best of my understanding, Overclan Prime, yes," Thrr't-rokik said. "My knowledge of the Human-Conqueror language is admittedly limited, but I believe I understood their speech correctly."

"Whose speech, the prisoners?"

Thrr't-rokik nodded. "Yes."

"Probably lying," Oclan-barjak grunted. "You can't trust something the enemy says."

"But why would they lie?" Thrr't-rokik asked reasonably. "They didn't know I was there listening. Why would they lie in private conversation with each other?"

"An interesting question," the Prime agreed. "Ask Searcher Nzz-oonaz if he believes them."

"I obey," Thrr't-rokik said, and vanished.

He was back half a hunbeat later. " 'I don't know, Overclan Prime,' " he quoted. " 'I don't trust the Human-Conquerors, of course. But I don't trust the Mrachanis anymore, either. I had a conversation with Thrr-gilag before the pathways were closed down about the Mrach ambassadors who died on Oaccanv.' "

"Yes, I read your report on that," the Prime nodded. Along with Commander Thrr-mezaz's report about the explosives attack on Dorcas, too. "All right, here's what I want you to do. On some pretext, without causing alarm, I want you to quietly bring your contact group back into the

Closed Mouth. That goes for your support technics, too. The only ones who are to be outside the ship are the warriors on guard duty, and they're to stay close. You have all that, Thrr't-rokik?"

"Yes, Overclan Prime." Thrr't-rokik vanished.

"If it comes to a real fight, the *Closed Mouth* is going to be in trouble," Oclan-barjak said quietly. "Most of the ship's weaponry was removed before they left Oaccanv."

"Yes, I know," the Prime said grimly, running through in his mind the Elders' description of the hangar area where the *Closed Mouth* had been hidden. Scooped out of the base of a solid stone hill, it wasn't going to be an easy place to make a quick exit from.

Especially since he seemed to remember that the Mrachanis had positioned the ship in such a way that its lasers couldn't be brought to bear on the hangar door. Odd that no one had noticed that before now.

Thrr't-rokik returned. " 'Understood, Overclan Prime. I'll alert the others immediately. Will you be returning to Unity City now?' "

The Prime glanced around the dark hills, curves of darkness against the blazing stars overhead. There was certainly no reason for him to stay here once this pathway was closed. A potential Mrach attack had nothing political about it, which meant Nzz-oonaz's usual pathways should be adequate for the situation. Besides which, the pathways he had available back at the Overclan Complex would be better for getting to the bottom of whatever was happening on Dorcas.

And yet, there was something about this situation. . . .

He flicked his tongue impatiently. Vague feelings were not something to base policy decisions on. Certainly not vague feelings generated by the shifting winds and shadows on top of a hill at latearc. "Yes," he said. "Let me know via the usual pathways when everyone's aboard the *Closed Mouth.*"

" 'I obey, Overclan Prime,' " the reply came a few beats later.

"Good luck." The Prime nodded. "All right, Thrr't-rokik. Go ahead and close the pathway."

"I obey." Thrr't-rokik hesitated. "Overclan Prime, what about the three Human-Conquerors?"

"What about them?"

"What if the Mrachanis decide to kill them before launching their attack on the *Closed Mouth*?"

"Again, what about it?"

"Well, shouldn't we do something to stop it?" Thrr't-rokik asked.

"They're our enemies, Thrr't-rokik," Oclan-barjak reminded him. "The more of them that die, the better it is for us."

"I'm not talking about death in warfare, Commander," Thrr't-rokik said stubbornly. "This would be flat-out murder."

"Of alien creatures who started a war—"

The Prime cut him off with a gesture. "I understand your concern, Thrr't-rokik," he said. "As a matter of fact, I do indeed sympathize. But I don't see what we can do to help. Not without some of Nzz-oonaz's warriors risking premature Eldership."

Thrr't-rokik's tongue flicked out. "What if they didn't start the war?" he asked. "Would that make a difference?"

The Prime frowned. "We've been through all this before, Thrr't-rokik. Who have you been talking to?"

An unreadable expression flicked across the translucent face. "My son, Thrr-gilag, has always wondered about that," he said. "He said Pheylan Cavanagh seemed so sure."

"The issue has been laid to rest," the Prime said, putting some ice in his voice. "The Human-Conquerors attacked first; and unless you want to challenge the honesty of the Elders who were at that first battle, I don't want to hear anything more about it. Understood?"

"Yes," Thrr't-rokik muttered.

"Good," the Prime said. "Then I thank you for your assistance. Go back to Nzz-oonaz and have him keep me informed of his situation."

"I obey."

The Elder vanished. "Thank you for your assistance, too, Protector," the Prime said, looking at Thrr-tulkoj. "I trust you understand that what has transpired here is to be kept totally confidential."

"Of course," Thrr-tulkoj said. "If you'd like, I can keep myself available in case you need to talk to Searcher Nzz-oonaz through Thrr't-rokik again."

The Prime eyed him, the other's name belatedly clicking. Thrr-tulkoj: the Kee'rr protector who'd been on duty the latearc when Speaker Cvv-panav's agents stole Thrr-pifix-a's *fsss* organ from the Thrr-family shrine. He probably had a good deal of time on his hands right now. "Yes, that's probably a good idea," he said. "Go back to where you were in Cliffside Dales. If I need you or Thrr't-rokik, I'll contact you there."

"I obey," Thrr-tulkoj said. With a nod he passed through the ring of warriors and headed down the hill toward his transport.

Oclan-barjak threw the Prime a lopsided smile. "You're just an old soft-tongue, Overclan Prime," he said quietly. "You know that, don't you?"

"Everyone needs to feel needed, Commander," the Prime said tiredly. "Come on, let's go home."

Two other Elders were just flicking away as Thrr't-rokik returned to the *Closed Mouth.* "There you are," Nzz-oonaz said. "Did the Overclan Prime have anything else?"

"Just that you were to keep him informed," Thrr't-rokik said.

Another Elder appeared. "Svv-selic and Gll-borgiv have been alerted," he reported.

"You warned them not to move too quickly?"

"Yes," the Elder confirmed. "Don't worry, I gave them some tips on how to do quiet evacuations—I handled such maneuvers myself a few times during the Etsiji occupation. The Mrachanis will never notice anything amiss."

Nzz-oonaz grunted. "I hope not. Take some other Elders and go monitor the Mrachanis' movements. Thrr't-rokik, you go back and keep an eye on the Human-Conquerors."

"I obey," Thrr't-rokik said. He moved along his anchorline, and a beat later he was back in the Human-Conquerors' cell.

Nothing had changed since his last time there except that all three Human-Conquerors were stretched out on their cots now. Their eyes were closed; apparently, they were asleep.

He drifted briefly outside the room. Standing across the hallway from the door, positioned where he could see anyone attempting to leave, was an amazingly wide-bodied alien of a sort Thrr't-rokik had never seen or heard of. Obviously, a guard.

He drifted back into the cell, disturbing uncertainties tugging at him. The Overclan Prime had been so certain that the Human-Conquerors had started this war. But the Human-Conqueror on the cot over there had been equally certain that they hadn't. As had Pheylan Cavanagh, according to his son Thrr-gilag.

Someone was lying, or else someone was wrong. But who?

"Hello."

Thrr't-rokik started at the soft voice, dropping reflexively toward the grayworld. One of the Human-Conquerors, the one called Cavanagh, had awakened, his eyes searching the area Thrr't-rokik had just vanished from. "I won't hurt you," the alien added, his voice even softer here in the grayworld. "I just want to talk."

Thrr't-rokik hesitated. But why not? "About what?" he asked, mouthing the alien words with difficulty as he rose again to the edge of the lightworld.

"There you are," the Human-Conqueror said. "My name is Lord-stewart Cavanagh. Pheylan Cavanagh is my son."

"I know," Thrr't-rokik said. "You said that already."

"Yes," the Human-Conqueror said. "Do you have a name?"

Again, why not? "I am Thrr't-rokik; Kee'rr. Thrr-gilag is my son."

The alien's eyes seemed to grow larger for a beat. "Thrr-gilag's father. I'm honored to meet you."

"Why did you come to this place?" Thrr't-rokik asked.

"We don't trust the Mrachanis," the Human-Conqueror said. "We came here to find out what they were doing."

"Why don't you trust them?"

"Because we now know they have lied to us many times," the alien said. "May I ask a question?"

"Yes," Thrr't-rokik said cautiously.

"What are you?" the Human-Conqueror asked. "What I mean is, what are the Elders? Are you the (something) of the dead?"

Thrr't-rokik eyed him, thinking furiously. What should he say? Everything about the Elders, even their very existence, was supposed to be kept a black secret—he'd lost track of how many times the language instructors and warrior commanders on the *Willing Servant* had pounded that into them.

But on the other side, he'd already slipped up by giving away his existence to Lord-stewart Cavanagh and his companions. And besides, these particular three would soon be dead. "We are Zhirrzh whose physical forms have failed," he said, hoping he was getting enough of the words right. For some reason, understanding the Human-Conqueror language was considerably easier than speaking it. "We're anchored to our *fsss* organs, which are stored at the family shrines on Oaccanv."

"So you are dead," the Human-Conqueror said, his voice sounding strange. "And yet you aren't. (Something.) How long can you live this way?"

"Many cyclics," Thrr't-rokik said. "A *fsss* organ wears out only slowly."

For a few beats the Human-Conqueror was silent. Thrr't-rokik moved closer, noticed a liquid trickling from the corners of his eyes. "What is wrong?" he demanded.

The alien moved his head back and forth to the side. "I was just thinking of my wife, Sara. Pheylan's mother. She died five (something) ago. I would give anything to be able to see and talk with her again. Even just this way, as an Elder."

Thrr't-rokik gazed at him, emotions he'd striven to suppress stirring within him. Lord-stewart Cavanagh had lost his wife to death . . . just as Thrr't-rokik might yet lose his own wife. "My wife is named Thrr-pifix-a," he said. "She does not wish to become an Elder."

Lord-stewart Cavanagh rubbed the liquid away with his hands. "Why not?"

"She fears the loss of her physical form," Thrr't-rokik said. "She calls Eldership not a real life."

The Human-Conqueror looked at his hands. "Yes, I can understand that," he said. "Actually, I think Sara would have felt the same way. But I know that if I could have her back, I would be selfish enough to do so."

Selfish. Thrr't-rokik gazed at the Human-Conqueror, an unpleasant feeling gnawing at his tongue. He hadn't really thought about it that way before. Or else hadn't wanted to think that way. Was he being selfish to want to hold on to Thrr-pifix-a?

Lord-stewart Cavanagh inhaled noisily, wiping at his eyes again. "Do you speak with your own father and mother often?" he asked.

"There is little for an Elder to do except speak," Thrr't-rokik said. "To speak, and to watch the world near us. We can only go small distances from our *fsss* organs."

"Yet you're here," Lord-stewart Cavanagh pointed out. "How is that possible?"

More forbidden territory, no doubt. Again, it probably didn't matter. "A small piece can be taken from the *fsss* organ," Thrr't-rokik told him. "An Elder can then move between the two parts."

"I see," the other said. "That's how you're able to send messages over great distances."

"Yes," Thrr't-rokik said. "I would ask that you not speak of these things. It is not permitted to tell anyone."

The muscles in Lord-stewart Cavanagh's neck moved. "Don't worry about it," he said. "We'll probably be dead soon. As may some of your people. You'd better warn them that the Mrachanis may soon attack them."

"They are warned," Thrr't-rokik said, rather surprised that the Human-Conqueror would even bother to say anything about that. Thrr-gilag's doubts about the presumed levels of Human-Conqueror aggression came floating back through his mind— "They are preparing for attack."

"Good." For a few beats Lord-stewart Cavanagh was silent. "I appreciate your telling me this," he said at last. "Actually, though, I have to agree with your leaders who want to keep it hidden. There are many Humans who would resent your ability to live on after physical death, even as Elders. We probably would eventually have been at war no matter what."

He propped his head up on one arm. "May I ask another question?"

"Yes," Thrr't-rokik said.

"Tell me about your world. Not anything that your leaders wouldn't want me to know; just what your world is like. Its plants and animals, its hills and streams. Tell me what you liked to do when you were alive."

When you were alive. Thrr't-rokik listened to the words echoing through his mind, an odd sadness seeping into him. Because he *was* still alive . . . and yet, at the same time, he wasn't.

The Human-Conqueror was right. Thrr-pifix-a was right. Could it have been the rest of the Zhirrzh who'd been wrong all these cyclics?

"My world is very beautiful," he told Lord-stewart Cavanagh, the alien words coming out with difficulty. "The home where I grew up was in a wide valley. . . ."

"Stand by," Daschka's voice came tautly in Aric's ear. "Almost there."

"Acknowledged," Quinn said from the Corvine's pilot seat in front of Aric. "We're ready."

Aric took a careful breath, held it a few seconds, then slowly let it out. This was it. If Cho Ming's estimate was right, they were about to mesh in at the spot where those three Conqueror warships had disappeared.

Unfortunately, that was all they had here: an estimate. They might arrive a hundred thousand kilometers away, or they might land right on top of them.

"Here we go," Daschka said. "Meshing in . . . now."

The relays cracked; and in front of the Corvine the forward cargo hatch dropped open to the stars. Without missing a beat Quinn fired the fighter's thrusters, and five seconds later they were outside. "In position," he called. "Situation?"

"No contact yet," Cho Ming's voice said. "Stand by."

An invisible weight leaned onto Aric's chest and right side, the stars outside the canopy spinning dizzily as Quinn threw the Corvine into an accelerating spiral around the *Happenstance*. "You see anything, Maestro?" Aric asked, not sure he really wanted to hear the answer.

"Some comets," Quinn replied. "Nothing that looks or reads like a Zhirrzh warship."

"Or even a Mrach heavy-hauler," Cho Ming's voice said. "Looks like they've flown the coop."

"Interesting," Quinn said as the Corvine eased out of its spiral into a more leisurely circle. "Where could they have gone?"

"To ground, obviously," Daschka said. "Also obvious how they did it. The Mrachanis picked up our wake-trail, figured out when we were going to mesh in here, and made sure they were already meshed in at that time."

"Hence, no wake-trail." Aric nodded understanding. "Question is, How do we find them again?"

"I don't know," Daschka growled. "Actually, I don't think we can."

"Why not?" Aric asked. "All we need to do is stay here until they get tired of waiting and mesh out again."

"*If* they get tired of waiting," Cho Ming pointed out. "They might not."

"Actually, it's worse than that," Quinn said. "All they really need to do is drop a static bomb to cover their wake and mesh out."

"Exactly," Daschka agreed. "So let's go ahead and beat them to the punch. You two get back here; Cho Ming, get our static bomb ready to drop."

"What's this supposed to accomplish?" Aric asked as Quinn turned the Corvine back toward the *Happenstance*.

"For starters, it may make them sweat a little," Daschka said. "Maybe make them wonder if they got away quite as cleanly as they thought, or if we're instead bearing down on them with a couple of Nova-class carriers coming in from the other side. Meanwhile, it'll give us cover while we head back to the *Trafalgar* and raise the alarm."

"We're going back to Phormbi, then?" Aric asked.

"Unless you have somewhere else you'd rather be."

Aric gazed out at the stars. "Actually, as long as we're this close already, I was thinking we might want to go to Mra."

There was a brief silence. "Any particular reason why?"

"That message you got at Phormbi said my father and Bronski were headed there," Aric reminded him. "Now that we know that the Mrachanis and Zhirrzh are working together, I'm thinking they might be in trouble."

"Bronski can generally take care of himself," Daschka said. But his tone was thoughtful. "Besides, alerting Montgomery about these missing Zhirrzh warships ought to be our priority here."

"On the other hand, Montgomery's going to be out of action for a while," Cho Ming put in. "Mra gets diplomatic skitters, too—we can send a report just as easily from there as we could from Phormbi."

"Point," Daschka admitted. "I wish we'd followed the other Zhirrzh warships . . . but that's over and done with. All right, what the hell, let's go to Mra."

"I just hope we'll be able to find them," Aric commented as Quinn sent the Corvine curving back. "A planet's a pretty big place to lose a couple of people in."

"Oh, we'll find them," Cho Ming promised. "Trust me."

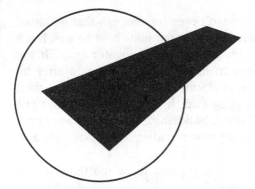

27

It was a long way back up to consciousness, Pheylan thought dimly as he drifted slowly through a tunnel filled with cotton-dense fog and randomly variable gravity. But finally he made it and opened his eyes.

And even through the fog the trip was suddenly worth all the effort. "Melinda?" he croaked.

"I'm right here, Pheylan," she said, stepping over to where he lay and smiling down at him.

A smile that seemed curiously tight . . . and then, suddenly, it all came rushing back. The frantic trip through Dorcas's atmosphere, Max's incredibly competent landing, his own incredibly stupid clumsiness—

And his capture by the enemy.

He lowered his eyes from his sister's face and looked at her body. Her outfit was all too familiar: the same type of obedience suit he'd been issued during his previous captivity, optical sensors and electromagnetic arm and leg rings and all.

Carefully, he turned his head to the side. A couple of meters to his left two Zhirrzh were looking back at him. "Right," he said, closing his eyes.

"That's not very sociable," Melinda chided him lightly. "Aren't you even going to say hello to an old friend?"

"I am pleased to see you recovering, Pheylan Cavanagh," a Zhirrzh voice said.

Pheylan opened his eyes, lifting his head from the table he was lying on and frowning again at the two Zhirrzh. The alien on the left . . .

No. It couldn't be. "Thrr-gilag?"

The Zhirrzh flicked his tongue. "I am pleased you remember."

"You'd be a little hard to forget," Pheylan muttered, laying his head back down and looking up at Melinda. Terrific. It wasn't bad enough he'd been recaptured by the enemy; it wasn't even bad enough that his sister, whom he'd come here hoping to help, was in the same boat he was. But it was humiliating to wind up with the same old interrogator again. It was like the time he was hauled back to his summer-camp cabin after his abortive attempt to go over the wall. "So who's your friend?" he asked.

"This is Klnn-dawan-a," Thrr-gilag said, his tongue darting out and curving around to point to the Zhirrzh beside him. "She and I were once bond-engaged. The Dhaa'rr clan has now repudiated that bond-engagement."

"I'm sorry," Pheylan said, since that seemed to be the thing to say. "Was it because I got away from you?"

"For that and for other reasons."

Pheylan grimaced. "Well, you've got me again. That ought to get you back in their good graces."

"In the meantime, we've got work to do," Melinda said briskly, stepping over to a table against the wall. There was some kind of electronic-equipment box sitting there, its face turned toward the wall. "Thrr-gilag and Klnn-dawan-a are here to study you," she continued, picking up a multitool and setting to work on one of the fasteners on the box's back. "Alien physiology must be an interesting field. Reminds me of the way I used to practice medical work on my Carrie Mantha doll. You remember?"

"Uh . . . sure," Pheylan said cautiously, the hairs on the back of his neck beginning to tingle. The main thing he remembered about that doll was Melinda driving him and Aric crazy with it until they'd hidden it in the back of the kitchen revamperator. Unfortunately, their mother had come along and turned the appliance on—

In the *back* of the revamperator?

He threw a quick glance at the two Zhirrzh, finally catching on. Something was hidden in that box Melinda was fiddling with. Was it his job to distract the aliens while she got it out? "I don't feel so good," he muttered, wincing for their benefit.

"Where do you feel ill?" Thrr-gilag asked, stepping to his side.

"I'm sure you'll feel better soon," Melinda said, coming up beside the alien and laying a reassuring hand on Pheylan's left leg.

The touch felt odd. Pheylan looked down, noticing only then the tattered flight suit and the membrane cast immobilizing the leg. Almost as good a restraint as the Zhirrzh obedience suit Melinda was wearing, at least as far as escape was concerned. Whatever she was up to, he hoped it wouldn't call for acrobatics on his part. "You think so, huh?" he asked, looking back up at her.

"I'm positive," she said firmly, catching his eye and shaking her head minutely. "We're all playing the Flying Muskers here."

Pheylan frowned, more confused now than ever. The Flying Muskers had been the private club the three of them had formed with their next-door neighbor Lizza Easley when Pheylan was seven, modeled on their enthusiastic youthful reading of *The Three Musketeers*. All for one and one for all; and two of the four people present were enemy Zhirrzh, and what the hell was going on?

"Just be patient, Pheylan," Melinda soothed him. "Patience is a virtue."

Pheylan looked at the two Zhirrzh. Clearly, they'd heard what Melinda had said. Just as clearly, she hadn't been trying to hide it from them. What the hell *was* going on? "Sure," he murmured back. "Patience is a virtue."

It has been 7.43 hours since Commander Pheylan Cavanagh and I were captured by the Zhirrzh, 4.94 hours since I was brought here to my current location in the former Commonwealth colony, now clearly under enemy control. Four Zhirrzh have been with me since my arrival, while three others have come and gone at irregular intervals. They have been studying me and other pieces of equipment brought here from the fueler.

I also infer from their posture and the movements of their eyes when they speak that there are conduits of communication I cannot detect. I compute a probability of 0.77 that there are three of these conduits, and a probability of 0.97 that they are mobile.

I regret the loss of my peripherals, which occurred when Commander Cavanagh detached my core from the fueler. With active sensors at my disposal I estimate a probability of 0.60 that I would be able to detect the unknown conduits. Again from the movements and reactions of those in the room, I calculate a probability of 0.86 that communication is in both directions, with messages being brought to the Zhirrzh as well as taken from them.

The loss of my libraries has also reduced my language-analysis capabilities to 0.14 of normal, with the result that it has required the entire time of my captivity to collect sufficient data on the language being spoken by my captors. However, I now estimate a probability of 0.80 that I have enough information to initiate communication with them. One of the Zhirrzh has spoken approximately 32 percent of the words I have heard. I choose his tonal pattern for maximum auditory acceptance, varying the waveform structure so as not to duplicate his voice exactly, and attempt to speak.

{Can you understand me?}

All six of the Zhirrzh currently in the room stop what they are doing or saying and look at me. I file the facial and postural reactions, tentatively labeling them as surprise. One of the Zhirrzh moves 0.67 meter closer to me; I note the center pupil of each eye has narrowed to approximately half its previous width.

{Who are you?}

{My name is Max. Will you tell me where Commander Cavanagh has been taken?}

The Zhirrzh takes another step toward me. {Where are you?}

I find the question odd, given that his eyes appear to be directly focused on me. {I am on the table directly in front of you.}

{Inside the metal container?}

I spend 0.03 second pondering the intent of his question. I am of course not contained in the metal container itself, but in the Porterdale lattice within the container. Still, I estimate a probability of 0.70 that the question seeks only general spatial information. {Yes.}

One of the other Zhirrzh steps to the first Zhirrzh's left side. {Are you a Human-Conqueror?}

{No.}

A third Zhirrzh extends his tongue for 0.15 second. {It's a trick. It has to be.}

The first Zhirrzh extends his tongue in similar fashion for 0.23 second. {Are you a *kabrsif*?}

I examine the unknown word carefully for 0.54 second, comparing it to the other words in my vocabulary list and attempting to interpolate its meaning. But I am unable to do so. {I do not know the meaning of that term.}

{Are you the *kassmi'fss* of a Human-Conqueror?}

{I do not know the meaning of that term. I have traveled far with Commander Pheylan Cavanagh, and would like to know where he has been taken.}

The first Zhirrzh steps 0.27 meter closer to me. {How long have you known Pheylan Cavanagh?}

I spend 0.04 second reviewing my core database, confirm that information on Lord Cavanagh and his family was among my primary programming. {I have known of his existence for three years. I met him in person approximately twenty-one days ago, during the mission to rescue him.}

{You were present at his rescue?}

{Yes.}

There is a general stirring among the Zhirrzh, and a low-level buzz of conversation too faint and mixed for me to decipher. {What did you do during the rescue?}

{I guided the rescue team to his position. I also performed a primary analysis of the poison in his body as he was being brought from the surface to the fueler.}

{During that flight? While he was in the small fighter warcraft?} {Yes.}

The Zhirrzh's posture changes, and I compute a probability of 0.87 that he is listening to one of the unknown communication conduits. {Yes, I know. But the *kabrsifli* stated there were only Human-Conquerors aboard the fighter spacecraft—}

He stops, listening again, and after 4.79 seconds he bobs his head in a short nod. {Yes. You'd better alert Second Commander Klnn-vavgi.}

His center pupils narrow another 30 percent. {Tell him that Thrr-gilag may have been right. That the Human-Conquerors may indeed have *kabrsifli.*}

"Small probe," Klnn-dawan-a said, holding out her hand.

"Small probe," Thrr-gilag repeated, choosing the instrument and handing it to her. Pheylan Cavanagh was looking warily at the probe, but Thrr-gilag's attention wasn't really on him. Three Elders were still keeping watch on them from various corners of the room. Thrr-gilag had no idea which Elders they were, or whose side they were on, and until they left, he didn't dare allow Melinda Cavanagh to release Prr't-zevisti's cutting from that metal box. She had indicated that a diversion would be coming soon, but what that diversion might be she hadn't said.

"Thrr-gilag," an agitated voice whispered at his ear.

Reflexively, Thrr-gilag stepped back behind Klnn-dawan-a, giving the Elder a little more visual cover from the two Humans. "Yes?"

"There's news from the technic examination room," the Elder said, the words tumbling over themselves in his hurry to get them out. "The Human-Conquerors may have Elders after all—they think they have one in there now!"

Thrr-gilag felt his tail twitch violently. Could that dubious hunch of his actually have been right? "What?"

"Yes—Human-Conqueror Elders," the Elder repeated. "Do you need us to keep watching here?"

Was this Melinda Cavanagh's diversion? Even if it wasn't, it was the perfect opening. "Not at all," he assured the Elder. "The Human is immobilized, and there are two warriors outside. Go on, and take the other Elders with you."

"Thank you," the Elder said. "I'll let you know what they find out as soon as I can."

"There's no hurry," Thrr-gilag said. "I'd rather you stayed there and learned everything you can."

The Elder flicked his tongue and vanished. Slowly, carefully, Thrr-gilag looked around the room. All three Elders were gone.

"What is it?" Klnn-dawan-a asked.

"Our chance," Thrr-gilag told her, motioning Melinda Cavanagh toward the metal box. "Quickly," he said in the Human language.

"I heard something about Human-Conqueror Elders," Klnn-dawan-a said as Melinda Cavanagh set to work on the last two fasteners.

"The technics think they've found one," he told her, looking around the room again. Still clear. "I have no idea what's going on, but this is our chance to sneak Prr't-zevisti's cutting out."

"What's happened?" Melinda Cavanagh asked.

"Something about the technics discovering a Human Elder," Thrr-gilag told her. "But there are no such things, are there?"

She shook her head. "Not unless you believe in ghosts."

"What do Elders have to do with ghosts?" Pheylan Cavanagh asked.

"They're the Zhirrzh version of the afterlife," his sister told him. "I'm told you saw one once." She finished the last fastener and pulled the metal plate off—

And with a rush like smoke escaping from a bubble, Prr't-zevisti appeared.

There was a sharp inhalation from Pheylan Cavanagh. "You've heard everything?" Thrr-gilag asked Prr't-zevisti as Melinda Cavanagh set to work digging the sampler out from where she'd wedged it.

"I have," Prr't-zevisti rumbled. "And I will have strong words for the Overclan Seating concerning the Speaker for Dhaa'rr."

"Only if you can get those words to someone who'll pass them on," Klnn-dawan-a reminded him tartly. "You've heard the situation— Speaker Cvv-panav's agents have the whole encampment legally under their command. Are there any Elders here you can trust to take a message back to Oaccanv without asking permission first?"

"There are several who have nothing but contempt for this kind of clan politics," he assured her. "As soon as Melinda Cavanagh has freed my cutting from the confines of this box, I'll go find them."

"And try not to let anyone else see you," Thrr-gilag warned. "If word gets back to Mnov-korthe before anyone back home knows about you, we could still lose it all."

With a final tug Melinda Cavanagh's hand emerged from the box with the sampler—

And suddenly Prr't-zevisti's face was infused with the most amazing expression of pure joy that Thrr-gilag had ever seen. "Thrr-gilag—my fsss—"

And without another word he was gone.

" 'All is quiet here, Overclan Prime,' " the Elder quoted. " 'There have been no attempts by anyone to enter your private chambers.' "

"Thank you," the Prime said. After that hilltop conversation with Thrr-tulkoj and Thrr't-rokik he'd decided that that possibility was reasonably remote. Still, it never paid to underestimate the subtlety of one's enemies. "Keep alert." He nodded to the Elder. "You may close the pathway."

"I obey, Overclan Prime." The Elder vanished.

The Prime adjusted his position on his couch, gazing out the transport window at the dark landscape rolling by beneath them and feeling like a contact juggler trying to handle five crystal orbs at once. The situation on Dorcas had some serious political implications; but the question of possible Mrach duplicity had a far greater potential for widespread disaster. As soon as he got back to Unity City and secure Elder pathways, he would have to contact Warrior Command and let them know what was happening on Mra.

After that he would have to get hold of Speaker Cvv-panav on Dharanv. Let him know about the Mrachanis and hint to the Speaker that he knew what the other was up to on Dorcas. Perhaps the time was right to strike another deal.

An Elder flicked into view across the transport's darkened cabin. Yet another bored and nosy Elder from the shrines below, no doubt, checking out the group of aircraft flying by so late. The Prime opened his mouth to suggest that the Elder leave—

And to his surprise the Elder's initial expression of relief and joy turned suddenly into terror. "What in—?" he gasped, looking frantically around him. "Where—how—?"

"Can I help you?" the Prime asked.

The Elder darted over to him, his eyes clinging to the Prime as if to the last lifeline of a rescue ship. "A Zhirrzh," he said, already starting to sound calmer. "I thought I was—" He broke off, flicking his tongue. "Please—where am I?"

"You're aboard an official transport of the Overclan Seating," the Prime told him, frowning at his face. It wasn't anyone he recognized. "I'm the Overclan Prime. Who are you?"

Another jolt of emotion passed across the Elder's face. "The Overclan Prime?"

And then, abruptly, he straightened up into full warrior posture. "Overclan Prime, I am Prr't-zevisti; Dhaa'rr," he said formally. "I have

recently been released from captivity among the Humans on the world
called Dorcas.

"And I have a vitally urgent report to make to you."

"Sara died soon after that," Lord-stewart Cavanagh said, those drops
of liquid running from the corners of his eyes again. "For a long time
after that I wasn't interested in doing much of anything."

"I understand," Thrr't-rokik said, bittersweet memories of his own
drifting across his mind. Only half a cyclic since he'd been raised to
Eldership, but already it sometimes felt as if this were the only life he'd
ever lived. "I felt much the same after I was raised to Eldership. I stayed
at the shrine by my *fsss* and did little else."

"That's not the same at all," Lord-stewart Cavanagh said, moving his
head back and forth. "You speak as a Human might who had lost a hand
or a leg. You were still there, but simply no longer had a body. Your wife
and children could still see and talk to you."

"If they so chose," Thrr't-rokik said quietly. "Thrr-gilag was across the
stars at his studies when I was raised to Eldership and could not come to
be with me." He hesitated, the pain edging through him again. "My wife,
Thrr-pifix-a, did not wish to see me this way at all. She moved away from
our home, too far away for me to reach her."

"I'm sorry," the other said. "Some Humans handle shock better than
others. I imagine it's the same for Zhirrzh."

"Yes," Thrr't-rokik said. "But it is not only that. For her—"

He broke off as a new voice swept suddenly through his mind. "Thrr't-
rokik?"

It was the voice of one of the protectors at the Thrr-family shrine, the
sound being transmitted directly to him through his *fsss*. "I have to go,
Lord-stewart Cavanagh," he said. "I will return."

He flicked back to Oaccanv and the shrine. It was latearc there, with
the stars twinkling faintly down from the sky. "I'm here," he said, remembering just in time to switch back to the Zhirrzh language.

"Protector Thrr-tulkoj wants to speak with you," the protector said.
"He said he'd be waiting where you last met."

"I understand," Thrr't-rokik said, frowning. Trouble? "Thank you."

He flicked along his anchorline to the hills west of Cliffside Dales—

Thrr-tulkoj was indeed waiting on the hill for him. So, to his surprise,
was the Overclan Prime and an unidentified Elder. "I'm here," Thrr't-
rokik said. "Is there trouble?"

"There is disaster," the Prime said bluntly. "You said you had listened
to those Human-Conqueror prisoners on Mra. Can you talk to them as
well?"

"I believe I can," Thrr't-rokik said cautiously. Did the Prime know he'd violated the ban on communications with the Humans?

"Good," the Prime said. "I need you to ask them a question. A vitally important question."

"So," Bronski said quietly from across the room. "You two having a nice chat?"

Cavanagh looked over at him, maintaining his mental count. Thrr't-rokik had been gone for nearly two minutes now. "What?"

"You and Thrr't-rokik," Bronski said. "You've been getting on together like a house on fire."

Cavanagh cocked an eyebrow. "I thought you were asleep."

Bronski shrugged. "Light sleeping is a habit you pick up in the commandos. Right, Kolchin?"

"Right," Kolchin's fully awake voice came from the other cot. "What do you think, sir?"

"About Thrr't-rokik?" Cavanagh shrugged. "My gut feeling is that he's sincere, that this isn't some sort of trick. Though I presume Bronski thinks differently."

"Not necessarily," Bronski said, his voice thoughtful. "We're seeing evidence that the Mrachanis are masters of this sort of verbal maneuvering; but, then, what else have they got? They can't fight, so they have to win with words and chicanery. The Zhirrzh, on the other hand, have one hell of a war machine. They don't need to use psychological trickery."

"Though subtlety and hardware aren't necessarily incompatible," Kolchin pointed out. "A lot of aggressor regimes have used both."

And then, suddenly, Thrr't-rokik was back. "Lord-stewart Cavanagh, I have an urgent question from the Overclan Prime," he said, his voice sounding oddly strained. "He wishes me to ask you if Human spacecraft communicate with below-light energy."

Cavanagh blinked. "With what?"

"With below-light energy," Thrr't-rokik repeated. "Wait."

He vanished again. "Any idea what below-light energy is?" Cavanagh asked the others.

"Infrared?" Bronski asked doubtfully. "Some of our short-range comm lasers use that."

"Or does he mean radio?" Kolchin suggested. "Radio signals have a lower frequency than light waves."

Thrr't-rokik reappeared. "It is called *radio*," he said. "Is this below-light energy?"

"I suppose you could call it that, yes," Cavanagh agreed. "We do use radio for some communications. Who is this Overclan Prime?"

"He is the leader of the Overclan Seating," Thrr't-rokik said, a strange expression on his translucent face. "Lord-stewart Cavanagh, this war is a mistake."

Cavanagh frowned. "What do you mean, a mistake?"

"A wrong happening," Thrr't-rokik said. "Your radio is what we call Elderdeath weapons."

"What do Elderdeath weapons do?" Bronski asked.

"They affect *fsss* organs," Thrr't-rokik said, turning to face him. "They cause great pain to Elders and children. Less effect on warriors, but still some. They are terrible and hated weapons."

"Oh, hell," Bronski murmured.

"What?" Cavanagh demanded. "Bronski, what?"

"Commander Cavanagh's report," Bronski said, his face carved from stone. "He said the Zhirrzh kept insisting that the *Jutland* fired first."

The back of Cavanagh's neck began to tingle. "Are you saying it *did*?"

"Yes, if what he's saying is true," Bronski said. "The *Jutland*'s first-contact package was transmitted by radio."

There was a long moment of silence. A hard, brittle silence. "Oh, my God," Cavanagh said. "What do we do?"

"I must return to the Overclan Prime," Thrr't-rokik said. "Tell him confirmation."

He vanished. "Bronski?" Cavanagh asked.

Bronski took a deep breath. "We can't just take their word for this. But it's certainly possible."

Thrr't-rokik reappeared. "The Overclan Prime says war must stop. How can we do this?"

"Not so fast," Bronski said, gazing at the Elder. "That first battle might have been a mistake; but after that you came down very hard against us. I want to know why."

"I will ask," Thrr't-rokik said, and vanished.

"Because excuses or not, they've still been acting like conquerors since day one," Bronski pointed out to the others. "This whole radio/Elderdeath thing could just be a ploy to buy them some time."

Thrr't-rokik returned. "The Overclan Prime says our attack was designed to protect us from you. He learned about weapon called CIRCE and wanted to stop your putting it together."

Cavanagh looked across the room at Bronski, feeling sick. CIRCE, the hoax of the millennium, the threat that NorCoord had used to maintain political supremacy over the rest of the Commonwealth nations.

And now the Zhirrzh had bought into the hoax, too. With disastrous results.

"Not a word, Cavanagh," Bronski warned sharply. "Thrr't-rokik, ask the Overclan Prime if he'd be interested in stopping their aggression against us if I could promise CIRCE wouldn't be used against the Zhirrzh."

"I obey."

He vanished. "Bronski, we have to tell him," Cavanagh said.

"No, we don't," Bronski growled. "And we're not going to. It's a military secret."

"A military secret?" Cavanagh echoed. "What in blazes does being a military secret have to do with anything?"

"For starters, the simple fact that we only have his word for any of this," Bronski shot back. "For all we know, fear of CIRCE's the only thing holding them back from leveling every world in the Commonwealth."

"Do you really believe that?" Cavanagh demanded.

"Personally?" Bronski said. "Probably not. But that kind of policy decision isn't my job. The diplomats can handle that one after we get a cease-fire arranged."

"Which is going to be a bit difficult to do from here," Cavanagh pointed out.

"Right," Bronski agreed. "Which gives us the perfect chance to see how sincere the Zhirrzh really are."

Thrr't-rokik was back before Cavanagh could ask what he meant. "The Overclan Prime agrees," he said. "How can we stop the war?"

"We need to get in contact with Peacekeeper Command," Bronski said. "But we obviously can't do that from here. You're going to have to send some of the soldiers from that ship of yours and free us. If you can get us back to our ship, we can do the rest."

Thrr't-rokik gazed at him. "You can promise that?" he asked.

"I can," Bronski said firmly. "Lord Cavanagh is an important man. He can get the war stopped while we figure this out."

"I will tell the Overclan Prime," Thrr't-rokik said. "He will decide."

He vanished again. "What now?" Cavanagh asked.

Bronski shrugged. "We wait."

Commander Oclan-barjak flicked his tongue in a negative. "No," he said firmly. "If you want my advice, Overclan Prime, I say no."

The Prime grimaced. "Thrr't-rokik? Your opinion?"

"I don't know, Overclan Prime," the Elder said. "I believe I would trust Lord-stewart Cavanagh. But I don't really know this Bronski."

The Prime eyed him. "But you *do* know Lord-stewart Cavanagh?"

A flicker of startled guilt shimmered across Thrr't-rokik's face before he could hide it. But it was enough. "What I meant—"

"What you meant is that you've been talking to him," the Prime interrupted.

"You arrogant fool," Oclan-barjak growled, glaring at Thrr't-rokik. "Warrior Command has instituted a strict ban on communication with the Human-Conquerors—"

"That's not important anymore," the Prime cut him off. "Thrr't-rokik, you said Bronski said Lord-stewart Cavanagh was important. Is he?"

"He was once," Thrr't-rokik said. "He was a member of the Humans' version of the Overclan Seating. But he left a short time before his wife died."

"But he probably still has contacts with other Human-Conqueror leaders," the Prime nodded. "That may be all we need."

Oclan-barjak flicked his tongue. "Overclan Prime, I strongly suggest you reconsider. Thrr't-rokik's illegal conversations aside, we know virtually nothing about this alien."

"We have no choice, Commander," the Prime said flatly. "We have exactly two direct contacts with Human-Conquerors right now: Lord-stewart Cavanagh, and his son and daughter."

Thrr't-rokik jolted. "His son and daughter?"

"Yes," the Prime said, gesturing Prr't-zevisti forward. "That's right, you don't know. This is Prr't-zevisti; Dhaa'rr."

"Yes, I remember the name," Thrr't-rokik murmured. "Rumor has it that the Human-Conquerors on Dorcas destroyed you."

"I was merely their unintentional guest," Prr't-zevisti said. "With the aid of Melinda Cavanagh and a visiting Zhirrzh searcher, I was able to escape."

Thrr't-rokik leaned closer. "A visiting searcher? Do you know his name?"

"It's your son, Thrr-gilag," the Prime confirmed. "I sent him there to do some studies for me. Go tell Lord-stewart Cavanagh we have an agreement. Then go to the *Closed Mouth* and tell Searcher Nzz-oonaz that he's to send as many warriors as it takes to get the three Human-Conquerors out."

"I obey," Thrr't-rokik said, and vanished.

Oclan-barjak flicked his tongue in a negative. "I hope you know what you're doing, Overclan Prime," he said. "If Speaker Cvv-panav had even a taste of this, he'd have you staked out for the savagefish by midarc."

"Speaker Cvv-panav is too busy playing politics on Dorcas to bother right now," the Prime said grimly. Which was true enough; but what Oclan-barjak probably didn't see was the potentially dangerous connection that now existed between the situation on Dorcas and that on Mra. Lord-stewart Cavanagh's son and daughter were in the middle of Cvv-panav's scheme . . . and if anything happened to them, their father might not be nearly so willing to help arrange a truce.

And then, abruptly, Thrr't-rokik was back, a look of fear and consternation on his face. "There is trouble!" he blurted. "The Human-Conquerors are attacking!"

"What?" Oclan-barjak barked. "Attacking who?"

"The *Closed Mouth*," Thrr't-rokik said. "And Nzz-oonaz says they are using the weapon called CIRCE!"

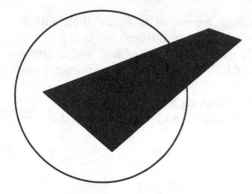

28

"Please," Valloittaja begged, his voice echoing from across the empty hangar to the half-open hatchway. "You must send warriors to help us, Searcher Nzz-oonaz. Otherwise none of us will survive this attack."

Commander Sps-kudah flicked his tongue impatiently. "Searcher, we can't simply sit here in safety and let our allies be destroyed," he snapped. "Whatever this CIRCE thing is he's talking about, it must be something terrible to get them so worked up."

"Your warriors will remain with us here in the *Closed Mouth,* Commander," Nzz-oonaz said, trying to keep his own tail and his resolve steady. The pleading was wrenching at him, too, but he still suspected this was nothing more than the Mrachanis' response to his bringing all of the Zhirrzh into the ship. A trick to lure them outside again; and he wasn't going to fall for it.

But if it wasn't a trick, and if the Human-Conquerors were really about to use CIRCE on them . . .

An Elder appeared. "We've completed our search of the rooms and corridors around the hangar," he reported. "There are no signs of Mrach warriors or obvious attack preparations."

"There—you see?" Sps-kudah said. "Now can we slash this misdirected paranoia and get our warriors outside and in defensive positions?"

"Two aircraft approaching, Commander," another Elder reported tightly. "Flying low and fast from the west toward the fortress."

Another Elder flicked in. Nzz-oonaz glanced at him; it was Thrr't-rokik. "Searcher Nzz-oonaz, I have a message from the Overclan Prime—"

"Not now," Nzz-oonaz snapped. "Can't you hear the alarms? The Human-Conquerors are attacking. Maybe even with the CIRCE weapon."

Thrr't-rokik gaped. "The Human-Conquerors are attacking?"

"Elder, what about those aircraft?" Nzz-oonaz called, turning away from him.

"Still incoming," the Elder said.

"Has Warrior Command been alerted?" Nzz-oonaz called. "Who's talking to Warrior Command?"

"I have a pathway to them," another Elder called back. "They're requesting more information on the situation."

Nzz-oonaz slashed his tongue in frustration. By the time the Elders finished their briefing, it might well be too late.

Or rather, it was already too late. "Aircraft still incoming," an Elder snapped. "Five beats away."

"Seal that hatchway!" Nzz-oonaz snapped. "All Zhirrzh, prepare for attack." With good luck maybe the hull would protect them. Silently, he counted the beats down to zero—

Nothing happened.

Nzz-oonaz continued his count, looking around in bewilderment. Everyone in the control room, physicals and Elders alike, seemed fine. "Elders, check the ship," he ordered.

The Elders vanished. "Perhaps that was just a surveillance check," Commander Sps-kudah suggested darkly. "They may be coming back to use the weapon on us."

"Or maybe they already have," Nzz-oonaz said, his tail spinning hard with delayed reaction. "Maybe our hull and the cliffs above us were able to block its effect."

An Elder appeared. "No one has been hurt, Searcher Nzz-oonaz," he reported. "There is also no obvious damage to the *Closed Mouth*."

"Go check on those aircraft," Sps-kudah ordered. "See if they're coming back."

"I obey."

"One way or another, Searcher, we need to move the ship out of this hangar," Sps-kudah said.

"If we can," Nzz-oonaz said, looking at the external monitors. The doors the Mrachanis had used to seal the hangar looked pretty strong. If they couldn't persuade the Mrachanis to open them, he'd have to send warriors out to do it the hard way—

"Searcher!" an Elder gasped, appearing in front of him. "Searcher, we're sealed in. We can't get out."

"What?" Nzz-oonaz demanded. "What do you mean?"

"There's a metal barrier covering the cliff over the hangar," a second

Elder said, popping in beside the first. "It's very thin—I checked the edge. But it covers the entire hangar. And it blocks all anchorlines to Zhirrzh space."

Nzz-oonaz looked at Sps-kudah, a horrible taste oozing beneath his tongue. So that was what the aircraft out there had been doing. An attack, all right, but like nothing he would ever have expected. "They've figured it out," he said, the words coming out mechanically. "And they've locked us in."

"Yes," Sps-kudah murmured. "And with our anchorlines blocked . . ."

He didn't finish the sentence. But he didn't have to. With their anchorlines blocked the Mrachanis could now destroy them all at their leisure. Not just raise them to Eldership, but destroy them.

And no one would ever know what had happened.

"CIRCE?" the Overclan Prime murmured. "You're sure that's what he said? CIRCE?"

"I think so," Thrr't-rokik said, his voice trembling despite his best efforts to control it, the taste of dread collecting beneath his tongue. What in the eighteen worlds was this CIRCE that it could provoke such a reaction from the Overclan Prime himself? "I might have misunderstood."

"No, CIRCE's the word, all right," the Prime said, gesturing peremptorily to Oclan-barjak. "Commander, have you gotten through to Warrior Command yet?"

"I have a pathway open to them now," Oclan-barjak said, jogging back toward him from the transport's hatchway. "No response yet."

An Elder appeared. " 'Warrior Command to the Overclan Prime,' " he quoted. " 'We confirm: Searcher Nzz-oonaz has warned that use of CIRCE against the Mrach study group is imminent.' "

"And?" the Prime said. "Come on, Communicator, snap to it. Get me a report."

"I obey," the Elder gulped, and vanished.

"Overclan Prime?" Thrr't-rokik spoke up gingerly. "If you want, I could go back to Mra and find out what's happening."

"You'll stay here until we have more information," the Prime growled.

Thrr't-rokik drifted away, the dread growing more bitter by the beat. Was whatever was happening back there his fault? His unauthorized talk with Lord-stewart Cavanagh—could that have been the cause of this?

And then the Elder was back. " 'We've lost all contact with the *Closed Mouth,*' " he quoted, his voice trembling with emotion. " 'All at once, with all the Elders still at their cuttings aboard.' "

For a handful of beats the only sound on the hilltop was the whistling of the latearc breezes through the trees. "What about the Elders who went to Mra with the supplies from the *Willing Servant?*" the Prime asked.

"They're still checking the list," the Elder said. "They'll know in a hunbeat."

Prr't-zevisti came over beside Thrr't-rokik. "What's all this about?" he asked quietly, motioning him away from the Prime.

"I don't know," Thrr't-rokik said as the two of them drifted a few strides away across the hilltop. "But I'm very much afraid that I've helped betray the Zhirrzh on Mra."

Prr't-zevisti seemed to ponder that. "No," he said. "No, I don't believe that. Melinda Cavanagh has acted most honorably toward me. She has trusted me and helped me at great risk to herself. I cannot believe the father of such a child would use you to betray your own people."

"We hardly know enough about any of these beings to presume how they'll behave," Thrr't-rokik scoffed. But he did feel marginally better. "What's Melinda Cavanagh's condition? Lord-stewart Cavanagh has expressed concern for her."

"She's unharmed," Prr't-zevisti told him. "Her brother Pheylan Cavanagh is injured, but Melinda Cavanagh is a healer and has treated him."

"What about my sons, Thrr-gilag and Thrr-mezaz? Are they all right?"

"Thrr-gilag is all right for now," Prr't-zevisti said, his voice turning ominous. "But Commander Thrr-mezaz has been placed in detention by two agents of the Speaker for Dhaa'rr. I don't know why, but I suspect it has to do with clan politics. And with me."

"Thrr't-rokik?"

Thrr't-rokik looked over to see the Overclan Prime gesturing to him. "Do me a favor," he murmured hurriedly to Prr't-zevisti. "Tell Pheylan Cavanagh that his father is a Mrach prisoner. He's a warrior—perhaps he'll have some ideas."

He went over to the Prime. "Yes?"

"Warrior Command can't open pathways to any of the Elders on Mra," the Prime told him. "So it's up to you. Go back and see what's happened to the *Closed Mouth*. But be careful."

"I obey." Thrr't-rokik flicked back along his anchorline to his hidden *fsss* cutting. The supply room where it had been stored was deserted. Carefully, keeping as deep in the grayworld as he could, he moved through the stone corridors and walls to the hangar area. He passed a dozen scurrying Mrachanis on the way; none of them seemed to notice him.

The *Closed Mouth* was still where it had been, looking unharmed. Bracing himself, prepared for the worst, he moved through the hull into the control room.

And stopped short in confusion. All the Zhirrzh were also still there, also apparently unharmed. "Nzz-oonaz?" he said, coming up again to the edge of the lightworld.

A dozen physicals and Elders spun around at the sound of his voice. "Thrr't-rokik?" Nzz-oonaz said with obvious surprise. "I thought you'd been caught on the other side."

"The other side of what?"

"Of the metal sheet covering this hangar," Nzz-oonaz told him. "Didn't you notice it?"

"Those aircraft that came by dropped it over the cliff above us," a Zhirrzh wearing commander's insignia growled, stepping to Nzz-oonaz's side. "Probably with help from the Human-Conquerors."

Thrr't-rokik flicked upward, through the hull and stone cliffs to the metal covering. "I see," he said, returning to the *Closed Mouth.* "That explains why Warrior Command hasn't been able to open pathways to the Elders—"

"Wait a beat," the commander cut him off. "You've talked to someone on Oaccanv? Recently?"

"Of course," Thrr't-rokik said. "As I tried to tell you before, I've been speaking with the Overclan Prime. He sent me back here just now to find out what happened to you."

Nzz-oonaz flicked his tongue suddenly. "Of course. That *fsss* cutting of yours—it's outside the metal covering. Get back and tell him that we expect to be under attack soon."

"I obey," Thrr't-rokik said, and flicked along his anchorline back to the Oaccanv hilltops and the Zhirrzh waiting there.

The Prime was speaking to another Elder but broke off as Thrr't-rokik arrived. "Well?" he asked.

"They're all alive and well," Thrr't-rokik told him. "What happened was that the Mrachanis have covered the hangar area with a metal sheet, blocking all anchorlines."

"I see," the Prime said, eyeing him. "And how is it that you aren't affected?"

Thrr't-rokik braced himself. If he hadn't been in trouble before, he was likely going to be so now. "Because I'm not part of any official group of Elders," he said. "I stowed away on the *Willing Servant.* My *fsss* cutting is hidden in a supply box that was moved to the study group's quarters."

"I see," the Prime said, his expression unreadable. "Any particular reason you stowed away on that particular ship?"

"I was following the two Zhirrzh who stole my wife's *fsss*," Thrr't-rokik said. "They got on the *Willing Servant* but then got off after my cutting was already aboard—"

He broke off, a sudden horrible thought striking him. Prr't-zevisti had said two Dhaa'rr agents had taken command of the Dorcas ground warriors. If they were the same ones he'd been following—

"There must be something about the Thrr family and illegal *fsss* operations," the Prime grunted. "But never mind. The issue here is how we're going to stop this war."

Thrr't-rokik grimaced. "Understood," he said. "What do you want me to do?"

For a long beat the Prime gazed out unseeingly at the waving treetops in the distance. "We need Lord-stewart Cavanagh's help to arrange a truce," he said at last, as if thinking aloud. "That much is clear. But with a Mrach attack on the *Closed Mouth* imminent, there's no longer any way for us to release him."

"Are we certain the Mrachanis are attacking?" Commander Oclan-barjak asked. "Could that metal sheet have some other purpose?"

"Not after they told Nzz-oonaz the attackers would be using CIRCE," the Prime said. "If it hadn't been for the accident of Thrr't-rokik's presence there, we would certainly have concluded that all the Zhirrzh had been killed instantly, leaving the Mrachanis free to take the ship apart at their leisure."

Oclan-barjak spat a curse. "So the Mrachanis have betrayed us."

"Valloittaja's group has," the Prime agreed. "We don't know if the betrayal extends to all Mrach clans. All the better, though, that we didn't agree to that attack on Earth he wanted. The point is that as long as he's a prisoner, Lord-stewart Cavanagh won't be able to influence the Human-Conqueror warriors. But perhaps he can influence his son and daughter. Prr't-zevisti?"

"Yes, Overclan Prime?" the other Elder said, coming forward.

"You said you'd spoken at length during your captivity with Melinda Cavanagh," the Prime said. "Did she seem to have any influence with the Human-Conqueror commander there?"

"Some influence, yes," Prr't-zevisti said. "I don't know if she has enough for your purposes."

"We'll have to hope she does," the Prime said. "All right. Prr't-zevisti, Thrr't-rokik—go back and explain the situation to your respective Human-Conqueror contacts. Then we'll set up a pathway between them."

He flicked his tongue. "And then," he added, "we shall see what happens."

· · ·

"It is time," Valloittaja said, standing two steps into the room. Behind him, filling the doorway, were two Bhurtala. "Come with me, please."

"Time for what?" Bronski asked, not making any move to get off his cot.

"Time for you to fulfill your purpose here," the Mrachani said.

"You're going to kill us, in other words," Bronski said, waving a hand negligently. Out of the corner of his eye Cavanagh saw Kolchin easing his position on his own cot. The signal had been given, and the two former Peacekeeper commandos were preparing their attack.

An attack that everyone in the room already knew was predestined to failure.

"Of course," Valloittaja said calmly. "I trust you didn't think you were here on holiday."

"I take it that means you've started your attack on the Zhirrzh," Bronski said. "Any progress?"

"Enough," Valloittaja said. "Please come cooperatively. I have no desire to order unnecessary pain inflicted on you."

"I'm sure you don't," Bronski agreed, his tone almost flippant. "Especially since we're probably supposed to die in combat of one sort or another. Can't have bruises from Bhurtist fingers all over us confusing the medical examiners."

"There will be no medical examiners," Valloittaja said, starting to sound irritated. "At least, no human ones. The Zhirrzh won't even notice them."

And then, from the stone wall behind Cavanagh's head, came Thrr't-rokik's faint voice. "Ask him how long it will take them to enter the Zhirrzh spacecraft."

With an effort Cavanagh resisted the urge to turn around. "Tell me, Valloittaja, how long do you think it'll take you to get into the Zhirrzh ship out there?" he asked.

The mouse face frowned delicately. "We'll be inside soon enough," he said.

"They are trying to make it look like an attack with CIRCE," Thrr't-rokik's voice murmured again in Cavanagh's ear. "All must die together."

Cavanagh frowned. CIRCE? What on Earth was the Elder talking about? Or trying to get him to say? "I don't suppose you could tell us exactly how this attack is going to be staged," he improvised, stalling for time. "The traditional last request?"

Valloittaja made some sarcastic-sounding reply. But Cavanagh didn't hear it, his full attention on the voice whispering from the stone behind him. "They told Nzz-oonaz that Human-Conquerors were attacking with

CIRCE," Thrr't-rokik whispered. "But if you and Zhirrzh do not die at same time—you see?"

"Yes," Cavanagh said to Valloittaja. "Still, I assume you're trying to stage this as if it all happened at once. We can't be the big, bad human attackers if we die a few days before you even get to the Zhirrzh on that ship."

Valloittaja's frown hardened. "What are you talking about?" he demanded suspiciously.

"I'm talking about the logical approach to this fraudulent attack," Cavanagh said, aware that Bronski and Kolchin were also staring at him. "I take it from your reaction I've hit close to the mark?"

Valloittaja drew himself up. "It will hardly require days to break into that ship. A few hours, at the most. By the time any Zhirrzh investigators arrive, such a difference in death times won't even be noticeable."

Bronski snorted. "You *are* joking," he said scornfully, finally picking up on the cue. "A few hours? Try a few days. If you're lucky."

"Bronski's right," Cavanagh agreed. "You'd better give that hull a try before you make rash promises. My guess is that it'll take you at least a week to get through it. Even without the Zhirrzh warriors inside shooting at you."

For a few seconds Valloittaja gazed at Cavanagh, not speaking. Cavanagh held the gaze, mentally crossing his fingers. "Your analysis is most interesting," the Mrach said softly. "Still, you disappoint me, Lord Cavanagh. You plead like small animals for a few more hours of life." He paused. "Or do you still have hope of escape?"

"Of course we have hope of escape," Bronski said. "You don't think we'd help you lie to the Zhirrzh just for the fun of it, do you?"

Valloittaja smiled thinly. "Very well; you have bought a few more hours of life. Enjoy them."

He turned and strode out, the Bhurtala moving aside for him and then closing the door behind him. "That was interesting," Bronski commented. "Where did you learn how to read Mrach minds, Cavanagh?"

"Insider information," Cavanagh told him, shifting back on his cot to block the spy-eye camera and motioning Bronski to do the same. "Thrr't-rokik?"

The Elder appeared in front of the door. "Beware," he cautioned. "The two large beasts still wait outside."

"So what the hell is going on?" Bronski asked.

"The Mrachanis have covered the area around the *Closed Mouth* with metal," Thrr't-rokik said. "It is blocking the Elders from returning home. First, the Mrachanis said that Human-Conquerors attacking with CIRCE weapon."

"With CIRCE?" Cavanagh echoed, looking at Bronski. "That's—"

"That's a lie," Bronski interrupted, throwing him a fiercely warning look. "What are your people going to do?"

"They will defend," Thrr't-rokik said. "But the Overclan Prime still wants to stop the war. He says perhaps you talk to your son Pheylan Cavanagh."

Cavanagh frowned. "Talk to my—"

And then, suddenly, he got it. "You're with Pheylan?"

"I am not," Thrr't-rokik said. "But Prr't-zevisti on Dorcas is with him."

"Dorcas?" Bronski demanded. "What's Pheylan doing there?"

"I do not know," Thrr't-rokik said. "Perhaps you can ask him."

"Yes," Cavanagh said. "How do I do this?"

"You speak," Thrr't-rokik said. "I will relay your words to Prr't-zevisti."

"I see," Cavanagh said, taking a deep breath. "All right, here we go. Pheylan, this is your father, Lord Stewart Simon Cavanagh. Are you there?"

Twelve more Zhirrzh have entered the room in the past 7.94 minutes. From their expressions and postures, I have deduced that more of the imperceptible communication conduits are also present. I estimate a probability of 0.70 that there are currently twenty of the latter, with a probable deviation of plus or minus four. The original questioner has spoken twice to me during that period but has merely asked simple permutations of his earlier questions. Most of the conversation in the room has been between the Zhirrzh and the unseen conduits, which has enabled me to strengthen and corroborate my earlier language studies.

Two new Zhirrzh have now entered the room, and with their arrival I detect a significant alteration in the body language of the other twelve present. I compare their altered postures to those of the original occupants of the room toward the Zhirrzh whose tonal pattern I copied and whom I presumed to be an authority figure. From this comparison I estimate a probability of 0.70 that the newcomers are also in positions of authority and estimate a further probability of 0.90 that this authority exceeds that of any of the room's original occupants.

A pathway is opened through the room, and the two Zhirrzh step to within 1.44 meters of me. The one on the left is 3 centimeters taller than the other; he also stops 18 centimeters closer to me. {Who are you?}

{My name is Max. I'm currently the travel companion of Commander Pheylan Cavanagh.}

{You cannot be a *kabrsif.* Human-Conquerors do not have *kabrsifli.* Admit to me that you are not a *kabrsif.*}

I spend 0.03 second examining his expression and posture and comparing them with all I have learned about the Zhirrzh. His expression is one I haven't yet seen. From his words I estimate a probability of 0.40 that he is angry and a probability of 0.50 that he is suspicious of me. {I cannot respond to that question, nor can I admit anything. I do not know the meaning of that word.}

The Zhirrzh continues to look at me for 3.50 seconds. His companion, still standing 18 centimeters behind him, is not looking at me, but is instead looking slowly about the room. I study the movements and brief pauses and compute a probability of 0.74 that he is looking in turn at each of the unseen communication conduits.

The first Zhirrzh extends his tongue toward me for 0.43 second. {Take it apart. All of it.}

The Zhirrzh beside him holds his right hand in an unfamiliar gesture. {Just a beat, Mnov-korthe. You have no right to order such a *minzhorh*.}

The first Zhirrzh turns his head to face the second. {Take caution, Second Commander Klnn-vavgi. I am commanding now, and you may yet end up in the same position as your commander.}

His expression changes abruptly, to a variation of the look I had tentatively identified as suspicion, and he spends the next 8.77 seconds looking around the room the same way Second Commander Klnn-vavgi has been doing. Mnov-korthe's tongue extends for 0.93 second, pointing upward at an angle of approximately forty degrees. {You—*kabrsif*. What are you doing here?}

Mnov-korthe holds his same posture for 10.22 seconds. I calculate a probability of 0.95 that he is listening to one of the unseen conduits. {He did, did he?} *There is a pause of 3.92 seconds.* {No, you stay here now. I'll see to this.}

He turns around and walks toward the door. As he takes his first step, he makes a hand gesture toward two of the Zhirrzh. {You two: take this so-called *kabrsif* across the landing field to the optronics assembly area and begin taking it apart.}

He makes another gesture toward Second Commander Klnn-vavgi. {You will come with me, Second Commander. The brother of your commander needs to be dealt with.}

"Pheylan, this is your father, Lord Stewart Simon Cavanagh," the ghostly figure said, its voice as faint and insubstantial as its appearance. "Are you there?"

Propped up on one elbow on his table, Pheylan looked at Melinda, standing a couple of meters away beside Thrr-gilag. The second Zhirrzh, Klnn-dawan-a, was across the room, her head pressed listening against the door. "Go ahead," Melinda coaxed. "It's all right. He'll repeat everything you say to Dad."

But would he? That was the big question. And if he altered things, even blatantly, how would any of them know it? "Hello, Father," he said to the ghost. It occurred to him even as he said it that he hardly ever called the elder Cavanagh *Father*—usually it was just *Dad*. But there was something about this whole setup that encouraged formality. "This is your son Pheylan David. Are you all right?"

The ghost nodded and vanished. "That's it," Melinda said encouragingly. "That's all you do. It's just like relaying messages through someone else when your own phone's broken."

Which Pheylan had always hated doing. "You were starting to tell me what all this was about."

"It's our radio signals," Melinda said. "It turns out they're extremely painful to Zhirrzh Elders."

"To be accurate, to the *fsss* organs of the Elders," Thrr-gilag put in. "To us they are called Elderdeath weapons—"

He stopped as the ghost reappeared. " 'I'm fine, Pheylan,' " he said. " 'We're in a bit of a tight situation at the moment, though. Do you have any way to get a message off Dorcas?' "

Pheylan looked at Melinda. "Do we?"

"Colonel Holloway has two Corvines," she said. "They're the ones who decided not to go on Aric's mission to rescue you. The question is whether the Zhirrzh blockade ships out there would let them pass."

Pheylan gestured at the ghost. "Go ahead, take that back."

The ghost vanished again. "What you call radio is to us Elderdeath weapons," Thrr-gilag said, picking up the thread of the earlier conversation. Probably standard practice with the Zhirrzh, Pheylan decided, given the built-in time lags of their communication system. "They were used once in a war, by the Svrr family of the Flii'rr clan. That family was afterward destroyed."

"What do you mean, destroyed?" Melinda asked.

"The *fsss* organs of the adults were destroyed and the adults executed," Thrr-gilag said, his voice taking on an oddly unsettling tone. "The Elders' *fsss* organs were also destroyed. The children were renamed and scattered to other clans."

The ghost returned. This time, instead of speaking to Pheylan, he jabbered at Thrr-gilag in their own language. "The Overclan Prime sends you a message," Thrr-gilag said. "He does not know your language, so I will translate."

His tone changed. " 'Pheylan Cavanagh, this is the Overclan Prime. I have asked Warrior Command about the warship over Dorcas. It is damaged and cannot maneuver, but it is still capable of attack. Any messenger you send must be warned to avoid it.' "

"Can't he just order it not to shoot?" Melinda asked.

"I will ask." Thrr-gilag spoke to the ghost, who vanished.

Melinda crossed the room to Pheylan's side. "I know this is pretty new for you, and probably hard to accept," she said quietly. "But I really believe they're telling the truth."

Pheylan thought back to that first battle. To the attack on the *Jutland,* as it transmitted the first-contact package . . . the widening of that attack to the other ships, as they all switched from laser communication to battle-coded radio signals . . . the systematic destruction of the honeycomb escape pods with their blaring emergency radio beacons.

And his rescue from a similar death, after he'd disabled his own beacon. "No," he told his sister slowly. "Actually, it's not all that hard to accept."

The ghost returned and again held a brief conference with Thrr-gilag. "From the Overclan Prime," Thrr-gilag said. " 'Warrior Command has not been informed of this conversation. Many of the clan leaders would violently not approve of negotiations with you, especially with the current attack on the Zhirrzh ship trapped on Mra. Many will believe the Mrachanis and Human-Conquerors are cooperating in this attack.' "

Pheylan chewed at his lip. "Does the Overclan Prime know if the Mrachanis have begun trying to get through the Zhirrzh ship's hull yet?"

"Why?" Melinda asked as Thrr-gilag translated for the ghost.

"I'll tell you after we find out," Pheylan said. "If they are, I want to know what method they're using."

The ghost vanished. Ninety seconds later he was back.

"The Mrachanis are indeed attempting to penetrate the hull, Pheylan Cavanagh," Thrr-gilag confirmed after the usual consultation. "They are using metal cutting tools, focused light, and explosive devices."

Pheylan smiled grimly. "In that case you can tell the Overclan Prime that no official human groups are involved in this. We know how to break Zhirrzh hulls, and it's not the way the Mrachanis are trying."

Thrr-gilag's tail twitched out of its usual steady corkscrewing motion. "You have found a way? How?"

"We had a tech team studying the buildings you left behind after I escaped," Pheylan told him. "They figured it out. The method's probably already back on Earth; it certainly could be on Mra by now if the Peacekeepers were involved."

Thrr-gilag's tail twitched again. "I will inform the Overclan Prime."

He spoke to the ghost, who vanished. "Are you sending all this to my father, too?" Pheylan asked. "He needs to know what's going on."

"He is hearing everything," Thrr-gilag assured him. "The Overclan Prime has insisted. It is by his authority that he hopes to persuade the other Human leaders."

"Good," Pheylan said. "Then when your communicator gets back, I've got some suggestions to make to him."

Beside the door Klnn-dawan-a suddenly hissed something and jumped toward Pheylan's table. "Someone is coming," Thrr-gilag said, grabbing two of their instruments and tossing her one of them. Pheylan dropped back flat on the table, wondering fleetingly whether he should feign pain or nervousness or defiance or whether it really mattered—

Abruptly the door slammed open against its stop, and a tall Zhirrzh strode in, three others behind him. Two of them, Pheylan noted, were carrying the well-remembered riflelike weapons. The tall Zhirrzh snarled something, and the two guards took up positions flanking the doorway, weapons angled just over the occupants' heads. Thrr-gilag said something, was answered by the tall Zhirrzh. Again Thrr-gilag spoke, gesturing. "Is there a problem?" Pheylan asked loudly into the conversation.

For a moment the tall Zhirrzh eyed him with what was probably a glare of some sort. Then, with a contemptuous-sounding noise, he spat something. "He asks you to be silent," Thrr-gilag translated.

"Why should we?" Pheylan demanded. The tall Zhirrzh was looking around the room now, his eyes searching the tables and miscellaneous human and Zhirrzh equipment in a way Pheylan didn't like. "We're involved in this too, you know. We deserve to know what's going on."

"Please be silent," Thrr-gilag said, his tone sounding urgent. "He is Mnov-korthe, agent of the Overclan Seating, and he has command here now. You will merely get us into trouble—"

He broke off, his tail twitching again. Mnov-korthe's roving eyes had abruptly stopped. With two long strides he stepped to the equipment table off to Pheylan's right, pulling away a rumpled piece of material from Pheylan's jumpsuit leg to reveal the short, slender cylinder that Melinda had hidden there. The cylinder she had earlier had hidden inside the vital-signs monitor.

Pheylan shifted his gaze to his sister. Her face was rigid, her eyes wide with the dismayed awareness of imminent disaster. Slowly, as if deliberately playing to the sudden tension in the room, Mnov-korthe picked up the cylinder. He turned to Thrr-gilag, lifting it triumphantly in front of him—

And then, through the open door, came the hard thunder crack of a distant explosion.

Mnov-korthe spun around toward the door, barking something to the guards and flicking his tongue toward the dusky village landscape outside. The last part of his speech was punctuated by three more explosions, this group coming in rapid succession. Pheylan hoisted himself back up into a sitting position, trying to look past the Zhirrzh to see if he could tell where the blasts were coming from. He couldn't; but even as one of the two guards stepped out through the doorway, he caught a glimpse of two ghosts outside. No doubt reporting on the explosions—

And then another ghost appeared directly in front of Mnov-korthe. It was their ghost, Prr't-zevisti, the one who'd been carrying their messages back and forth.

The other unarmed Zhirrzh who'd come in with Mnov-korthe shouted something, jabbing his tongue out at the ghost. Mnov-korthe took a step backward, then stepped forward again directly into and through the ghost, saying something and waving the cylinder emphatically. Thrr-gilag said something, jumping forward and making a snatch at the cylinder. But Mnov-korthe was faster, taking a quick step to the side and deflecting Thrr-gilag's rush with his free hand. Klnn-dawan-a started toward him, but the unarmed Zhirrzh caught her arm and pulled her to his side. Recovering his balance, Thrr-gilag tried again; again Mnov-korthe took a step back, easily batting his flailing hands away. From outside came a sudden flurry of noise and alien shouts—

"Melinda Cavanagh," the ghost called, his thin voice barely audible over the noise. "He must stop!"

Pheylan had no idea what the ghost meant, and he doubted that Melinda understood the situation any better than he did. And if he'd had the chance, he would have warned her to keep out of it.

But he never had the chance. Suddenly, to his dismay, Melinda broke away from where she stood rooted to the floor and threw herself toward Mnov-korthe.

Again the Zhirrzh was too fast. He twisted away like a cat, her hand missing his wrist by bare millimeters. Off balance, she lunged for him with her other hand; again he evaded her. Out of the corner of his eye Pheylan saw the second guard swing back into the room, his hand fumbling up the barrel of his rifle.

And suddenly Melinda's arms slammed to her sides, her legs snapped together, and she toppled toward the floor.

Mnov-korthe made no effort to cushion her fall, jumping back instead out of her way as she crashed to the floor with a grunt of pain. The Zhirrzh spat something, waving at the guards with one hand and pointing down at her with his tongue. The guards lowered their rifle barrels toward her—

And clenching his teeth, Pheylan launched himself off the side of his table toward Mnov-korthe.

His feet hit the floor, a jolt of pain from his broken leg lancing straight up to his skull despite the numbing effect of the anesthetics. His arms snaked around the Zhirrzh's torso and neck, and he yanked back, pinning Mnov-korthe solidly against his chest.

And nearly lost his grip an instant later as the Zhirrzh's left foot swung violently backward to slam against his broken leg, turning the throbbing ache into a red-tinged blaze of agony. Pheylan swore viciously, tightening his grip, resisting the sudden urge to break the alien's neck. A subtle movement in Mnov-korthe's right shoulder warned him, and he snaked his right hand down the other's arm just as the Zhirrzh's hand emerged from a waist pouch gripping a small hand-weapon-sized object. Twisting them both to the left, he slammed Mnov-korthe's wrist onto the edge of the table, then whipped the arm down and to his right, sending the weapon clattering to the floor. "Guns up!" he snarled toward the guards. "Thrr-gilag—tell them!"

The Zhirrzh holding Klnn-dawan-a's arm had already barked an order, and the rifle muzzles had moved uncertainly off their targets. Though not very far off their targets. "Tell them to lay the guns down on the floor," Pheylan said, breathing hard with exertion and trying to ignore the rekindled pain in his leg. He looked along the second guard's barrel, spotted the obedience-suit trigger that the alien had strapped halfway along it. "And have them release Melinda's suit," he added. "Go ahead, tell them."

Thrr-gilag translated. The Zhirrzh holding Klnn-dawan-a flicked his tongue out and said something in return. "Second Commander Klnn-vavgi will not so order," Thrr-gilag said, his voice as agitated as the blur of his tail spinning behind him. "He orders you instead to release Mnov-korthe unharmed."

"You know better than that, Thrr-gilag," Pheylan bit out. "We've been here before, you and me, remember? I'm not letting him go."

"It will serve no purpose, Pheylan Cavanagh," Thrr-gilag said. "Second Commander Klnn-vavgi cannot allow you to escape. The warriors are already gathering; and if you are killed, it will greatly harm the chances for us to stop the war."

Pheylan shook his head. "This is a matter for diplomats, Thrr-gilag. I'm one solitary soldier. I can't stop any wars."

"But the diplomats will not hear unless you take word to them," Thrr-gilag persisted. "We have no direct contact with any other Humans who can tell them."

Pheylan clenched his teeth, uncertainty twisting through his gut. "What was Mnov-korthe ordering just before I grabbed him?"

Thrr-gilag looked down at Melinda, still frozen in place on the floor. "He had ordered the warriors to shoot Melinda Cavanagh."

Pheylan tightened his grip around Mnov-korthe's neck a little. "And you said he was in command here?"

"Yes."

"So if I let him go, and he tells them to shoot her, they will?"

Thrr-gilag hissed softly. "Yes."

"Then I can't let him go," Pheylan told him. "And I won't."

"Pheylan, this is crazy," Melinda said, her voice sounding slurred with her cheek pressed against the floor. "This is a chance to stop the war. You can't throw that away for one life. Not even mine."

"I came here to help you, Melinda," Pheylan said, the words sounding bitter in his ears. He'd certainly done a terrific job of it. "Getting you killed is not exactly how I intended to do it."

"Pheylan, listen—"

"Besides, who says this Mnov-korthe character even wants peace?" he cut her off. "Or that any of the Zhirrzh really want peace? You heard the Overclan Prime—he can't even order the blockade ships over Dorcas to let anyone out."

"That is why we need you alive," Thrr-gilag said. "Through you the Overclan Prime may negotiate a stop to the fighting."

"And that's also why Mnov-korthe will probably order us killed the minute he has the chance," Pheylan told him tightly. "If his boss is one of those who wants the war to continue, killing us here and now is the simplest way to accomplish that." He nodded toward the spot where their ghost had last appeared. "You'd better get word back to the Overclan Prime."

"He has been informed," Thrr-gilag said. "Perhaps he can do something to help."

"Right," Pheylan murmured. But he doubted it. It sounded as if the Overclan Prime was in the middle of a major political fight on this one; and he'd seen enough of his father's own battles in the NorCoord Parliament to know their outcome was never certain. And if the Prime lost this one . . .

"So what do we do now?" Melinda murmured.

Pheylan looked around the room. "We start by staying calm," Pheylan told her. "We don't want to do anything to provoke them."

"I think I can handle that," she said dryly. "What then?"

He shook his head. "I haven't the faintest idea."

"All attack units are in the air and in formation," Takara reported tightly. "Transports lifting now, falling in behind. ETA, sixteen minutes."

"Acknowledged," Holloway said, gazing out the aircar canopy at the hills rolling by beneath them. Ahead, the last glow of sunset was fading from the sky, leaving a hyphenated layer of purple clouds behind it. "Have Vanbrugh and Hodgson lifted yet?"

"Their Corvine's lifting now," Takara said, pressing his headphone closer to his ear. "Gaining altitude. Base reports no enemy response yet."

Holloway grimaced. It was a terrible risk, sending one of their irreplaceable Corvines into the free-fire zone of the Zhirrzh blockade like this. But it was a risk that had to be taken. "Have there been any more explosions in the enemy camp?" he asked.

"Just those four," Takara said. "The spotters think they've located the affected building, at one of two centers of increased enemy activity."

"Probably means they had Janovetz and the Cavanaghs split up," Holloway said. "You have both centers marked?"

"Yes." Takara touched a key, and an overlay appeared on the canopy view.

Holloway studied it briefly. Two buildings fronting onto the landing field, no more than a hundred meters apart. Perfect. "Send that to the rest of the force," he ordered. "We'll be putting down midway between them; everything around those zones is free-fire. Remind everyone that the objective here is to take out the antiaircraft weaponry, not to rack up enemy casualties."

"They've been so informed." Takara threw him a sideways look. "You sure you want to do this, Cass?"

Holloway gazed out at the horizon. No, he wasn't at all sure. He'd been three-quarters convinced already that this batch of Zhirrzh weren't nearly as savage or bloodthirsty as the group who'd hit the *Jutland,* even before Melinda Cavanagh's ghost had shown up with this radio/Elderdeath-weapon theory of his. Up to now, in fact, the war here had been remarkably clean, almost civilized.

But Holloway's job wasn't to keep the war civilized. It was to protect the people under his authority. And right now that meant finding a way to get them off-planet before the halucine epidemic condemned them to slow starvation.

And if he had to flatten that entire village over there to accomplish that, then that was what he would do. Civilized warfare or not. "We're doing what we have to, Major," he said.

Takara nodded. "Understood, sir."

29

"What kind of attack?" Cavanagh demanded, his chest tightening painfully. "From whom?"

"I do not know more," Thrr't-rokik said, his thin voice as agitated as Cavanagh felt. "Prr't-zevisti says that human aircraft coming toward Zhirrzh encampment. I must go hear what is happening."

"Wait a minute," Cavanagh called. "What about Pheylan and Melinda? You said something had gone wrong—?"

"Don't bother—he's gone," Bronski said grimly. He was up off his cot now, pulling his shirt off and stuffing it into the wall slot where one of the Mrachanis' hidden cameras was located. "Do what I'm doing over the camera on your side. Kolchin, I need two bolas and a slingshot."

"Right," Kolchin said, pulling out the impromptu screwdriver he'd used earlier on the door. Pushing his mattress onto the floor, he set the metal cot frame up on its side and got to work on the hardware holding it together.

"What's going on?" Cavanagh asked, taking his shirt off and wedging it into the slot as instructed.

"We're getting out of here," Bronski told him. He had his own mattress on the floor and was balancing the wire-strung frame on its side against the wall opposite the door.

"What about the Mrachanis?" Cavanagh asked.

"They're the reason we're getting out," Bronski said. Leaving the frame propped against the wall, he squatted down beside the discarded mattress and began tearing carefully through the fabric of the outer enclosure. "You remember Thrr't-rokik quoting the Overclan Prime earlier as saying he was glad they hadn't agreed to an attack on Earth?"

"Yes," Cavanagh said.

"Well, he was wrong," Bronski told him. "Because when Valloittaja was marching us in here, he pretty well confirmed they *had* conned the Zhirrzh into launching a major attack."

"Maybe he was just playing games with you," Cavanagh said, watching the two of them in fascination. Kolchin was making a small collection of nuts and bolts pulled from the cot frame; Bronski had gotten a tear started in the mattress fabric and was carefully making it longer. "Or else planting disinformation."

"I don't think so," Bronski said. "I know the Mrachanis. From the level of gloating I think he was telling the truth."

"So you're saying the Overclan Prime lied to us?"

"No," Bronski said bluntly. "I'm saying that one of his political opponents is pulling a fast one. He's made a private deal with the Mrachanis."

Cavanagh swore gently. Obvious, of course, now that they knew how the Mrachanis worked. "Why didn't you warn Pheylan?"

"I was trying to find a way to say it that wouldn't tip off the Zhirrzh that I knew." The slit was long enough now for Bronski to begin pulling one of the tube-shaped floater pads out of the mattress. "Someone from the wrong political side might have been listening in. This communication system might be handy, but it has security holes you could fly a carrier through."

"I think the time for subtlety has passed," Cavanagh said. "You'd better warn the Overclan Prime. There must be a way for him to stop the attack."

"Not if this enemy of his is smart," Bronski said. He had all the floater pads from his mattress laid out on the floor now, lined up neatly from where he'd propped up the frame to a point about halfway to the door. "I'm sure you've played enough steamroller politics in your day to know how it's done. Anyway, from the sound of things the whole question's academic. If the Dorcas Peacekeepers have launched an attack, it's going to be a while before Thrr't-rokik comes back to talk to us. Even assuming the Overclan Prime lets him do it."

"They want peace, Bronski," Cavanagh said. "At least the Overclan Prime does."

"You just hold that thought. Kolchin?"

"Slingshot's finished," Kolchin said. He held up one of the leg frames of the cot, now sporting an elastic band from his tunic waist strung between two of the right-angle sections.

"What about the bolas?"

"One's done," Kolchin said, indicating a lumpy assortment of bolts and nuts connected by long cords pulled from somewhere else in his clothing. "I'll be another minute on the other one."

"Good." Bronski stepped back to the cot frame and began working at the loose wire mesh that normally supported the mattress. A minute later he had one end loose; leaving the other end fastened to the frame, he began unweaving it from the other wires.

"All right, I give up," Cavanagh said. "What in the world are you two doing?"

"You saw how that Bhurt came charging in here earlier," Bronski said. He had nearly three meters of wire loose now. Peering briefly up at the ceiling light rectangle, he unwrapped another meter. "Bhurtala like to make that kind of grand entrance. Kolchin, do you have a spare nut and bolt over there?"

"Sure." Kolchin lobbed them across to him. "The second bola's ready."

"Start poking holes in those floater pads," Bronski ordered. "Make sure the outer mattress cover doesn't touch the liquid that comes out— they're usually treated with catalytic sealer coagulant. Cavanagh, go stand there in the corner away from the door and be ready to run. And don't get any of the floater liquid on your boots—it's slippery as hell."

Silently, Cavanagh complied. Bronski wrapped the loose end of his wire around the bolt and secured it with the nut, then took up position off to one side of the room with Kolchin's slingshot. Kolchin was busily puncturing the floater pads, releasing the dark, faintly noxious-smelling fluid inside. By the time he'd finished and collected his two bolas, the pool had spread out to cover a good half of the floor. "Ready?" he asked Bronski, stepping over to the door.

Bronski set his wire-wrapped projectile against the elastic and pulled it back. "Ready."

Kolchin nodded. Keeping clear of the door itself, he eased the end of his stiffener into the gap he'd opened earlier in the edge of the lock cover. For a moment he probed around; then, with a distinctive *snick*, the lock tripped.

As the one Bhurt had earlier, the two Bhurtala outside must have just waiting for their opportunity. With a horrendous crash the door was flung open and both of the big aliens charged into the room, eager for trouble.

They got it, but not the kind they were expecting. The first Bhurt was no more than a long pace into the room when Kolchin's bola caught him squarely at the knees, the spinning weighted cords wrapping themselves instantly around his legs. He bellowed in rage, his forward momentum faltering as he flailed for balance.

With Bhurtist muscle behind it, it took only half a second for him to snap the cords. But even as he did so, his fellow guard, already crowding too close behind him, caught the second bola around his legs and slammed into him.

They hit the floor together, hard enough for Cavanagh to feel the vibration right through the stone, splattering the walls with a splash of floater-pad fluid. The enraged bellows took on a slight gurgling as their forward momentum sent them surfing helplessly through the slippery liquid to collide with the cot frame across the room.

And as it came crashing down on top of them, Bronski fired his weighted wire directly into the overhead light fixture. There was a spatter of sparks as the wire made its connection to the power line—another spatter where the Bhurtala touched the cot frame—

And then Bronski's hand was on Cavanagh's shoulder, shoving him around the still-quivering door and out of the room. Kolchin was already outside, looking back and forth along the corridor. "Clear," he said.

"Won't be for long," Bronski grunted, pulling the door closed behind them and locking it. "Didn't get as good a contact as I'd hoped—they'll be up and making faces at the spy-eyes in a minute or two."

"Then we'd better get going," Kolchin said. "Back out the way we came in?"

"Probably our best bet," Bronski agreed. "You take point; let's go."

"This is insane, Thrr-gilag," Second Commander Klnn-vavgi said, his voice tight, his tail spinning hard. "Tell him that. It's insane."

"He won't listen to me," Thrr-gilag said mechanically, his full attention on Pheylan Cavanagh and the catastrophic situation the Human's actions had now put them all in. Whatever Mnov-korthe had hoped to gain politically from his discovery of the illegal cutting, it would have been blown away like dust by the fact that they'd succeeded in rescuing Prr't-zevisti.

But Pheylan Cavanagh hadn't understood that . . . and in his attempt to protect the cutting, he'd now sliced to shreds any hope of dealing with this matter quietly.

"This is your fault, Searcher," Mnov-korthe said softly. The Human arm across his neck made his voice sound a little odd, but the rage beneath it came through with no trouble at all. "You're the one who took the illegal cutting; you're the one who brought this female Human-Conqueror here; you're the one who let this male Human-Conqueror escape from you in the first place. You're finished, Thrr-gilag; Kee'rr. You and your entire family."

"You're not exactly helping the matter, either," Thrr-gilag told him, glancing at Klnn-dawan-a and Klnn-vavgi. Whatever happened, he had to keep both of them as far out of this as possible. There were probably legal limits as to what an agent of the Dhaa'rr could do to a Kee'rr. He doubted such limits existed for members of his own clan. "You're the one who ordered the warriors to shoot Melinda Cavanagh—"

"She attacked me," Mnov-korthe snapped.

"*And* you could probably resolve this right now by pledging not to harm either of them," Thrr-gilag snapped back.

Mnov-korthe flicked the tip of his tongue in contempt. "I will make no such pledge," he said. "Not to enemies of the Zhirrzh."

"Why, because Pheylan Cavanagh was able to grab you?" Thrr-gilag said with some contempt of his own. "Get it through your head, Mnov-korthe, that there are bigger things at risk here than your pride. Maybe even an end of the war."

Mnov-korthe smiled thinly. "The war will end soon enough," he said with quiet assurance. "With a victory for the Zhirrzh."

Thrr-gilag felt his midlight pupils narrow. What did he mean by that—?

"Second Commander!" a thin Elder voice broke into his thoughts. "The Human-Conquerors are launching an attack!"

"Where are they?" Klnn-vavgi demanded.

"Still in flight, coming from the east," a second Elder reported. "Coming in force. One of their spacecraft appears to be attempting to leave the planet—"

"Second Commander, the other Human-Conqueror prisoner has escaped!" a third Elder shouted. "Those explosions—they tore an opening in his holding room. He has disabled both warriors guarding him and has taken one of their laser rifles."

"Things seem to be falling apart around you, Second Commander," Mnov-korthe suggested, his voice smooth with menace. "You'd better get outside and deal with them. Just leave me those two warriors and some Elders I can give orders to."

"You can't do that, Klnn-vavgi," Klnn-dawan-a said urgently. "He'll kill the Human-Conquerors if you leave. You can't let that happen."

"I'm in command on Dorcas, Second Commander," Mnov-korthe reminded him. "You will obey my orders."

Klnn-vavgi grimaced . . . and then, even as Thrr-gilag watched, he seemed to straighten up to a decision. "Communicator, go to the warriors at the base of the Human-Conqueror aircraft," he ordered. "Tell them that Commander Thrr-mezaz is to be released immediately and returned to command."

"I absolutely forbid that," Mnov-korthe snapped before the Elder could reply. "I'm in command here—I have a document so stating from the Overclan Seating."

Prr't-zevisti reappeared. "A message from the Overclan Prime, Second Commander: 'I concur with your decision to reinstate Commander Thrr-mezaz—' "

"You will keep silence, traitor to the Dhaa'rr," Mnov-korthe said, his voice a vicious snarl that sent a twitch along Thrr-gilag's tail. "I reject your claim that you're in contact with the Overclan Prime. It's utterly impossible. You are speaking criminal lies."

"But I can prove it," Prr't-zevisti insisted. "Ask any question you wish—"

"And even if you were, the significance and importance of this particular Overclan Prime will very shortly fade into the mists of history," Mnov-korthe added, his eyes flicking back and forth now between Klnn-vavgi and the two warriors. "When the Speaker for Dhaa'rr has exposed his treason, those who have stood by him will fall along with him."

Thrr-gilag exchanged startled glances with Klnn-dawan-a. "What treason?" he demanded. "There's been no treason here."

"Keep silence, Kee'rr." Mnov-korthe flicked his tongue at the two warriors still flanking the doorway. "You two are Dhaa'rr, sworn to obey Warrior Command and the Overclan Seating. Will you stand with me, with my proved authority from the Seating? Or will you stand with criminal liars and traitors to the Zhirrzh?"

The warriors glanced at each other. "We stand by our oath," one of them said cautiously. "But—"

"Wisely spoken," Mnov-korthe said. "And there will thus be no need afterward for your families to be destroyed. Elder?"

"Yes?"

"Inform my brother Mnov-dornt that he is to assume command of the battle preparations," Mnov-korthe ordered. "Tell him I'll be joining him soon. Warriors, you will escort Second Commander Klnn-vavgi to the Human-Conqueror aircraft to join with Commander Thrr-mezaz."

"You can't do that," Thrr-gilag said, taking a step forward.

"But before you do," Mnov-korthe amended, "you will carry out one other task." His tongue flicked out toward Thrr-gilag. "This Kee'rr is a traitor to the Zhirrzh and, through his contacts with the Human-Conquerors, is a clear danger to this warrior force. I therefore order him raised to Eldership.

"Now."

"They won't listen to me," Prr't-zevisti said, his voice trembling with fear and frustration. "That Dhaa'rr—Mnov-korthe—refuses to believe I'm delivering messages from you. He's denouncing me as a criminal liar; and he's saying that *you're* a traitor."

The Prime flicked his tongue savagely. He would have expected an agent of Speaker Cvv-panav to be ruthless, but not to be so audacious as to cry treason. What in the eighteen worlds did Cvv-panav have poised that he could even think of taking such a stupendous risk? "Go to Commander Thrr-mezaz," he bit out. "Tell him that I order him to resume command."

"I can't reach him," Prr't-zevisti said. "He's inside the Human's metal aircraft."

"What about the warriors guarding him?"

"Both are Dhaa'rr," Prr't-zevisti said, his voice sounding distracted. Listening to what was happening on Dorcas. "Mnov-korthe is ordering his brother Mnov-dornt to be put in command. Ordering Second Commander Klnn-vavgi to be put in detention with Commander Thrr-mezaz—"

He jerked suddenly. "He's ordering the warriors to raise Thrr-gilag to Eldership!"

"Get back there," the Prime snapped. "Order them not to obey."

Prr't-zevisti was already gone. "Overclan Prime," Thrr't-rokik breathed. "My son—will he—?"

The Prime looked at him. For perhaps the first time really *looked* at him. At that pale Elder face, echoing a lifetime of simple honest labor. A face that had no doubt been filled with shame for his wife when the *fsss* theft he'd helped to organize had branded her a criminal. A face now filled with anxiety for the danger his son was in.

Back when all of this had started, the previous Primes had insisted that it was sometimes necessary for individuals to be sacrificed for the greater political good. Distantly, the Prime wondered if any of them had ever had to face the individuals they had so sacrificed.

"ETA, twelve minutes," Takara reported. "We'll be in range of those outer laser installations in ten."

"Understood," Holloway said. "Stand by."

"Yes, sir."

He gazed out the canopy at the scattering of lights ahead marking the Zhirrzh encampment, a small voice in the back of his mind reminding him that Melinda Cavanagh was not going to approve of this at all. Considering her feelings toward the Zhirrzh in general and Prr't-zevisti in particular, in fact, she might well decide to hate him for what he was about to do.

But, ultimately, that didn't matter. It was her life that was at stake here, and her brother's life, and the lives of a lot of good Peacekeepers.

And if the loss of her respect was the price he had to pay to protect those lives, then so be it.

"Activate," he ordered.

Slowly, almost reluctantly, the two Zhirrzh warriors turned their weapons away from Pheylan. Melinda sighed with relief—

And gasped as the muzzles turned to line up instead on Thrr-gilag. "Wait!" she shouted. "No. Stop!"

"It is too late, Melinda Cavanagh," Thrr-gilag said. He drew himself up, his corkscrewing tail slowing down as he apparently accepted the inevitable.

"Wait," Melinda pleaded, twisting her head around to look at him more fully. "Tell him we'll make a deal. If Pheylan lets him go—"

And then, to her horror, Thrr-gilag suddenly gasped, a violent convulsion running through his body. Twisting at the waist, he bent over to one side and toppled to the floor.

"No!" Melinda gasped. She wrenched her head back around toward the other Zhirrzh—

To an incredible sight. Klnn-dawan-a was on her knees, only Klnn-vavgi's slack grip on her arm keeping her from collapsing completely. Klnn-vavgi himself was gripping the edge of the table with his other hand, swaying back and forth as if suddenly gone drunk. The two warriors were similarly staggering, leaning on their laser rifles for balance.

And then Prr't-zevisti screamed, a bizarre, unearthly sound . . . and abruptly Melinda understood.

"Pheylan, get their weapons," she called. "Quickly."

Mnov-korthe was twisting dizzily in his grip; shoving him aside, Pheylan hobbled across to the warriors. Wrenching one of the weapons away, he touched something on the barrel, and suddenly Melinda was free of the grip pinioning her arms and legs. She scrambled to her feet as Pheylan relieved the second warrior of his weapon. "What the hell's going on?" he demanded.

"Holloway put a white-noise radio transmitter in the vital-signs monitor," she said, taking one of the rifles from him. "He didn't bother to tell me that he'd set up a remote trigger for it."

"I guess that pretty well proves this Elderdeath-weapon theory," Pheylan said, the beads of sweat on his face evidence of what his trek across the room had cost him. "What now?"

"We shut the thing off, that's what," Melinda said, studying the laser rifle in her hands. She'd seen Holloway's techs demonstrating how it worked. . . .

"No, Melinda Cavanagh. You must not."

Melinda looked up, a shiver running through her. It had been Prr't-zevisti's voice, but so distorted by pain as to be almost unrecognizable. "Prr't-zevisti, I have to shut it down."

"No," Prr't-zevisti said, his transparent face as agonized as his voice. "You must . . . let it continue. It is the . . . only way for . . . you to stop . . . the attack."

"But I can't let you suffer like this," she protested.

"You have to," Pheylan said, taking the rifle from her hand. "He's right—you've got to get out there and stop Holloway before he wrecks everything. The radio's all that's keeping the Zhirrzh off balance—you won't get ten meters without it."

Melinda bit hard at her lip. But it was hurting them all so horribly— *But it's not killing them,* she told herself sternly. *Neither the Elders nor the warriors. You're a surgeon; start thinking surgical priorities.* "All right," she said. "How do I do it?"

"First get out of that obedience suit," Pheylan told her, reaching over to unfasten the suit's neck. "They'll have another trigger for it out there somewhere. Then get over to that aircar parked at the south end of the landing field, the one you said Janovetz came here in. There should be a laser comm built in. You know how to use one?"

"I think so," Melinda said, pulling off the last leg of the suit and shivering as the evening air hit sweaty skin. "What then?"

"Then you say whatever you have to to get Holloway to pull back," Pheylan said grimly.

She looked at Thrr-gilag, clutching dizzily at the floor. "Thrr-gi-lag . . . ?"

"I will explain to Klnn-vavgi," the other panted. "And the Overclan Prime will also understand. Go. Quickly."

"All right." Melinda opened the door; paused. The radio over there, still blaring its Elderdeath pain . . . "Give me two minutes," she told her brother. "Then destroy that radio. If I can't stop Holloway, I won't have the Zhirrzh being sitting ducks for him."

Pheylan's jaw tightened, but he nodded. "Two minutes. Good luck."

They were perhaps halfway down the hallway leading to the back door they'd entered the fortress by when Kolchin abruptly stopped. "Someone's coming," he whispered, taking a step back and pushing open the door he'd just passed. He glanced in and nodded, and three seconds later they were inside. Kolchin closed the door to a crack, peering out through the narrow gap, and a moment later Cavanagh heard the rhythmic thudding of heavy feet approaching down the corridor. The footsteps passed, faded away— "Valloittaja?" Bronski asked quietly.

"No," Kolchin said, easing the door open and looking out after them. "A different Mrach and two Bhurtala."

Bronski nodded. "Let's hope they're not the guard change."

"Clear," Kolchin said, opening the door the rest of the way and slipping outside.

They reached the tunnel leading to the exit door without seeing or hearing anyone else. There Bronski stopped, peering cautiously down the tunnel. "Well, come on," Cavanagh urged. "What are we waiting for?"

"I don't know," Bronski muttered. "Something feels wrong about all this. It's a little too easy."

"They're planning to kill us," Cavanagh pointed out tartly. "What could they have planned that's worse?"

"Point," Bronski conceded. "All right, let's give it a try." He stepped into the tunnel—

"Lord Stewart Cavanagh."

Cavanagh spun around toward the voice. Thrr't-rokik had finally returned. "Thrr't-rokik!" he said in relief. "We thought something had happened to you—"

"What's happening on Dorcas?" Bronski interrupted.

"There is still trouble," the Elder said, his words tumbling over each other. "But there is new trouble here. The Mrachanis have wrapped a second metal sheet directly around the *Closed Mouth*. The Elders are now sealed inside, and I cannot talk to Speaker Nzz-oonaz. They are also putting many objects on the ceiling of the hangar."

"What do the objects look like?" Bronski asked. "Long, narrow tubes?" He demonstrated with his hands.

"Yes," Thrr't-rokik said. "Many of them in a single bundle. And many bundles."

Bronski swore. "Fracture explosives," he said. "Damn it all—Valloittaja's trying to collapse the cliffs above the hangar."

Cavanagh felt his chest tighten. "With the Zhirrzh ship still inside?"

"Yeah, it's called burying your mistakes," Bronski said, starting down the exit tunnel and gesturing the others to follow. "I knew this would be coming—I just didn't figure on the Zhirrzh being able to get another ship here this fast."

"But—oh, God," Cavanagh murmured as it finally clicked. Of course: the Overclan Prime would have immediately dispatched another ship to investigate. It had closed to within six light-years of Mra now, and its distinctive tachyon wake-trail had appeared on the Mrachanis' detectors.

And Valloittaja, whose best efforts had probably not even been able to scratch the *Closed Mouth*'s hull, had decided to settle for a stalemate.

"So they're going to drop a million-ton mountain on top of the ship and kill everyone aboard," he said. "And undoubtedly try to blame us."

"Which means," Kolchin said quietly, "those two Bhurtala we saw were probably heading to our room."

"To get us ready for our grand finale," Bronski agreed. "Human bodies to show to the Zhirrzh when they arrive."

They had reached the end of the tunnel now and the door they'd entered the fortress through. "What will you do?" Thrr't-rokik asked.

"Try to stay a jump ahead of them," Bronski told him, easing the door open. The cool night wind whistled in through the crack, accompanied by a sliver of pale moonlight. "I'll be damned. Our rented aircar's still out there. Maybe Valloittaja's missed a bet after all." He pushed the door open—

"Hold it," Cavanagh said suddenly, gripping his arm. "They're trying to stage this as a human attack, right? Well, to do that, don't they have to produce human bodies from an aircar wreck?"

"Sure do," Bronski agreed. "My guess is that's why we haven't heard any noise over our escape. They were probably expecting us to demolish that group who just went to get us and make a run for it. Probably why Valloittaja sent one of his stooges instead of coming along himself for last-minute gloating—he didn't want to put his own skin at risk. All we did by taking out our guards was move up the timetable a bit and save them the trouble of herding us out here."

"You mean they *want* us to get in that aircar and fly away?" Cavanagh asked.

"That's my guess."

"That's terrific," Cavanagh gritted. "So what exactly is this bet you think he's missed?"

"You'll see." Bronski started to push the door open, then paused. "Thrr't-rokik . . . look, there's a fair chance this isn't going to work. If it doesn't, the three of us are going to die here. In case that happens—"

He took a deep breath, throwing a sour look at Cavanagh. "In case that happens, there's something the Overclan Prime needs to know. The weapon CIRCE that he's so afraid of doesn't exist. Never has existed. Do you understand?"

"I am not sure," Thrr't-rokik said, his expression odd. "The Zhirrzh have read about it. Pheylan Cavanagh spoke of it."

"He was lied to," Bronski said. "All of us were, for a long time. But what I'm telling you now is the truth. The Zhirrzh have nothing to fear from CIRCE, or from the Commonwealth. Make sure the Overclan Prime knows that."

"I obey," Thrr't-rokik said. "I thank you, and I will return your trust to you."

He vanished. "What did he mean by that?" Cavanagh asked.

"No idea," Bronski said. "But we haven't got time to wait and find out. Come on."

He led the way out into the night. All three of Mra's moons were in the sky overhead, bathing the ground in a pale yellowish light. "What now?" Cavanagh whispered as Bronski moved carefully forward. "We make a run for it?"

"I'm worried about those sentry holes," the brigadier said, nodding toward the flanking rock walls where the Bhurtala had been hidden earlier. "We're only assuming this is what Valloittaja has in mind."

And then Thrr't-rokik was back. "There are three Mrach aircraft waiting around the curve of rock," he said, his tongue flicking to point to the left. "Two more there"—the tongue flicked right—"and five behind the rock above."

"Check over there," Cavanagh told him, pointing to the sentry holes. "Inside holes in the rock. See if anyone's hiding there."

The ghost flicked away; flicked back. "No one is there."

"I could get used to having these guys around," Bronski said dryly. "Go."

They made it to the aircar without incident. Bronski slipped into the pilot's seat and gave the control board a quick but careful scan. He keyed the main power control, and the board lit up with muted light. "Cross your fingers, gentlemen," he said. "Here goes."

"How are you going to evade those Mrachani aircars?" Cavanagh asked.

Bronski threw him a tight smile. "As a matter of fact," he said, "I'm not even going to try."

The roar of approaching aircars was audible as Melinda flattened herself against the side of the Peacekeeper aircar, her breath coming in quick, hot gasps. There were Zhirrzh all across the field, dimly visible in the sunset's fading afterglow. Some were still on their feet, swaying with the disorienting loss of balance the radio was causing; most had already conceded defeat and were lying on the ground twitching. Helpless and harmless.

But that would change. In approximately thirty seconds.

"Cavanagh?"

Melinda jumped. "Who—"

"Janovetz, Doctor," the other identified himself, rolling out from beneath the aircar. He, too, had gotten rid of his obedience suit. "Figured you'd come here if you got free. Where's Commander Cavanagh?"

"He's all right for now," Melinda told him. "We've got to get inside the aircar and tell Colonel Holloway to stop his attack."

"You've got to be kidding," Janovetz said. "Something's happened to all the Zhirrzh—this is the perfect time for an attack."

"I know what's happened," Melinda said. She had a flash of inspiration— "It's a trap."

"I should have guessed," Janovetz muttered. "Come on."

They circled around the aircar's nose to the landing ramp. Two Zhirrzh were twitching on the ground at the foot; passing between them, Janovetz ran up the ramp and ducked through the hatchway. Hopping up behind him, Melinda followed—

And suddenly Janovetz tumbled back out again, flopping with a terrible crash onto his back on the ramp.

"Janovetz!" Melinda gasped, dropping onto her knees at his side. Even in the dim light she could see the dark bloodstain slowly spreading over his chest and shoulder. Reflexively, she reached for a sleeve to tear for a bandage, stopped with a curse as her fingers hit bare skin, and instead felt for the wound. Not in the neck as she'd feared, but higher up on the cheek. At least he wouldn't bleed to death.

But there was Zhirrzh tongue poison in the wound. If it wasn't treated quickly . . .

His eyes fluttered open. "Leave me," he whispered. "Warn . . . the colonel."

Melinda blinked away sudden tears. "I will," she promised. She scrambled back to her feet—

And stopped. A Zhirrzh was standing in front of her, just inside the hatchway, one hand gripping his side, but otherwise apparently unaffected by the Elderdeath weapon blazing across the landing field.

Standing inside the shielding effects of the metal hull.

"I have to get through," she said, knowing even as she spoke that her human words probably wouldn't be understood. "Please. I have to stop this attack."

The Zhirrzh didn't reply; but suddenly there was a sharp word from behind her.

Slowly, she turned around. The two Zhirrzh at the foot of the landing ramp were on their feet again, their weapons and eyes pointed directly at her. All around the landing field, the rest of the Zhirrzh were coming back to life.

Following her instructions, Pheylan had destroyed the radio.

A half-dozen other Zhirrzh were hurrying up now, forming a semicircle around the foot of the ramp. As with the first two, their weapons were trained on her. "I have to call Colonel Holloway," she said, raising her voice. Surely someone out there could understand her. "I have to tell him to stop his attack."

None of the warriors replied. But suddenly, from off to her left, came a familiar voice. "Melinda Cavanagh?"

"Thrr-gilag?" she called back in relief. "Come quickly—you have to explain."

Thrr-gilag raced up to the ring of warriors, already talking. The Zhirrzh in the hatchway said something; was answered— "There's no time to argue," Melinda insisted. The sound of the incoming aircars was growing dangerously loud. "Tell him I have to get in there."

Thrr-gilag made a hissing sound. "I am sorry, Melinda Cavanagh," he said. "My brother believes me but cannot order the warriors away. Mnov-korthe has taken command away from him—"

He broke off as a faint Elder voice spoke. Melinda looked around, spotted the pale image beside the Zhirrzh just outside the hatchway. "It is Prr't-zevisti," Thrr-gilag told her. "He is bringing orders from the Overclan Prime for you to be allowed in."

Melinda looked down. Most of the warriors had reluctantly lowered their weapons.

But the original two hadn't moved. One of them spoke— "Thrr-gilag?" Melinda asked.

Thrr-gilag hissed again. "They are Dhaa'rr," he identified them. "They will not accept that Prr't-zevisti is speaking for the Overclan Prime. They will only accept orders from—"

And then, from somewhere across the landing field, another voice joined in. "From Mnov-korthe," Thrr-gilag said, sounding surprised. "But now he too is ordering the Dhaa'rr to let you pass."

Melinda blinked. Considering Mnov-korthe's last views on the subject . . . but there was no time now to reflect on his change of heart. The last two warriors had lowered their weapons— "Come on," she told Thrr-gilag, hurrying up the ramp. "We'll need your brother, too."

The aircar's control board was laid out differently from the civilian aircars Melinda was used to, but it took only a few seconds to locate the laser comm. "Here goes," she muttered, keying it on and hoping the Zhirrzh techs who'd undoubtedly studied the craft hadn't accidentally disabled it. The lights went on; changed color as the tracking control searched out and found the incoming attack force— "Colonel Holloway, this is Melinda Cavanagh," she called into the mike. "You have to break off the attack. Repeat, you have to break off the attack. Colonel Hollo-way—"

"This is Holloway," the colonel's voice boomed from the speaker. "Explain."

"The Zhirrzh leaders now know the war's been a mistake," she said. "We've got the beginnings of a cease-fire started, but a battle now could ruin it. Please break off."

There was a long moment of silence. "Thrr-gilag, tell your brother to order his warriors not to fire on the human aircars," she said hurriedly. "Or at least not unless fired on themselves."

"I obey." Thrr-gilag spoke rapidly to his brother, who stepped back to the hatchway. Melinda glimpsed a group of Elders gathered there around him—

"This makes no sense at all, Cavanagh," Holloway's voice came back. "You haven't got authority to make deals with the Zhirrzh."

"So court-martial me," Melinda retorted. "But damn it all, don't attack."

There was another long pause. Melinda clenched her hand into a fist—

"I'll tell you what," Holloway said at last. "I'm still not buying this yet; but what I'll do is order my troops not to fire unless fired upon. If you can persuade your new friends down there to do likewise, that ought to show enough good faith on both sides to try to sort this out. Fair enough?"

Melinda's hand opened up again, the fingers trembling with reaction. "Very fair, Colonel. Thank you. As a matter of fact, the commander here has already given his troops that same order."

"Then we're in business," he said. "I presume you're going to want me to come down there and talk about this?"

"Please. And bring a full medical pack with you—Janovetz has taken some Zhirrzh tongue poison."

"Acknowledged," Holloway said. "We'll be down in three minutes."

"All right," Bronski muttered. "Here we go."

"Wait a second," Cavanagh told him, glancing around. Kolchin was nowhere in sight. "Kolchin's not in yet."

"Don't worry, we're not going anywhere," Bronski assured him. Reaching to the control board, he touched a switch—

And hovering just inside the canopy, Thrr't-rokik suddenly stiffened.

"Bronski!" Cavanagh snapped, suddenly understanding. "Thrr't-rokik—"

"I'm sorry, Thrr't-rokik," Bronski said, adjusting the frequency control. "But we don't have a choice here."

"I understand," the Elder said, his face contorted in pain. "Do what you must."

Bronski nodded. "This is Bronski," he called. "Code four; condition red; situation red. If you're out there, Daschka, get your rear over here fast."

"Daschka?" Cavanagh said, frowning. "Where—I mean how—?"

"Because I left a message drop for him back at the ship, of course," Bronski grunted. "We're hardly amateurs here, Cavanagh. If he got the skitter message at Phormbi, he and Cho Ming ought to be lurking out there somewhere."

"And if they didn't?"

"Then we go to Plan B," Bronski said. "Come on, Daschka, look alive."

There was movement outside. Cavanagh jumped, but it was just Kolchin. "Farewell gift from the Mrachanis," he said, holding up a cluster of blue cylinders with a set of wires attached. "I guess they didn't want to trust in their marksmanship to bring us down."

Cavanagh looked at Thrr't-rokik. "You'd better go check on the hangar," he told the Elder. "See if the Mrachanis have finished planting their explosives yet."

"I obey," Thrr't-rokik gritted, and vanished.

"Daschka, this is Bronski," Bronski called again. "Code four."

Again there was no response. "Looks like we've flared out, gentlemen," Bronski said, keying the board. "Plan B: we run like hell."

From behind Cavanagh came the distinctive whine of the engines. "What about the *Closed Mouth*?" he asked.

"Sorry, Cavanagh," Bronski said, shaking his head. "I don't think there's anything we can do to help them."

And then Thrr't-rokik was back. "Beware, Lord-stewart Cavanagh," he said. "The Mrach aircraft are raising into the air."

"Damn," Bronski bit out. "So much for engine warm-up. Here we go."

"Wait," Kolchin said, touching his arm. "Out there—two o'clock. Incoming."

Cavanagh peered out into the moonlight. Sure enough, a dark shape barely illuminated by the moonlight was lumbering through the sky toward them.

But the Mrachanis were on it. From both sides and over the top of the cliffs the aircraft Thrr't-rokik had identified blazed forward to intercept, assembling into a pair of attack formations as they flew. From a large rock outcropping in the near distance another group appeared, falling into backup position above and between the first two. Like wolves charging toward a tottering elk . . .

And then, abruptly, a smaller shape burst into view from the concealing shadows beneath the incoming vehicle. It flashed ahead; and as it turned toward the Mrach aircraft, a stray glint of moonlight flickered across it, reflecting off the distinctive black-and-white hull—

"I'll be damned," Bronski breathed. "It's a Corvine. It's a damned Copperhead Corvine."

The attackers' own reaction was immediate and frantic, the confident multipronged attack floundering as the aircraft suddenly recognized what they faced and scurried like mad to get out of the way. But the wolves had met the tiger; and for the wolves it was far too late. The Corvine sliced straight through the center of their formation, its cannon sputtering in all directions with deadly accuracy. Five of the aircraft flashed to vapor in midair, lighting up the sky like a Founding Day fireworks display. Four others survived long enough to hit the ground, turning there into instant bonfires. The rest scattered, clawing for the relative safety of distance.

Bronski keyed the radio again. "Corvine, this is Bronski. There's a hangar door in the fortress about five klicks south of my position. There's a trapped spacecraft inside. Free it."

"Corvine acknowledging," a familiar voice responded. "Is Lord Cavanagh there with you?"

"I'm here, Aric," Cavanagh said, leaning forward toward the mike. Why Aric would be there with Bronski's men . . . but they could sort that out later. "Hurry with that hangar door. The Mrachanis are planning to bring the mountain down on it."

The Corvine was already driving south. "Hang on," Bronski said, lifting into the air and following. "Thrr't-rokik?"

"They have stopped work," Thrr't-rokik said. "I fear it will be happening soon."

"Let's hope your captain's smart enough to run when the door opens," Bronski said, touching the radio control again. "Seconds count here, gentlemen."

There was no reply; but suddenly the Corvine swooped in close to the cliff wall and rolled ninety degrees to its right. The cannon stuttered again, the shells stitching parallel lines of miniature explosions across the width of the hangar doors. The fighter pulled back and around in a tight curve, swinging around to drive directly at the doors. At the last second it pulled sharply up, the twin flashes of missile launchings sparking toward the doors.

And with a roar and double flash of roiling fire the doors shattered and collapsed.

And through the smoke and still-flaming gas the Zhirrzh ship appeared, its glittering new metal sheathing torn in a hundred places by shrapnel and flying rock. It battered its way out through the opening, its hull scraping repeatedly against the crumbling remains of the door. There was a half-strangled gasp from Aric as the Corvine came around in another tight loop—

"Hold your fire," Bronski barked. "We've got a truce with the Zhirrzh."

"No—let them fire," Cavanagh suggested. "They can't hurt the hull, but it'll help clear off that metal sheathing."

"Good idea," Bronski agreed. "You copy, Corvine?"

"We copy," Quinn's cautious voice came. "Lord Cavanagh?"

"It's all right," Cavanagh assured him. "Your responsibility is to the family, and to obey all family orders."

"Acknowledged," Quinn said.

"We ought to get out of here," Kolchin said. "The Mrachanis may have heavier weaponry in the area."

"Yes," Cavanagh said, looking around and finally spotting Thrr't-rokik. "Thrr't-rokik, what about your *fsss* cutting?"

"Leave it there," the other said. "It would be dangerous to try to retrieve it now. And the Overclan Prime may wish me to continue observing."

"All right," Cavanagh said. "Can you get to Nzz-oonaz and his group yet?"

Thrr't-rokik flicked away, returned a few seconds later. "He is informed of new truths," he assured them. "He will not attack you. The Overclan Prime wishes to know if Lord-stewart Cavanagh and Bronski will accompany the *Closed Mouth* to a Human world to discuss peace."

"Sounds like a plan," Bronski said. "Edo's our best bet, I think. Daschka can send a skitter on ahead to warn them we're coming."

Cavanagh braced himself. "What about my daughter and other son?" he asked. "Is there word yet?"

"They are unharmed," Thrr't-rokik said. "The Human commander is soon arriving to discuss matters with Thrr-mezaz."

Cavanagh closed his eyes, exhaling a breath he hadn't realized he'd been holding. "It's over," he murmured, a wave of fatigue and released tension rolling over him. "We've done it."

"It's not over yet," Bronski said grimly. "There's still that rogue attack force heading for Earth. My guess is we haven't got more than a few hours to stop them."

"Why can't the Elders just take them a message?" Kolchin asked. "Warrior Command's in charge, isn't it?"

"But Warrior Command still does not know about this," Thrr't-rokik said. "And if it is a Dhaa'rr fleet as the Overclan Prime thinks, only Speaker Cvv-panav will be able to stop the attack."

"Then call him," Bronski said.

"That is problem," Thrr't-rokik told him. "Speaker Cvv-panav now on Dhaa'rr world of Dharanv. Not accepting any communications."

Bronski swore gently. "Waiting at home for word of his grand victory, I imagine. This is going to be trouble."

Cavanagh opened his eyes again. The Zhirrzh ship was settling to the ground nearby, Quinn and Bronski's men flying high cover for it. "Actually, I don't think so," he told the brigadier. "I think I know how to get through to him. Let's go aboard and discuss it with the Overclan Prime, shall we?"

Melinda keyed off the laser comm and stepped out of the hatchway. Prr't-zevisti was waiting there for her, his face looking strange. "It's all over, Prr't-zevisti," she assured him. "We've done it."

"Yes," he said. "And I thank you deeply, Melinda Cavanagh. But I am confused. I have now been to see your brother. Mnov-korthe is still there with him, under guard of Second Commander Klnn-vavgi. Yet we heard him call from the landing area and order you to be allowed inside the aircraft."

"Yes, we did." Melinda frowned, peering out into the darkness. Holloway's incoming aircar was visible now, circling around to get into landing position. Its lights flicked on, illuminating the area where the voice had come from—

And Melinda's frown smoothed into a wry smile. Of course; she should have guessed. "Hello?" she called. "Max?"

"Hello, Dr. Cavanagh," Max's smooth voice came from the meter-long silver cylinder lying ignominiously in the dust of the landing field. "The Zhirrzh assigned to transport me seem to have run off to other duties."

"And so you listened in," she said. "And decided to lend a hand."

"You appeared to require assistance," the computer said. "I hope I have not acted improperly."

"No, Max," she assured him. "Your timing and your voice were absolutely perfect."

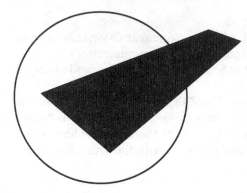

30

Speaker Cvv-panav had gone to sleep smiling, with firm orders that he was not to be awakened for anything but the most momentous information.

Five hunbeats ago he had indeed been awakened. And was no longer smiling.

"How in the eighteen worlds could this have happened?" he thundered to the Elder hovering nervously before him. "You had everything you needed."

" 'It wasn't enough,' " Mnov-korthe's tart reply came a few beats later. " 'We found the illegal cutting, all right, but Prr't-zevisti was alive. And somehow in contact with the Overclan Prime.' "

Cvv-panav slashed viciously at the air. And that part was his own fault. But how could he have known—? "Never mind," he growled. "The Prime may have won a battle, but the war is still ours. He wants peace? Fine; we'll give him peace. The peace that comes with final victory."

The Elder nodded and vanished. Yes, they would have peace, all right, Cvv-panav told himself as he keyed his reader for current status of the warships being towed toward the heart of Human-Conqueror territory by their Mrach allies. A little over a tentharc away from Earth now, still off the Human-Conqueror detectors. And when they did appear, looking merely like a fleet of harmless Mrach spacecraft—

The Elder reappeared. " 'There is news of that, as well, Speaker Cvv-panav,' " he quoted Mnov-korthe. " 'As Mnov-dornt and I were being taken to confinement, I overheard one of the Human-Conquerors tell Commander Thrr-mezaz that the spacecraft that had escaped Dorcas had taken with it the final piece of the CIRCE weapon.' "

"So it was there after all," Cvv-panav said, a flicker of his earlier satisfaction returning. "You were right: the Mrach intelligence reports were indeed wrong. Excellent. That means there will be no chance at all of our assault force having to face that weapon."

" 'Yes,' " the reply came. " 'I suppose that's something.' "

"That's everything," Cvv-panav countered. "It's the upcoming victory at Earth that will vault the Dhaa'rr back to power. What's going to happen to you now?"

" 'The Overclan Prime will be sending a ship to return us to Oac-canv.' "

Cvv-panav flicked his tongue in contempt. "Don't let it worry you," he said. "Long before you reach Zhirrzh space, the Overclan Prime will have ceased to exist as a political force. Farewell."

"Close the pathway," he told the Elder. Yes, the ship commanders of his warships would find this good news indeed. As would the Mrachanis towing them; and this would be an excellent opportunity to demonstrate to those nornin-furred aliens that the Zhirrzh weren't dependent on them for information about their enemies. "And open a pathway to the *Trillsnake.*"

Mra was receding behind the *Closed Mouth* when the word finally came from Oaccanv. "It has happened, Lord-stewart Cavanagh," Nzz-oonaz said, his voice sounding both excited and surprised. "Exactly as you predicted. The Dhaa'rr warships have reported to Warrior Command that the Mrach spacecraft have broken their tow cables and fled into the tunnel-line. The commanders are close to panic—they say they are now within enemy detection range."

"Have the Overclan Prime tell them that as long as they stay where they are, they can't be detected," Cavanagh said. "It's only in the tunnel-line that we can find them. Once we get a proper and official truce established, they'll be able to leave. You can let them know when that happens."

"I obey," Nzz-oonaz said. He turned back to the waiting Elders and began to speak.

Beside Cavanagh, Bronski shook his head. "You called it," he conceded. "But I'm still not sure I believe it. Why would the Mrachanis cut and run that way?"

"Because the only reason they allied with the Zhirrzh in the first place was because they were convinced CIRCE didn't exist," Cavanagh told him. "They'd drugged Ezer Sholom on Mra-mig, remember—they must have learned about CIRCE's nonexistence from him and then cleared out just before we got there. At that point it became a typical Mrach power game: manipulate the Zhirrzh against the Commonwealth and see what advantage they could get out of it. By having Pheylan and Commander Thrr-mezaz plant that story with Cvv-panav's agent, all I did was give them strong evidence that Sholom was wrong."

"Ah," Bronski said, nodding. "Which instantly changed all the percentages they were playing. If CIRCE really did exist, the last thing they'd want would be to get caught in the company of a Zhirrzh war fleet. But how did you know Speaker Cvv-panav would even bother to tell them?"

"Because I've known too many politicians just like him," Cavanagh said. "Politicians who like to gloat and show off their knowledge to allies and enemies alike. And who never let prudence get in the way of their personal agendas."

"Mm," Bronski said. "Speaking of politicians like that, I'll bet Parlimin Jacy VanDiver is going to want your head over this one."

Cavanagh smiled tiredly. "Let him try."

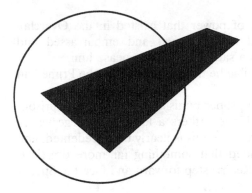

31 "Searcher Thrr-gilag; Kee'rr," the Overclan Prime called, his voice echoing across the Overclan Seating chamber. "Come forward."

Bracing himself, steadying his tail as best he could, Thrr-gilag walked down the aisle toward the front of the chamber, gazing straight ahead and trying to ignore the eyes of the Thousand Speakers and the thousands of Elders in the room. Trying not to wonder what they were thinking.

The chamber was quiet as he reached the front. He performed the *kavra* ceremony; then, at the Prime's nod, he turned to face the Speakers.

"You all are aware of the events of the past few fullarcs," the Prime said. "And of the role of Searcher Thrr-gilag within them. His actions, and the actions of his family, have helped to end an unnecessary and tragically pointless war.

"But some of those same actions have also violated the most deeply consecrated areas of Zhirrzh law and custom. Those violations, and the consequences stemming from them, cannot be ignored."

In the center of the front row Thrr-gilag could see his mother and brother and Klnn-dawan-a, looking terribly out of place among the powerful and distinguished Speakers around them. His father was there, too, a pale figure hovering between Thrr-mezaz and Klnn-dawan-a. A few couches away to their right was Speaker Cvv-panav, his eyes glittering with malice and anticipation. It was he who had insisted on this confrontation, Thrr-gilag knew, in revenge for the devastation of his grandiose plans.

It apparently didn't matter to him that there was now a genuine hope for peace between the Zhirrzh and Humans; didn't even matter that he had escaped the rubble of his scheme with his position and public prestige intact. In the quiet circles of power that existed in the Overclan Complex back rooms, he had been shamed and embarrassed and thwarted, and nothing less than a sacrifice would appease him.

He had demanded that Thrr-gilag be that sacrifice. And the Prime had agreed.

"Under some circumstances a proper punishment would be imprisonment," the Prime continued. "Under others a loss of privilege would suffice. But the situation we have before us is nearly unprecedented; and in the face of that I have decided that something far more drastic is called for. Searcher Thrr-gilag; Kee'rr: step forward and face the Speakers of the Thousand Clans."

Thrr-gilag took a step forward, his tongue pressing hard against the inside of his mouth. Here it came: the end of life as he'd known it. Distantly, he wondered how it would feel.

Off to his right the chamber hailer stepped forward. "Hear, all members of this chamber," he called, his voice booming across the room. "The Overclan Seating and Overclan Prime hereby decree that Thrr-gilag; Kee'rr shall no longer bear his family or his clan name. He is from this hunbeat forward a Zhirrzh with neither clan nor family, neither home nor territory, and is cut off from all rights and responsibilities and privileges which those names and those associations require and permit. By this action too shall any and all crimes and violations of Zhirrzh law be satisfied and declared void. Gilag is now above and outside of Zhirrzh law."

The last word echoed across the chamber as the hailer stepped back again. Thrr-gilag—no; just Gilag now—looked down at Speaker Cvv-panav. The Speaker was smiling back at him, the bitter, self-satisfied smile of one who has finally seen an enemy trampled beneath his feet and is fully enjoying the spectacle.

The Prime stepped forward to stand again at Gilag's side. "I said earlier that the situation here is nearly unprecedented," he said to the assemblage. "But it is not entirely so. Once before, five hundred and eight cyclics ago, a group of clan leaders met under similar circumstances, and for a similar purpose. Then, it was to seek a way to end centuries of clan hatred and to bring peace from the devastation of the Third Eldership War. Now, it is to seek a way to deal with the Human Commonwealth in such a way that no single clan benefits at the expense of any other.

"For both purposes, the same answer has been chosen."

Gilag looked at Speaker Cvv-panav again. The smile had vanished, his entire face going suddenly brittle as he suddenly understood the full scope of the Prime's plan.

And how his own demand for vengeance had played directly into that plan.

"And so, as the clan leaders did then," the Prime continued, "we have come here this fullarc to separate from our midst one who will begin a new family. Like the Overclan family, it will be a family without a clan, one that will stand above clan rivalries in all our dealings with the leaders of the Human Commonwealth."

He turned to face Gilag. "Gilag, do you accept this burden on behalf of the Zhirrzh people?"

Gilag took a deep breath. "I do," he said.

"And what say the Speakers of the Thousand Clans?" the Prime called.

For a handful of beats the chamber was silent. Then, gravely, Hggspontib, the Speaker for Kee'rr, rose from his couch and lifted his arms into the air. Another Speaker followed, and another, and another; and within a few beats the chamber was filled with the muted rustle of cloth as the rest of the Speakers rose to indicate their support.

"It's over, Gilag," the Prime murmured from beside him. "Or rather, it's just beginning. Are you frightened?"

Gilag considered. "Not frightened, Overclan Prime. A little overwhelmed, though. There'll be so much to do: the trading of goods and technology between our peoples, exchanges of diplomats and culture, adjustments of all sorts. And the Elders will be deeply involved, too— Bronski has already expressed interest in hiring them for interstar communication within the Human Commonwealth."

"Yes, you'll be busy," the Prime agreed. "But you can handle it. Your brother and father have already indicated their willingness to give up their family and clan names to join you in your new family. And your contacts with the Cavanagh family will stand you in good stead, too; I'm told that Lord Stewart Cavanagh will likely be one of the delegates the Human Commonwealth will be sending to deal with you."

He flicked his tongue. "But of course you'll need to begin your own family soon so that your work can expand and be carried on to future generations. I presume you'll be asking Klnn-dawan-a to join you?"

To join him outside Zhirrzh law, and outside the power of the Dhaa'rr clan to forbid their bonding. "She's already agreed," he said, looking down at her. She smiled at him; feeling a little awkward at the focus of so much official attention, he nevertheless smiled back.

And then his eyes moved over to his mother. His father was hovering at her shoulder now, talking earnestly to her. She wasn't looking at him, but even as he watched, she said a few words back.

They had a long way to go to rebuild their relationship. But it was a start. "What about my mother?" he asked.

"You're outside Zhirrzh law now, Gilag," the Prime reminded him soberly. "So is she, if you choose to bring her across into your new family. Whether or not she'll be forced to become an Elder will be for you two to decide."

"I see," Gilag murmured.

"Perhaps it's time for a change in the old customs," the Prime continued. "Or perhaps not. Whatever you and she decide, the rest of the Zhirrzh will watch and evaluate and learn."

Gilag felt his tail twitch. "And if I make the wrong decision?"

"Oh, you'll make plenty of wrong decisions," the Prime said matter-of-factly. "That's the way life is. But to be honest, it really won't matter all that much. The Zhirrzh are great survivors, Gilag. Whatever happens in your dealings with the Humans and Yycromae and Mrachanis, we'll ultimately come out of it all right."

"Yes," Gilag said, gazing out at the rows of Speakers standing together in acceptance of this new legacy of peace for their future. The Thousand Clans, all acting and working solidly together to create benefits for themselves, and to further the overall interests of the Zhirrzh race.

It was a new life and a new world they were all entering. And Gilag could almost feel sorry for the Humans.

ABOUT THE AUTHOR

TIMOTHY ZAHN is one of science fiction's most popular voices, known for his ability to tell very human stories against a well-researched background of future science and technology. He won the Hugo Award for his novella "Cascade Point" and is the author of numerous science fiction novels and story collections, including the *New York Times* best-selling STAR WARS® trilogy, which includes *Heir to the Empire, Dark Force Rising,* and *The Last Command.* Timothy Zahn lives in Oregon.